# Praise for THE LIGHTLARK SAGA

"Fantasy that reads like a breath of fresh air. Filled with secrets aplenty and enthralling magic, *Lightlark* will have you gasping then swooning while these valiant rulers fight to break their curses." —**Chloe Gong**, #1 *New York Times* bestselling author of *These Violent Delights*

"Gorgeously lush and cinematic, *Lightlark* is the kind of fantasy that indulges all your senses, makes you swoon, and then knocks you sideways with twists. You won't want to put this down." —**Marie Lu**, #1 *New York Times* bestselling author of *Skyhunter*

"If *The Hunger Games* was a dark fairy tale, you'd get the vicious and enchanting *Lightlark*. Get ready to be transported into a dazzling world where love is a death sentence and the romances between competitors are even fiercer than the curses plaguing the islands."
—**Adam Silvera,** #1 *New York Times* bestselling author of *They Both Die at the End*

"Alex Aster's *Lightlark* is an ebullient, fast-paced fantasy with a beautifully rendered world that seethes with intrigue, romance, and tension. I couldn't turn the pages fast enough." —**Sabaa Tahir**, #1 *New York Times* bestselling author of *An Ember in the Ashes*

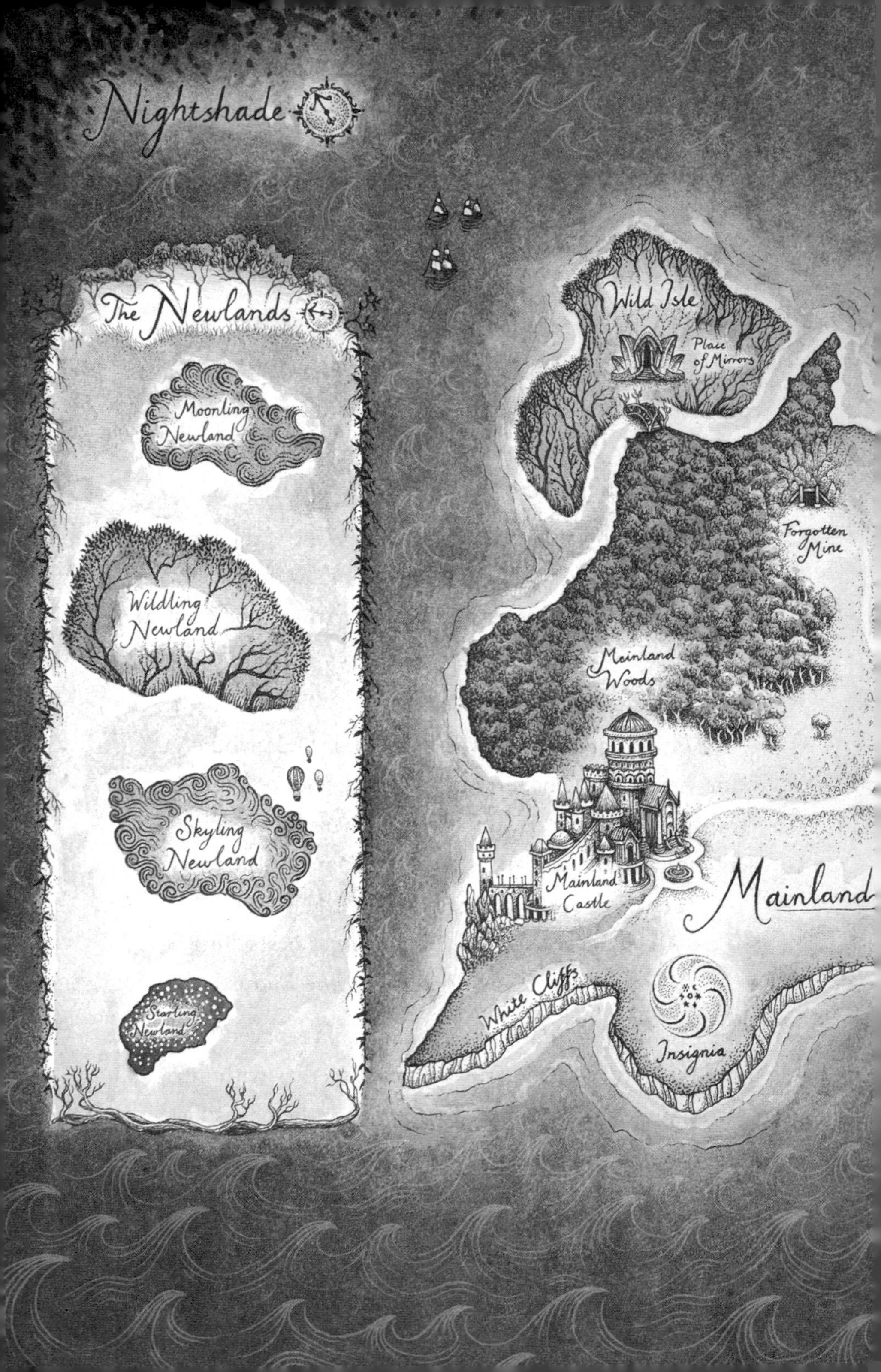

Nightshade
The Newlands
Moonling Newland
Wildling Newland
Skyling Newland
Starling Newland
Wild Isle
Place of Mirrors
Forgotten Mine
Mainland Woods
Mainland Castle
Mainland
White Cliffs
Insignia

The Isles
Vinderland Territory
Moon Isle
The Oracles
Broken Harbor
The Gates
Sun Isle
Singing Mountains
Agora
Hive
Abbey
Sky Isle
Bay of Teeth
The Last Tower
The Craters
Star Isle
Lightlark

*For my love. I couldn't write our love story if I tried.*

PUBLISHER'S NOTE: This is a work of fiction. Names, characters, places, and incidents are either the product of the author's imagination or used fictitiously, and any resemblance to actual persons, living or dead, business establishments, events, or locales is entirely coincidental.

Library of Congress Control Number 2022007680

Paperback ISBN 978-1-4197-9509-1


Map illustrations by Justin Estcourt
Vine artwork courtesy STOCKMAMBAdotCOM/Shutterstock.com
Book design by Chelsea Hunter

This paperback edition published in 2026 by Amulet Books, an imprint of ABRAMS. Originally published in hardcover by Amulet Books in 2022. 

Printed and bound in China
10 9 8 7 6 5 4 3 2 1



ABRAMS is represented in the UK and Europe by Abrams & Chronicle Books, 22-24 Ely Place, London EC1N 6TE and Média-Participations, 57 rue Gaston Tessier, 75166 Paris, France.
abramsandchronicle.co.uk and media-participations.com
info@abramsandchronicle.co.uk

**ABRAMS** The Art of Books
195 Broadway, New York, NY 10007
abramsbooks.com

# LIGHTLARK

ALEX ASTER

AMULET BOOKS • NEW YORK

# LIGHTLARK
## CURSES AND POWERS

### Wildling
**Curse:** Must eat human hearts to survive—
and kill anyone they fall in love with
**Powers:** Control of nature and affinity with animals

### Starling
**Curse:** All die at twenty-five
**Powers:** Can harness energy from the stars and
perform telekinesis

### Skyling
**Curse:** Have lost the ability to fly—
thousands fell to their deaths from the sky
**Powers:** Control of wind and weather

### Moonling
**Curse:** The sea becomes deadly every full moon
**Powers:** Control of water, healing abilities,
and the power to freeze

### Sunling
**Curse:** Will burn in the sunlight
**Powers:** Control of fire, light, and heat

### Nightshade
**Curse:** Will perish outside after nightfall
**Powers (vary based on strength):**
Ability to turn invisible and read emotions;
stronger individuals may be capable of mind control,
shadow-wielding, and spinning curses

# PROLOGUE

Bodies fell from the sky like stars that had lost their grip on the galaxy. Children in gold burned in the marketplace. Silver-clad people painted the island in heaps of lustrous gray, limbs still knotted together in the last throes of panic. The hearts of lovers were stabbed through with shaking hands and sharpened blades.

The curses were spun and felt in minutes, and Lightlark became more dead than alive.

It is said that by the end of the day, six rulers of six realms came together before an oracle who spoke a prophecy.

*Only joined can the curses be undone*
*Only after one of six has won,*
*When the original offense*
*Has been committed again*
*And a ruling line has come to an end*
*Only then can history amend.*

Blood and pain allowed access to the deepest depths of power. With the island on the brink of destruction, the six rulers sacrificed themselves to give their heirs the chance to break the curses, and with that power, the Centennial was created. Lightlark would disappear and emerge every hundred years for one hundred days, to give the six realms a chance to use the prophecy to save them all.

A cursed storm began to overtake Lightlark as it vanished to somewhere else entirely. The new Sunling ruler—and the new king of Lightlark—stayed on the island, while every other new ruler fled, taking some of their people with them. They formed the newlands, hundreds of miles away from each other and where the island once was.

Every hundred years, rulers returned to Lightlark, desperate to break the curses.

Every hundred years, they failed.

# CHAPTER ONE

# ISLA

Isla Crown often fell through puddles of stars and into faraway places. Always without permission—and seemingly on the worst occasions.

Even after five years, portaling still made her bones groan. She held her starstick tightly, her breath bottled in her chest like the rare perfumes on her vanity, the glass room spinning and fractured colors bleeding together, until gravity finally pinned her down like a loose thread in the universe.

And it was safely tucked down the back of her dress, along her spine, by the time the door swung open.

"What happened to your hair?" Poppy shrieked so loudly, Terra came rushing in behind her, the many knives and swords at her waist clanking together.

Her hair was the least of her worries, though she didn't doubt it resembled a bed of moss. Traveling between the realms' newlands with her starstick had the habit of undoing even Poppy's most tightly wound coils and firmly made braids—an unexpected perk, really.

Isla didn't pretend to be an expert at using the device. In the beginning, the puddle of stars took her unexpected places. The snow villages of the Moonling newlands. The airy jubilees of the Skyling newlands. A few lands that hadn't been settled by any of the six realms at all. Little by little, she learned how to return to locations she had been to before. And that was the extent of her mastering of the starstick. All she knew for certain was that somehow the mysterious device allowed her to travel hundreds of miles in seconds.

Terra sighed, hand dropping from the hilt of her blade. "It's just a few loose strands, Poppy."

Poppy ignored her. She rushed over to Isla, wielding a brush and a vial of syrupy leaf oil the same way Terra had taught Isla to brandish weapons years before. Isla grinned at her fighting teacher over her charm teacher's shoulder and cried out as Poppy roughly removed the pins. Poppy shook her head. "Have to start from scratch." She stuck the clips between her lips and spoke around them. "I leave you alone for an hour, and you're a mess. Even locked the door for good measure! How in the realm did you manage to mess it up in your own room, little bird?"

*Own room*. Her room was not her own. It was an orb of glass, the remnants of an ancient greenhouse. But the panes had been painted over. The windows had been sealed. All except one door had been removed.

She was a little bird, just like Poppy and sometimes even Terra called her.

A bird in a cage.

Isla shrugged. "Just some swordplay." Poppy and Terra were her only family—though they weren't family at all. Everyone who shared blood with her was long dead. Still, even they didn't know about the starstick. If they did, they would never let her use it. It was the only key out of the bird's cage. And Isla had been locked inside not just for her own safety—

But for everyone else's.

Terra eyed her suspiciously before turning her focus to the wall. Dozens of swords hung there in a shining row, a makeshift mirror. "Pity you can't bring any of them," she said, a finger trailing across the wall of blades. She had given Isla every single sword, presented from the castle's ancient store. Isla had *earned* them after each training achievement and mastery.

Poppy scoffed. "That's one Centennial rule I agree with. We don't need her reaffirming all the other realms' horrible views of us."

Nerves began to swirl in Isla's stomach, leaves dancing in a storm.

She forced a smile, knowing it would douse Poppy's frustration—her guardian always *was* telling her she didn't smile enough. Isla hadn't met many people, but the ones she had were simple to figure out. She just needed to uncover their motivations. Everyone wanted something. And some things were easier to give. A smile for a charm teacher who had spent nearly two decades teaching her student manners. A compliment for a woman who prized beauty above all else. "Poppy, pretty as you are, all of their horrible views are true. We *are* monsters."

Poppy sighed as she slid the last pin into Isla's hair. "Not you," she said meaningfully.

And though her guardian's words were wrapped in love—*good*—they made her stomach pool with dread.

"They're ready," Terra said. She took a few steps toward the vanity. Isla watched her through the mirror, its edges spotted with age. "Are you?"

*No*. And she never would be. The Centennial was many things. A game. A chance at breaking the many curses that plagued the six realms. An opportunity to win unmatched power. A meeting of the six rulers. A hundred days on an island cursed to only appear once every hundred years. And for Isla—

Almost certain death.

*Are you ready, Isla?* a voice in her mind said, mocking and cruel.

Her fear was only tempered by her curiosity. She had always longed for more . . . everything. More experiences, more places, more people.

The place she was going—Lightlark—was made of more. Before her guardians had discovered it and had it sealed, Isla used to sneak through a loose pane of glass in her room and down into the forest. It was there that she met an Eldress who had once lived on Lightlark, the way all Wildlings used to before the curses were spun. Before most of the realms fled the island to create new lands in the chaotic aftermath. Her stories were fruits in a tree—sweet and limited. She spoke of kings who could grip the sun in their hands, white-haired women who could make the sea dance, castles in clouds, and flowers that bloomed pure power.

That was before the curses.

Now the island was invisible. It had vanished somewhere else entirely, surrounded by its cursed storm.

One night, Isla had found the Eldress at the base of a tree, on her side. She might have thought the woman was sleeping, if her tanned skin hadn't become bark, if her veins hadn't turned to vines. Wildlings wielded nature in life and joined it in death.

But there had been nothing natural about the Eldress's passing. Even at over five hundred, even away from the strength of Lightlark, she had died too soon. Her death had been the first of many.

And the fault was Isla's.

Terra repeated her question, dark-green eyes the same color as the leaves and ivy that wrapped around the Wildling palace, a skin over everything. The same color as Isla's. "Are you ready?"

Isla nodded, though her fingers trembled as she reached for the crown in front of her. It was a simple gold band, adorned with golden buds, leaves, and a hissing snake. She placed it atop her head, careful not to interfere with the clips that kept her long, dark-brown hair out of her face.

"Beautiful," Poppy said. Isla didn't need to hear the compliment to know it was true. Beauty was a Wildling's gift—and curse. A curse that had gotten her own mother killed. Which only made the fact that she supposedly had her mother's face all the more unsettling. Poppy met Isla's eyes through the mirror and said fiercely, "You are enough, little bird. Better than any of them."

If only that was true.

Isla could feel a jolt of panic breaking her features in half. What if this was the last time she ever saw her guardians? What if she never returned to her room? Her hands acted on instinct, reaching for each of them, wanting to touch them one last time.

Before she could, Terra gave her a stern look that made her go still.

*Sentimentality is selfish,* her stare seemed to say.

The Centennial wasn't about her. It was about saving her realm. Her people.

Chastised, Isla straightened her spine. She stood slowly, the heaviness of her crown far greater than its weight. "I know what I must do," she said. Each ruler arrived at the Centennial with a plan. Terra and Poppy had hammered theirs into Isla since she was a child. "I will follow your orders."

"Good," Terra said. "Because you are our only hope."

The Wildling castle was more outside than in. The halls were bridges. Trees extended their arms into the corridor, branches catching gently on her dress as if to say goodbye. Leaves rustled at Isla's sides as she walked through the endless chambers she wasn't allowed access to, Poppy and Terra right behind her. Vines crept across walls. Birds flew in and out as they pleased. Wind howled through the halls in a breeze that made Isla's cape billow behind her. She wore deep green to honor her realm, a fabric that clung to her ribs, waist, knees, and pooled at her feet. Her cape was made of gossamer, sheer enough to make its traditional purpose for modesty obsolete. And that choice represented her realm just as much as its color.

Wildlings had always been proud of their bodies, beauty, and ability. They had always loved wildly, lived freely, and fought fiercely.

Five hundred years before, each of the six realms—Wildling, Starling, Moonling, Skyling, Sunling, and Nightshade—were cursed, their strengths turned into their own personal poisons. Each curse was uniquely wicked.

Wildlings' was twofold. They were cursed to kill anyone they fell in love with—and to live exclusively on human hearts. They turned into terrifyingly beautiful monsters with the wicked power to seduce with a single look.

Thousands of Wildling men and women had been killed off since. Love became forbidden. Reckless. Fewer children were born . . . and daughters had always been more common for their realm. Though love had various forms, men were killed more often when the rules were broken, and they had slowly become a small community of mostly warrior women. Feared. Hated. Weak, since fewer people meant less power being used. The Centennial was the only chance to end their curses, to return to their previous glory again, to regain the power they so badly needed. *Isla* was their only chance.

*You are our only hope . . .*

She heard them before she saw them. Chanting their ancient words, clashing their blades together like instruments. Wildling control over nature was on full display. Flowers bloomed and spilled over the balcony, down into the hall, not stopping until they reached her feet. They grew exponentially, doubling over themselves in a puddle of petals and rising to her ankles. According to lore, a thousand years before, Wildlings had been able to grow entire forests with half a thought, move mountains with a flick of their wrists.

Now, hundreds of years after the curse and just as much time away from the island's power, their abilities had dwindled to barely more than party tricks.

Isla walked carefully over the flowers until the castle walls ended and she faced hundreds of cheering Wildlings.

The trees above bloomed cherries and berries and bloodred blossoms, which fell onto the crowd in a colorful rain. Animals crept from the woods and into the group, sitting beside their companions. Wildling powers varied in their mastery of nature, but they often included affinity with animals—Terra had a great panther named Shadow she spoke to as easily as she communicated with Isla. Poppy had a hummingbird that liked to nestle in her hair.

When Isla nodded, the crowd fell silent.

"It is my honor to represent our realm this Centennial." Isla's pulse quickened, a drum along her bones. She looked across the crowd, at stunning, hopeful faces. Some Wildlings wore dresses made from bits of fabric woven through with leaves and vines. Some wore nothing at all except for the swords draped down their backs. Some had clearly just fed, their lips stained deep red. Isla looked and tried her best not to tremble. Not to let her voice crack, or stumble, or make them question for a moment why their ruler often hid behind the thick walls of her castle. Why attendants were banned from entering her quarters. She tried not to wonder how many of these Wildlings had heard this same declaration a hundred years before, from a different ruler—how many of them were even left, after the recent string of deaths. She made a promise, because that was what her people were looking for. Reassurance. Strength. "I vow to shatter our curse once and for all."

They would have every right to be worried. Isla's failure would doom them all for at least another century. And there had been four failed Centennials already. Isla clenched her back teeth together, waiting for them to see right through her—waiting for her perception of what they wanted to be wrong.

But the morning air ignited with yells and blades raised high overhead. Birds screeched from the treetops. Wind rustled leaves into a roar. Relieved, Isla walked down the stairs, smeared in petals, nature blossoming at her feet as the crowd parted, making a path toward their most ancient twin trees.

Their roots crested into the air, then braided together, forming a towering archway, round as a looking glass. The other side of the forest waited beyond, safe and familiar. But that wasn't where she was going. Isla swallowed. She had been preparing for this moment her entire life. Terra's and Poppy's hands found her shoulders.

Isla walked through the portal that only worked once every hundred years, her last words to her guardians fresh in her mind: *I will follow your orders.*

And wished they hadn't been a lie.

## CHAPTER TWO

# THE ISLAND

The portal rippled closed behind her, choking the cheers into silence. Only Isla's ragged breath remained. She took a single step forward, and light like a thousand dying stars and suns blinded her.

She teetered to the side. An arm reached out to steady her.

"Open your eyes," a voice said, dark and striking as midnight.

Isla hadn't even realized they were closed. With a blink, the world stumbled then steadied, this portaling far worse than using her starstick.

The face belonging to the man looking down at her was amused. And familiar, somehow. He was so tall Isla had to tilt her chin to meet his eyes, black as coals. His hair spilled ink across his pale forehead. Nightshade, no question. Which meant . . .

"Thank you, Grimshaw," Isla said firmly. She quickly straightened and looked around, hoping no one had seen her stumble. She could practically hear Poppy and Terra in each of her ears, scolding her.

But besides Isla and the Nightshade, the cliff was empty. She turned, and a tiny choking sound rasped against the back of her throat. The sea raged angrily hundreds of feet below. She had almost joined the jutting rocks and ended her plans at saving her people before the Centennial had even started.

Ended *all* her plans.

"That would have been inconvenient." The Nightshade ruler grinned, revealing a single dimple, completely out of place in his cruelly cut face. "Call me Grim, Isla."

*Grim.* What a terrible word, Isla thought, worn with pride. Still, the name suited him. There *was* something grim beneath that grin, a faint shadow that might become monstrous in the dark.

"Have we met before?" It wasn't that he knew her name, no. That was expected. It wasn't even that he pronounced it perfectly, like a snake's hiss, with all the letters sounded out. There was something else . . .

That grin faltered. "If we had"—his eyes dipped for just a moment—"it wouldn't have been just once."

Isla could feel her face get hot beneath his gaze. Other than rare, closely monitored interactions or her secret travels to the other newlands with her starstick, she hadn't spent much time with men.

Especially men who looked like him.

Especially men who didn't seem to be terrified of her and her Wildling curse.

She frowned. He *should* be afraid. If a Wildling wished, they could make a person fall off a cliff in pursuit of them. Their power to beguile was impossible to resist—though forbidden during the hundred days. The Nightshade must have thought he was safe.

He was not.

Each Centennial was a giant game, a chance to gain unparalleled ability. It was said that whoever broke the curses by fulfilling the prophecy would be gifted all the power it had taken to spin them—the ultimate prize.

Was his flirting meant to distract her?

Isla glared at him.

And Grim grinned even wider.

Interesting.

Every hundred years since the curses had been cast, the island of Lightlark appeared for just a hundred days, freed from its impassable storm. Rulers of each realm were invited to journey from the new lands they had settled after fleeing Lightlark, to try to break the curses binding each of their powers and the island itself. Every realm except for Nightshade, that was. Nightshades had the power to spin curses, making them prime suspects for having created them in the first place, though they denied it. This year, it seemed as though the Lightlark king was desperate.

It was the first Centennial Nightshade had been invited to.

Grim took her arm once more. Before Isla could object, he gently moved her to the side. A moment later, the giant marking on the edge of the cliff—an insignia representing all six realms—glowed gold, and someone else appeared from thin air, right where Isla had been.

A pale-blue cloak cracked with wind before settling against bare, very dark shoulders and muscled arms. The man had eyebrows larger than his eyes, a sculpted chin, and perfectly coiffed stubble that framed his pink mouth. Azul, ruler of Skyling. Isla had known their names since the time she could talk. Azul and Grim were both ancient, more than five hundred years old. Alive the day the curses had been cast. They were legends—compared to them, she was no one.

Centuries were apparently not enough time for Azul and Grim to have become friends. The Skyling nodded curtly at the Nightshade, and Grim's smile turned wicked. Mocking. Azul turned to Isla and bowed fully, reaching for her hand.

"Nice to have new Wildling blood this Centennial," he said. His bright eyes met hers, then studied her fingers, each covered in rings with gems as big as acorns. Though the rest of the realms liked to view Wildlings as savages, their wealth was unquestionable. Control of nature had its advantages. "Clouds, I've never seen a diamond that big."

To Isla, it was just a rock. Pretty, of course, but nothing in spades ever seemed too special. Jewels were made when great power was wielded over nature, and over the centuries the glittering gems had bloomed beneath the ground in the Wildling newland, rising up eventually, blossoming like flowers. It was difficult *not* to trip over some sort of precious stone in Isla's lands, which she only knew from texts, and certainly not from personal experience.

As far as Terra and Poppy were aware.

Terra always said those glittering rocks were the reason they had such a steady supply of hearts. Thieves from other realms, foolish and bold and wicked, sneaked onto their territory for the diamonds.

Isla smiled. So, the Skyling liked jewels. She slipped the ring right off her own hand and onto Azul's longest finger without missing a beat. "It complements you much more than it does me."

Azul looked like he might object—but didn't.

Someone else appeared, stepping easily past them, as if walking through portals was as seamless as the tide coming in. She turned to Isla. Her frown seemed to come as easily as most people's smiles. "So, this is the new pet?"

An ember lit in Isla's chest. The rest of the realms viewed the women warriors as savage temptresses, predators that lured lovers, then feasted on their hearts.

And Isla really couldn't blame them. Because that was very nearly the truth.

But Wildlings were so much more. At least, they had been. And still could be.

Though part of her wanted to say something she would likely regret, Isla knew the ruler *wanted* her to bite back. She was trying to tempt the monster out of Isla, to show the rest of them she was nothing more than a bloodthirsty beast. Instead, Isla bowed. "An honor to meet you, Cleo," she said, nodding her head in slight reverence. Cleo was the oldest among them, even older than the king of Lightlark, who also ruled over all Sunlings. Her age was at odds with her perfectly smooth, youthful face. Though most of the rulers were hundreds of years older, it was almost difficult to tell the difference between them and Isla. Almost.

Instead of making another insult, Cleo simply raised her chin at Isla and sneered, looking at her green dress as if she had stepped onto the island naked. Compared to the Moonling's clothing, she might as well have. Cleo's white gown had long sleeves like milky beams of moonlight, a neckline that reached her chin, and a cape that completely covered three-fourths of her body. The skin Isla *could* see was so fair, her veins shined through, blue streaks on a slab of white marble. She was not only many shades lighter than Isla but also far taller. Her face was long and pointed in three places, cheekbones and chin, sculpted like a diamond.

The insignia glowed a final time, and a girl stepped forward, stumbling ever so slightly. She was the silver of stars, from her long, straight sheet of hair to her twinkling dress to her gloves, which reached her elbows. She smiled sheepishly at them, heart-shaped face going wide, then stood tall. "I suppose I'm the last to arrive?"

Cleo channeled her distaste right at the girl. The ruler of Starling, like Isla, was new. Starling's curse had been one of the cruelest. No one in their realm lived past the age of twenty-five.

Isla stepped forward and offered her hand. "Celeste, is it?"

The Starling smiled warmly. "Hello, Isla."

"Enchanted," Grim said, offering a bow that seemed to mock the one that Azul had given just moments before.

The Skyling frowned for just a moment before he offered Celeste his own fingers, now glimmering with Isla's diamond. "More new blood. I have a good feeling about this Centennial."

Cleo raised an eyebrow at him. "She better hope so," she said, nodding at Celeste. "She won't be here for the next one."

The Starling's face fell. And the Moonling simply turned around, her white cape floating slightly behind her.

"Don't feel too special," Azul said with a wink. "She's this unpleasant to everyone."

The rulers began the path to the palace, and Isla's heart tripped in anticipation. She had been so focused on them, she hadn't gotten a chance to truly take in her surroundings. The rest of the century, the island was encased in its storm. But now the clouds had cleared.

Lightlark was a shining, cliffy thing. Its bluffs were white as bone, and sunlight rained down in sheets of misted gold. One of the original sources of power, its ground still thrummed with it, singing to Isla in a humming siren song. She could feel its force with each step, each breath. She drank the island in greedily, like the wine she was never allowed to touch. Equally addictive and dangerous.

Poppy's lessons ran through her head, facts on paper that were now real and solid before her.

Thousands of years ago, the island was cut into several pieces, so each realm could claim a shard. Nightshades left the island shortly afterward to form their own land. Wildlings left after the curses. The pieces that remained were Star Isle for the Starlings, Sky Isle for the Skylings, Moon Isle for the Moonlings, and Sun Isle for the Sunlings. Then, there was the Mainland, where all the realms had traditionally gathered together. It was the Centennial's base.

It was also historically home to Lightlark royalty.

The Mainland castle loomed nearby, set high on a cliff like a crown jewel, jutting precariously out over the sea. Large enough to be its own city. Which was good, considering its main inhabitant could not leave it.

Not during the day, at least.

Isla must have been staring at it, because Celeste sighed next to her. "Do you think he's watching us?" she said quietly.

*He.* The Sunling ruler and king of Lightlark. The last remaining Origin, with blood from each of the four realms that still had a presence on the island. He could wield each of the four Lightlark powers.

And, by all accounts, he was insufferable.

On Lightlark and beyond, love had a price. Falling deeply and truly in love meant forming a bond that gave a beloved complete access to one's abilities. They could do whatever they wished with it. Wield it, reject it. Even steal it.

Knowing very well how many people wanted access to his endless stream of power, the Lightlark ruler was untrusting. Paranoid. Cold.

Isla dreaded meeting him. Especially given the first step of Poppy and Terra's plan for her.

She stared back at the castle and resisted the urge to flinch. Instead, she broke through her mask of charm and made an obscene gesture at the palace.

The game had officially started.

"I hope so."

Crowds awaited them at the castle doors. Starlings. Moonlings. Skylings.

On the night of the curses, five hundred years before, all six rulers perished. Their power and responsibility were transferred to their heirs, and all of them except for the new king fled the island's instability to create the newlands, hundreds of miles from the island and each other.

Some subjects had remained on Lightlark.

Once, Isla had asked the Wildling Eldress why anyone would stay in the near constant cursed tempest that had overtaken it.

*Power is in the island's blood and bones,* she had said. *Lightlark lengthens our lives, gives us access to a power much greater than our own. And more than that, to many . . . Lightlark is home.*

No Wildlings remained. She would get no aid from her people.

She was alone.

"Don't worry," a deep voice said mockingly at her side. "I don't have any adoring fans either."

The crowd watched Grim with a healthy mix of fear and disdain—Isla studied their reactions carefully. He looked like night come to life, his clothing shadow spun into silk. If Wildlings were looked down upon on Lightlark, Nightshades seemed to be outright hated. And, according to Terra and Poppy's lessons, never fully accepted on the island. They had their own land, a stronghold they had maintained for thousands of years.

The war between Nightshade and Lightlark hadn't helped either.

Isla didn't meet his gaze, though she felt his eyes all over her. It was unnerving. Her skin felt inexplicably electric. "I'm sure you get more than enough attention back home." She smiled politely at the crowd, testing their own reaction to her. Some of them returned the gesture warily. Others visibly recoiled from the sight of her, the heart-devouring temptress. She wasn't surprised. Everything she represented was forbidden. A Moonling woman covered her child's eyes and made a figure in the air, as if warding off a demon.

"I do," he admitted. "Yet, I'm left . . . unsatisfied."

Isla ignored him. She wasn't going to play this game with him, whatever it was. She had her own game to play.

The interior of the castle looked like a sun had burst inside and bathed the walls in its glow—an ode to the Sunlings who had built it. Everything was gold. Buttery sunlight spilled from long windows, coating the foyer in glittering light that reflected off the smooth, shining floor. Isla squinted as if she was still outside. A raging fire burned in a ring high above them on a chandelier, flames peaking in place of crystals.

The Sunling ruler was not there to greet them. He couldn't be, even if he wanted to, which Isla truly doubted. Sunlings had been cursed never to feel the warmth of sunlight or see the brightness of day—forced to shun that which gave them power. The king of Lightlark was trapped in the darkness of his chambers, only able to surface at night. In that, Isla supposed they were similar. She had spent a lot of time trapped inside too.

A woman in Starling silver bowed before them. Behind her, a small group of staff echoed her movement. Each ruler received an attendant for the entirety of the Centennial. "It would be our pleasure to escort you to your chambers."

Each ruler was led away to completely different parts of the castle. Far from each other. Isla didn't know what to think about that. Intentional—every detail at the Centennial was intentional, that was what Terra had taught her.

A young Starling girl walked toward her slowly, slightly sideways, the way a child might approach a coiled snake. "My lady," she said, voice so soft Isla had to lean in to hear her, which only made the girl flinch. Isla resisted the urge to roll her eyes. Did the girl actually think she would feast on her heart in the middle of the foyer? Her kind was wild, but they weren't *animals*. "Follow me."

"Isla," she said at the girl's stiff back as she raced away with a noticeable amount of trouble. Isla would likely need the girl's help during some point—which meant she would need to earn her loyalty somehow. "You can call me Isla."

"As you wish," the girl murmured.

She led Isla up a sweeping set of stairs that ran through the center of the castle and down an impossible tangle of hallways that jutted over and across each other like bridges. But, unlike her palace in the Wildling realm, this one became more and more enclosed the deeper she went. It reminded her of a maze in a cave. Or a prison. She suddenly imagined the king as an ancient beast, trapped in the dark. Lost in the labyrinth that was his castle. They reached a stretch without a single window. The halls grew colder, the walls thicker.

The girl stopped in front of an ancient stone door. With about all the strength it seemed she could muster, she pushed it open.

Someone had managed to plant a tree right in the middle of the room, an oak with blush-colored blossoms and blooming fruit Isla didn't recognize, its roots dug right into the stone floor. Ivy crept across the ceiling in a pretty design, leading to the wall her bed rested against, which was covered in leaves down to the floor.

There was more. Isla walked across the room and onto a wide, curling balcony that jutted right over the sea. Dangerously so. Waves churned below. The castle was a curious child perched at the top of the mountain, leaning way too far over the edge.

Isla frowned. "How sturdy is this?" It seemed like the balcony could break off at any moment, or that the castle itself could simply slide off the cliff during a storm.

"As sturdy as the king himself, I suppose."

Right. Isla knew that from her lessons. The king of Lightlark didn't just control its power—he *was* its power. If something happened to him, the entire land would crumble away, and every Lightlark realm would fall. That was why he trod so carefully. Not in fear of being killed, but in fear of someone stealing that terrible power right from under him.

Another similarity. Isla couldn't fall in love either.

Well, she *could,* but everyone lived in fear of a Wildling loving them. Their curse made love a death sentence.

Not exactly the fodder for romance, admittedly.

It hadn't been an issue so far, in Isla's relatively short, halfway-contained life. Yet—

How cruel would a king who had been afraid to fall in love for more than five hundred years be?

It seemed she would soon find out.

"Dinner is at eight chimes," the Starling girl said before beginning to stoke the already monstrous fire burning in the hearth across from her bed.

"It's hot enough," Isla said. "Don't trouble yourself."

The Starling continued, moving the coals around in a practiced way. "The king has given strict orders for the fires to remain burning constantly."

*What a strange command,* Isla thought. Before she could ask why, the Starling was across the room. She bowed once before quickly closing the door behind her.

Isla was just finishing surveying her bathroom—more spacious than the one back home, even, with a tub she could do laps in—when a knock sounded on her door.

She tentatively opened it.

And found Celeste standing there.

Isla immediately threw her arms around the Starling ruler. They jumped in a tiny circle, embracing and laughing so hard, Isla kicked the door closed to keep it from echoing down the hall.

Celeste raised an eyebrow. "Celeste, is it?" she said, doing a shockingly good and unflattering impression of Isla. She threw her silver head back and laughed.

Isla's smile strained, wondering if she hadn't been convincing enough. "Do you think they—"

"They don't suspect a thing," Celeste cut her off. She clicked her tongue and reached to pull a lock of Isla's hair. "I thought you were going to cut this."

Isla sighed. "I tried. One look at the scissors, and Poppy almost stabbed me with them. She confiscated every set in my chambers."

"Confiscated?" Celeste raised an eyebrow. "Do I need to remind you that *you're* the ruler of your realm?" Isla laughed without humor. She turned to walk deeper into her quarters, and Celeste's hand went straight to her back. "You brought it?"

She caught her reflection in the mirror. Something along her spine was faintly glowing—it must have been Celeste's presence. She cursed, hoping no one else had noticed, and pulled the starstick out. "I couldn't leave it behind."

Celeste frowned. "It's risky. Hide it well." She was right. If anyone found out Isla had the enchantment, their secret alliance would be compromised.

Isla had found the starstick in her mother's things, five years prior. More desperate for freedom than fearful of being portaled somewhere dangerous, she had traveled the realms' newlands with it for months before finally coming across Celeste. That was the first time they had ever met.

Celeste had instantly recognized the starstick as an ancient Starling relic. Isla had no idea how her mother had gotten her hands on it before her death. And, since Celeste's own family had died long before, thanks to the curse that killed all in their realm at twenty-five, she didn't know either.

Though it belonged to the Starlings, Celeste had never asked for it back. That had marked the start of their friendship—two rulers of realms, their lands separated by hundreds of miles, with one thing in common: they both desperately needed to break the curses *this* Centennial.

For Celeste, breaking her curse was the difference between life or death. Not only for her, but for all her people.

For Isla . . . things were even more complicated. No one realized how small their realm had gotten. Many more Wildlings had died than been born. Their powers had gotten weaker with every generation. Forests had shrunk. Wildlife had gone extinct. At the rate her lands and people were deteriorating, there wouldn't be any Wildlings *left* by the next Centennial.

Isla had never agreed with Poppy and Terra's plan. It was too complex. Too uncertain.

So, she had created a new strategy with Celeste.

"I should go," her friend said after fully appraising Isla's room. "For the record, your quarters are nicer than mine. Though my room isn't in such a drafty old corner of the castle."

Isla rolled her eyes. "I'll see you at dinner."

Celeste turned on her way to the door and formed a wicked smile. "So, it begins."

## CHAPTER THREE

# BLOOD

The sun had fallen. It was just a yolky smear, halfway consumed by the horizon, when Isla opened the double doors and stared up at the incoming moon. She was in the middle of getting ready, just in her slip. The gauzy white curtains blew back in the breeze, trailing her arms, falling against her bare knees, her toes. She crept out onto the balcony, the stone cold beneath her feet. Breathed in salt and brine.

She carefully climbed onto the wide stone ledge, knees to her chest. And just like she did back home when she was alone in her room, whenever she felt anxious and lonely and trapped, she began to sing.

Singing brought her peace. It was something she was born good at, without really having to try. Isla's voice was unnaturally good, like silk and velvet and deep dreams. She knew it and liked the sound. Liked how her voice could be as deep as the ocean floor and as high as wind chimes. She didn't need music. The sea below was instrument enough, its waves crashing roughly against the island's harrowing white cliffs as if trying to get a good look at her.

She sang and sang, meaningless words and melodies, letting her voice ripple and peak and dip, like drawing on an endless canvas. She sang to the sea, to the moon, to the rising darkness. All things she hadn't been able to see from her painted-over windows in the Wildling realm. Finally, she ended on a high note, letting it drag out as much as she could without taking another breath. She smiled to herself, always surprised by what came out of her mouth. Always relieved by how it put to rest even her darkest thoughts.

And there was clapping.

Isla whipped around to see a man on another balcony yards away, tucked so far back into the castle she hadn't even noticed it. Practically in her underclothes and caught completely off guard, Isla gasped. She whirled too quickly, startled. Her arms pinwheeled at her sides, but it was no use—gravity was too great.

She fell straight back, clean off the ledge.

Her breath spooled out of her chest, and she screamed soundlessly as she fell, grasping at the night air like the stars were footholds.

But only air passed through her fingers, and she fell, fell—

Until the sea roared below, and her head cracked against its surface.

Isla sat up so quickly she retched sea water. Her throat burned with it. She blinked and blinked. Wiped her mouth with the back of her hand.

And found that she was back on her balcony, in a puddle of water. Her hair was dripping wet. Her slip clung to her body, completely soaked through. Her head pounded in pain from its very crown. When her fingers gingerly ran over the spot, she expected there to be blood. There wasn't.

She was very much alive. Not drowned, the way she should have been. That person, the one who had been watching her . . . he must have saved her.

Then dumped her here, not even bothering to see if she would wake up.

Who would do such a thing?

The more surprising part wasn't that he had discarded her . . .

But that he had *rescued* her.

After the curses were spun, there was chaos. That same night, the six rulers of realm sacrificed themselves in exchange for a prophecy that was promised to be the key to breaking the curses. Terra and Poppy claimed her own ancestor had been the one to lead the sacrifices, the first to die.

True or not, Isla could never imagine the strength it must have taken to give up their lives for the chance at their people's salvation. The power the six injected into the island and transferred to their realms made the Centennial possible. Every hundred years, for a hundred days, the six realms were given a chance to save themselves, because of that sacrifice.

The prophecy to break the curses had three parts, which had been interpreted in several ways throughout the centuries. One was clear. For the curses to be eradicated, one of the six rulers had to die. It was why the Centennial was such a risky affair, feared and prepared for, why Terra had trained Isla to fight since the time she could walk.

Isla's sudden death by drowning might have been the first step to fulfilling the prophecy. But for some reason, the person on the balcony wanted to keep her alive.

*Why?*

Bells rang through the castle, making Isla almost jump out of her skin. She counted them, then cursed.

For the first dinner, she was supposed to have spent an hour on her hair, arranging it in a complicated design atop her head. She was supposed to choose the perfect gown, rub rose-scented lotion on her skin until it gleamed, and apply her makeup with precision, using tools she had learned to wield just as expertly as her throwing blades. All things Poppy had drilled into her.

Instead, she combed her wet hair with her fingers and almost slipped in the trail it made, threw on the first gown she could get her hands on, put on a pair of silk slippers, and grabbed her crown at the last moment, placing it haphazardly on her head as she tore through the door.

And almost ran into her Starling attendant. Her tiny mouth was open in shock, and she put her hands up on instinct, shielding from an attack. "This way . . . Isla."

A dozen hallways later, the doors to the dining hall opened, and everyone turned to look at her.

Isla wished she was a Nightshade, just so she could disappear.

Celeste sat back in her chair, eyebrows raised.

Azul put down the goblet he was holding.

Cleo regarded her with even more disdain than before. In her rush, Isla had grabbed one of her most brazen dresses, one she had been instructed to wear far later in the game. The bones of the bodice were visible, the panels nearly sheer. The skirt had a slit that ran up her leg, to the top of her thigh. Her cape was green lace, attached to a dipping neckline.

Grim looked amused, eyeing her every step in a way that made her flush, mortified.

There was someone else at the head of the table. The same person who had been watching her sing—who must have both saved her and abandoned her.

Oro, king of Lightlark, ruler of Sunlings. Hundreds of years old, yet nearly as youthful-looking as she was. He had hair like woven gold and mean, amber eyes that pinned her in place. He frowned and nodded curtly at her in welcome, purely out of obligation.

Why had the king saved her?

Only to regard her so dismissively.

She returned the cold nod and took the empty seat at his side, cursing whoever had placed her there.

Isla's wet hair draped over her arm, dripping down her skin and onto the floor beside her in a puddle. Her body shook slightly, freezing, the flimsy, practically fabric-less excuse of a gown doing absolutely nothing to warm her.

The taunting voice was back: *Are you ready, Isla?*

Of course she wasn't. How had she been foolish enough to accept the Centennial invitation? To walk directly into such a deadly game?

One of the six rulers had to die. As the youngest and least experienced, she would be a fool to believe it wouldn't be her. Especially when she had nearly died twice already, less than a day into the ceremony.

If she was smart, she would leave that night, using her starstick.

If she wanted to live, she would abandon the island, her realm, her people, her duty, and never look back. Lands beyond Lightlark and the newlands were largely unexplored. She had always wondered about them. It would be risky traveling beyond them, but certainly not more dangerous than the Centennial . . .

She couldn't. Not if she ever wished to be truly free. Her curse would never allow her to have the full life she wanted, with the people she cared about most. Terra. Poppy. Celeste.

If all went to plan, she would never have to be hidden away like a secret again. She would never feel ashamed about who she was. She could lead her people to prosperity and travel the newlands at will, visiting Celeste whenever she wanted to.

Isla had spent countless hours of her life studying other people, guessing at their motivations.

Freedom was hers.

Oro studied her dripping hair, and he had the nerve to smile. "I know our seas are irresistible . . . but please, in the future, do limit your swims to earlier in the evening so as not to keep the rest of us waiting." He raised his chin slightly. The crown atop his head was gold and gleaming, its spikes sharp enough to draw blood. "Very rude—though perhaps my expectations of your realm were too high to begin with."

Cleo's eyes glittered with amusement, relishing the red that Isla could feel spreading across her cheeks. "A swim in *that* sea, at *this* hour? She certainly is a wild pet. Even a Moonling wouldn't think to do such a thing during the Centennial. Only a fool would."

*Wild. Pet. Fool.* The Moonling had managed to insert multiple jabs in just a few short sentences.

"Certainly not on a full moon," Isla said smoothly, the words slipping out before she could stop herself.

Silence.

Silverware clattered together somewhere across the room.

Moonlings' curse meant that every full moon, the sea claimed dozens of lives from their realm, drowning anyone who found themselves too close to the coast. It made faraway trade nearly impossible, made living near the ocean a danger, and had completely crippled the Moonlings' economy.

Isla regretted her words immediately. The way Cleo's eyes narrowed, right at her, like an arrow marking its target, made her feel like she had just officially made her first enemy.

Before anyone could say another word, a plate was placed in front of Isla. On it sat a bleeding heart.

"Sourced from the worst of our prisons," Oro said smoothly. "A murderer of women."

It took all of Isla's will to smile warmly at him. "How kind of you. However, I prefer to eat in private. Some find it . . . disturbing." She looked around for the Starling who had led her to the dining hall. "Could I have this sent to my room for later?"

"Nonsense," Oro said. He stared down at the heart, then at Isla. "Eat."

She could feel everyone's gaze on her. It had been a while since they had encountered a Wildling. Isla carefully took her fork and knife, nodded graciously at her host, and cut a piece of the heart, blood pooling out of it, filling her plate. She breathed in the metallic sent.

Then she took a bite.

Grim roughly placed his goblet of wine down onto the table. "Isla, as much as the blood on your lips suits you, I sense my good friend Azul's distaste for Wildling . . . pleasures." Indeed, the Skyling, though clearly trying to be polite, looked ill. Grim motioned for the staff. "Please send this to her quarters."

He spoke as if this was his castle, not Oro's. The Sunling ruler blinked but did not stop the Skyling boy from taking Isla's plate away. "Weak stomach, Grimshaw?"

The Nightshade grinned, the dimple returning. "We all have our weaknesses, Oro," he said. "I'm counting on them."

Somehow, Isla made it through the rest of the dinner without having to excuse herself.

Then she spent the night retching blood.

## CHAPTER FOUR

# RULES

Isla had been born without the Wildlings' curse—or their power. Since birth, she'd lived locked away, protected by Poppy and Terra, in fear that her realm would discover her secret.

According to her guardians, her mother was to blame. She broke the most important Wildling rule—she fell in love. Then she somehow failed to kill him. Isla didn't know the details, but the end of their story was clear. Isla's father had murdered her mother moments after Isla was born, and their spawn was powerless—her own curse. Isla's malediction was not eating hearts or killing a beloved. But being a ruler born without powers was just as deadly.

Rulers were expected to inject their power into their lands to keep their people strong. It was why Lightlark was so engorged with energy, and how the realms had survived in the newlands they had formed after they had fled the island. Without power to give, her realm was steadily dying. So far, her people had blamed their curses and length of time away from Lightlark for the deaths. But some were beginning to become suspicious of Isla.

It was her greatest secret. One that would be a death sentence at the Centennial.

One of the six rulers had to die to break the curses, according to the oracle's prophecy. But it was worse than that. A ruler's power was the life force of their people. So, if one died without an heir—

All their people would die along with them.

Those were the stakes of the game. Breaking the curses meant eliminating an entire realm.

The first Centennial had been a bloodbath. All the invited rulers set out to kill each other, and many of the islanders were caught in the cross fire. But the heads of realm were too skilled, too ancient already. The hundred days ended with all of them alive and the curses intact. It was decided that future Centennials would have order.

It was decided that there would be rules.

Oro stood on the steps in front of his golden throne, instead of on it. That was the first thing Isla noticed as she entered the grand hall. Leaders seemed to be constantly reminding people around them of their authority. During the few times she had visited the Moonling newland, she had seen countless ice statues carved in the likeness of their ruler, heard Moonlings speak of paying their monthly dues, saw the patrol Cleo kept constantly roaming the streets.

Was there a reason the king was hesitant to sit on his throne?

The next thing she noticed were the half dozen chandeliers of fire, overlapping across the ceiling. They echoed the flames of four hearths, burning brightly. She thought back to her attendant's comment. The king never wanted any of the fireplaces going out.

*Why not?*

The rulers gathered in a circle, and Isla stood tall, ignoring the pang of hunger in her stomach. She had sneaked into the kitchens early that morning, but all she had been able to procure was some stale bread, fruit that vaguely resembled mura from the Wildling newland, and a cup of milk. A longer-term solution to her food problem would be necessary.

Celeste, across the way, looked well rested, her skin vibrant. Isla imagined her friend had visited Star Isle for the first time that morning. Perhaps there had been a ceremony honoring her. Without regular access to their leaders, the Skylings, Starlings, and Moonlings who had remained on Lightlark had created their own subgovernments. Their rulers had become seen as almost gods, figureheads they deferred to and only saw for a few months every hundred years. All rulers traditionally spent most of their time on the Mainland during the Centennial. But there were occasional exceptions.

Isla had always wondered what the different isles that made up Lightlark looked like. She longed to ask her friend all about it, wishing she knew how to work her starstick between small distances so that she could simply appear in Celeste's room whenever she wanted. Instead, they would have to rely on using the hallways for that. And meeting up often, this early in the game, was too great of a risk.

She turned and accidentally put herself in Cleo's path. The Moonling eyed her with too much interest. There was a sharp gleam in her gaze—a predator sizing up its prey.

Isla would pay for her comment the night before. She was sure of it.

Oro finally spoke. "Let us begin by stating the rules of the Centennial."

The air was electric, buzzing with energy.

"The first rule. A ruler may not assassinate or attempt to assassinate another ruler until after the fiftieth day." The rule was a relief to Isla. For at least half of the Centennial, powerless or not, she would be safe. Which was why she and Celeste planned to be off the island before the ball on the fiftieth day even took place. "And, when pairs are decided on the twenty-fifth day, a ruler may not assassinate their partner."

After the chaos of the first Centennial, the hundred days became more structured, split into parts. The first twenty-five days were dedicated to demonstrations hosted by each ruler, designed to test one another's strengths—and worthiness of staying alive. Each test had a winner. The ruler who won the most trials would decide which pairs the rulers would split into for the remainder of the Centennial.

"The second rule. All rulers must attend and participate in every Centennial event." That rule seemed innocuous but was dangerous, depending on what it was.

"The third rule. To participate, no ruler can have an heir." So, their death would successfully eliminate their familial line and break the curses, according to the prophecy. It would also mean the end of their realm forever.

Each ruler received an invitation to the Centennial containing these rules. Acceptance of it meant acceptance of the three ordinances.

But every good promise was sealed in blood.

With a flick of the king's wrist, a fire erupted in the middle of their circle. Isla knew exactly what was to happen next.

Poppy had made her practice the act, over and over—*again, until you don't flinch!* Her wound would be stitched up, only to be sliced open again and again and again, until she had no visible reaction to the pain.

In sync with the others, Isla removed the crown from her head—and used its sharpest point to form a deep cut across her palm.

She did not flinch. Poppy would be proud.

Before she offered the stream of blood to the flames, there was another part to the ceremony that she had practiced. With great use of power and control, each ruler's blood could display special properties. Wildling blood was supposed to bloom flowers during ceremonies like these.

Isla was prepared, petals hidden between her fingers. When her blood finally dripped down her palm, it held a miniature rose.

Cleo's blood hardened into ice before being seared by the fire. Grim's blood became dark as ink. Azul's blood suspended in the air, separating into parts, before finally falling. Celeste's blood burst into a mess of sparks. Oro's blood burned brightly before even reaching the flames.

The fire turned crimson, stained with their blood—then vanished.

Now, they were bound to the rules. Breaking them had consequences. For Isla, Celeste, Grim, Cleo, and Azul, it meant forfeiting claim to the Centennial's prize: the unmatched power the oracle said would be gifted to the one responsible for breaking all the curses. Oro, as king and host of the Centennial, was bound to the rules with his life.

Was that why Oro had saved her? Did he have a responsibility to? It was unclear how accidental deaths factored into the prophecy.

What *was* clear was that the king of Lightlark had a plan. And it apparently involved Isla staying alive.

At least, until he wanted her dead.

## CHAPTER FIVE

# GRIM

The next morning, when Isla's attendant knocked on her door, she was ready.

She hadn't been allowed weapons, but she *had* been allowed a trunk of belongings. She applied kohl to her green eyes, in perfectly arched streaks. Her lashes were already thick and long, but she curled them even more. Spread a balm across her full lips that brightened their natural shade. Her skin was naturally tan, but she still looked too pale for her liking, having spent far too much of her life inside.

That would be easily remedied. Now that she was free to explore, she had no intention of locking herself in her room.

The few dresses from her trunk looked more like a collection of sewn-together ribbons. Sheer, bare, and so smooth they looked liquid. In the Wildling realm, in the constant seclusion of her chambers, she could get away with wearing loose, soft clothes. But this was the Centennial, and Poppy had chosen these gowns for a reason.

A reason that made Isla want to throw them all into the closest fireplace.

That day, she chose a dress the pink of tulips, with a plunging back and fabric that clung to her like it was wet. It was tradition to wear the color of one's power source. Starlings wore silver, Sunlings wore gold, Skylings wore light blue, Nightshades wore black, and Moonlings wore white. Because nature was multicolored, Isla was not bound to one shade, as long as she did not infringe upon anyone else's.

The Starling girl startled when Isla answered the door so quickly.

Isla did not waste a moment. "What is your name?" she asked.

"My name?" the girl said with such confusion, Isla couldn't help but laugh.

"I'm assuming you have one?" she joked, hoping her smile made it seem good-natured, not mean.

The girl smiled back tentatively. *Good.* "Of course. It's Ella, lady." She shook her head. "I mean, *Isla.*"

Isla dipped her head, the way she had watched people do when they were about to speak in confidence. She had heard many a secret whispered in a back alley, or on the outskirts of a village, thanks to her starstick. Over time, she had learned how to go undercover, to blend into a crowd so seamlessly that no one would guess she didn't belong. "I notice you walk with a limp, Ella," she said.

The Starling girl looked taken aback. She took a shaky step away, and Isla wondered if she should have waited longer . . . or if she had been too direct. The girl's hand went instinctively to her leg. "My—my bone," Ella finally said. "It broke a while ago and never healed right."

Isla frowned. "Aren't there Moonling healers here who could help?" Their skills were legendary. Beyond controlling water, healing was their power.

"At a cost," Ella said, smiling weakly. "If at all, lately." Isla wondered what she meant, but before she could ask, Ella added, "Also . . . I'm not so far from twenty-five. It wouldn't, it wouldn't—"

*Be worth it.* Isla winced. Even with Celeste as her best friend, sometimes she forgot about the cruelty of their curse. No Starling had lived past twenty-five in hundreds of years.

"Well," Isla said, reaching into the pocket in her dress. "This should help." She handed over the tub of paste, a Wildling healing elixir made from specially grown flora. The same potion that had healed the cut on her palm from the ceremony the day before.

Ella just stared at the tub placed in her hand until finally Isla curled the Starling's fingers around the container and gently pushed her hand away, signaling for her to take it.

"Now," Isla said brightly. "I need something from *you.*"

With the means to getting regular meals delivered settled, Isla set off for the marketplace, an invitation from the tailor that Ella had brought in her hands. Before participating in any of the six demonstrations, she needed new clothes. There were only so many outfits one could pack in the allotted luggage, so each Centennial, every ruler was gifted a custom wardrobe.

Today was Isla's appointment.

She heard Poppy in her ear.

*Your dresses are your armor—your jewels are your weapons.* They were the tools of a seductress.

It was the role Poppy had trained her for, as the first step of her guardian's plan—which Isla had no intention of following. She might not have powers, but that didn't mean she was *powerless.*

She could blend in. Listen. Hide. Strategize. All skills her and Celeste's plan required.

Ella had insisted on escorting Isla to the agora at the center of the Mainland, where the tailor operated. The Wildling Eldress had mentioned it in her stories, as *an enchanting place that blooms at night, like a flower facing the sun.*

Isla had insisted on going alone. It would give her a good opportunity to scope out this part of the island, to watch the islanders from a distance, unnoticed for as long as possible.

With three words, that plan went out the window.

"You're up early." *Grim.*

Isla swallowed, suddenly too aware of how tightly the fabric of her gown clung to her as she turned around.

Only to find him inches away.

Isla stumbled back. It took her a moment too long to find her voice. "So are you."

Grim lifted a broad shoulder, looking down at her just as she was forced to crane her neck up to maintain eye contact. "I like to take advantage of any time I can be out."

Right. His curse was the mirror of Oro's. Nightshades could not feel the energy and calm of night. Though they used to be nocturnal, choosing to live in darkness, that all changed five hundred years before.

"And I have business in the agora."

"As do I," Isla said.

Grim grinned. "Good. I hate walking alone."

Guards stood along the entrance and noticeably stiffened as Grim passed. Isla tried not to think about all the terrible things she had heard about Nightshades. About *him.* She tried and failed, and though her chin was held high, her legs went boneless beneath her.

Terra always said they were the most dangerous of the realms. Nightshades drew power from darkness, while all others drew from light. Rumors of their abilities abounded—the power to disappear, move through walls, spin nightmares, wield darkness itself.

Grimshaw had a reputation. There had been a war between Lightlark and Nightshade, just decades before the curses were spun. He had been the most fearsome warrior. It was rumored that by the end of a battle, his cloak was always soaked through with the blood of his enemies. Which only made his clear discomfort at Isla eating the heart at dinner more confusing.

Despite Grim's skill, Lightlark won the war, and a treaty was made. There was peace between all realms for a while.

Then the curses were cast, and most were convinced Nightshades had spun them in revenge.

Isla didn't know what to think. Nightshade had suffered a great loss thanks to their curse. Their realm's leader, Grimshaw's father, had died for the prophecy. His son had come into power immediately, back when having an heir was the norm. They weren't allowed anymore. Rulers attended the Centennial at their own realm's risk.

Isla knew why *she* was on the island. Grim's reasons were more of a mystery. If the rulers of realm wanted anyone dead more than Isla, it was Grim. He would find no allies during the Centennial. Winning the prize of the power promised would be nearly impossible without true partnerships. So why attend—why take the risk?

What did *he* want?

A knowing grin overtook Grim's sharply cut face as he studied her right back. His black hair was smooth down his pale forehead, ink across a page. "Deciding if I'm a villain?"

Isla narrowed her eyes at him. "Can you . . ."

"Read minds?" His head knocked gently from side to side. "Not really. I can read flashes of emotions. Fear. Anger." His lips raised into a half smile. "Curiosity."

Isla's next breath was as unsteady as if rocks had been piled in her lungs. She was an impostor, a powerless ruler in a pack of wolves. She was skilled at playing the part of a Wildling ruler, of keeping up the facade, but her emotions were far harder to control. This power of his could be her unraveling if she didn't learn to manage her feelings around him.

Mind abilities were common in Nightshades. It was part of what made them so dangerous. Rulers also often had one additional ability—rare powers carried through bloodlines, popping up generations later. They had nothing to do with the stars, moon, sun, nature, darkness, or sky.

Isla wondered if on top of this, Grim had one of those.

"You're nervous now." He stopped and looked at her. "Why are you nervous?"

*Nervous* wasn't something a powerful Wildling ruler should feel, even around the Nightshade ruler. She looked up at him, into eyes so dark they seemed endless, two galactic black holes, and pulled herself together enough to boldly ask, "Do you have a flair?"

Grim's head tilted back in understanding. "You're worried I have an ability I'm not telling you about. One I'm using against you at this very moment."

No use in hiding it. In her hundred days on the island, she would have to lie, steal, and possibly kill.

Grim wasn't part of the plan. Not yet.

Isla nodded.

He raised a shoulder and started down the walkway once more. "I do. But it's something I'll keep to myself, for now." Grim glanced at her. "It's not mind reading, however. Or anything else I could secretly use on you."

The hill ended, the grass stopped—and below, in the valley between two mountains, sat a marketplace.

Grim sighed. "Five hundred years, I haven't been back. And nearly nothing has changed." He turned to her, a gleam in his eye. "Hearteater—can you have chocolate?"

Isla tried to keep the hunger off her face. "I can eat my weight in it."

Islanders flooded the marketplace, pockets clinking with coin. The hubbub was unnerving. The Centennial was a deadly game. Didn't they understand that if the rulers were successful, one of their realms would perish? Weren't they afraid?

It seemed the hundred days of sunshine, outside of the storm, outweighed any terror.

The agora was made up of tiny houses, all pushed together and different as each of the realms. One shop resembled a turned-over teacup, its walls made of frosted glass. Another stood tall as a redwood, smoke spilling from a chimney like a string of storm clouds. The next was held up on stilts. Yet another resembled a star roped down from the heavens, silver and glittering.

The one they entered was shaped like a winter ornament, painted bright blue. "Skylings make the best sweets, I'll admit it," Grim said over his shoulder before opening the door with so much force its hinges screamed. The moment Isla walked inside, she groaned from somewhere deep in her chest.

Chocolate—velvety, nutty, sugary, silky cocoa.

She had only tasted chocolate on her forays to Skyling villages on their newland, during their quarterly celebrations. Skylings made constant excuses to host parties—before storms, after storms, even *during* storms. But nothing like this. Nothing like the thick slabs of fudge she watched a Skyling slice into rounds with a long knife.

Grim glanced at her, amused.

The man behind the counter paled at the sight of him. He shot a look over his shoulder at his associate, who had conveniently slipped into the back room. He didn't even register Isla.

*Interesting.* Being around Grim was like being a slightly smaller lightning rod in a storm—all wrath went to him.

Though he was one of the most powerful rulers, and she didn't have *any* power, in the islanders' eyes, they were both villains. Isla knew how important this was. Though, if they were successful, the rulers would decide which of them would die to fulfill part of the prophecy, the islanders' opinions and actions could shift the course of the Centennial. Their help—or lack of it—could mean the difference between life or death, especially for Isla, who didn't have any of her own people on the island. They were also typically invited to witness all six demonstrations.

Grim didn't seem to notice the way they all looked at him. Or, if he did, he didn't seem to care, unnervingly willing to play into the villainous role.

Though maybe he wasn't playing at all.

"Two of everything," he said lazily, pulling a handful of coin from his pocket and not bothering to count it. He set it on the counter and didn't wait for a reply, didn't look the man in the eye as he found a seat.

It was laughably small. His knees bumped against the top of the table. Isla slipped slowly into the chair across from him. "That's a lot of chocolate."

He shrugged. "You said you could eat your weight in it. I'm taking that at face value."

Soon, the owner of the shop placed a monstrous silver tray on the table. He bowed quickly, once at Isla, then at Grim, before hurriedly joining the rest of the staff in the back room.

Isla raised an eyebrow. "Did you set fire to the agora the last time you were here?"

Grim's knee bumped into her own, and she pulled her legs back so quickly, he grinned. "Let's just say the islanders' memories are long."

Before she could ask for clarification, he plucked a truffle between two enormous fingers. "Try this one first."

She tentatively took it, chewed it—and her eyes bulged.

"Divine, isn't it?"

Isla sank into her chair, her head lolling back. She shouldn't be wasting precious time on a chocolate tasting. But getting to know the Nightshade—perhaps getting him to trust her—could be useful. She closed her eyes, caramel on her tongue. "Wake me up when all of this is over."

A chuckle. Eyes still closed, she felt something rough against her lips.

"Open."

She did, and Grim dropped another truffle against her tongue. This one had a berry cream filling. A hard outer shell.

Isla tried every single one he offered. The fudge, the mint thins, a banana butter bar. Everything except for the chili pepper–powder praline.

"It's not that spicy," Grim said, throwing one carelessly into his mouth. He shrugged. "A hint of heat, nothing more."

"I like my tongue *functioning,* thank you."

Grim strung his long fingers together and rested his chin on the bridge they made. "So, you'll devour hearts and blood, but not a chili-dusted chocolate?"

A joke, but dangerously close to the truth. "Fine," she said, mumbling something else under her breath that made him grin wickedly.

Isla put the chocolate in her mouth and instantly regretted it. Her eyes watered, her mouth burned, her tongue immediately swelled. She spit it out, forgetting every manner, not even caring that the shop owner was peering at them through the kitchen window. Her nostrils flared. "*You,*" she said between deep gulps of water that made the pain even worse.

Grim laughed and laughed and laughed, that stupid dimple bright on his face. He tried to say something, then laughed some more, not stopping even when he got up, even when he used his Nightshade abilities to walk *through* the counter as if it was nothing and helped himself to a jug of milk. Not even when he placed a glass of it in front of Isla and said, "Drink."

She stared daggers at him the entire time she gulped it down, so desperately it dripped down her chin and the front of her dress. Villain indeed.

"Demon," she said.

He raised an eyebrow at her. "Not quite." He frowned at her dress. "We'll have to replace that. You're headed to the tailor now?"

"And you know that how . . . ?"

He only answered once they were out of the store. "I was also offered a consultation with the Lightlark tailor."

"I'm guessing your wardrobe doesn't have much range."

Grim frowned down at his black shirt, black pants, black boots, and black cape. "I told them I'm capable of dressing myself."

The streets were filled with dozens of torches dug into the stone, burning even though the day was warm and the sun was out. Sunling guards seemed to be in charge of keeping them lit, flames curling from their palms.

They reached a shop with crystalline glass windows, each pane cut in an emerald shape. Inside sat a rainbow of Wildling colors—spools of fabric, ribbon, thread, and piles of pins.

All for her.

"Enjoy," Grim said mockingly, and then he was gone.

Vanished. There one moment and gone the next. A chill tripped down her spine.

What would it be like, having a power like invisibility?

She entered the shop.

A bell rang, announcing her presence. A young Starling man with pins stuck into a cushion on his wrist froze. Isla waited for his eyes to widen in disgust or fear.

But the tailor bowed gracefully. "Isla, ruler of Wildlings. Pleasure. What happened to your gown?" Before she could respond, he lifted a hand. "Not to worry—*I* only use giant spider silk in my shop . . . Doesn't stain . . . strong as steel . . . and the fit is unparalleled." He motioned for her to step onto the platform.

"Preferred colors?"

The answers that came out of her mouth might as well have come from Poppy's, hundreds of miles away in the Wildling realm. Isla had been taught exactly what to say.

"Green. Red. Purples and pinks, on occasion."

"Preferred fit?"

"Tight."

"Length?"

"Long."

He examined her. "How attached are you to this dress?"

She looked down at it and shrugged. "Not especially."

"Good," he said, and snapped his fingers. At once, everything in the shop floated. Thanks to Celeste, Isla knew this realm's powers well. Starlings channeled energy from the stars, allowing them to move objects. He pointed a finger, and a spool of rich, bloodred fabric flew across the room, wrapping around Isla in a flash, so fast that it replaced the pink she had been wearing before, and she only realized it when she saw her old dress in ribbons on the floor. The red wrapped breathtakingly tightly around her waist; floating scissors made rough slices; flying threads and needles sewed at an impossible speed. The tailor directed it all like leading an orchestra, hands moving gracefully in front of him. Another sheet of fabric formed a silky, gauzy cape. A bodice was expertly crafted around her, and she was tied tightly into its corset, sucking her breath.

In seconds, she was in a new, beautiful gown.

She turned to face the tailor and found someone else sitting in the shop, elbows on his knees.

"How did you get in here?" she asked incredulously.

Grim looked bored. He raised an eyebrow at her, as if to say, *Is that a serious question?*

The tailor eyed him—remaining surprisingly calm compared to the other islanders they had encountered—and turned his attention to Isla. "How does it feel?"

She regarded herself in the many mirrors. "Like water. The fabric . . . it's smooth as a rose petal."

"Giant spider silk, Ruler. I'll get to work on your wardrobe."

Keeping her voice as low as possible, and shooting another look in Grim's direction, she said, "If it isn't any trouble, in addition to the dresses, I require something more suited for fighting. Pants. Armor." *Those* instructions came from Terra. As the tailor wrote down some notes, she peered behind him, getting a good look at the back room . . . and the lock on its door.

The tailor placed his hands perfectly together, as if in prayer. He *did* seem to worship clothes more than most people did their rulers. "My pleasure. I will have everything sent to the castle shortly."

Isla thanked him and glared daggers at Grim as she left the shop, knowing he would like it. Sharing chocolate had seemed to put some of her fears about Nightshades and their powers to rest. Part of her was surprised that she felt so comfortable around a man after only a few days of knowing him. And perhaps that was just what he wanted—for her to let her guard down. "Could you be less of a creep?" she said.

Grim's expression turned serious. "If you would like me to leave you alone, I will. Say the word, and I'll vanish."

Isla said nothing. She wondered what Grim was playing at. Whether she could use him, and this, to her advantage.

He started walking, and she fell by his side. Islanders turned to stare as they passed and looked at her for just as long as they did Grim. She supposed she stood out in her red dress, so bright against the light blue, white, and silver the day-dwelling islanders wore. Like blood spattered in the marketplace. "You're curious again, Isla."

She didn't meet his gaze. "Don't read me. It's rude."

He laughed. "It's not like I can help it."

Isla gave him a look. "The famed, all-powerful Nightshade ruler can't control his own abilities?"

The corners of his lips turned deviously. "Famed? Well, at least I know rumors of my greatness have reached even the Wildlings." He looked down at her, and the smile faded. "I'm glad you are having armor made," he said, pulling something from his pocket. It was a sheet of gold foil, the same paper her Centennial invitation had arrived on. "My demonstration is first," he said, returning the card to his black cloak before she could make out the words. He leaned low, lips getting dangerously close to her ear. "You will also need a sword."

By the time Grim's words sank in and the chill from his proximity had disappeared—so had he.

And Isla was left alone in the market, wondering why the ruler of Nightshade was helping her.

## CHAPTER SIX

# BONDBREAKER

Isla threw the weapon at Celeste, who caught it in the air, in her power's invisible grip. "What is this?"

"A sword," Isla said, pulling her own from behind her spine, where she had smuggled them both into the castle. "And an expensive one, at that."

Celeste gave her a look. "I *know* what it is, Isla," she said. "What I'm wondering is why you've brought the ghastly thing into my quarters."

Isla had long ago learned that the Starling didn't have the same appreciation for weapons, though her realm was famous for making them with their proprietary techniques and metals. Why would she? Celeste had the power of energy at her fingertips—she could wound an enemy from across the room. In her eyes, a sword was a clunky misuse of iron.

Which, Isla imagined, was exactly why Grim had chosen a duel as his demonstration. Well, he hadn't said the word *duel,* but with his clues, he might as well have.

"Our first trial is a duel," she said. "We'll need these."

Celeste crinkled her nose as if she had smelled something foul. "And who told you that?"

"Grimshaw."

Celeste blinked. "Is that who you were with this whole time?"

"No, just for a bit. Why?"

Celeste gave her a look. "Really, Isla?" She didn't need to say anything else. Grim was bad news. Dangerous. Untrustworthy.

"I know, I *know.* But I got this information, didn't I? Don't you think he could be useful?"

Celeste shook her head firmly. "No, Isla. I think, if anything, he'll use *you.* Us."

Was that what their trip to the agora had been? Just strategy by the wicked Nightshade ruler?

Of course it was. It would be foolish to believe it to be anything else.

Isla started to wonder if Grim's heads-up was even accurate. Maybe it *wasn't* a duel, or any type of demonstration involving a sword, and he was just trying to fool her into thinking so.

She frowned.

Celeste sighed in a long-suffering way. She placed both of her delicate hands upon Isla's cheeks and said, "My lovely, lovely, *naive* friend." Isla would have balked if it had been anyone other than Celeste saying those words. But even though they were practically the same age, Isla had learned priceless lessons from the Starling. Celeste had taken her under her wing when she had no one other than Poppy and Terra. "You will stay away from him," she said steadily, a sister warning a misguided sibling who should know better.

Celeste was right. Grim was a distraction. She wouldn't be the fool who fell for his tricks. Especially when her own mother had died because of her affection toward a man.

Especially when she had made it her mission to prove she was more than the temptress her guardians had trained her to be.

The first step in Terra and Poppy's elaborate plan was to seduce the king. Steal his power by making him fall in love with her. Without this step, the rest of their strategy was useless. And Isla was willing to do many things to save her realm. But that wasn't one of them.

Luckily, her friend had thought of another way for Isla to get everything she wanted.

"Good. Now. Even though we haven't started the demonstrations, the sooner we start preparing for finding the bondbreaker, the better," Celeste said.

*The bondbreaker.* That was their plan. In a room full of manuscripts taken from Lightlark, Celeste had discovered a text speaking of an enchanted relic. A giant glass needle with two sharp points on either side that could break any bond that imprisoned a person and their family line—including curses.

But everything on Lightlark had a cost.

The bondbreaker's cost was blood. Enough to kill even a ruler. That was why, to their knowledge, it had never been used before. On Celeste's chamber floor, they had come up with a plan to split the cost between the two of them.

And hope it wouldn't kill them both.

According to the text, the bondbreaker was hidden deep within a library on Lightlark. They didn't know which one, and each isle had its own. So, they would have to search them all.

Celeste would search Star Isle's library first. Hopefully, it would be there. If not, the Starling would have to go to great lengths to procure the tool Isla would need to access the rest of the libraries.

And, with their tight timeline, Isla needed to operate under the assumption that she would have to.

The bondbreaker would only break *their* realms' curses, not the rest. They wouldn't win the prize of the power promised in the prophecy. But Isla didn't care. By breaking the curse of being born powerless, she would finally receive the Wildling ability that had been denied to her at birth. And her realm would be rid of its suffering.

She could return to the Wildling newland free at last—no need to hide in her room any longer. She could inject power back into the land and make it prosper once more. She would have the life of an immortal ruler, centuries to explore the world with Celeste.

Everything she wanted hinged on finding the bondbreaker and its ability to break all the curses that affected her and her realm.

"I'll start tonight," Isla said.

To secretly search the libraries on Sun Isle, Moon Isle, and Sky Isle, Isla would need to blend in.

Her dark hair would be the first giveaway to her identity. But she had arrived prepared. Before leaving for the Centennial, she had sneaked into Poppy's quarters. Wildling elixirs ranged from healing remedies to enchantments to beauty products. Creams that tinted one's lips, or cheeks, or even, temporarily, *hair.*

She would have to mix the right color herself, which would be its own challenge, but at least she had the materials.

Clothing was the other problem.

Far past midnight, she crept out of the castle. She committed landmarks along the way to memory. The abbey with a giant single stained-glass eye. The insignia she had arrived upon just days before. A pile of ruins that she liked to think might have once been a lighthouse, powered by Sunling beams. She had read about those in one of the few books she was allowed a year.

Terra learned early on that she liked to read. So, she used books as incentives. If Isla didn't complain about her split knuckles or sore muscles during training, if she mastered a certain fighting technique, if she threw her throwing stars right at their marks, she was rewarded with a trip to the library.

Isla cherished them, wrote her favorite lines down on paper. Felt pangs of grief when she was forced to give them away in exchange for another.

*Only one book at a time,* her guardian told her. *Don't be greedy.*

She stopped just short of the agora, surprise making her still.

The marketplace transformed when the sun went down. Most shops were closed, their windows dark, but the ones that were open were . . . *open.* Just as the Wildling Eldress had described.

Somehow, some of the stores had been turned inside out, their walls completely folding out into the streets, no doors to be seen, the ceiling stretched out and wide like a fan. Patrons walked freely inside pubs and, moments later, out, holding foaming, overflowing drinks. Skylings danced in the middle of the road to music that spilled into the night, drums and guitar and voices that forced the darkness to obey its wild rhythm. Sunlings were specks of gold everywhere, enjoying the hours they could be outside.

The agora was lively, disorienting, but Isla remembered the roads from earlier. She took a back way, choosing alleys instead of main streets, following the lines of lit torches until she ended up at the back door of the tailor.

Every light was off. Every window was locked.

When she was sure there was no other way inside, she got on her knees and pulled out her pins. On one trip to the Skyling newland with her starstick, she had trailed a group of thieves, curious. She had watched from the shadows as they used pins and curved needles to work their way into a lock.

A useful skill for breaking into Poppy's and Terra's rooms later. For breaking out of her own room too.

The door popped open, and Isla gathered her tools, careful not to leave anything behind. She squinted through the darkness, not daring to turn any of the lights on. A tailor wasn't typically a place prone to robbery, therefore guards wouldn't be focusing on this street, but who knew how long it would take someone to stumble into the alley and see her through the window?

*Quickly.* Her eyes zeroed in on the colors she needed—every Lightlark realm's hues other than Starling, which Celeste would take care of.

White. She grabbed a simple long-sleeved and high-necked Moonling dress.

Light blue. She took a dress with pants that were supposed to be worn underneath, a fashion she had seen a few Skylings in the market wearing.

Gold.

There was no gold. Come to think of it, she didn't remember seeing the color in the store during her appointment.

Did Sunlings not use the same tailor as the rest of the realms?

*Why not?*

A voice at the window sent her to the floor. Two friends were leaning against the store, laughing merrily, clinking glasses together. She crawled to the wall and put her back against it, determined not to make a sound.

Half an hour passed before the men moved along, and Isla was gone moments later, careful to close the door on her way out, hoping the tailor would assume he left it unlocked by mistake.

With an armful of silk, she returned to the castle, one step closer to the bondbreaker.

## CHAPTER SEVEN

# DUEL

On the fifth day of the Centennial, the invitation to the first demonstration arrived. The paper was charred, black, burned. Only a few words were visible, carved into the page with a knife.

*Be ready to duel.*

Isla couldn't help but smile. Grim *had* helped her.

But why?

The time of the event was scrawled at the bottom—in one hour. Instead of having to scramble for a weapon, Isla had already purchased the ideal sword. One that was light enough for her to wield almost weightlessly, but sharp and firm enough to strike true. It had taken hours to choose the right one in the Starling weapons shop. The realm's metalwork really was unparalleled . . . though she longed for the familiar feel of one of her own blades from home.

The tailor's wardrobe had arrived the day before. The man worked at a remarkable speed. His commitment to his craft only made Isla feel worse about stealing from him.

*By finding the bondbreaker, I'm saving him and his realm,* Isla convinced herself to counteract the guilt.

One gown was the dark blue of sapphires, with crystal-shaped shards cut out of its sides. One was the purple of fresh lavender with an eye-rollingly low-cut bodice and skintight pants, finished with a glittering cape that tied around her waist, creating the illusion of a skirt. One, the green of emeralds, was tight and light and sheer enough to make her blush. Another, she discovered, had pockets.

For this demonstration, she wore the armor. Ella helped tie the many pieces together, grunting as she lifted the metal.

To Isla, it was a second skin. Terra had made sure of that.

How many times had she been left abandoned in the middle of the woods, or in the center of a rain forest storm, with fifty pounds of chain mail and armor on her? Getting back took more than a day. Without water, without food, with the howls of wolves and patter of panthers at her heels.

The last half mile was always done on her stomach as she dragged herself back to her room, nails digging into roots and dirt for purchase.

In comparison, the smartly made Starling fabric and thin sheets of iron were nearly weightless. They had been fashioned into parts that accentuated her figure while also protecting it—metal shoulder pads, chain mail sleeves and tights, metal-plated boots that ran up to the top of her thigh, a sculpted breastplate.

"Done," Ella said, slumping over after the last of Isla's outfit was assembled.

"Thank you," Isla said before taking a bite of the vegetable skewer and grains Ella had brought her for lunch. In exchange for the healing elixir, the Starling girl brought Isla regular meals, believing them to be indulgences, in addition to the hearts she planned to secretly throw off her balcony. "For *everything.*"

Ella bowed her head and gently tapped at her leg. She walked almost evenly now, and her brow wasn't set in its constant tension at the pain. "Thank *you,*" she said.

The duel took place at an arena in the farthest reach of the castle, one that used to be open but had been covered with a dome after the curses. It made the crowd's cheers echo and braid together, forming a single taunting voice from a thousand mouths. Rulers controlled many variables about their trials—what it would test, where it would take place, if there would be any advance notice, and who was allowed to witness it. Grim had invited all islanders. They sat separated by realm, filling every seat, rows lined by dozens of lit torches. Starling in their glittering silver. Skyling in their bright blue. Moonling in their immaculate white. Sunling in their polished gold.

Demonstrations were a spectacle. She knew that. Meant to test different skills. Meant to manipulate favor. Meant to decide who deserved to die.

Or, at the very least, who would determine the teams they would break into, which would, in some way or another, change the course of the Centennial by forcing alliances.

Each trial was also a risk. Though killing was not permitted until after the fiftieth day, Isla's own ancestor had lost one of her hands during a demonstration. It had weakened her ability to wield power significantly, and she was forced to have a child after the Centennial ended, as a better representative for the next one.

Grim's voice rumbled through the applause, silencing the room.

"Welcome to my demonstration," he said, somewhere. She couldn't place him—it was as if his voice was coming from everywhere at once. "You are all very menacing *with* your endless powers . . . but how will you fare without them?"

He announced the first pair—Oro against Azul.

The king's sword was made of solid gold to match his priceless armor. Isla wondered if the duel would end up embarrassing the king in front of his people, and the thought nearly made her smile. She had never heard anything of the king's fighting abilities in her years of lessons, which might mean he relied heavily on his fire instead.

Azul's own weapon was covered in precious jewels, sapphires mixed with diamonds. He didn't wear armor at all; much of his chest was exposed. But he *did* wear the ring she had gifted him. Was he so good he didn't require protection?

Both of Isla's assessments were wrong.

The duel finished within seconds. The king struck so quickly, she almost missed it. One moment, the tip of his sword was dug into the gravel of the arena—the next, it was at the Skyling's throat.

Azul only smiled graciously and bowed, admitting defeat.

Sunlings were on their feet, roaring in approval, waving long lengths of golden fabric above their heads.

Celeste and Cleo were next.

Isla's manicured nails dug into her palm, watching her friend enter the arena. The Moonling wore a serpentine grin. She didn't wear armor either, but she had opted for pants. Her weapon was long and thin like an ice pick.

Celeste held her sword steadily. Isla had chosen a lighter one for her friend, one that would be easy to maneuver by someone who didn't have extensive training. Her silver hair was plaited, stuck firmly to her scalp.

At the bell, Cleo lunged—

"Nervous, Hearteater?"

Grim's voice was at her ear. She didn't dare take her eyes off the action. Cleo had missed Celeste's arm by inches, and her friend had just unsuccessfully struck back.

"Don't call me that," she said quietly, wincing as Celeste nearly tripped right into Cleo's blade.

It was like she could hear the grin in Grim's words as he said, "Is that the thanks I get for my help?"

She spared him a quick withering look, retort on her tongue, and—

Froze. Grim was a fearsome warrior. He wore a helmet of spikes like daggers that shot from the crown of his skull. One dipped between his eyes, shielding his nose. His shoulders had the same sharp metal points that ran down the lengths of his arms, spikes everywhere.

He was a demon, death itself.

She swallowed. He watched the movement, staring at her neck far too intently, before almost absentmindedly baring his teeth, like he wanted to bite her there. Her skin inexplicably prickled at the thought.

*No, that's disgusting.* Isla forced herself to get it together. He didn't want to bite her. That was just in her head.

Why was that in her head?

The ringing of a bell tore her attention away, back to the arena.

Celeste's sword was on the ground. Cleo's blade was tapping recklessly against the Starling's heart. Then, it too dropped to the floor.

Relief washed over her. Celeste had lost, but that didn't matter. They both planned to perform adequately. Not badly enough to be marked as weak, but not strong enough to be chosen as a partner. While they couldn't control the pairings that would be decided on the twenty-fifth day unless they won the most trials—which would instantly identify them as competition to be potentially eliminated—they were relying on the fact that whoever *did* win would pair the youngest, most inexperienced rulers together. It would be the smartest choice, they reasoned, tying the weakest links together as easy prey for the rest of the matches.

*Don't draw too much attention to yourself,* Celeste had warned.

"Our turn, Hearteater," Grim said before strolling past her into the ring.

*Oh.*

Somehow, Isla hadn't put together that *they* would be dueling. She had been too distracted by Celeste's battle.

She didn't move a muscle, watching the center of the arena as Grim reached behind him for a broadsword thicker than her thigh.

Her throat was suddenly too dry. Grim chose the matches. This was his demonstration. He must have paired them together for a reason.

A theory formed in her head, pieces coming together. They were the only two rulers without their people present. The two most hated. Did he purposefully match them to show his superiority over her? To make sure, from the very first demonstration, that the island rooted for *him* over her?

Celeste was right. She couldn't trust him.

"*Go,*" her friend whispered sharply, suddenly at her side.

Right. Isla stepped into the exposed center on legs that weren't as steady as they had been a few minutes before.

Not one person cheered. When Isla's sword knocked into the metal plating her long boots, feeling uncharacteristically off-kilter, the sound was projected through the silence.

*Get yourself together,* she told herself, thinking of her training. Of Terra.

The Nightshade might be plotting against her. All she could do was ensure his plan was foiled before it even began.

With a steadying breath, Isla drew her weapon and took her stance. It was second nature, like tumbling into sleep or taking a breath. The only time she ever felt like she had a whisper of power. Part of her still wanted to cower. But Isla knew how to handle a blade better than a quill.

The bell rang out, loud and clear.

Grim struck first.

Isla twirled to the side, fast as the wind. His blade met air. She pivoted on her heel and aimed for his chest.

Grim was too quick. He dodged the blow, then struck again, only for his blade to meet hers. Her arm shook for a moment from the sheer strength of it. Quickly, she regained her balance and slid her sword right down his, the metal against metal making her wince, slicing through the room.

His eyes widened in surprise as he shot backward, barely missing the tip of her blade.

*See? Maybe you should have chosen a different opponent,* she thought.

"You're feeling confident, Hearteater," Grim purred. He advanced, and she blocked his blow. Tried again, only to meet steel. For a few stumbling, dizzying seconds, their blades met over and over and over, touching, skimming, clashing. Somehow, he was at her ear. "Tell me, how will you feel when you lose?"

She swallowed and whipped around—then ducked, air shooting out of her nostrils as he went for her neck. And barely missed. *Too close.*

She shot up and forward, one arm completely outstretched, the other tight behind her back. She was light as a dandelion on her feet but strong as the steel of her blade with every advance. It was a part of her, another limb, an old friend. Each of her motions was faster than the last as she slipped into her rhythm, her flow. Her dance. She felt the room like she was barefoot, the air like it was electric. A growl sounded from the back of her throat as she pushed Grim farther down the arena, toward its wall, at the crowd sitting high above.

His mouth was a line as he focused; she could have sworn a bead of sweat shot down his temple.

"You're feeling surprised, *Grim,*" she said, her voice deep and raspy.

His eyes were fierce, no gleam in them anymore.

Isla grinned, spun fast as a maelstrom to gather more strength, and struck like a cobra—so hard that Grim stumbled, just the slightest bit.

It was all she needed. She leaped off the floor with a warrior's cry and landed right in front of him, pinning him to the wall.

Her blade was at his throat.

His clattered to the ground.

She was panting, right in his face. He was looking at her like he hadn't ever seen her before.

"Everyone seems to forget," she said, not breaking his gaze, even though it meant tilting her head. They were both panting, their chests flush with every breath. "That Wildlings are, above all, warriors." Isla might not have had powers. And she might have been trapped like a bird in a cage her entire life because of it. But she could fight as well as any ruler—Terra had made sure of that. She dropped the blade from his throat.

And there was clapping.

Isla whipped around, stunned by the sound, the only cheer in the room of hundreds.

The king. He was clapping for her.

Again.

She turned back to the Nightshade ruler, expecting him to hate her. But he was grinning, his eyes filled with something like delight.

He was *thrilled* that she had beaten him.

Which made no sense.

Her eyes narrowed at him, trying to read him. Never had anyone's motivations been more of a mystery.

What did Grim want?

What game was he playing?

Spurred by their king, a few claps sounded in the crowd, then spread like wildfire until everyone was cheering, celebrating her victory, the lesser of two evils overcoming the other.

Still confused, Isla made her way to the sidelines, only to find a concerned Celeste. Her friend couldn't say anything, not in front of the other rulers, but Isla knew she had made herself stand out too much.

The islanders and rulers were certainly noticing her now.

Cleo and Oro dueled next, as winners of their pairs. The Moonling put on an impressive display. In less than a minute, the king succeeded, however. But not before Cleo was able to tear a line down his arm. The skin flayed open. Blood stained the arena, sizzling. He did not make a move to heal himself before moving on to the next duel.

Part of Isla wondered how the Moonling dared wound the king. Nervous energy seemed to swirl through the arena, some of the islanders perhaps thinking the same thing.

Oro did not even bother leaving the ring. He stood, blade dug into the ground before him, hands resting on its hilt. Still bleeding. Staring at her. His final opponent.

His eyes were hollow. Emotionless.

She did not shy away from his lifeless gaze as she stepped back into the arena. This time, there was no applause for her. The crowd's loyalty had shifted as quickly and predictably as the tide.

A bell, somewhere.

Then a sword, slicing the air before her to pieces. She managed to get her own up in time, just barely, but the strength of the king's first blow echoed through her bones. She felt the force of it in her teeth.

A groan escaped her lips as she deepened her stance, digging in, absorbing the impact, shielding against his advance.

He kept pushing, and her back foot slid, compromising her posture. He was forcing her to make a move, to make herself vulnerable.

Did he think she was a fool?

She added a second hand along the hilt of her blade, then shoved back as hard as she could.

He did what she expected, pressing back in equal measure—

And she spun at the last moment, leaving him stumbling forward.

Isla was quicker on her feet, she knew that. It was her advantage.

But Oro was stronger. Even while wounded.

The king's sword found hers before she could truly recover, and Isla fought to keep up, mostly on the defense, blocking blow after blow after deafening blow. He knew his strength. His strategy was to tire her, to use up her energy on taking his hits instead of making her own. Until her arms gave out.

She almost smiled.

He didn't know that when Isla was twelve, Terra had left her hanging onto the branch of a tree, fifty feet above the ground, for five hours.

*Fall, and you'll break your legs,* she'd said. *They'll heal, but you won't be allowed to go on the tour of the newland if you're injured.*

She had been looking forward to her first tour of her lands for years.

The first hour wasn't so bad. She had been training for a while at that point. Her arms were strong.

By the third hour, she was screaming.

By the fourth, her voice gave out.

By the fifth, one of her shoulders had popped out of its socket.

She never let go.

But she wasn't allowed to go on the tour. A punishment for the screaming.

*You take the pain like medicine,* Terra had said in response to her tears. *You swallow it down with a smile.*

Then she popped Isla's shoulder back into place without medication. Another lesson.

The king would not be the one to wear her down.

Still—it was to her benefit for him to think he would. She slowed her movements slightly, bent her wrist just a degree. Angled her sword the way someone trying to shift its weight might.

He advanced faster in response, sensing her weakening.

She took a step back. Another, this time with a slight stumble.

He made his final, bold move.

And Isla unleashed the strength she had stored.

The king was caught off guard by the force of her blow. His blade shook with the impact. She advanced, seizing her chance, aiming everywhere. He was now forced to retreat, deflecting her hits, his brows coming together in focus.

She was going to win.

Her blade became a serpent, the one on her crown come to life, striking for the kill, fangs and all. Again, again, again, she pounced, nearly reaching his heart. Almost grazing his neck.

She leaped forward, ready for the final blow—

And hesitated.

Celeste was a silver reminder in the wings, right behind the king. She wasn't supposed to win the trial. This wasn't part of the plan.

*Don't you want to be free?* a voice in her head said. That was more important than her pride. Than winning. Than anything.

At the last moment, Isla aimed lower, to a place Oro would easily be able to deflect. When he did, she loosened her grip on her hilt.

So, when his sword struck, her own went flying across the stadium.

Cheers erupted, not only Sunlings, but every Lightlark realm getting to their feet. Honoring their king.

But he only watched Isla, eyes narrowing.

He *knew*.

Somehow, he knew she had let him win.

The tip of his sword eventually, half-heartedly, slid up her stomach, to her heart. Then away. But the king's gaze was relentless, studying her far too closely.

Isla shrank under it, folding herself over, bowing, recognizing defeat.

She retreated to the wings as Oro was crowned the winner of the demonstration.

Her eyes didn't meet his again. But she could feel his gaze on her, not lifeless any longer—but merciless as flames.

# CHAPTER EIGHT
# CELESTE

The first time Isla met Celeste, she'd felt relief. She had learned about the other rulers of realm her entire life. Four of them were terrifyingly old and skilled, alive when the curses were spun. The original heirs of the fallen rulers who had sacrificed themselves for the prophecy. They were the stars of her nightmares, each of them killing her in her dreams a thousand times before the Centennial invitation had even arrived.

The Starling was a mystery. Young like Isla. Disadvantaged because she would have no Terra or Poppy, no one ancient and wise to guide her, thanks to their curse.

Still, Starlings were powerful.

*She is your enemy,* Terra would tell her. An informant had long ago announced to her guardians that the latest in the long string of Starling rulers was a girl. *One of you will lose.*

Terra convinced her that as the youngest two, they would be preyed upon to fulfill part of the prophecy. Only one of the two would live.

*It must be you.*

So, when Isla accidentally portaled her way directly into the Starling ruler's newland castle with her starstick, and the girl just looked at her and smiled, a weight was taken from her chest.

"I think the starstick knew I needed you," Isla would tell Celeste years later during one of their many secret sleepovers.

"And that *I* needed *you,*" Celeste replied, squeezing her hand tightly.

Not enemies—

Friends.

*Sisters*. That word did a much better job at encapsulating their bond, a relationship Isla could have never prepared for after a life alone. She loved Celeste more than anyone. Even her guardians.

It was only natural to tell the Starling her secret, three years after they met.

It was because of her love for her friend that she had been honest.

"I understand if you don't want to work together anymore," Isla had said. "Truly, Celeste. I would understand."

Celeste had held her tightly as they both cried. Knowing Isla's powerlessness complicated everything. Knowing there was a big possibility that the other rulers would find out during the Centennial, and Isla would die once the rest of the prophecy was fulfilled.

"No," the Starling whispered into Isla's shoulder after a long while. "We work together. Always." Taking her face into her hands, she looked right into Isla's eyes and made a promise. "I will protect you. We will walk away from the Centennial and into the rest of our very long lives together."

That was why Isla listened—or tried to. Celeste had put herself and her entire realm in danger, forming an alliance with her.

And Isla might have already ruined it.

"I'm sorry," she said, looking at the floor of Celeste's room. It was past midnight, so no one would hear their whispers. They had barely seen each other, knowing being caught visiting each other's rooms would mean the end of their secret plan.

But tonight, Isla had taken the risk.

Celeste shook her head. Sighed. She was braiding her silver hair just to do something with her hands. Her friend often busied herself when she was anxious. Before the Centennial, Celeste had made a blanket with her stress, knitting for hours on end, until Isla had finally hidden the needles. "We can't mend what is done," she said simply.

Silence spread, and it always made Isla uncomfortable. She filled it with excuses. "I mean, was I just supposed to lose against Grim? I couldn't. That's what he *wanted.*" Though his grin at being defeated hinted otherwise . . .

She had no idea what he wanted.

Celeste gave her a look. "You weren't supposed to make yourself a target."

Isla didn't know why she rolled her eyes, but she did, suddenly annoyed.

That was when the Starling stood. Energy crackled in the room, a sure sign that she was angry. "You need to think long term," she said sharply, hands in fists at her sides. "Islanders were watching. All the rulers were watching. You beat *Grimshaw.* You nearly beat the king. Do you mean to make enemies, Isla? Do you mean to become someone the other rulers want to *get rid of?*"

Isla looked away. "Of course not."

"Then you need to *listen.* We have a plan. Complete the demonstrations without notice. Be the young, inexperienced rulers they already see us as, so the winner of the demonstrations hopefully pairs us up. That allows us to search for the bondbreaker, to work together." Isla was surprised when Celeste's voice broke. She had only seen the Starling cry a handful of times before. "It allows me to spend time with *you* without making anyone suspicious. To protect you." A silver tear shot down her cheek. She took a shaking breath as Isla made her way to her friend, instantly ashamed. "I can't protect you if you won't listen."

Isla threw her arms around Celeste, holding her close.

The truth was, if the Starling ruler only wanted to survive and save her realm, she would have abandoned Isla. She knew her secret, after all. It would be easy to share it with everyone else. To guarantee Wildling would die, over Starling, when the time came to choose a ruler and realm to sacrifice.

But she hadn't. Because they were sisters.

Celeste was a better friend than she deserved.

"I'm sorry," Isla said. "I promise, I'll think of the plan. I promise to listen."

Later, Celeste told Isla that she had searched the Star Isle library.

"It wasn't there," she said. One library off their list.

A pang of disappointment rattled through Isla's stomach. Their plan would have been far easier if the bondbreaker had ended up being a Starling relic.

"I'm going after the gloves next," she said.

Isla's head jerked up. She met Celeste's eyes.

"Don't look at me like that," she said quietly. "Like you didn't know this was next." She dipped her chin. "Like this wasn't *your* idea."

Of course Isla knew this part of their plan was next. If the bondbreaker wasn't in the Star Isle library, they would need a way to get into the protected sections of the other isles' collections.

The gloves were crucial to getting inside them.

This particular type of enchanted accessory was well-known throughout even the newlands—gloves that were able to harness a whisper of a realm's power. Isla had researched them obsessively, believing they could help her during the Centennial. All she would have to do was capture a bit of Poppy's or Terra's ability to wield nature and use them to pretend . . .

Unfortunately, the gloves were dangerous to procure. It was said they were made of skinned human flesh. Only dark markets in the newlands would dare sell such a thing—and Isla had searched nearly all of them.

They were rarer nowadays. Not regularly made. Doing so wasn't typically worth the hassle. The power they held was minimal. Inconsequential.

Unless someone found a very specific use for them.

Isla had suggested the gloves when they needed a way to get into the libraries, as a last resort.

"You look ill, Isla," Celeste said, frowning at her.

She swallowed. "How are you going to get a pair?"

Her friend studied her. Sighed. "Don't ask questions you don't want answers to."

Perhaps she *would* be ill. "If you have to make new ones, go to the prison. Pick a killer, someone terrible—"

Celeste grabbed Isla's shoulders almost painfully, bringing her back into the moment, steadying her. "This is my part of our plan," she said. "Focus on yours."

Right. Hers. Isla had volunteered to search the other three libraries. Once they had the gloves, her role would truly begin. "Speaking of my role . . ." she said. It was her turn to share her bad news about not being able to secure the Sunling clothing.

Celeste's brows folded together. "That's strange . . ." She pursed her lips. "Though, on Star Isle, the nobles *did* tell me suspicious things have been happening since the last Centennial. Sunling has separated itself more than ever from the other realms. They stay mostly on their own isle."

"Do you think the king is behind it?"

Celeste frowned. "I'm not sure. But I don't trust him at all."

Neither did Isla. Even if he had saved her the first day of the Centennial. After their duel, she was willing to bet he didn't trust her either.

"That's not the only thing," Celeste said, and Isla braced herself for an added obstacle. "Moonling has also been acting oddly. My nobles said they have guards on their bridge every day. *All* day."

Isla cursed. How was she supposed to sneak onto Moon Isle and search its library with guards at its entrance?

She was allowed to enter, but her movements would surely be shared with Cleo.

Who would immediately become suspicious.

"Did you check?" Isla asked.

Celeste nodded. Her friend was always thorough. "I went for a stroll along that part of the isle and confirmed it. Two guards, right at the front, checking everyone in."

Two Moonlings would not stand between them and their plan.

"I'll find a way," Isla said, eager to help after her display at the duel.

And hoping it wasn't just one more promise she couldn't keep.

## CHAPTER NINE

# CROWN

Thankfully for Isla, the rulers did not dine together every meal. Some nights, Celeste, Azul, Cleo, and Oro ate on their isles. Others, they ate separately in their chambers. Group dinners were preceded by an invitation and were awkward affairs, for Isla especially, since she would sit with an empty plate in front of her. Ever since their first dinner, eight days ago now, the king had honored her request to eat in her room. It made her time at the Centennial easier, she had to admit. Hearts were to be provided at her convenience—and secretly disposed of.

Cleo's constant insults also made dinners uncomfortable. The Moonling had made her distaste for her well-known, ever since that first meal when Isla had foolishly bitten back. She had regretted it ever since, especially when Celeste's eyes would meet hers, a reminder of why it was important to stay under the radar.

Unnoticed. Unremarkable.

Isla was about to enter the dining room for one of these group dinners when she stopped suddenly.

There were too many voices inside. Dozens.

The doors opened by someone else's hands, revealing a room filled with nobles from every Lightlark realm. Many turned to watch Isla, fear and curiosity in a battle across their features, studying her as carefully and critically as a jeweler searching for flaws in a diamond.

Every one of Poppy's lessons pummeled into her head at once.

*Back straight.*

*Chin up.*

*Shoulders down.*

*Look right ahead—pay them no mind.*

*Fingers relaxed at your sides.*

This was clearly a demonstration. Whoever had planned it had decided only to invite Lightlark's nobles.

No invitation had preceded it. There were often surprises during the Centennial. *You must be prepared for anything,* Terra had told her.

Demonstrations were opportunities for the rulers to assess each other. To decide who was weak. To potentially win the power to choose the pairs that would work the remainder of the Centennial to figure out the prophecy.

Isla racked her head for what kind of trial this could be. Her guardians had a list of demonstrations from past Centennials. Some were more elaborate than others. Quests. Challenges to tame a wild beast. Scavenger hunts, even. Tests of physical strength, or strategy, or the mind.

There weren't any clues around her. All she saw were tables set with wineglasses and crystal plates.

It really did look like a dinner. Her nerves curbed a bit. Perhaps it *was* just a meal and the nobles were simply invited as guests.

They had seen her during the first trial, from a distance. And she had clearly caught their attention. Some of them looked too long at the parts of her dress that hugged her body. Others watched her like she might be getting ready to shed her clothes or burst into flames. A few backed away, eyes trained on her mouth and fingers, as if half expecting to see claws.

She was a temptress. A monster who subsisted on the hearts of easily seduced prey.

They thought they knew her.

They knew nothing.

A few people gasped as Grim appeared beside her from thin air, making himself visible. His expression did not change.

The people who weren't watching her before were certainly looking now. The temptress and the ruler of darkness. A winning pair.

"Grim," she said curtly, avoiding meeting his gaze. Remembering she knew nothing about him or what he was after.

"Hearteater," he whispered, so only she could hear it. His eyes dipped, studying every inch of her new crimson dress. The two thin straps. The simple scrap of silk of a bodice. Her waist, where the dress cinched tightly before tumbling into more sheets of fabric that clung to her body. Gloves to her elbows, which she rarely wore but had opted for, if only for a bit more coverage, the same color and material as her dress.

He looked shamelessly, eagerly, like it was important to commit every inch to memory. She had never been studied so thoroughly.

Did he mean to embarrass her?

Or seduce the seductress?

His dark eyes seemed to get even darker as they met hers, and he said, "I'm not sure what I enjoy more. Seeing the way you grip a sword . . . or the way your dress grips you."

If looks could kill, the Nightshade would be dead, and Isla would have broken the first rule of the Centennial. Grim's lips formed a devious smile in response to her glare.

She took a step toward him, emboldened. She still wasn't sure what game Grim was playing, but she *did* know he enjoyed it when she bit back.

"And I don't know what *I* enjoy more. Replaying the image of my sword against your throat . . . or thinking about how your heart might look on my plate."

Grim's dark eyes flashed with amusement. "Careful, Hearteater," he whispered, towering over her, standing far too close. "I might just give it to you."

For the last few moments, it might as well have been just her and Grim in the room.

Applause brought her back into the crowd. Isla turned to see that Azul had positioned himself at the head of a table already filled with the other rulers. "Welcome," he said. "If you could all make your way to your seats, we'll get started."

Isla rushed to the table, grateful for an excuse to put some distance between her and the Nightshade. Though the only two remaining seats were next to each other. Perfect.

It was clear this *was* a demonstration, not an elaborate dinner event, even though food was being brought out by dozens of staff. Her mind began spinning possibilities. She was alert, studying every detail, mentally preparing herself for whatever trial she might face.

The nobles had settled in their seats. Isla studied the suits and dresses, all made from dazzling fabrics. The tailor must have been busy in the prior months. She wondered if he had noticed his two missing pieces yet.

But the shop had hundreds of clothes . . . it would be nearly impossible to take inventory each day.

Then again, the tailor seemed deeply committed to his profession. Perhaps he *had* noticed. Would he report the theft?

Would he suspect the Wildling who had been in his shop that same morning of being the culprit?

"Let us begin," Azul said heartily, smiling widely. The Skyling ruler had the most perfect, shining teeth she had ever seen. Tonight, he wore robes with triangle cuts along the sides, revealing markings painted across his dark skin, symbols she didn't recognize. Some Wildlings inked themselves with needles and paint after their training or honorable feats. Isla was never allowed. Her body did not belong solely to her, Poppy said. It belonged to the realm. She was its representative, its lifeline. Even after having been born so wrong.

"Tonight, I would like to celebrate the tremendous abilities that will allow us to succeed in shattering our curses," Azul said. "Rulers of realm, would you honor us with a demonstration of your power?"

Isla almost dropped the goblet of water in her hand she had absent-mindedly reached for.

Grim's eyes were on her cup. Her fingers were shaking against the stem, water rippling inside her glass. If she thought her legs would be steady beneath her, she might have run right out of the room.

She had no powers to demonstrate.

*Grim*—he could make the lights go out. He could make her disappear, or at least cause a diversion. If she asked, he would. He would love the chance to cause chaos. And, though his intentions were murky, he had helped her before.

But then she would have to explain why. She swallowed, weighing the risks.

Before she could say a word, Azul said, "Grim. We haven't had a Nightshade on our island for centuries." His voice was tight. Untrusting. "Would you go first?"

Grim stayed seated for a few moments, and Isla wondered what would happen if he simply ignored the ruler of Skyling. Finally, he stood.

He opened his palm.

The room changed. Suddenly, there were a hundred Grims, standing between each chair. All smirking. The ceiling cracked open, the floor split, large slabs of stone fell right onto their heads, screams pierced the air—

Everything disappeared. The room was back to normal. There was just one Grim, looking bored, as if the display hadn't used even a whisper of his power.

The room was silent. Someone dropped a glass.

Nightshades had mind abilities, Isla knew. But this was more, a vision on a grand scale.

How dangerous would that skill be in war?

Or *now,* in this game?

She looked over at the king. Oro watched Grim with hard eyes, like his display was a threat. A declaration of exactly what he was capable of.

"Cleo, if you would," Azul said, a bit less excitedly.

She had to come up with something. Quickly.

Terra and Poppy had prepared her for this very possibility. But *their* complicated plan had hinged on her already having gotten close to the king and stolen one of the enchantments he supposedly had in his personal collection, a Wildling flower able to multiply and live forever. She'd had specific directions to get it as soon as possible.

Something she had completely forgotten about, in favor of her and Celeste's plan.

She hadn't even spoken to the king directly since that first dinner, avoiding him as much as possible. Perhaps *too* much, in blatant defiance of the first degrading step of her guardians' strategy.

Now, what would she do?

Admit her secret not only to all the nobles, but to the rulers as well?

She might as well count herself dead the second the clock chimed midnight on the fiftieth day. Not even Celeste could protect her from all the rulers. She had admitted as much.

*Celeste*. Isla finally looked at the Starling ruler, who was staring her down, clearly trying to get her attention for a while.

Her expression was strained, eyes wide in worry.

Isla was a burden. Always needing to be looked after. Cared for.

She didn't know why, but she smiled back, easily, nodding her chin slightly as if to say, *Not to worry, I have a plan*.

Though she never had her own plan, did she? She'd only ever gone along with others' strategies. Never her own. Not really.

Cleo was in front of their table now. Her arms lifted dramatically.

Wine red as blood shot up from every goblet, into the center of the room. She moved her hands as if petting a wild beast, and from the wine emerged a massive shark with three rows of teeth. It rushed at the crowd, falling from the sky, its monstrous jaw coming apart—but before it could reach Cleo, her hand made a fist, and the shark froze into ice. Its teeth became mauve icicles that landed in a perfect circle around the Moonling, digging deep into the floor. The rest became a dizzying steam.

Applause rang through the room, the nobles not looking upset in the slightest that their goblets now sat empty. Cleo looked very smug as she walked back to the table.

"Celeste?"

The Starling slowly stood, shoulders tense. Isla knew her friend wasn't nervous, at least not for her *own* demonstration. She walked carefully to the front, hair shimmering below the chandelier flames. Celeste raised a finger to the air.

And the room exploded.

Fireworks burst from every corner, silvery sparks showering down like miniature shooting stars. They screeched and roared, flying through the room, before shattering against the walls into silvery specks.

The crowd cooed, some reaching up to touch the stardust that fell like confetti, draping the tables in glitter. Some of it landed in Isla's hair.

It was beautiful.

Isla's stomach lurched, waiting for her name to be called. She needed a plan . . . a way out—

"My turn, I suppose," Azul said, smiling good-naturedly.

The Skyling stood with grace, his cape curling behind him in a self-created breeze. He spun his wrist toward the ceiling, and the air began to ripple. Three clouds like spun sugar appeared, growing wider and wider, until their corners touched. They darkened, then lit with flashes of light—storm clouds. Thunder echoed through the room, before the clouds calmed and became white as parchment. The audience looked up in wonder as they floated down toward their heads. Their fingers went right through them. When the clouds reached their table, even Isla reached a gloved hand up, trying hard to smile while dread boiled in her stomach.

She needed to think . . . she needed help . . .

Azul took a deep breath and blew with so much force that everyone's hair flew back, their capes cracking behind their chairs. And the clouds were no more.

The Skyling turned toward her and grinned.

Now there was no doubt.

Isla's heart was a drum in her chest as Azul spoke her name.

*Powerless, powerless, powerless*—the word was a chant, a taunt, so loud in her head, she wondered how no one else could hear it.

Compared to all the other rulers' demonstrations, she felt as useless and unremarkable as a piece of coal among diamonds. But she still had to pretend for a few more weeks—long enough to find the bondbreaker.

Celeste couldn't help her. Her guardians couldn't help her. Grim couldn't help her.

She had to find her strength.

Isla stood, feeling eyes on her like stage lights. Nobles whispered, disgust and fear clear on their well-powdered faces. She pressed her lips together, her plan a roughly made puzzle still forming in her head, then smiled, trying to look confident, though her knees trembled beneath her dress.

"King? Would you assist me in my demonstration?"

Oro blinked at her. Now, in his nearly always lifeless eyes, she read many things. Curiosity. Irritation. Perhaps even worry. All of it gone in an instant. He was expressionless by the time he stood, towering over her, offering his hand.

It was foolish garnering his attention after their duel, after he had looked so suspicious of her actions. But being bold was the only way she was going to get through this demonstration without having everyone question her and her abilities.

She led the king to the front of the table, her grip too tight on his hand, a sign of her nerves. "Stand there," she ordered. Then, trying not to look at the faces that showed their outrage at her audacity at commanding the king, that were as hungry for her to fail as they were for the red meat on their plates, she walked to the opposite side of the room.

Slowly, willing her fingers not to shake, she shed her many rings, placing them on the nearest table, before a Sunling who gasped at the wealth piled in front of him. She took her gloves off and kept one clenched in her hand. With the other hand, she pulled a pin from her hair.

Not any ordinary pin. A throwing star, disguised to look like an accessory.

The room was silent, so Cleo's voice carried as she said, "I didn't realize you came to dinners *armed,* Wildling."

Isla lifted her chin slightly, taking the cool metal into her palm. "I'm always armed," she said.

She could have sworn she heard someone near her gulp.

Oro did not make a move, standing still before her, yards away. She did not break his gaze as she took the throwing star between her teeth. And tied her remaining glove over her eyes.

The crowd gasped, but she couldn't see their expressions anymore. She couldn't see anything behind the dark-red fabric.

She took the star from between her lips and put it between her fingers, its deadly sharp points digging into her skin.

Isla breathed in, slowly, as Terra's lessons ran through her mind.

*Be still, child.*

*Do not be easily troubled.*

*You are a warrior.*

*Let them fear you.*

*Let them see what it means to be wild.*

The star flew.

Isla heard the unmistakable clang of metal against metal as it found its mark.

She lifted the fabric from her eyes—and couldn't help but smirk as she saw Oro, king of Lightlark, still glued in place, his gaze not on her but on the crown she had knocked from his golden head.

It clattered loudly on the ground before settling, echoing through the silent room.

Isla sauntered over to Oro, forgetting her rings. His eyes finally went to hers. She couldn't read him in that moment and didn't try to. Instead, she bent down and picked up his crown.

"You dropped this," she whispered before handing it over and taking her seat once more.

She hadn't used a drop of power in her demonstration. But no one questioned her, shocked at her nerve. Outraged.

And for just a slice of a second, she felt like the most powerful ruler in the room.

Oro was the last ruler to perform.

Isla expected fire. A raging inferno from his hand.

Instead, the king stood, placed a palm on the table—

And the stone turned to gold. It happened in waves. The metal overtook the marble, then dripped down the side and smothered the floor. In seconds, it was all gilded.

An impossible power. Thousands of years ago, it was said Starlings could make diamonds. Wildlings could make emeralds and rubies grow in their palms like flowers.

Sunlings could turn goblets to gold.

It represented a complete mastery of power.

Could he turn a person to gold? Kill them by gilding them?

Rulers decided how their trial would be judged. Azul announced that the nobles would be voting for the winner, with the caveat that they could not vote for their own realm. As if that made it fair.

It was no surprise the king won, again. He *deserved* to, Isla had to admit, with a display that had rendered them all speechless.

Even the Sunling nobles looked shocked. They had clearly never seen Oro use this power before.

Which only made Isla wonder what else the king was keeping secret.

# CHAPTER TEN
# JUNIPER

The night tasted of salt. Wind blew the scent of the sea up and over the cliffs and trees, to where Isla crouched, on the outskirts of the agora.

Patterns formed for the patient, Isla knew, and she had learned to be a very special brand of persistent while trapped within her glass castle. It had been five days since Azul's demonstration. Celeste was busy sourcing the gloves. No other trials had been announced. So Isla had focused on her part of their plan. She had visited the agora almost every night, watching. Waiting.

She knew the nobles who frequented a storefront that sold art during the day but turned into a secret brothel past midnight. She knew the shops that had back entrances and exactly what time they truly closed. She counted the number of songs the band played before packing up for the night—always fourteen—and noted the members who would go to a bar before setting off for home.

The important information was gleaned when the Sunlings were long gone, lest they burst into flames with the rising sun. When the first rosy hint of day coated the horizon and the only people left in the marketplace were too full of drink to notice her, she would walk the back streets, paying attention. Listening.

That was how she learned about the barkeep.

The man locked his door for the night with a key he kept in the pocket of his immaculately pressed light-blue pants. There was a strange rhythm to the jingle of his lock—it took five turns to get it right.

He turned around and startled.

Isla sat on an unsteady stool, hands clasped in front of her. The place reeked of alcohol. Sharp, pure, concentrated liquor. She had never tried a sip, thanks to Poppy and Terra, but she knew the smell well.

*Your head is already in the clouds,* they said. *No need to cloud it even more.*

"It seems business is booming," she said, motioning at the dozens of empty glasses left discarded on the tables, the leftovers from a euphoric night.

The barkeep grinned, making his strangely shaped mustache curl upward on either side. "Well, the years haven't been kind. But bad times are good for business."

Isla wasn't wearing her crown, or any of her brighter colors, but the barkeep stared at her eyes. "You know who I am, then," she said.

The Skyling's gaze remained fixed upon her as he made his way to the other side of the bar. He uncorked a bottle, poured it directly into a glass, and took a sip of the honey-colored substance, eyes never leaving hers. "Of course I do, Wildling. The question is . . . do you know who I am?"

Isla had watched countless islanders walk in and out of this bar, too quickly to have had a good time, without any drink in their hands. Some left without smelling of alcohol at all. She had followed some of them, brushed past them, seen there was nothing new in their pockets. Which meant the barkeep was selling something other than liquor. Something invisible, yet priceless. Gossip on the street had all but confirmed it.

"You're the person islanders come to for information."

The Skyling pursed his lips, considering. Finally, he put his drink down and bowed. "Juniper, at your service."

"What is your price?" she asked. She had arrived prepared. Without waiting for him to answer, she dropped a handful of precious gems on the counter, next to a large pile of coin. Ready to pay whatever she needed to for the right information.

Juniper looked at the display and grinned. "I require a different sort of payment . . ." he said.

Her breath hitched. What was he implying?

He must have seen her tense, because he added, "I deal in secrets, dear."

"Secrets?"

Juniper nodded. "Give me one of yours . . . and I would be happy to provide you with any information you require."

The mention of secrets made her blood go cold. Her secrets would mean death. Isla straightened her spine. "I have none," she said steadily.

Juniper only smiled. "We both know *that's* not true."

She swallowed. What exactly *did* he know?

Panic rose in her chest, bile up her throat.

Part of her wanted to flee.

But to get into the Moon Isle library, Isla needed information. She took a steady breath and, before she could stop herself, said, "I let the king win during the first demonstration. I could have bested him—but didn't."

Juniper took a deep breath, as if the secret invigorated him, then said, "That will do. What is it you wish to know, Ruler?"

Isla leaned in so she could whisper and he would hear her. "How do I get past the guards on Moon Isle?"

He put a finger against his lip, considering. "There are no guards during the full moon, when the Moonling curse is at its strongest. All Moonlings retreat to the safety of their castle then."

Good. "And when is the next full moon?"

Juniper answered immediately, as if he'd known that would be her next question. "The twentieth day of the Centennial."

That was in a week.

She nodded. "Thank you." Part of her wanted to ask about all the remaining libraries. Where they were. Tips on getting inside them.

But she couldn't trust the barkeep with any more of their plan. Doing so would be foolish. Dangerous.

Isla turned to go.

"Oh, and, Wildling?" Juniper said, thrumming his fingers against the bar.

She froze. Looked back at him over her shoulder.

"The tailor is missing clothing. *You* wouldn't know anything about that, would you?"

Isla's stomach twisted into a braid. But her face revealed nothing. Poppy's training ensured her emotions were always left off her face.

This was a game. For *all* of them. The islanders' lives were also at risk. She needed to remember that. Needed to remind herself she couldn't trust anyone. Especially not Juniper.

She grinned. "A secret for another time," she said before leaving through the back door.

## CHAPTER ELEVEN

# FEAR

The tailor knew his clothes were missing. It was more important than ever for them to find the bondbreaker before any of the rulers learned of the robbery and became suspicious.

A problem—she couldn't begin her search of the libraries until after Celeste's demonstration. It would provide them with the final thing Isla needed to locate the bondbreaker.

Luckily, the Starling's crisp gold letter from Oro arrived the very next morning. A ruler had the right to choose the time their trial took place, as long as it was within two days of receiving their paper.

Celeste chose to host hers immediately.

When Ella knocked upon Isla's door, she took her time answering it, as if she wasn't already dressed in the perfect attire for the next trial. As if she hadn't been running scenarios through her head for the last few hours. As if she hadn't coincidentally requested her meal to be delivered early.

The paper she was handed was silver, sparkling. The words were made in Celeste's perfect cursive.

*A test of fear,* it read.

*Location: The Hall of Glass*

*Time: Now*

Isla followed Ella through the Mainland castle. She had never been to this wing before, a part that looked ancient, nearly untouched for hundreds of years.

The walls were covered in paintings. Portraits. Sunling leaders.

She saw what had to be Oro's predecessor, his brother, King Egan. He had ruled for centuries before sacrificing himself on the night of the curses. Isla recognized the same golden hair. A similar set in their brows.

King Egan, however, had lively eyes. A glimmer of joy in them.

Nothing like his brother.

Isla wondered if Oro had always been the way he was now . . . or if five hundred years of curses had taken their toll on the king.

The Hall of Glass was frosted over, sunlight choked and muted, a protection for Sunlings. She wondered if Oro ever even bothered opening the blinds of his windows at night, knowing that forgetting to close them again would mean death in the morning.

Then she remembered when he had saved her. He had been on the balcony as soon as the sun went down, as if desperate to be within inches and minutes of sunshine. Sunshine adjacent.

A cruel curse.

All of them were so very cruel.

Celeste was already there, speaking to a group of Starling nobles. Her friend's cape was magnificent, specially made for her demonstration. Somehow, a tailor in the Starling realm had managed to make silk that was so thin, so translucent, it almost resembled glass. Faintly silver, with stars sewn into its edges, crystalline and glittering.

Isla had to stop herself from smiling at her friend, from acknowledging her at all.

The king was there too, surrounded by his own nobles and advisers and by wealthy islanders who wore gold cuffs and necklaces, who were so decked in gold, they looked like statues gilded by their king.

Cleo entered, joined by her entourage, who trailed her like guards.

Azul laughed with a group, interacting with them more like friends than a leader speaking to his subjects.

Isla was alone. Not surrounded by anyone. Even Ella had left her side, waiting in the wings with the other attendants.

So was Grim. He appeared across the room, making the nobles closest to him scuttle like roaches.

His dark eyes found hers, and she saw an understanding there.

Both were alone.

Was that why he had helped her?

Was it because he knew what it felt like?

No. He was her enemy. She had to remember that.

"Welcome," Celeste said. She was standing by something tall and cloaked. It looked like a statue with a sheet shrouding it.

It was not.

"My demonstration is a trial of fear. Whoever conquers their greatest fear first is the winner." A silver hourglass sat across the room, counting the seconds down.

Demonstrations were planned carefully. Some were chosen to showcase the hosting ruler's superiority. Some were chosen to demonstrate a particular opponent's weakness. Some, like this one, had a more mysterious purpose.

With a silver-gloved hand, Celeste tugged at the glittering sheet, revealing a towering mirror.

It was an ancient Starling relic the ruler had brought from her own realm. Isla had watched it for over a year, standing in the corner of Celeste's room like a specter. It could only be used by a person once, so Isla hadn't been able to practice. But she was almost certain about what her biggest fear would be.

"Who would like to begin?" Celeste asked.

Fear was perhaps a ruler's greatest weakness. What they feared most could doom their realm. It was a good test.

But it was not why Celeste had chosen this challenge.

The king stepped forward. The moment he pressed his palm against the mirror, its glass rippled, water shifting in a goblet.

Suddenly, it stilled. And so did he.

For minutes, the king went on a journey none of them could see. Oro just stared blankly at the mirror, hand still pressed to its face, brows occasionally jerking together.

Everyone had a fear. Isla wondered what the king was so afraid of. According to Celeste, the mirror trapped someone until they succeeded in besting their greatest fear. Someone could be stuck inside it forever. Many had died using the relic.

Oro straightened, the spell broken. The king's hand was released.

He had conquered it.

In just three minutes.

Isla swallowed. The king had been alive for more than five hundred years.

What if she kept the crowd waiting here for hours? What would that say of her and her abilities? Of her worthiness of surviving the Centennial?

What if she *never* bested it, and the mirror kept her?

Isla knew how important the use of this relic was to their plan. But she suddenly wished her friend had chosen a different trial.

Azul was next. He took five minutes. More than the king, but not by much.

When he left the mirror, Isla couldn't help but notice that his smile was a little duller than usual. Something in his expression looked haunted.

What had he seen?

What fear had he been forced to face?

Isla's palms began to sweat. She brushed them against her cape and took a deep breath. *Get it together.*

The moment Cleo placed her pale hand onto the mirror, Isla knew things would be different. The glass didn't ripple nearly as much. Her eyes closed and she froze completely, a ruler turned to ice.

It was not two minutes later that they reopened.

Gasps sounded among the crowd. Cleo had beaten even the king. By over a minute.

Isla's teeth ground against each other. The Moonling must be heartless. Or fearless. Both dangerous qualities in an enemy.

Grim finished his exercise in just under three minutes.

Celeste did hers in five.

Then it was Isla's turn.

The room was silent as she made her way over to the towering object. Her heels echoed through the hall. Her knees trembled beneath her dress, and she was grateful for its length.

Too soon, Isla found herself holding up her hand. Her fingers shook slightly before pressing against the mirror.

It moved—shifted.

Then something yanked her through the glass.

## CHAPTER TWELVE

# SHATTERED

Isla was pulled through the mirror into a crystal world.

In the many months she had anticipated this demonstration, she had determined her greatest fear: failing her realm.

She had readied herself to see a field of fallen Wildlings. Burned forests. A dead Poppy and Terra at her feet.

Now that she was in the trial, there were no bodies, no flames, no dying wildlife.

Only a room. *Her* room, in Wildling.

It looked exactly like it did when she left it. Clean. Proper. Her wall of swords glimmered at one side, winking their hello.

She expected to feel a rush of relief at being back, at being in a place so familiar after two weeks surrounded by strangers. In a strange land ruled by secrets.

But all she felt was dread.

If she failed, this was where she would return. She would live out the rest of her short, cursed, powerless, mortal life hidden away again. The realm would need a better heir for the next Centennial, so she would be forced to have a child.

She would continue to be sheltered.

One book from the library at a time.

Visits to her people from a distance, if at all.

Choices made for her by Wildlings who knew better, who knew more than just these glass walls.

Secret travels with her starstick.

Not even training, because there would be nothing left to train *for.*

Forests and people that would continue to die, flowers that would become extinct, Wildlings forced to kill for survival, unable to ever fall in love, turning them more and more into the beasts the rest of the realms believed them to be.

*No.*

She couldn't bear a life like that.

Lightlark was dangerous but full of wonders. Now that she had tasted freedom, she couldn't be locked in her glass box again and be content.

She wanted more than she had ever wanted in her life.

Isla watched herself reflected in the glass windows before her. As if spurred by her thoughts, her reflection began to move of its own free will.

She watched as it paced around the room. Lay in bed. Read a single book. Again. Again. Again. The reflection sped up, her movements a blur, and the days passed by too quickly, like time had tripped over itself, again, again, again. This time, instead of reading the book, her reflection tore its pages out. Banged on the windows instead of staring out of them. Pulled at her hair instead of braiding it. Forced back the floorboards, one by one, searching for something, fingers bleeding. Her starstick? *Had her guardians found and gotten rid of her starstick?* Years seemed to flip by in seconds, and eventually the reflection stood still in the middle of the room as time continued to pass her by, her body weakening, hair falling out, her soul scooped out of her chest. Her eyes had gone lifeless.

She couldn't see herself like this. Empty. All the best parts of herself stripped away. Isla reached a hand out to touch her reflection, to comfort it—

And suddenly, she was looking back at her own self.

Her heart was beating too quickly.

Was that her fate, should she fail? Was that what she was destined to become? A hull of herself?

A prisoner?

Something lurched, screeching—

The room became smaller.

Isla startled, moving closer to its center. Somehow, the walls had moved, the floor had been eaten up.

Smaller.

The glass rattled as it shrank. Perfumes fell from her vanity and smashed against the tile, her leftover makeup soon joining them, blots of color bleeding, bright powders making plumes of dust.

Smaller.

Isla's heartbeat rang through her ears in warning; her fingers shook, and sweat dripped down her forehead. The room was going to swallow her whole, press its glass against her skin, make her and her reflection one and the same.

Smaller.

The ceiling concaved, nearly skewering her in place. The walls folded together, getting smaller, smaller, smaller.

Her bed was gone, her things were mangled in the mess, and the room was getting smaller still, shrinking all around her.

This was her fate. The reflection had told it to her.

Locked forever in a room.

A secret too shameful to share.

A curse too painful to bear.

The room creaked, and Isla's bones vibrated with the movement of everything around her being eaten up, enclosed, matted over.

*No.*

She refused.

Isla hadn't worked for years for her efforts to be useless, to be a victim of this room and her circumstances.

She hadn't even known how much she was missing. Now that she saw how much the world had to offer, she wanted it all.

She wanted *everything*.

Isla wouldn't return here. She would either break her curse—or die trying.

Before she could make a single move to stop her fate, however, it seemed she was too late. There was nothing she could do as the remaining walls all fell down atop her.

The bites of a million pieces of glass were a constellation across her body as the room shattered. Before she could move out of its path, a massive solid pane crushed her without breaking. Her breath was torn from her chest. The world was black and silent. Her face pressed against the glass, so closely she couldn't breathe.

Was she permanently in the mirror?

Had she joined the girl in the reflection?

She tried to move a foot, a leg, *anything*—and finally managed to feel around with her fingers. Only one hand hadn't been crushed by the wall.

*Give me a chance,* she told her broken bones. *Give me a chance, and I'll make sure we never become her.*

Her fingers searched blindly, desperately, until a blade cut through her skin like butter. She grinned beneath the rubble. It was one of her swords. She gripped its hilt—

And broke through the glass that had smothered her.

Isla gasped.

She was back in the hall.

The mirror had gone still again. Her rattled reflection stared back at her. This time, it did not move of its own accord.

Isla tore her hand away, her palm cold as ice.

There was no applause. No sound as she backed away, and the demonstration ended. Cleo was crowned the winner.

Isla remained in the hall until it was just her, the mirror, and Celeste.

"How long?" Isla finally asked. She was certain her time had been far longer than everyone else's. *That* was why the crowds had left so suddenly. *That* was why no one had caught her eye, why Celeste hadn't nodded at her or touched her nose or done any of their subtle tricks to speak to one another in secret.

Celeste frowned. "Six minutes," she said simply. "Why didn't you look at the hourglass?"

*Six minutes*. That wasn't bad.

Isla didn't bother answering Celeste's question, because she didn't want to admit that she had been afraid to look. That she felt on edge.

She might have faced her fear in the mirror . . . but she had never been more scared.

Now she had seen her worst fear embodied, brought to life.

She would do anything to keep that fear from becoming reality.

And that, perhaps, scared her most of all.

The Starling ruler was circling the mirror, looking at it carefully. Isla watched from a distance as Celeste strung her fingers together and smiled. "It worked."

Isla straightened. "How do you know?"

Celeste snapped her fingers, and sparks illuminated the hall. Handprints glowed silver across the mirror's glass. Every ruler's print and essence had been stored by the relic.

The Starling pulled a pair of gloves from her pocket. They were so thin they looked translucent. Isla nearly retched. She had done it. She had completed her part of their plan.

Isla opened her mouth, ready to ask if Celeste had truly managed to find a pair of the gloves in a dark market somewhere on Lightlark. The alternative—

Celeste shot her a look that made her think better of it.

Frowning in focus, the Starling slowly rolled on the new gloves. They sounded both papery and leathery, crinkling as they slid down her skin. Isla winced. When they were fully on, Celeste carefully pressed them against each handprint, letting the marks soak into the gloves. They would absorb the energy the enchanted Starling mirror had taken from all the rulers, to be used later. It was an inconsequential amount. Not enough to be used in battle or make any meaningful display.

But every library on Lightlark had a protected section, a home for each realm's most valuable relics. Each was guarded by enchantments that only allowed a ruler and their essence to enter.

Wearing these gloves, Isla would be granted access.

Now, she had everything she needed to begin searching the libraries for the bondbreaker.

## CHAPTER THIRTEEN

# TOWER

The next night, Celeste stared at the materials between them and frowned. "Is this really everything?"

"Yes." Or, at least, what Isla *thought* she needed to make the elixir.

It was the fifteenth day of the Centennial. Isla was anxious to search the next library for the bondbreaker as soon as possible. It hadn't been on Star Isle, but perhaps they would get lucky and it would be in the Sky Isle collection. If not, she would have to wait until the full moon to go to Moon Isle. And she still hadn't come up with a plan to get onto Sun Isle unnoticed.

She tried to remain positive. She could very well find the bondbreaker that night. Then they could use it, and both of their bloodlines would be rid of all the curses that afflicted them. Isla would get her Wildling powers she had been denied at birth. The Wildling realm wouldn't have to kill their beloveds or live on hearts any longer. Celeste and all Starlings would live to see their twenty-sixth birthday.

The bondbreaker was the key to both of their freedoms. And right now, they were counting on some sparse hair dye instructions to get it.

Isla held the torn piece of parchment between them. She couldn't have asked Poppy for help with this alternate plan, so she had taken a page from one of her guardian's books, swiped some Wildling-specific ingredients, and hoped for the best.

She read the list out one last time.

"Rose water."

Check. She had swiped a vial of it from Poppy's vanity.

"Ash-leaf extract."

She had only been able to find an ash leaf during a last-minute expedition in the forest and hoped that would do.

"Soil from the ever-changing tulip."

Check. She had grabbed a small shovel of it from Poppy's collection. The enchanted flower only grew by the coast in the Wildling newland, where her great-great-grandmother had planted it, straight from the island's soil. Many of Lightlark's flowers had been transplanted there in the aftermath of the curses, attempting to create some sort of ecosystem like their island.

And many of them had died since Isla had been born.

She poured a portion of the small pouch of dirt into the pot of hot water Ella had brought her, supposedly for tea.

Finally, she needed some of the color she wanted her hair transformed to. Though Azul's own hair was dark, many Skylings had hair the color of their realm. Maybe it was fashion, or a way to honor their power source, or perhaps it was natural, like Celeste's own silver hair—she didn't know.

All she knew was that she needed to fit in, and this would be the most inconspicuous color.

The recipe called for a flower petal with the shade, but there weren't any in Wildling. As a substitute, she carefully ripped the bottom of her stolen dress's hem and threw the fabric into the potion.

It bubbled a bit, thickened. Isla and Celeste watched as it became a paste.

The Starling peered into the pot carefully. "Is it supposed to look like this?"

"I don't know," Isla mumbled. Nerves flurried in her stomach. She wasn't just sneaking onto another ruler's isle. She was *impersonating* another realm. None of the Centennial rules stated against it, but it was still dangerous.

No one could recognize her. It would immediately put her and their plan in jeopardy.

The enchanted dye had to work.

"It's cooled," Celeste said. She had dipped a gloved finger into the mixture.

They took the bowl into the bathroom, and Isla sat in the bathtub as her friend coated her long brown hair in the light-blue paste.

Celeste worked in silence, her fingers careful, rubbing into her scalp, then making her way down to the ends.

"How does it look?" Isla finally asked after most of her hair felt like it had been covered.

Celeste said nothing.

She whipped around to look at her friend's expression.

And found a smile tugging on the corners of her lips.

"What?"

She finally laughed. "It— You just look different," she offered. "But it's good. The color is nearly exact."

*"Nearly?"*

Celeste waved her concern away. "No one will be able to tell in the moonlight," she said. "And no one will be in the library this late . . ."

Isla groaned. So many excuses, so many elements out of her control that had to go right.

The mixture was enchanted, thanks to the ever-changing tulip soil. Without it, the color wouldn't have stuck nearly as quickly or effectively on her dark hair. Still—the blue would only last a few hours.

Her friend took her stained gloves off and gripped her hand tightly. "This will work. You do this all the time."

Isla gave her an incredulous look. "I sneak onto another realm's isle *all the time?*"

"No. But you sneak into other realms' *newlands* all the time. Wearing stolen clothing. Impersonating another ruler's people. With your starstick."

That was true. But this was different.

This was the Centennial.

"You move like a shadow," Celeste continued. "You can blend in anywhere—I've *seen* you."

Her friend was right. She had spent years unwittingly gaining the skills she now needed to find the bondbreaker.

Isla washed the paste out of her hair, combed it, and hoped it would dry by the time she reached her destination.

"Right," Isla said, staring at her reflection, feeling strange in a color she had never been allowed to wear. "So far, I've been a thief. A liar." She sighed. "Time to become a fraud."

It took forty-five minutes to reach the Sky Isle bridge. Once, the island was whole. Then, thousands of years ago, it was sliced into pieces, so each realm could have its own. All the isles were connected to the Mainland by rope and wood that didn't look even remotely steady. Wind whistled through large gaps between each plank. The strings holding them together were thin and frayed. The entire thing rocked back and forth like a pendulum. Isla looked down at what had to be two hundred feet, the water churning roughly below, a soup ready to boil her.

"No," she said simply, the word slipping out of her mouth, into an empty night.

She had read about these enchanted bridges. Though everyone was traditionally allowed on any isle they wanted to visit, some realms had been known to restrict access during political turmoil. If Azul or the Lightlark-based Skyling government had decided those outside their realm weren't allowed to pass, the bridge would collapse, sending her hurtling hundreds of feet below.

It was unlikely—but not impossible. If she fell, no one would hear her screams. Worse, if someone did, there would be nothing left of her to save.

Her entire realm would die in an instant, just because she was foolish enough to fall off a bridge.

It was too big a risk.

Isla took a step back.

Right into someone's chest.

She stilled, forcing herself not to scream, then whirled around, hands splayed in apology.

A tall, freckled Skyling man stood there, eyes half-closed, a large cup of drink in his hand. "Crossing?" he said merrily, staring down at her as if nothing was amiss.

He didn't question her hair.

Didn't stare at her clothing or face like he recognized her.

His gaze narrowed then, and Isla froze, wondering if he was about to yell to all Lightlark that Isla Crown, ruler of Wildling, was trying to get onto Sky Isle.

Then she remembered he was staring at her strangely not because he was putting the puzzle pieces of her identity together but because she had been gaping up at him for several seconds without responding.

"Yes, of course," she managed to say, forcing a smile.

He smiled back. His eyes flickered behind her, as if saying, *So, are you going to cross, then?*

Now she had no choice. Isla took a step, feeling at least a glimmer of comfort that should she plummet hundreds of feet, someone would know her fate right away.

Her foot was met by a steady plank.

Relief needled down the backs of her legs.

The rest of the way across was unsteady and filled with at least half a dozen more stomach-sinking feelings, but she made it to the other side in one piece.

Only to stop and stare at the world she had entered.

Sky Isle was a floating city. Giant chunks of rock hovered high above, strung together by bridges like beads on a bracelet. Waterfalls spilled right off levitating mountain ranges, their triangular bases and roots trailing far beneath them, almost to the ground. On the largest floating piece sat a palace with spires that shot so far up into the clouds they must have scratched the sky itself.

The ground beneath the floating city was far inferior—Isla felt like someone walking on the seafloor, looking up at the surface in wonder. Poppy had taught her that Skylings used to be able to fly, once upon a time. Before their curse bound them forever to the ground.

The only person who could fly now was Oro. As an Origin, he had all the Lightlark realms' powers. But not their curses. Only Sunling's, since his family had claimed the realm as their own long ago.

The second city, built beneath the first, covered every inch of a mountain. At its peak stood a tower tall enough to reach the very bottom of the closest floating rock. Isla wondered if *that* was how one entered the flying city—and who was allowed to. At the mountain's base sat a marketplace that smelled of peppermint and ale.

Mostly ale.

Someone tumbled from the closest pub, right into the street, face bright pink, barely missing a puddle of vomit.

Skylings were well-known for their celebratory nature. Part of her wanted to rush into the closest bar and down her first drink, knowing it gave others courage.

But she couldn't risk the distraction or an adverse effect. Not tonight.

Celeste had found out the location of the library through her attendant, a Skyling boy with pale skin and a voice so soft it was hard to even hear him. It supposedly used to be located high above but now had taken over a tower in the newer Sky Isle castle, at the base of the great mountain.

Isla had wondered about the best way to sneak into the palace—but, it turned out, Skylings weren't as pretentious or paranoid as other realms. The castle doors were open, welcoming any of its people, from nobles to other islanders, inside. No guards were present.

This late at night, there were just a few visitors milling through the halls. A couple, walking hand in hand, sharing a foaming drink between them. A cluster of teenagers, taking turns throwing a ball at each other, only using their power to harness wind.

The people of the realm were not unlike their leader. Content. Happy.

It was a bit unnerving, more than two weeks into the Centennial. Weren't they anxious? Did they know something she didn't? Did Azul have a plan for this Centennial that he had shared with his people?

Isla made a turn to the east side of the palace. She studied it carefully. It was surprisingly well-kept for being the home of a ruler who only returned for a few months every century. It was just a fraction of the size of the Mainland castle and painted light blue, a giant bird's egg. Its ceilings were designed to resemble a massive, endless sky and were remarkably tall. Wind whistled through the corridors, from various windows left open.

Free. Airy. Light.

The tower wasn't difficult to find. It was one of just a few and had unlocked glass doors, which revealed its interior.

Books. Floors of them, in a circular shape, going around and around, in a spiral leading up to a rounded skylight. All empty. Celeste was right. No one seemed interested in reading at this hour.

Now she just needed to find the protected section.

She studied the space and frowned. There were no hidden back rooms. Everything in the library was on full display, shelves built into the walls. Isla started up the spiral walkway, forcing herself not to look too carefully at the books. If she saw any of their titles, she wasn't sure she would be able to resist the temptation to sit down and read.

*You will have plenty of time to read once your curses are broken,* she told herself. After using the bondbreaker, she would have the freedom to pillage the library in the Wildling realm and devour every book if she wished.

She just needed to find it.

The tower was taller than it looked from the bottom—it took several minutes to reach its top.

When she did, she frowned. No protected section.

No relics. Just books. Thousands of them.

Isla gripped the railing, staring a hundred feet down at the bottom. The library was empty. Hollow. She barely resisted the urge to fill it with her frustrated screams.

But she hadn't colored her hair and stolen her clothes and stepped foot on another realm's Lightlark territory to give up so easily.

Every isle's library had a protected area.

This one must just be hidden.

Isla backed toward the wall and felt it carefully, knocking gently. It was solid, books covering nearly every inch of the tower's interior. Its middle was air.

No room for a secret.

Unless—

She looked up at the skylight. If she stood on her toes, she could reach it.

Her stomach roiled as she carefully grabbed the gloves from her pocket. They felt rough and thin enough to tear if she wasn't careful. She tried not to think of what they were made of, of *who* they were—

No. She had to keep her mind on the mission, lest she retch her dinner.

Hoping Celeste was right, and Azul's essence was indeed imprinted on the fabric, she rolled them on, then pressed her gloved palm against the glass—

It dropped open, along with an elegant pair of metal stairs that unfolded before her eyes.

Isla's grin was pure satisfaction. She had uncovered a ruler's secret. She had figured it out alone. A powerless young ruler.

*There is no time to celebrate.* Terra's scolding was in her brain. Whenever Isla beamed after mastering a skill or managing to disarm her guardian, she would be chastised.

*Time can stand still for just a moment,* Isla once said.

*Not for you. From the moment you were born, the clock began counting down,* Terra had replied. Any time not used to prepare for the Centennial was wasted. Wanting anything more than to defend and protect her realm was selfish. Her life had never been her own.

With the bondbreaker, it could be.

Isla took the first step up the ladder.

The skylight was a door, leading to a small glass room awash with moonlight. There was a bundle of ancient scrolls. A scepter with a gemstone top that was milky, the color of someone blending clouds and sky together with their thumb. A sword with a braided blade, two sheets of metal intertwined, locked together like lovers.

But there was no oversize glass needle.

There was no bondbreaker.

Disappointment made her reckless. Isla entered the Mainland castle without her normal precautions. She did not wait in the shadows to ensure no one was around. She did not cloak her steps, which would require slowing her pace. She did not take the long way, through halls that were always empty because they were ancient and let cracks of moonlight and cold drafts through holes in the stone and didn't have any of the monstrous hearths that filled the rest of the palace.

All she wanted was to get to her room as soon as possible, wash the dye out of her hair, tear the light-blue clothes to pieces, and get any remainder of sleep the night allowed.

By the time she quickly turned a corner into the main hall, it was too late.

Cleo had already spotted her.

Isla was gone in an instant. She kept walking straight instead, not knowing where she was going, heart thundering, wondering how good a look the Moonling ruler had gotten at her face.

It was dark. She had been on the other side of the hall.

*No,* not close enough to have seen it was her.

But certainly close enough to make her suspicious.

Seconds later, Isla heard the unmistakable sound of steps behind her.

Following her.

Just a few long strides and the Moonling would catch up to her, confirm that the girl with the light-blue hair and Skyling clothing was a fellow ruler.

An impostor.

The discovery would spin so many questions and stab so many of her secrets, Isla began sweating, panting.

Cleo wouldn't give up until she had Isla backed into a corner. Her steps were just a few moments behind hers.

Another turn came up, and Isla took it, using the few seconds that the Moonling ruler couldn't see her to take off at full speed.

She ran, ran, then took another turn—

And crashed into something solid.

Her mind spun behind her eyes. She would have fallen backward if it wasn't for two strong hands catching her by the waist.

*Grim.*

Footsteps sounded behind her, echoing through the last hall. One turn, and the Moonling ruler would find her there, *both* of them.

The Nightshade ruler stared down at her, confusion drawing his brows together. His eyes caught on her colored hair, her clothes, a question in his expression.

No time to explain.

"*Please,*" she said, gripping his arms, hating the way her voice broke on the word.

He seemed to know what she wanted.

Because before Cleo could turn the corner, Grim gathered Isla to his chest and they both disappeared.

The Moonling ruler froze at the entrance of their corridor, finding it empty. Isla might have found pleasure in the shock on Cleo's face, if she wasn't so afraid.

She was trembling. Cleo was just feet away. If the Moonling discovered her, Celeste's plans and help would be for nothing. Just because Isla was foolish enough not to be cautious. Just because she was upset that she didn't find the bondbreaker on her first try.

The Moonling took a step forward, right toward them. Silent as a shadow, Grim lifted Isla as if she weighed nothing and shifted them both to the side of the room. The rough stone wall dug into her back. Grim was shielding her. She could feel his breath against her forehead.

Isla tried not to focus on what *else* she could feel. His tight grip on her waist, the cold emanating from him searing through the thin fabric of her stolen clothing. The chill that licked her spine like night blossoming in her bones.

Out of fear, she told herself, fear of being discovered. Nothing else.

The Moonling walked the entire length of the room—before finally retreating the way she had come.

Only after her steps were too faint to hear did Grim make them visible again.

And Isla was shocked by his proximity.

She was pressed against the wall, and he towered over her, head bent so low his nose almost grazed hers.

He looked down at her. "Have you decided to change realms, Hearteater?" he said, reaching up and taking a strand of her colored hair between his fingers. "If so, you might consider Nightshade. We can't compete with Skyling when it comes to sweets or inventive drinks, but if debauchery is what you're after . . ." His dark gaze gleamed in amusement. "We are most famed for our thorough exploration of pleasure."

What was he implying? His hands were still on her waist, his fingers long against her ribs. She took a shaky breath.

Then batted him away, scowling. "Count me uninterested," she said.

But Grim only grinned as he took a step back.

Of course. The demon could feel her emotions, the heat pooling in her stomach as she thought about his surprisingly gentle touch. The way his lips had curled around the word *pleasure* . . .

*No.* What was wrong with her? She had always judged the Wildlings reckless enough to begin to have feelings for someone. They risked the relationship ending in death.

Isla's actions put her entire *realm* at risk.

She wanted freedom. She wanted to break her and her people's curses. That was all.

That was *everything*.

"Thank you," she said simply.

Then she darted out of the hall as quickly as she could.

# CHAPTER FOURTEEN
# AZUL

Isla's invitation arrived the next morning. Her demonstration was next.

All night, the Nightshade had haunted her dreams. Their brief encounter in the hallway had affected her more than she cared to admit.

Grim had made her invisible, just because she had asked. He had no reason to help her. If it hadn't been for him, Cleo would have discovered her, and all of Isla's plans would have been ruined in one disastrous night.

She knew she would regret this. If Celeste ever found out, she might seriously reconsider their friendship.

It was foolish, *dangerous*, but Isla set off looking for the Nightshade.

She knew all the rulers' habits by now, thanks to her regular snooping during the last sixteen days. Azul was always with his people and spent a surprising amount of time walking along the coast. Cleo was always surrounded by nobles she seemed to keep at an arm's length and visited her isle far more than the other rulers. Oro left the castle nearly every night, and she still hadn't had the nerve to follow him.

Grim's movements were more of a mystery, since he was often invisible, traveling from place to place unnoticed. A few times, though, she had caught him slipping into a bar in the marketplace in the middle of the afternoon. That was where she headed.

She was nearly at the agora when her name was spoken.

Isla whirled around, only to find another ruler standing there.

Azul.

Her blood went cold. Did he know that she had been on his isle the night before? Had someone seen her?

Had *Grim* told him? They didn't appear to be friends, but alliances were easy to hide during the Centennial. Isla and Celeste were the prime example of that.

If she hadn't been distracted, she would have heard him approach. She wouldn't have leaped in surprise at his voice.

She pasted a practiced smile on her face. "What a pleasant surprise," she said, her tone sounding so genuine, Isla wondered when she had become such a good liar.

"Likewise," he said, matching her expression. "What brings you to this part of the Mainland, Ruler?"

Isla tried her best not to let her voice tremble, the way her hands were. She clasped them behind her back. "The castle was getting a bit dreary. I thought I would do some exploring."

Azul's grin grew, but it did not reach his eyes. They remained as cold as the gems he hoarded. Was it possible she hadn't been as discreet on Sky Isle as she thought?

Or perhaps he was just wary of her. And why wouldn't he be? She was wary of him too.

"If it's the Mainland you'd like to see . . . allow me to take you to one of its greatest wonders."

She didn't want to go anywhere with a ruler who might or might not know that she had been disguised as one of his people the day before. Their chance encounter was too great of a coincidence.

He must know.

Refusing his offer would make him even more suspicious of her, though. "How generous of you."

They started in the direction of the mountain range that framed the Mainland. The rock was brown and red in some places, marbled in others.

"How are you enjoying the island?" he asked lightly, as if the Centennial was a vacation, and not Isla's only chance at living.

Of course, he couldn't know that. A Wildling ruler was supposed to be nearly immortal.

"I can understand its appeal . . . though I have much to explore." She had learned that it was better to let others speak when she had much to hide. Most people liked to talk about themselves, anyway. "And how is your fifth Centennial?"

He laughed without humor. Something about that laugh was strange, Isla thought. Bitter, maybe. "It's . . . interesting." He pursed his lips. "The first Centennial, I'm sure you've heard, was a nightmare. Almost worse than the war . . . With the second came rules, and some order. We had plans. Strategies. But no alliances. None of us trusted each other, you see, after the first time. For good reason too."

His voice trailed off, and Isla saw something flash in his eyes.

Was it pain?

"The third was better. It was the first time we split into teams. We believed we were very close to breaking the curses—to figuring out all parts of the prophecy. We were wrong, of course. By the fourth, it seemed most had lost hope. Cleo did not even attend . . . did you know that?" Isla nodded, though she most certainly hadn't known.

Any ruler who didn't attend wasn't eligible for the grand prize . . . and their curse wouldn't be broken with the rest, should someone find a solution. Why would Cleo stay away?

More importantly—why had she returned this year?

Dread danced in her bones, and Isla had the feeling there was something everyone else knew that she didn't.

"Even without her, we really thought we had it." He shook his head. "The curses have ruined so much. But one of the worst things it has done is tear our realms further apart. Before, we were very close to unity."

Isla knew this from Poppy's history lessons. She was happy to speak about anything that didn't involve her sneaking into the Sky Isle library. "That's why King Egan was getting married to another ruler, wasn't it? To try to bring the realms back together?" Isla used to wonder if the king had decided, atypically, to marry outside his realm for love. That was certainly how Poppy told King Egan and Aurora's story. A Sunling and a Starling finding love, despite their differences. It was the only time her guardian hadn't spoken about love as a cautionary tale.

"Precisely." Azul sighed. "Now, here we are at the fifth." He looked at her briefly over his shoulder, pity in his eyes. "And I'm afraid I don't know if I have it in me to attend a sixth."

Isla swallowed at his dark tone. Was this a warning?

Was he telling her that, despite his typically jovial disposition, he wasn't above killing her if it meant this Centennial was the last?

Isla was desperate to change the subject. "Are you close to your nobles?"

Sky Isle had been surprisingly well-kept. The nobles seemed to be doing a good job of running it in their ruler's absence.

Azul frowned. "There are no Skyling nobles." She must have looked confused, because he continued. "We've had a democracy since I came into rule. The Skylings who are invited to the smaller events are elected officials. All big decisions are made based on voting from my people."

Isla blinked at him. "So, if they decided they didn't want you as ruler . . ."

He shrugged. "I would step down. Though that would certainly complicate things, what with the Centennial and the way our powers are passed down," he said. "I'm lucky they have been happy with my rule."

She had never heard of a realm being run that way.

As she considered Azul's words, she found him watching her.

*Studying* her.

What was he looking for?

They had stopped at the base of a mountain that looked peculiar, but not special enough to have made the trek. Azul had told her many things, things she wouldn't have expected another ruler of realm to be so up-front about during the Centennial.

Was it because he knew she wouldn't be alive long enough to use what knowledge he had shared?

The fiftieth day was just over a month away. Isla tensed, wondering if the Skyling was counting down the hours before he could kill her without breaking the rules. Perhaps his people had already cast their votes, wanting her to be the one who died when the time came to fulfill the entire prophecy.

Azul only stared upward. Isla followed his gaze warily and saw that there were tunnels dug above them, high into the sky. If she squinted, she could see bright blue on the other side, through the mountain. She counted seven, all lined up next to each other, perfectly carved through the stone.

"I used to come here as a child, with friends," he said, smiling. This time, it did reach his eyes. "We would fly through the tunnels as fast as we could, timing ourselves. We made a game of it."

It had been five hundred years since he had flown. It appeared he missed it as much as Grim missed night and Oro missed day.

He turned to her. "Nowadays, it has a different use." He planted his legs in a wide stance and shot up with his fist.

Isla instinctively backed away, then watched a burst of air travel through one of the tunnels. A moment later, it made a beautiful sound.

"It's an instrument," she said loudly, her excitement real this time.

In response, he sent air through all the tunnels, one after the other, fast as wind.

A song broke through the afternoon.

Isla hummed, matching the pitch, overjoyed. The mountain was an instrument . . . she couldn't believe it. Azul indulged her, playing song after song, his air never weakening. The wariness from his eyes disappeared, little by little.

She found herself happy that Azul had happened upon her, if only for a limited distraction.

By the time Azul escorted Isla back to the Mainland castle, it was nearly dusk. Grim would have already left the agora.

Instead of finding him in the bar, she had to go to his bedroom.

Isla had figured out the location of all the rulers' rooms several days before. She could have asked Ella where the other rulers were staying. It would have saved her hours of snooping. But Isla felt safer spreading her requests around, not allowing anyone to know too much about what she needed, lest they put any pieces of her plans together. The rulers were harder to follow through the castle without notice, so she had trailed their Lightlark-provided attendants.

That was how she knew Grim's chamber was on the other side of the castle, farthest from another ruler than anyone.

Isla had already made up her mind, knowing the potential consequences. Knowing what she was putting at risk. She had traveled here regardless.

Standing in front of his door, though, she hesitated, her knuckle inches from the stone.

Before she lost her nerve, it swung open.

Grim stood there, looking down at her with an eyebrow lifted.

"I'm sorry I ran off," she said. It really was rude, after he had helped her. "I came to thank you, again. And to offer something to you, in thanks for—for what you did."

A grin began to overtake his face at the mention of an offering. "Oh?" he said, voice somehow growing even deeper.

Isla glared at him, as if to say, *Not that kind of offering.* He was shameless. Was he like this with everyone? Was she only the latest person he had decided to flirt with?

It had to be part of his plan. Which only made what she was about to do all the more foolish.

His eyes only glimmered deviously.

"My demonstration is next," Isla said, the words rushing out of her before she could change her mind. "Tomorrow. It requires preparation."

Grim's face went surprisingly serious. "Hearteater, you don't have to—"

No. She did have to. Grim knew one of her secrets now, after finding her in the Skyling clothing. He had *helped* her, by turning her invisible to avoid Cleo. Isla was beholden to him. She didn't like that. She would tell him this information, then be done with it.

"It's demonstrating the worth of your realm by showing something of value it's created, for the future of Lightlark."

The Nightshade did not break her gaze. He did not grin. He did not thank her. He simply nodded.

She nodded back.

It was only late that night, staring up at her ceiling instead of sleeping, that she wondered if she had made a grave mistake.

## CHAPTER FIFTEEN

# ELIXIR

Isla had given them an hour.

Instead of a trial focusing on the power of their ruler—for obvious reasons—Isla wished to test the ability of their realm. Her people might not be on the island, but it was a chance for her to show Lightlark all they were beyond their bloodthirsty curse.

Her guardians had wanted the demonstration to be something different. An opportunity to further their own strategy.

Isla had convinced them that showing that her people could *heal* just as much as they could *kill* might convince the other rulers of Wildlings' value, especially over Nightshade, who only destroyed.

Her warning Grim of the demonstration negated some of that strategy. Complicated everything.

They were back in the arena. Isla wanted as many islanders as possible present to see what she had brought from her newland.

She had already announced her trial to a wary audience. Her voice had been surprisingly smooth, no hint of her nerves peeking through.

The rules had been stated as well. The audience would vote for which demonstration of a realm's abilities was most useful in securing the future of the island. No one could vote for their own ruler—though Isla was under no illusion that it would give Wildling a fair shot. She wouldn't win. But she didn't need to. All the crowd needed to know was that Wildlings were more than wicked seductresses.

The rulers stood on the sidelines. She wondered if an hour had been enough time to prepare—for the ones who didn't already know about the demonstration, anyway.

Their expressions gave nothing away, waiting for her to call out their names.

"Azul."

The ruler swept into the center of the arena, followed by a trail of other Skylings, who were aiding in the demonstration. "Our realm has been working on a form of communication that uses wind. Easier communication means more efficiency, streamlined processes . . . faster invitations to parties." The crowd laughed. Azul certainly knew how to present himself. Isla thought back to what he had said about Skyling's government the day before. His people did seem to adore him. Was it because he had given them choice? She of all people could understand the importance of freedom . . .

He grabbed a piece of parchment from an interior pocket of his cape and wrote a message on it. Then he folded it carefully into a square and used his power to fly it across the arena, right into Isla's hand.

All eyes were on her. She folded open the page and read the words the ruler had scrawled: *Of course, we also have our music . . .*

Isla couldn't help but smile.

"This can be replicated on a grand scale," Azul added. He motioned to the rest of the Skylings who had joined him. They carried stacks of sheets of parchment. Without warning, they threw all of it into the air. Before her eyes, each page folded neatly, then set off, one after the other, on dozens of paths the Skylings had created in the sky, wind currents for the messages to use as trails to their recipients. A true infrastructure for mass communication.

It was a grand display. An innovation that would surely make an impact on Lightlark.

The crowd certainly seemed to think so as well.

Isla wondered what the pages Azul had distributed even said. Perhaps an invitation to a festivity the Skyling was throwing in the agora after this.

"Cleo."

Isla hoped that the lack of time to prepare had flustered the ruler. She imagined the Moonling struggling to put together a demonstration and nearly smiled.

Cleo only radiated confidence as she strolled toward the center of the arena. She had no helpers. No tools . . . or anything visual to display.

Her words were simple. "We have ships," she said. "For the past two centuries, we have built many, *many* ships."

That was it.

The Moonling walked back to her place, and Isla felt a tinge of anger in her chest. She wondered if the crowd would be silent. Confused. If the other rulers would balk at her lack of display.

But no one did. Moonlings cheered, all but confirming that they had spent decades making the fleet Cleo had so casually described.

She could be lying. But Oro looked like he believed her.

He looked like he hadn't known about the ships at all.

*Interesting.* Celeste was right. There was tension brewing between some of the Lightlark realms.

Though a navy wasn't logical while the Moonlings were still haunted by the deadly full moon, it *would* be useful in a postcurse world. The ships could be used to bring the thousands of Moonlings, Starlings, Wildlings, and Skylings back to Lightlark, to unify the realms in one place once more. They could explore distant lands beyond the island and the realms' newlands.

They could also be used for war.

"Celeste," Isla said, wondering if the way she spoke her friend's name was different than she had said the others. Wondering if saying a person's name thousands of times made it sound different coming from a mouth.

The Starling was prepared, of course. A dozen of her subjects joined her.

"My realm has been developing a way to manufacture tools and weapons, using solely our power," she said, gesturing to her people, bidding them to begin.

The crowd watched in wonder as they demonstrated the way they pooled their energy, making it so concentrated that, before their eyes, a sword was created in just moments. They had turned energy to metal, almost like Oro had turned the table to gold.

Almost.

This took a dozen Starlings and much effort. For one sword.

The king could likely gild them all in a single breath.

Celeste took the finished sword in her hand and lifted it up, to the endless cheers of all the Starlings in attendance.

Isla wanted to smile, wanted to say something to her friend. But all she did was call out the next name.

"Oro."

The king did not meet her gaze as he took his place. He had always looked at her with disdain. Now, after likely knowing she'd let him win the duel and using him as a prop for Azul's demonstration, it seemed he deemed her below his notice.

"We have found additional ways to spread light and heat throughout the island." He lit a fire in front of him with a curl of his fingers. Then he dipped his entire hand inside it before dragging it out again quickly, fingers splayed. The flames came apart, the fire like spatters of paint, flying across the room. There were screams—some islanders blocked themselves using their power.

But the flames had been contained in dozens of orbs. They landed harmlessly in hands and laps. "They will not go out, as long as the original flame is lit."

Between the endless hearths inside the castle, torches across the Mainland, and this demonstration, the king clearly had an obsession with making sure flames were everywhere. Was it because they represented his rule? His realm?

He allowed the crowd a few more moments of inspecting the orbs of fire, throwing them in the air, marveling at their warmth, the light like a hundred fireflies lighting up the arena, before curling his hand. Smothering his flames.

The lights shriveled and died, just like he said they would.

Applause seemed to follow everything Oro did, and this demonstration was no different.

"Grimshaw" was the next name Isla spoke.

The Nightshade brushed past her. A stripe of chill danced down her arm at his slightest touch.

She needed to get herself together.

The crowd was silent. But they were clearly curious about what the Nightshade would show them. His realm had been a mystery ever since they had created their own stronghold. They were the enemy during the war. Even with a peace treaty, his kind weren't trusted at all. Many, Isla imagined, still believed Grim's people were responsible for the curses.

And maybe they were.

Grim stopped at the center of the arena. He gazed right back at the curious faces, turning to face them all to allow them to get a clear look at him.

"My realm has nothing productive to offer you," he said.

Then he left.

Silence. Whispers.

Isla felt her face go hot. With rage? With surprise?

She had given him more than enough time to prepare for her demonstration. Against her better judgment. Behind her friend's back. And he had made a mockery of it.

He had arrived empty-handed on purpose.

*Why?*

The Nightshade had the nerve to walk right toward her on his way back to the wings and say, "You're next, Hearteater," before becoming one with the shadows.

*Demon. Monster.*

She straightened. She wouldn't let him unnerve her. That was surely what he was after.

Isla didn't bother announcing herself as she readied for her turn. There was one thing she needed.

From the king.

"Would you make me a fire?" she asked him.

For a moment, he just frowned down at her. She wondered if he might ignore her, or refuse her, and she would have to ask some other Sunling for help. As if they would.

Then, with the smallest whip of his wrist, a column of fire appeared in the center of the arena.

"Thank you," she said tightly.

He did not nod, or even acknowledge her, before she walked toward the flames he had created.

All eyes on her. She should have been used to it by now, but their scrutiny was like a thousand knives, all turned in her direction.

Isla pulled a vial from her pocket, glass in the shape of a heart. It held a liquid thick and crimson as blood.

"Wildlings have developed advanced healing remedies," she said, holding the container up for all to see.

Now, she just needed to demonstrate its potency.

Before she could lose her nerve, the same way she had done a half dozen times before in preparation, Isla took a deep breath.

And put her entire arm in the flames.

Yells. Cries of horror. The crowd gasped, horrified, as Isla's skin charred. Melted.

She did not flinch. Even though the pain threatened to swallow her whole. Her arm shook in the fire. Her other hand was curled so tight, her nails drew blood in her palm.

*Just a little longer.*

Tears welled up in the corners of her eyes, and she lifted her head, willing them not to fall. She must have looked triumphant to the audience. Pain-free.

She was not.

Not being able to take it any longer, not without falling to her knees and breaking like an egg in front of them all, she removed her arm.

The skin had peeled off in coils, leaving only angry red.

It was sickening to look at, to smell. Her stomach turned—a moment more and she would retch.

She took the vial's top off with her teeth, lip quivering uncontrollably. Then she poured every drop of the liquid across the burns.

Before her eyes, and everyone else's, the skin calmed. Knitted itself back together. Grew back, until her arm looked just as it had a few moments prior.

There was no mark of the fire.

The pain was not gone—not even close—but she kept it off her face as she bowed her head, signaling the end of her demonstration.

No one clapped. But they didn't need to. Isla could see the wonder in their faces.

Moonlings were the only ones on Lightlark who were supposed to be able to heal, using water. If Celeste's intel from her nobles and Ella were to be believed, they had begun making their skills scarce on the island. Charging too much. Healing less and less.

Almost *wanting* the rest of the island to be weaker.

Isla had just proven someone else could do what they did. Perhaps even better. Which, she knew, would only make Cleo hate her more.

In the end, Azul won.

Some would say the decision wasn't fair, but neither was the game.

# CHAPTER SIXTEEN
# SHADOWS

Isla's skin was still sore that night. She flinched as she slowly inched the thin strap of her gown down her arm, cursing herself for not wearing a different dress.

Then there was the matter of the zipper. From where it was placed, it typically required both hands to maneuver, to reach it—

"If you need help undressing, allow me to offer my services, Hearteater."

She jumped at the deep voice, spinning around.

Grim sat in a chair bathed in shadows, nearly all the way hidden. He leaned forward, elbows on his knees, eyes trailing her now bare shoulder, the strap hanging off it. The top of her dress slightly slipping down . . .

She righted it with her bad arm, then groaned, the flash of pain lightning behind her eyes.

The Wildling elixir might have healed her, but it hadn't been advanced enough to completely dull the ache. It was either take away the pain or heal—one, or the other. Of course, the rulers and islanders didn't need to know that.

It was why it was so important Isla never flinched. Never let anyone else see her pain.

It was why Terra and Poppy had made her practice, again and again, until she got it perfect.

"How did you get in here?" she demanded, voice thinner than she would have liked. He was so crass. So suggestive. She might have claimed she hated it.

But she didn't hate it.

She hated *herself* for not thinking his words were repulsive.

He shrugged. "Through the walls." Of course.

Isla remembered his demonstration. Anger replaced her pain. "Good. I suppose you can *leave* through the walls too, then," she said, pointing at one.

Grim stood. She swallowed. His size was always surprising. The height. The power that emanated off him in invisible tendrils.

"I will admit," he said, wicked smile tugging the side of his mouth. A step toward her. "This is not how I imagined you would want to spend our time in your chambers."

She scowled. Glared at him. Neither had enough bite. Both were offset by the blooming emotions she knew he could sense.

He was trying to distract her.

"You made a mockery of my demonstration, demon," she said, lest she forget why she was mad. "I told you about the trial. I gave you time to prepare."

Her inexplicable hurt must have peeked through her expression, because his eyes softened. "Hearteater," he said, his voice surprisingly gentle. "I thought you would have guessed by now, but let me make this clear. I have no interest in winning the Centennial. Or forming alliances. Or playing this game at all."

There was silence as his words washed over her.

He could have been lying.

But she had always focused on actions above words. They reflected motivations much more accurately. And Grim's words matched his actions. He hadn't attempted to be allies with the other rulers. He hadn't taken any of the demonstrations seriously.

She felt her face twist in confusion. "Then why are you here?" she said, finally voicing the one question she had about him. The one that blared over and over in her head every time he got close to her. Every time she wanted to get close to *him*. The Nightshade did not answer, so she took a step toward him, filling the gap. Everyone wanted something. Everyone had motives. She had been trying and failing to uncover his the entire first fifth of the Centennial. Her gaze locked on to his, demanding an answer. "What do you want?"

Grim looked down at her, and she could have sworn his expression turned sad. But a moment later, the wicked smile was back. "I believe I've made it clear what I want," he said, running a finger down the arm that had been seared.

Isla braced herself for the pain—but it never came. It was as if, somehow, he was masking her hurt. His skin was cold to the touch. Soothing. Ice against a burn.

Still, she stepped away. "You didn't come to the Centennial for me," she said, refusing to allow him to get away with the nonanswer.

"No," he said simply. "I did not."

"Then why?"

He frowned. "Do you know how Lightlark was created, Hearteater?" he asked.

Her hands curled into fists. She couldn't help but feel he was evading her question, but she preferred him speaking to simply vanishing, so she played along. Perhaps she would get useful information from him anyway. "It was formed by Oro's ancestor, the first Origin Horus Rey."

"That is a lie. The island was created by *two* people. Not just Horus, but also Cronan Malvere."

Her eyebrows came together.

"My own ancestor."

Isla had only ever heard of Horus Rey forming Lightlark, thousands of years before. Nightshades weren't even welcomed on the island, didn't even have a dedicated *isle* anymore.

"Lightlark became more powerful than either founder could have anticipated. It made both men greedy. Turned friend against friend. It ended in a duel, and when Cronan lost, all of Nightshade fled to form their own land, one not nearly as strong as Lightlark."

His dark eyes found Isla's. And, though she wanted to, she found she couldn't look away.

"Nightshade power built this place just as much as Sunling's did. My father believed it was time for us to regain control of a land we had claim to."

That was the reason for the war between Nightshade and Lightlark.

No wonder Grim hadn't been invited to any of the previous Centennials. Isla wondered how Oro could host the person who had invaded his home and killed his kin. The king must have truly been desperate to end the curses.

Why? What was he hiding?

"And what do you think?" Isla asked, voice barely above a whisper and still feeling too loud.

Grim ground his back teeth together. "I told my father to sign the treaty. We had lost too many people. We were going to lose everything if we didn't agree to peace. As part of the agreement, I was sent to live on Lightlark. A reminder that if Nightshades slipped up, they could kill my father's only heir. I lived here for twenty years, until—"

Until. He didn't say the words, but Isla knew the next part well.

Until the curses were cast, and all the rulers of realm died in sacrifice on one horrific night. Until power was transferred to heirs for the last time. Until the new rulers and most of their people fled the island and the incoming storm that would engulf it.

Isla dreaded her next question. But she had to ask it. "Grim, did you cast the curses?"

He looked at her, really looked at her. "If I did, would you ever speak to me again?"

She moved back, tensed. Her nostrils flared. Her answer was immediate. "No. The curses killed countless of my people. Turned us into monsters." Her voice thickened. "It's the reason my parents are both dead."

Something like sadness flashed in Grim's eyes. "The curses killed my family too." His head dipped, and he did not break her gaze. "No, Isla, I did not cast those curses."

She knew it was foolish to believe any of the other rulers. But Grim's pain was real. And it mirrored her own.

"So why are you here?" she demanded. "To get revenge? To try to invade Lightlark again?" Another thought formed in her mind, and she paled. "To ensure the curses *don't* get broken?"

Grim raised an eyebrow. "Why are *you* here, Hearteater? What are you after?"

Her body went still. Lies filled her mouth, ready to be spoken, but Grim grinned. He had felt her nerves. Her hesitancy. He would know she wasn't telling the truth.

Isla did not break his gaze. But she also did not say a word.

The Nightshade only shook his head. "You know," he said, making his way toward the wall through which he'd come, "you ask a great deal of questions, Hearteater." He studied her from head to toe before frowning at her arm, as if he could sense the pain it still gave her. "For someone with so many secrets of her own."

## CHAPTER SEVENTEEN

# FROZEN

Isla spent the next day with her arm wrapped in ice. Ella had fetched a bucket of it from the kitchen and replaced it regularly, without question. The burns still hurt. But not as badly. She alternated the ice with her Wildling elixirs. The faster the skin fully healed, the less it would feel like a layer of herself had been sliced away.

Later, the lingering pain—and perhaps the equally pestering thoughts of the Nightshade—had made her restless. Instead of trying to find sleep that wouldn't come, she roamed the halls, doing her typical snooping.

That was when she noticed the commotion around the wing of the castle that held the arena.

They were setting up for a demonstration. Dozens of islanders milled around, yelling orders. She tried to get as close as possible, to get a hint of what the trial might be. But there were too many people. It wasn't long before her arm flared in pain again, calling for its ice.

Her efforts hadn't been fruitless, however. The vast majority of those wandering the halls wore white. Moonlings.

She shouldn't have been surprised when Ella knocked on her chamber door twenty-four hours later, in the dead of night.

Her skin still burned, but not as sharply. She had tried her best to speed up the healing process after seeing the signs of a trial being set up, doubling her creams and taking other elixirs by mouth. Still, she thought she'd have more time. Only someone as cruel as Cleo would plan their demonstration to happen at midnight.

"A test of desire," the Moonling ruler said, hands pressed together in prayer. She stood in the center of the arena, which had been transformed into a maze of waterways. Each of the rulers stood on points of its perimeter. Once they dove into the lanes, they wouldn't be able to see each other anymore, thanks to walls of ice that made the confines of the labyrinth.

There had been no warning. No time to change. That was how Isla had ended up in the freezing snow globe that the stadium had been turned into, in nothing but a tank top and tiny shorts. Surely, she would freeze in the water. The rest of the rulers weren't in their typical capes and elaborate dress. But they also weren't in sleepwear. Somehow, they had managed to put on clothes that would fare well in the water. Did something in their powers allow them to do so? Or had they insisted upon the time to change, while Isla had blearily followed Ella through the castle?

"A true ruler must deny the selfish wants of their heart, for the good of their realm. You will be guided through the maze by your own heart. It will lead you to what you desire most. The winner will be decided *not* by their desire, but by who can reach it first. For worse than desiring something above the good of one's realm is not being sure of what you want at all."

The king stood just a few feet away, eyeing the water like it had personally offended him. *He* wasn't wearing dainty pajamas. He wore gold trousers and a shirt, with sleeves he now carefully rolled up his wrists.

A patch of skin on his hand was slightly swollen, a rash forming.

"Giselroot, nasty thing," she said quietly, almost to herself.

He stiffened. Looked at her, as if it was the first time he noticed she had been positioned in the lane beside him. "You know what this is?"

She shrugged. "Of course. Plant with five points? Green spots? Yellow buds?"

Oro nodded slowly.

"Giselroot. Poisonous. Causes a rash, and bad dreams."

He blinked at her.

"All right, the bad dreams might have just been a tactic by my guardians to keep me away from them." Giselroot grew in the forest just outside the loose pane of her window. After Poppy and Terra had it sealed, they had warned Isla against the plant, lest she find another way out of her room. "You'll want to treat that with an elixir of milk, tomato paste, honey, willow bark, pasted ash, and crushed mulberries."

Oro's lips pressed together before he said, "Thank you." Like it was a very hard thing to say.

She narrowed her eyes. "Giselroot only grows deep in the woods, where the trees are close enough to touch. What in the realm were you doing in a place like that?" Her tone said, *Don't you know how dangerous it is?*

Oro fixed her with a strange look. Isla stared back.

Without warning, a bell sounded.

And Isla was forced to jump into her lane.

The water was a thousand needles piercing her skin. At first, the cold was almost welcome against her raw arm. But it quickly sharpened, becoming too much, making it hurt even more. She immediately gasped for air, her chest a block of ice, the tips of her fingers and toes already numb.

Hundreds of islanders greeted her above, yelling, relishing in her weakness, jeering at her, cheering for their rulers.

*Keep going,* a voice in her head said, though her body screamed to get out of the water. She was surely at a disadvantage, coming from a place like the Wildling realm, which never saw a winter.

But she had been tested in the elements before.

Terra knew some of the trials might involve harsh weather conditions. When Isla was seventeen, she was left blindfolded in the middle of the woods, during a hurricane.

By the time she tore the fabric from her eyes, her guardians were long gone. The trees were bent in grotesque shapes from the wind, dirt and leaves stuck to her skin, and bugs had already started gnawing at her ankles.

Forests were deadly to those who couldn't control them. It was why the king's choice to venture into them was so shocking.

It took her three days to get home. In that time, she drank spoiled water and sat shaking beneath a hastily made canopy of palm fronds, the fever in her head like a bell, ringing over and over. Knowing she would die if she stayed, she forced herself to walk, remembering her survival lessons. She hunted for food with bows and arrows she made herself, using the dagger she always kept strapped to her thigh.

In the haze, she cut her fingers, and the blood smeared her weapons, acting as a siren call to even more insects, which feasted on her flesh as if she was already dead.

By the time she collapsed outside the Wildling castle, she was so sick, it took their best healers weeks to bring her back to health.

*You could have killed me* were the first words out of her mouth once she could speak again, directed at Terra.

Her guardian had only smiled. *The only way not to fear death is to meet it.*

Isla knew what dying felt like. This wasn't it. So, she kept going, pushing, though the needles sank deeper, until they clicked against her bones, her entire body overcome with cold.

Ahead, there was a split in the maze. Isla wondered which route to take when she felt a faint pull in one direction.

Then, a pull in the other.

She stopped, angling her head to take a deep breath.

One direction felt like home—Poppy and Terra. Her people.

The other felt like more.

She couldn't quite make out what it meant, but the emotions were powerful. Intoxicating. Startling.

Cleo's words played back in her mind. Her heart was supposed to guide her. Why was it so undecided?

Time froze over as she treaded water.

Had it been a few moments?

Or minutes?

Or longer?

*Snap out of it,* a voice in her mind sounded.

She wanted freedom, that was for sure.

But was that truly all she wanted?

A whistle sounded somewhere, breaking her out of her thoughts. The first ruler had reached the end of their maze.

Isla was so far behind. It was time to make a choice.

To follow her heart.

She chose a direction and swam, reinvigorated, her chest full of frost, white plumes coming out of her mouth each time she gulped for air.

Her hair had divided into thick, frozen strands; her clothes did nothing to keep her warm. Her skin felt too stiff, her muscles fighting to flex in the unrelenting temperature of the water.

*Just a little longer,* she pleaded with her body, knowing it had been through worse. She had trained for this.

Her lungs began to shut down first, choking with water that had somehow broken through her mouth.

Another turn.

The maze appeared to be closing in around her; each time she went up for air, the crowd seemed blurrier. Their cheers farther away.

Was she even moving anymore? She couldn't feel her arms.

Everything became colder. Her lungs lurched.

Her eyes fought to blink open, one more time, and all she saw was light, retreating.

She was sinking.

If the trial killed her, she wondered if part of the prophecy would be fulfilled. Perhaps the Moonling ruler had chosen this trial, knowing it might kill one of the weaker rulers for her, without having to break the rules. At least, in that scenario, Celeste would live.

But her people wouldn't.

Terra and Poppy wouldn't.

This was not death. This death was too quiet. Too much like slipping into sleep.

She wanted all life had to offer. The long life of a ruler with powers, exploring all Lightlark, a lifetime of friendship with Celeste, perhaps even . . . love. Something she had judged others for. Including her own mother. Something she had always seen as reckless. She *wanted*, wanted so strongly, selfish things beyond just saving her realm and breaking the curses—

Slowly, her fingers uncurled from their fists. A groan sounded in the back of her throat, and she fought the urge to keep her eyes closed, willed her limbs back to life.

She clawed through the ice-cold water like it was the only thing standing between her and everything held in her heart.

Her vision went in and out, but she felt the end of the maze. She grabbed the glowing tablet of ice waiting there and hauled herself out of the water with all her remaining strength.

Isla didn't see what was written on the slab, didn't hear the crowd. All she felt was something warm washing over her body. Ella. The Starling draped a towel across her back.

She was shaking, her vision going in and out. "Please, get me to my room," she managed to say.

Isla owed Ella far more than pain cream, she thought as her attendant rushed her out of the stadium, using the cheers of the crowd and the crowning of Cleo as the winner as a cover. The Moonling had clearly chosen her trial to showcase her superiority over the others.

She might have been more concerned that Cleo was now tied with the king, and could potentially be choosing their matches, if she didn't feel so weak.

Ella was small but stronger than she looked, holding Isla up as they slowly made their way through the empty castle. Water dripped an endless puddle behind her. The rest was frozen. Her lungs ached, two buckets of ice in her chest.

"I'll draw a bath," Ella said when they finally made it to her room. "And get tea." She rushed out of Isla's room.

Isla was going in and out of consciousness. Her body had gone numb.

Her mind was full of her mission.

She needed to find the bondbreaker.

For so long, she had denied her desires. Pushed them down. Her guardians' warnings were always on her mind. Saying her life didn't just belong to her. Teaching that wanting anything but saving her realm was selfish.

Now, she couldn't lie to herself any longer.

She wanted many, many things.

And she was willing to do terrible things to get them.

Not just for her. Her desires made her understand her people more than she ever had before. They deserved to have what they wanted. So did Celeste's people—including Ella.

*I promise,* she might have said aloud, or maybe her words never reached her mouth. Ella had helped her into the bath, and the hot water scalded her frozen skin, made her scream out, too dazed to hide her pain. *I'll find the bondbreaker. I'll break the curses.*

*Even if it means breaking myself.*

## CHAPTER EIGHTEEN

# CASTLE

Isla awoke feeling on the brink of death. There was a relentless cold at the center of her chest. All day, she stayed in bed, drinking broths. Ella fed the fire. Kept bringing tea. Drawing hot baths. By night, Isla only felt a little better.

Celeste risked a visit, bringing a special Starling soup recipe she had procured from Star Isle. "I'll go instead," she said as soon as she saw her.

And Isla knew she must have looked on the brink of death too. A groan escaped her as she pushed herself off the bed. She shook her head.

It was the twentieth day of the Centennial. Tonight was the full moon. Her only chance to go to Moon Isle undiscovered. "No offense, Cel," she said, "but you can't move like I do."

Her friend sighed. "I know. But—"

Isla shook her head again, cutting the Starling off. "If you get caught, it's over. We can't risk it."

Celeste frowned. "Can we risk *you?*" she asked pointedly.

Isla waved her concern off. She stretched her limbs as she formulated the hair dye again. "I'm fine," she lied. Celeste knew it was a lie.

But she also knew as well as Isla did that they didn't have another choice.

Everything she wanted was on her mind as she forced down the pain of her arm, the cold with every breath, her need for rest.

None of it meant anything compared to their need to find the bondbreaker.

***

Juniper might be the most or least trustworthy barkeep on the island, Isla still wasn't sure. But his information had been correct.

There were no guards on the bridge that night.

The Moonling curse meant that every full moon, the sea sought out Moonling blood. Ships were cracked in half by hundred-foot waves; girls were swept off cliffs by monstrous surges. The sea swallowed them, then went still.

Tonight, it was ravenous.

The entire isle was empty. It was so quiet, Isla could hear the sea banging against the cliff of the castle, over and over, knocks on a door, death demanding its due.

Moon Isle was an ornament encased in ice, water, and glass. From the first step off the bridge, Isla felt the frost, cold in her chest like regret. Harsh as the ruler who ruled it.

And, also, just as beautiful.

Fountains and thin rivers snaked across Moon Isle, giving the water-wielding Moonlings constant access to their power. The ice palace sat perched above, watching her as closely as the moon. The paths were carved out of mother-of-pearl, lined with marble statues depicting sea creatures with winding tentacles, fish-tailed women, and ships floating on nothing. No guards anywhere.

Unfortunately, she was going right toward where they all were hiding.

Celeste had learned the Moonling library was deep within the castle walls. That was where Isla was headed.

Her hair had been painted white with Wildling elixir. She wore the right dress. But something told her that being a Moonling was much more than that—and if any of the guards took one look at her, they would immediately know she was an impostor. Being outside during the full moon was the greatest hint to her identity of all. No Moonling would survive being outside the palace tonight, so Isla needed to move like a ghost, get inside undiscovered. She stuck to the shadows, should anyone be watching from above.

The castle sat high on a hill of white rock. A thin, exposed path led from the gardens up to the castle entrance. Easy to monitor. Impossible for Isla to use without being detected.

She circled the mountain's perimeter, hoping to see another entrance. The rock was impenetrable—except for a window, fifty feet up, right at the bottom level of the palace.

There were no bars on its glass.

That was her way in.

Isla readied herself. Her palms were wet with nerves, so she smoothed them along the chalky rock, coating her hands in the stuff.

The cliff was nearly flat, but there were pockets. She had been trained to see the tiniest of holes, the invisible recesses.

Her hands found its first two placements, barely a few inches to cling to.

Then, with a grunt, she hauled herself up.

The first few moments of climbing were never too bad. The ground wasn't that far away. One wrong move, and she could just start over.

Things became more precarious thirty feet up.

She moved quickly, so as not to lose her momentum and not make time for fear, similar to swallowing down medicine too fast to taste it.

One of Terra's lessons. Her guardian had made her watch the monkeys that swept across the forest effortlessly, climbing trees with ease.

They didn't plan out every movement. They swung, knowing there would always be something for their arms or tail to latch on to.

*Climb until your muscles learn the movements; leave your mind out of it,* Terra said. And Isla climbed the tree, the cliff, the wall, again. Again. Again.

Her hands were used to this. They moved on their own, looking for grooves in the stone. Finding them. Going up. And up. And up.

Another move. One hand latched on to a slight bump. Her other fingers felt around for purchase.

But for once, the rock was smooth.

Nothing to hold on to.

Higher. She would need to look higher. Arm shaking with the effort, she lifted herself up, to find somewhere else for her other hand to hold. She barely muted a cry as her still-sensitive skin screamed in pain at the movement.

Nothing.

That was the problem with climbing an unfamiliar rock face. There were no guarantees. Still, there was always *something*. Some way to get up.

Her fingers were starting to get sweaty. The grip on the point of rock less secure. She felt both freezing and too warm. Did she have a fever? Was she sick?

No. Just weak. Her arm's skin was still slightly raw. The cold in her chest had intensified.

She needed to find placement for her other hand quickly.

Higher.

Despite her efforts to be silent, Isla grumbled with strain as she forced her arm to lift her even *higher*—

Only then did she find a slight hollow in the rock. She didn't waste a moment before shoving her fingers painfully into the pit, distributing her weight again.

That was close.

The window was just a few feet above. It was large enough for her to fit through, with a ledge, even, for support.

Isla made her next move. And just as her hand was about to lock on to another hold, the knob holding all her weight gave way.

She fell.

This high up, she might break her legs. Or, depending on how she landed, could crack her ribs. Or her spine.

In any case, she would be discovered. Found in a broken heap right outside the castle walls.

No bondbreaker.

No future that she wanted more than anything, a future that was changing every day the more she saw and experienced.

*No.*

So fast it was muscle memory, Isla unclipped the back of her necklace—a dagger made to look like a choker, sharp point instead of a clasp—and dug its hidden blade into the rock with all her strength.

She stopped falling.

Barely.

A moment later, the blade gave out.

By then, she had new hand placements.

She was twenty feet down from the window now. But she was alive. Whole.

Her stomach felt like it had been turned inside out, her heart drummed against the cliff.

*No time to celebrate.* Sweat licking the back of her neck despite the cold, Isla traveled the rest of the way up to the window. Roaring still filled her ears, from the sea, or the adrenaline, or her body warning that she wasn't ready to exert so much effort—she wasn't sure.

Minutes later, she hauled herself up the ledge, lifted the mercifully unlocked window, and dragged herself through.

The Moon Isle castle was quiet.

Every inch had been sculpted from white marble, dark-blue veins weaving through it like rivers. It reminded Isla of Cleo.

Spotless. Ageless.

Something about it was unsettling.

It was late. The Moonlings must have retreated to their rooms within the castle. Ever since the curses, Celeste said, most of them had moved into the palace, the only building on the isle high enough to escape the monthly surges.

Even inside, Isla could hear the snarl of the sea, desperately rising in curls toward its inhabitants.

Most people must be asleep. Or perhaps there were rules. Cleo seemed to take pleasure in wielding her power. There could be a mandatory curfew. Or restricted areas of the castle.

It was a labyrinth.

Isla didn't know where she was going, just that the library was at the very back of the castle, overlooking the sea.

So, she went deeper.

The occasional footstep sounded through the hall, followed by orders. Guards, patrolling certain corridors.

There were so many. Much, much more than she had seen on other parts of the island. Now that she thought about it, there hadn't been *any* guards on Sky Isle. There weren't many on the Mainland either, except for the ones who lit the torches in the agora.

What was Cleo up to?

Isla hoped the library wouldn't be as highly monitored. The restricted section required Cleo's touch to be accessed, after all. But the farther she made it into the palace, the more she heard. Whispers through the walls. The gurgle of water being wielded. The high-pitched crackling of water being turned to ice.

Was she close to the dungeons? Or were the guards simply practicing?

For what?

There was a flash of white at her side, and she darted into the closest room she could find.

Empty. Just four stone walls that chilled her to the bone as she pressed against them, hoping the passerby hadn't seen her.

For a few moments, there was just silence.

Then, she heard voices.

"Were you patrolling this hall?" A man.

"No." A woman.

"Was Lazlo?"

The woman grunted her no. "Why?"

A second. "I saw someone."

"Here?"

Isla froze. He *had* spotted her.

The man and woman were walking down the hall now; she could hear their boots clearly against the marble, clacking like clinking china. Every step brought them closer to her.

"How would they get past the legion?" the woman said.

*Legion?*

Cleo was building an army.

Why?

What was she planning?

Isla didn't have much time to wonder.

Because a moment later, the door of the room she was hiding in flew open.

## CHAPTER NINETEEN

# UNDERWATER

Isla didn't give the guards time to reach for their ice blades or wield the sloshing water held in vials across their belts.

Before they could even yell for help, she had hit them in six different places, special points Terra taught her to target.

Their muscles slackened.

One good hit each in the back of the head, and they slumped down to the floor, passed out. Not one drop of blood.

Terra would be proud.

The moment she stopped moving, she was panting. The climbing, the fighting—it had taken too much energy. She really shouldn't be out of bed, let alone deep in another ruler's territory.

Too late now. She was here. And things were already starting to get out of hand.

As quietly as she could, and with all the strength she could muster, she dragged them fully into the room, closed the door behind them, and ran down the hall.

Either they would wake up and call for help, someone would realize they were missing and would call for help, or someone else was about to stop her and call for help.

It was clear that the time for being a shadow had passed.

Now she just needed to get into the library. As fast as her quickly weakening legs could take her.

The next passageway was empty, but the one after that had four guards, pressed against the wall, chins up, ice swords to their chests like nutcrackers she once saw in a market. At the sound of her steps, they came to life, turning right to her.

*Time to go,* she thought, taking another turn instead, and hoping she was going in the right direction.

Their boots echoed loudly behind her, the sounds growing as more guards joined the pursuit. Isla ran as fast as she could, white dress curling behind her like a plume of steam. Her chest made concerning sounds with every breath. Her bones and muscles ached.

The halls were endless. Isla couldn't help but feel she must have taken a wrong turn. She wouldn't make it much longer.

Maybe she was getting farther away. Maybe she had become disoriented in her struggle to outrun the guards. Maybe—

Then she heard it.

The sea, louder than before, echoing like thunder. A beast shaking the walls of the castle with its firm grip.

The library had to be close.

She took off toward the sound of the sea, following its force, wincing at the pulsing of pain of her arm and her chest and her head, like the three of them were having a conversation. The farther she made it into the castle, the more the chandeliers on the ceilings shook, pale crystals clinking together. The more works of art teetered on their hooks. The Moonling curse was ruthless.

How many more cycles would it take for the castle to simply be knocked off its cliff, into the ocean's waiting mouth? When would the sea be rewarded for its efforts by getting the entire palace and its inhabitants in one fell swoop?

*Not tonight,* she hoped, as she ran and ran and ran, faster than the guards, as fast as she could without collapsing.

Until she nearly crashed into a wall.

A dead end.

No more halls. No more turns. No doors.

Just a wall.

She hunched over, hands on her thighs, and began coughing, the cold in her chest crawling up her throat. Her knees wobbled.

The steps behind her had turned into a stampede, and they were closing in. A few more seconds, and they would have her surrounded.

The ocean made another move against the palace, raging. She expected, this close to the exterior, to feel the hit in her bones, the sea colliding directly against the stone in front of her.

But as she braced herself for the impact, the wave hit—and the rock in front of her did not shake nearly as much as it should have.

Which meant there was something else behind this wall.

Just as the guards rounded the corner, Isla slipped on Celeste's gloves as quickly as she could and pressed against the bricks.

The stones began turning, a puzzle undoing itself, unlocking a door.

It opened. And she pushed herself through, then slammed it closed, hoping it would seal behind her.

The guards were a flurry of sounds on the other side, alerting more of their crew. The *legion,* perhaps.

"Intruder!" she heard. "In the library!"

She was trapped inside. Cornered.

But at least now she knew for certain she had found it.

Isla turned to find a frozen library. Perfect. As if she wasn't already cold enough. Every book was trapped in walls of ice. Slab after slab formed rows, an entire room of parchment and frost.

She should have suspected that Cleo would have made the *entire* library restricted, instead of a specific section.

Bangs sounded outside as the guards tried to break the wall down.

*No time to waste.* She took off, running through the icy rows, nearly slipping on the frosted-over marble floor. Her feet skated as she rounded the corner—

And came face-to-face with a monstrous wave. It hit the set of glass doors with a force that seemed to shake the castle to its foundations. If it wasn't for her last-minute gripping of an ice-coated shelf, she would have fallen to the floor.

The doors led to a curling white balcony now flooded with sea-foam like a rabid mouth, the aftermath of the sea as it retreated, gathering its strength to strike once more. It was a wonder the glass doors hadn't shattered. They must have been reinforced with enchantment somehow.

*Enchantment.*

Where were the relics? All she saw were books.

"She's inside!"

"Get the ruler!"

*Ruler?* Isla swallowed. Cleo was supposed to be sleeping in the Mainland castle. It was tradition to spend the most time there, especially during the first twenty-five days.

She had to hurry. Her eyes strained to take in every inch of the library. It only had one floor.

Nothing. Only books contained in ice, for as far as she could see.

She must have missed something.

Isla whipped around, ready to take a closer look at the front shelves, when another crushing wave sent her tumbling forward.

This time, she hit the floor.

There was a terrible cracking sound as her head smacked against it.

For a moment, there was just blinding white. She blinked, willing her vision to come back, telling her body there was no time to waste, no time to give in to pain.

Her cheek had nearly stuck to the ground. Her mind spun as she lifted it, and the world tripped before righting itself.

Her arms shook as she made to get up.

That was when she saw it.

The floor was frosted over. Her body heat had warmed it enough that the icy coating had cleared, revealing a second library beneath.

Water. Dozens of relics were encased in water, chained down, floating below the floor.

A cape, its fabric moving unnaturally, flipping this way and that.

An arrow with a snowflake point.

Crystal daggers.

Books with locks.

Keys long as her arms.

No bondbreaker.

Nothing that even resembled an oversize glass needle.

Disappointment quickly turned to anger as she stood on shaky legs, stumbling to the side, having to steady herself against a block of ice.

Something hot dripped down her cheek.

Tears?

Was she crying and she didn't even know it?

She lifted a trembling hand that came back crimson.

No. Blood.

Isla stepped forward and nearly collapsed.

Her other foot made to move, but her knee gave way.

First, her sore, burned arm. Then, the effects of the Moonling's demonstration. Now, this head injury.

It was too much.

Isla had sworn she would break her curse, even if it meant breaking herself.

Perhaps she should have worded her promise a little differently.

Bangs echoed through the room—but they weren't coming from the balcony or the sea. No, they were coming from the wall through which she had entered.

"We have the entire legion out here," a voice yelled from the other side. "The ruler is on her way. You are cornered. There is nowhere to run. There is no way out."

Isla smirked.

He was right. There was nowhere left to run.

But *no way out?*

In that, he was wrong.

"Good thing I never planned on getting out the way I came," she said to no one. Every part of her ached as she reached back her good arm and pulled her starstick from its place against her spine.

She didn't know how to use it accurately for small distances or places she had never been before. But her room in the Mainland castle was neither.

The wall came down just as she portaled away.

## CHAPTER TWENTY

# TEA

For two full days, Isla slept. She only awoke to eat and sip broth, then she drifted away again. She had strange dreams. Grim was in some of them. Flashes of him. Of her. Of *them*.

By the twenty-third day, when Ella came with news of afternoon tea, Isla knew it was time to get up. To shed the pain and weakness like the snake on her crown shrugging off its skin.

The bondbreaker wasn't in the Star Isle, Sky Isle, or Moon Isle libraries. Which only left one place.

Sun Isle.

The king's own land. It made sense that a relic as powerful as the bondbreaker would be kept there.

But Isla had no way of getting gold clothing. Barely any hair dye left.

And more problems than ever.

Cleo knew someone had attacked her guards, gotten into her library, and left without a trace.

She must have suspected Isla immediately. Ever since that first dinner, Cleo had had her sights on her. The physical description the attacked guards would have provided would have simply confirmed her suspicions.

Cleo didn't have proof it was her. But she *knew.*

She had to.

The wound to her head had mostly healed, thanks to her Wildling elixir. The white had washed out of her hair. She had thrown her Moonling clothing into the fire.

Still, Isla felt like the truth of her whereabouts three nights prior was written across her body as she walked inside the tearoom.

It must have been beautiful, once upon a time. Now the windows, giant arches every few feet, were covered with thick fabrics like mirrors in an old house. Like her room back home. The ceiling, domed and made of glass, had been painted over, trapping the sunlight outside. The only light came from hundreds of orbs of fire that floated precariously overhead, the same ones the king had displayed at her demonstration. Marble columns lined the room the way guards might if Oro allowed them inside. The king didn't need guards, however. Not even against rulers of realm. He was more powerful than all of them combined.

Isla felt that power ringing through the room as Oro entered it.

Cleo swept inside next, and her eyes immediately locked onto Isla's. Her expression revealed nothing.

But Isla's palms began to sweat. She forced herself to keep the Moonling's gaze until an attendant guided Isla to her seat.

The Moonling ruler knew. Isla felt it in her bones.

Cleo was a dangerous enemy. One who was building an army. For what? Did any of the other rulers know that between the legion and her supposed ships, the Moonling seemed ready for war?

Once all the rulers were seated, staff came pouring out of a large set of doors, carrying gleaming trays of china. They circled the table once, then stopped suddenly, their movements perfectly choreographed. Behind each chair stood a Skyling, a Moonling, and a Starling.

Oro nodded.

The Starlings lifted their hands, and tiny plates flew in a flurry, landing carefully on the table, followed closely by teacups, which fell atop them with a clink. Three cups total sat in front of Isla. Ornately decorated teapots hovered overhead, high above the table, heavy with liquid. Water-wielding Moonlings lifted their hands, and steaming tea Sunlings had no doubt heated fell from the pots like tiny waterfalls, through strainers the Starlings held steadily, rich red liquid that spilled into her first mug. The pots straightened and moved in a circle before her second cup was filled with honeyed gold. The third tea was the deep blue of sapphires.

The Starlings lifted their arms again, and cubes of sugar fell into each cup, followed by drops of honey and shots of cream. Each flavor of tea received its own treatment, the blue tea getting a slice of lemon, the red receiving a mint leaf, the gold gifted a candied orange peel.

Finally, the Skylings whipped their wrists, sending a gentle breeze over their drinks, cooling them.

Grim sighed. "I suppose this isn't the moment to mention I detest tea?"

Oro ignored him. "Please enjoy," he said.

Isla loved tea. She would have smiled under happier circumstances. Wildlings were experts at collecting the richest herbs, leaves, and spices that, when steeped, created the most delicious drinks.

She reached for the red one first. The drop of cream had turned it the pink of dahlias. She brought the cup to her lips tentatively, bracing herself for the burning liquid. But the Skylings had cooled the tea perfectly—she took a deep sip and almost groaned. It tasted like berries without the bitterness, honey without the heaviness.

Her eyes had fluttered closed, and she only opened them when the tea was drained from its cup. She lowered it and found Oro watching her.

"Any match to Wildling tea?" he asked.

"It's certainly drinkable," she said flatly. Then she reached for the second cup.

Cleo studied her. Too carefully. "How *do* Wildlings take their tea?" she asked, sharp eyes gleaming. "With a splash of blood?"

Isla sipped the second tea slowly. This one—the gold one—tasted of caramel. "And we drink it from the skulls of our conquests," she said steadily, smiling good-naturedly, like the Moonling's words were a joke from a friend and not a barb from a now certain enemy.

There were a few moments of clattering and quiet as they drank their tea. Isla finished her first cup and peered into it, noticing a strange pattern in the leaves that stuck to the bottom.

Her next one had something similar.

By the time she finished her third, her blood had gone cold.

Oro rose.

"Welcome to my demonstration," he said. Tension filled the room. Power surged.

*Demonstration?* But there weren't even any islanders present.

Though, she supposed, that wasn't truly a rule. Just a custom. Something most rulers preferred too, to display their excellence at their own trials.

The king's pointer finger circled the lip of one of his teacups. "This is no ordinary tea," he continued, his tone steady. "It is a truth tea."

Isla went still. Dread dripped down her spine.

"Your greatest secret is written in the leaves."

She risked a look down at her cups.

And saw her greatest truth written across the three of them, in careful script.

*I have no power.*

It took every drop of her training not to let her horror filter through her face. She remained calm, though inside she was a tempest, desperate for escape.

She studied the other rulers as a distraction from the panic that had turned her skin to thorns. Cleo had gone paler than usual. Azul simply frowned. Grim looked ready to coat the entire room in Oro's ash. Celeste darted a rare, risky look in her direction, eyes wide with a message.

*It's you,* she seemed to be saying. Of course. The Starling's greatest secret was one she was keeping for Isla.

The urgency of her glance said *run.*

Before Isla could debate any move, the king picked up his first cup and said, "Whoever shares their secret wins my trial."

There was a shatter of glass as Celeste dropped her cups to the floor, taking herself out of the challenge. She looked over at Isla meaningfully, for just a moment, and her heart swelled. Celeste was a better friend than she deserved.

Azul's broke next.

Without wasting another moment, Isla pushed hers to the floor and watched them break into a thousand pieces, her secret lost in the shards.

Grim let his own fall one by one, eyes trained on the king. Isla had never seen him look so murderous. He had transformed into the famed Nightshade killer, the ruthless ruler she had heard warnings about. His expression held promises of torture and darkness.

The force of his invisible power lashed out, waves of searing chill coating the room. For a moment, her bones felt hollow, dead.

One thing was for sure. Grim *did* have a secret. And if even the idea of it being revealed produced this much anger, Isla was afraid to know what it was.

Just Oro and Cleo were left.

This was the last trial.

The king had won the duel and the demonstration of power. Cleo had won her own trial and Celeste's.

They were tied.

Whoever won this one would decide the matches the rulers would break into. The decision was important. Because of the first rule, a ruler could not kill the person they were joined with. The choice would force alliances, guide their search for the meaning of the rest of the prophecy, shape the rest of the Centennial. Perhaps even decide who would be targeted to be killed.

Oro's gaze was unrelenting as he stared down the Moonling, daring her to reveal her secret. And for a moment, Isla thought she might.

But, thinking better of it, Cleo sent the glass to the ground.

The king had officially won the trials.

His eyes were lifeless as he stared down at his first cup, and said, "I."

He let it fall to the floor.

The second. "Am."

For the third, he looked up and caught Isla's eyes. He frowned a bit, as if disturbed his gaze had shifted her way. But he did not look away as he spoke the third and final word of his greatest secret: "Dying."

## CHAPTER TWENTY-ONE

# PAIRED

The king was dying. What did that even mean? Chaos erupted at his confession, but he said nothing more before sweeping out of the room. Claiming his win.

It was a secret that affected them all.

Oro's life-force was directly correlated with the island's. Did that mean Lightlark was at risk?

He was the strongest of them. An Origin, who was Starling, Skyling, Moonling, and Sunling combined. If *he* was dying . . .

What hope did the rest of them have?

Isla heard a soft knock at her door, far past midnight. *Celeste.*

The Starling hurried inside, looking as if she had seen a ghost.

"That was close" was all she said.

Isla's stomach dropped, remembering the words printed in her cup. She imagined Celeste's were nearly the same.

"I know." She frowned. "Thank you. You shouldn't have to protect me like this, but—thank you."

Celeste waved her thanks away, as if it was nothing. But it wasn't nothing. The only way Isla could ever repay her friend for the risk she was enduring on her behalf was to find the bondbreaker.

"What do you think it means?" Isla asked.

The Starling seemed to know immediately she meant the king's confession. She shrugged. "I'm not sure. But it's reason enough for us to hurry up and find the bondbreaker so we can get off this island."

She was right. Once they were free of the curses, they could be free of Lightlark. The king's death wouldn't affect them or their realms.

But there were even more factors that rushed their already limited timeline. And complicated their plan.

She told Celeste about the disastrous display in the Moon Isle castle and Cleo's almost certain knowledge that Isla had broken in.

Celeste walked around Isla's room, hands coated in sparks. Her emotions often triggered them, which was part of the reason she always wore gloves. To keep her energy in check.

"I'll do my best to get information on the Sun Isle library" was all she said after a long while. Isla nodded, though that wouldn't solve their biggest issues. How was she supposed to sneak onto Sunling land without gold clothing? Celeste finally stopped pacing and clasped her palms together, making the sparks fall away like ribbons, vanishing before they hit the floor. "In two days, teams are being decided. Oro will hopefully match us together. Then we won't have to work in secret. We will find a way for you to get onto Sun Isle undetected."

Isla didn't want to question her friend, especially when she had complicated everything by making Cleo suspicious of her, but she couldn't help voicing a doubt. "What if we aren't paired together?"

Celeste frowned. She placed a gentle palm, still buzzing with energy, against Isla's cheek. "*I* know how incredible you are, my brilliant friend," she said. "But they do not. The king is not going to pick you. Or me, for that matter."

Isla had to admit she was right.

"Now," Celeste said. "It's not all bad news, is it? We know for certain that the bondbreaker is in the Sun Isle library now. We will get you inside. You will find the bondbreaker. We will use it. Break our curses. You'll get your power. Our realms will be freed. We could be off the island in a week. Two weeks, at the most."

Said like that, it sounded easy.

But Isla knew now that nothing on Lightlark ever was.

***

On the twenty-fifth day of the Centennial, they returned to the throne room for the pairing ceremony.

"King." Azul's tone was steady, though his eyes flashed with urgency. "Are you going to explain your . . . *truth?*"

This time, the king sat on his throne, as if reminding the rest of them of his position.

Even if he was, supposedly, dying.

Oro's crown glinted beneath the light of the flames above. He frowned.

The rest of the rulers were silent, clearly wondering the same thing Azul had so helpfully verbalized.

Finally, the king spoke. "Since the last Centennial, the island has been steadily weakening. Elders have died. Buildings that have stood for thousands of years are now ruins. Our most ancient creatures have vanished." He gripped the sides of the throne so strongly, his knuckles turned white. "The curses. Centuries of rulers living away from the island. Thousands of our people leaving. It has all taken its toll on Lightlark. On *me.*"

Isla thought of her own realm. The same things had happened. All signs that too little power was being injected to the land and not enough ability was being used.

Oro rose from his throne. He looked at each of them, eyes hollow as ever. "I fear this Centennial is not simply *a* chance to break our curses. I fear this is our *last* chance."

The room was silent.

Surging power—from anger or fear or wariness, Isla didn't know—filled the hall.

Azul spoke again. "How do you know you're dying?"

With that, the king lifted his sleeve. Starting from his elbow, his golden skin had started to gray. It looked almost blue. "It's spreading," he said. "Quicker than I anticipated." His jaw locked. "Part of my power and role has been to keep the island warm and full of light for centuries, even during the endless storm." He frowned. "That power has weakened. The last decade has been our coldest in history. It is causing plants and animals to die. I have been trying to lessen its impact . . . but soon, I won't be able to stop it."

*That* was why he had commanded that all the hearths remain lit. Why there were so many torches across the Mainland, and fire in nearly every room of the castle. They were all masking the king's weakness.

He stepped down the stairs, putting him at their level. "I hope you see now why it is more important than ever to figure out and fulfill the prophecy."

The king motioned to the wall. Words began to be carved along the stone in large, fire-coated letters. The oracle's riddle, the one Isla had been taught years prior. The key to breaking the curses.

*Only joined can the curses be undone*
*Only after one of six has won,*
*When the original offense*
*Has been committed again*
*And a ruling line has come to an end*
*Only then can history amend.*

"'Only joined can the curses be undone,'" Oro read. "That is why we break into teams, to fulfill the prophecy. And attempt to solve it. A reminder of the first rule. A ruler is forbidden from assassinating their partner." To encourage trust, she knew.

Isla wasn't really concerned with the prophecy. Her and Celeste's plan didn't require it.

Still, she pretended to read the words on the wall while running ideas through her mind. Perhaps she could tweak her elixir potion to dye clothing . . . she might be able to make one of her own gowns gold.

It would never work. Plus, she barely had enough elixir for one more shot at dyeing her hair, let alone an entire swath of fabric.

She could rob a Sunling in the market and take their clothes?

Isla winced at that idea.

Horrible. Also, the Sunling would immediately report the crime, and Oro would know someone meant to sneak onto his isle.

Isla was so focused on feigning interest in the prophecy and plotting her attempt to sneak into the Sun Isle library that she didn't realize her name had been spoken until it was repeated so loudly she startled.

"*Isla,*" the king was saying.

Her expression must have given away that she had no idea what he had said previously, or if she had been asked a question, because the king gave her a grating look.

"My choice of partner," the king repeated through his teeth, clearly hating every word coming out of his mouth. The room fell away. She forgot to school her expression or control her emotions around Grim. Her mouth might have been hanging open. She might have accidentally shot Celeste a horrified look. "Is Isla."

# CHAPTER TWENTY-TWO

# DEAL

This was bad. Dangerous.

She was supposed to be matched with Celeste. They had a plan.

This was yet another factor that complicated everything.

Why in the realm would the king want to be matched with her?

The last thing Isla wanted was to be forced to spend time with the Lightlark ruler. Not just because he was insufferable, but also because doing so would surely mean having to use her powers in search of a way to break the curses, using the prophecy.

Powers she didn't have.

Would he be able to sense her powerlessness if they spent more time together? Grim hadn't. But Oro was the king of Lightlark—his abilities were endless.

She had to find a way out of it . . . an excuse. She waited for Celeste to knock on her door, to brainstorm.

*Celeste*. Her friend had been paired with the worse possible ruler. Cleo. She felt a pang of dread.

Everything had gone so wrong.

Because of the king.

Hours later, there was a knock on her door. She had done everything she could to distract herself, waiting for the Starling to finally arrive. Isla had taken a bath, as if she could wash the day off. She had put on her comfiest clothes, the pieces she had sneaked into her luggage before leaving the Wildling newland—an oversize long-sleeved shirt Poppy had let her wear at night. Tight pants that were just as soft as the shirt.

*Celeste, finally,* she thought as she threw the door open.

But it wasn't Celeste.

Oro's eyebrows were slightly raised as he took her in. She supposed she looked like a completely different person—makeup off, hair in a bun atop her head, shirt five sizes too large. She might have been worried that the king had seen her like this, without her Wildling temptress mask on, if she wasn't so annoyed.

She crossed her arms across her chest. "Do you normally call upon rulers at midnight?"

He matched her frosty expression before looking over her shoulder, into her room. "May I enter?"

Her chest tightened. There were many things in her room that would give her and her secrets away. Her starstick. Her reliance on elixirs. But she couldn't say no. It would only make him suspicious. "I suppose."

She should have anticipated he would seek her out. He *had* decided to pair up with her—for whatever reason. Isla had excused herself as soon as possible, fleeing to her room, fearing everyone in the hall would be able to hear the unsteady beating of her anxious heart if she stayed too long.

He strode past her and frowned at the state of her room.

It wasn't even that messy. There were a few dresses she hadn't managed to put away strewn across the furniture, and teacups littered her nightstand, but, what, was the king's room perfect?

She closed the door and didn't stray far from it. "Yes?" she said flatly.

Oro carefully picked up one of her dresses, placed it on the bed, and took a seat on the chair that it had previously occupied, leaning back as if it was his own room. And Isla supposed it was.

His fingers trailed the curling sides of the seat as he said, "I would like to make a deal."

For a moment, Isla considered grabbing her starstick from its hidden place in the wardrobe and portaling somewhere far away. It would be so easy . . .

Somehow, she forced herself to stand very tall and say, "Oh? What is it you propose?"

They were already paired. She didn't understand why he wanted to make a deal on top of that but decided it would be best to allow him to speak. Perhaps she would finally get some answers.

He laced his long fingers together. "I have a theory about the curses, one I've been working through the last half century. And I believe you are able to help me." She wanted to laugh and say if it was power he needed, he should ask someone else. She wanted to make any excuse she could. "You see, I require a knowledge of nature. One you clearly possess."

So that was why he had saved her that first day. Why he had paired them together. He *did* need something . . . "What is the deal?"

"You are, of course, aware of the second-to-last line of the oracle's riddle. One of our realms must fall for the curses to be broken." Isla nodded. "As we are a pair, I cannot harm you. And, if you help me find what I seek, I will do my best to protect you from the other rulers as well."

*Protect.*

She hated that word, though she clearly needed to be protected.

She wished she didn't.

Also—*his best?*

She gave him a withering look. Her unfiltered thoughts came out. Why bother playing the game she did with everyone else, acting a part, telling them only what they wanted to hear? Every time she looked at him, all she heard was the first step of her guardians' plan in her head. To seduce him. To steal his powers.

Did they think so little of her?

Did the *king* think so little of her that he believed she needed his protection?

"*You* want to protect me? I thought you were dying."

Oro's eyes turned hot as fire. She imagined if he didn't need her, or wasn't forced to adhere to the rules, he would have lit her aflame with a single look.

"Is it a deal or not, Wildling?" He spit out the last word like it burned his tongue.

Isla smirked. "I disgust you, don't I?" she said. She took one step toward him. "Is it the heart eating?" she asked, pleasure blooming as his frown deepened. "Or the dresses?" She feigned compassion. "What a shame the only person who can help you with your supposed *theory* repulses you so much."

Oro stood.

He didn't answer her question, but she could see it clear on his face. He *was* disgusted by her and her kind.

"You are wasting my time," he said through his teeth. "Do we have a deal, or not?"

For a moment, she considered.

She had no idea what the king's theory was and didn't care. What she *did* care about was that this proposed alliance offered her something she needed.

The closest chance she might have at getting into the Sun Isle library.

Isla didn't have to go along with his plan. He just needed to believe she would.

Still—

In case Oro's strategy did end up having merit, it could make a good backup plan. So, she needed to assure Celeste's safety as well. But if she asked outright, Oro would suspect their alliance . . .

"It's only a deal if I am able to decide a second realm that will remain safe."

His frown managed to deepen even further. "Is there one you have in mind?" he demanded.

She shrugged noncommittally. "If I'm helping you break the curses, I should at least get to determine one other realm that deserves to be saved." Her smile was feline. "And, since you *require* me, it seems there might be room for negotiation."

Oro's jaw tensed. It seemed he hadn't expected any opposition. Chimes sounded, almost making Isla jump, marking the hour. Officially midnight. When they were over, Oro said, "Fine. So, it's a deal?"

It felt good, deciding on her own. Forming a backup plan. Her entire life, she had listened to others. Her guardians. Celeste. Even though they only had her best interests in mind, it felt freeing, making this choice.

"It's a deal," she said firmly, wondering what in the realms she was getting herself into.

"Good."

She walked toward her door, eager to have this meeting be over. "When do we start?"

The king did not follow her the way she planned. "Now."

"Now?" Her voice was too panicked. But she needed time to figure out an excuse for her powerlessness . . . to prepare . . .

"Is that a problem?" he asked, gaze narrowing.

She glared at him. "Well, I did have plans to *sleep.*" Speaking of sleep . . . this close, she could see the king had purple crescents below his eyes. Was the king sleeping at all? Oro didn't budge, or react to her words, so she said, "Fine. Just let me get dressed." She reached for one of her new dresses. "If you could step outside—"

Oro frowned at the gown she had chosen, as bright and revealing as the rest. "You can't wear that."

Back when she was still preparing for the Centennial, Isla had dreaded meeting the king. She had wondered if she might cower in his presence, or if he would sense her lack of powers and kill her as soon as he could. Now, looking up at Oro and his disapproving frown, Isla realized that her main problem would be controlling her urge to throttle him.

"Are you telling me how to dress now?" she demanded.

Oro blinked slowly, annoyed. "During our excursions together, no one can know you are ruler of Wildling."

She stiffened. "Why?"

"Lightlark doesn't like you."

*No kidding.* Still, Isla scowled. "Excuse me?"

"Some ancient creatures on the island, the ones that still live in the deepest pockets of Lightlark, believe Wildlings abandoned them five hundred years ago. If they sense you, or hear rumors that you are near their lands, they will attack. Which would only end in spilled blood and too much attention to our efforts."

She knew Wildlings weren't liked but had never heard this reason. *Abandoned?* The bloodthirsty Wildlings had practically fled the island. Or, at least, that was what she had always been taught. "So . . . you want me to dress differently?"

"Not just that." He took a step toward her and lowered his voice. "I can't sense your abilities, Wildling."

Her stomach collapsed. She made to step back—

"I can tell that you're cloaking them," he continued, without missing a beat. "I just ask that you keep doing that when we're on the isles."

Isla blinked. Again. "So . . . you don't want me using my powers." She felt like falling over. This was a *good* thing. A great thing.

Lucky—she had gotten lucky. Isla was both grateful and anxious. Luck was dangerous.

Because just like any rare elixir, it was bound to run out.

He nodded. "If you do, those ancient creatures will be immediately drawn to you."

Isla wondered about these mysterious ancient creatures. And why even the king of Lightlark wanted to avoid them. She pretended to look pained, inconvenienced. Angry, even. "Fine."

"Good." He looked down at her clothes and said, "That will do."

"These are pajamas . . ."

He just blinked at her.

Isla wanted their time together to be over as soon as possible, so she shrugged, quickly braided her hair, and left without her crown.

# CHAPTER TWENTY-THREE

# STORM

Oro stepped out into the darkness with ease, a king of day who now walked only through night. Isla wondered if it pained him to be outside his castle, remembering how things looked in the sunlight. Or maybe he was used to it.

Five hundred years was a long time.

She didn't ask him any of it as she struggled to match his pace.

Isla assumed they were going to the agora, or to one of the isles beyond it. But, before they could reach the valley, he turned sharply to the left.

"Where are we going?" she asked.

Oro walked several steps without saying a word. They continued down the green hills of the Mainland, far away from islanders enjoying their night. Far from any trail.

"Are you going to ignore me?" Part of her wanted to stay silent. It didn't really matter where he was taking her as long as she got what she wanted from this pairing, right? But his disdain had turned disrespectful.

He kept walking, and she had a good view of his golden cape, floating gently with the nighttime breeze.

She stopped, arms crossed.

The moment she stopped, he did too. His back tensed before he slowly turned around. He opened his mouth, but she beat him to it.

"Just because you *asked* me to wear *this,*" she said, motioning toward her too-big shirt and pants fit to ride a horse, "and asked me not to wear *this*"—she reached up and flicked his crown, the metal singing in response. Her nail sang too, in pain, but she didn't dare wince—"doesn't mean I'm not *also* a ruler of realm. You will treat me with respect, *King*." She spat the last word out like it was poison.

Poppy would have dropped dead hearing the way she dared speak to the king of Lightlark. Especially with what her guardian had commanded her to do.

But she had tired of filtering herself, of shoving her emotions down, of telling everyone what they wanted to hear. What had it gotten her?

Cleo now almost certainly wanted to kill her. They hadn't yet found the bondbreaker. The matches had turned out to be a disaster.

He glared at her. No, he didn't like her tone or the crown flicking one bit. "We are going to the storm," he said sharply before turning around and continuing on his way.

*The storm?*

She had no idea what he meant. But she followed him again, content at least to have gotten a response.

They were walking toward the coast. The one she knew Azul often liked to visit. The air began tasting of salt. Her hair blew back, braid whipping wildly.

In Wildling lands, the wind whispered. It sang songs and passed along gossip and whistled melodies high-pitched as clock chimes. Before Terra and Poppy had it sealed shut, Isla had sometimes kept the loose pane in her room open during the day, hoping to catch bits and pieces of what the wind said.

The wind spoke of heartbreak, from Wildlings who had made the mistake of falling in love. Of hearts, eaten and torn apart by nails sharp as knives. It told her stories that seemed old as the trees themselves, born of seeds that were rumored to come straight from Lightlark.

The Wildling newland had been formed just five hundred years prior, but its foundation was ancient. It was said that after they fled the island and its cursed storm, a hundred Wildlings sacrificed themselves to create their new land, relinquishing their power to the dry, infertile dirt.

Flowers bloomed from their blood, forests grew in a matter of weeks, and the newland was born from their bones.

That was what the wind said, anyway. Isla had found it to be quite dramatic.

Sometimes, she would answer it. Confide in it. Trapped in her orb of fogged glass, she spoke her thoughts to the wind.

It never responded. Not once.

But Isla hoped it listened.

They reached yet another steep incline. Her calves began to strain.

She wasn't sure why the king would take her to this part of the Mainland. What was there even to see? The ocean?

Then, she spotted it. Something had swallowed the coast.

A storm gone still.

Dark clouds like blotches of ink stained the sky above the beach. Silver lightning strikes thick as blades shot out of them and down to the sand, glittering in jittering energy. A ringlet of fire hovered close by, its flames stuck in time. Enormous, deadly spouts leaked from gaps in the clouds, long sheets of water like beams of moonlight tinged in purple.

The sea had been pulled back like a blanket and stacked high—a wave tall as a tower crested but never fell. It was frozen, though not in ice. Even from her height, Isla could see the water running within it, bubbling. Waiting. It had left a long stretch of sea floor uncovered. Sparkling gems and long-lost ancient trinkets coated the sand, alongside shells.

It was the curse on the island, temporarily subdued. The enchanted storm.

Was this what Azul was always visiting?

There were whispers, calling her forward. The storm pulsed with power. She wanted to see it up close.

The cliff closest to the storm was broken into shards. Parts of it had fallen away, leaving two-hundred-foot gaps between half a dozen islands of rock. Some were connected by hastily made bridges, with planks so far apart it seemed easier to fall through than actually reach the next step. They made the bridges to the isles look safe.

The king took a step toward one.

"No," she said simply.

Oro turned to look at her.

"No?" he asked, as if he must have misheard her.

She didn't meet his eyes but could have guessed he was looking down at her with something like disgust.

The king sighed. She saw a flash of movement, like he had pressed his fingers to his temple in frustration. "It is steady. But if for some reason you did fall, I would obviously save you."

Isla turned and pinned him with a glare. "*Save* me? Like you did the first day?"

Oro stiffened. Then he returned her look and said, "*Yes, like I saved you the first day.*"

She barked out a laugh. "I hit the water! And you left me in a puddle on the balcony, like discarded trash, without even bothering to wait and see if I woke up!"

He scoffed. "You might have hit the water before I got to you, but you also had a head injury that you would *not* have woken up from if I hadn't healed you."

Isla remembered the pounding of her head, how there hadn't been any blood. She straightened. "You just admitted you didn't get to me until it was practically too late, so the only way I'm crossing this bridge is if you're tightly by my side. So, if I fall, *you fall.*"

Oro looked at her as if he might just shove her over the side himself. "Fine," he said through his teeth, and roughly took her arm in his.

Before Isla could hesitate, he dragged them both onto the bridge.

Isla didn't breathe. Wind blew up through the cracks, sending chills up her legs. They had suddenly gone as stiff as the thin planks of wood shifting wildly beneath them.

"Quickly," she whispered, closing her eyes. She stepped one foot in front of the other, trying not to think about how it had felt to plunge, plunge, plunge into the sea from the balcony. How her breath had been ripped from her chest. How she had—

"You can open your eyes now," he said, dropping her arm like it had burned him. And Isla had never been so grateful to feel solid ground.

She did as he said and looked around. They had reached a shard of mountain that was narrow at the top but joined the rest of the hill toward the bottom. If she slipped from here, she would only plummet about a hundred feet before ending up in some crack of the cliff. She winced. Not that that sounded much better than simply falling off the side of the island.

The storm seemed close enough to touch, curled toward them in its frozen dance. The whispers she had been able to hear at the cliff were louder now. Insistent, almost.

Oro had stopped at a gaping hole a few feet away, perfectly round like a well. In the near darkness, Isla couldn't see a bottom. It went all the way through the mountain, for all she knew.

"I'll go first," Oro said from her side. "Then you."

He made to take a step forward, into the black hole, and she gripped his elbow. *Go first?* They were jumping *inside?*

"Will something . . . break my fall?"

"Obviously."

She peered into the hole and squinted. It was as dark as the backs of her eyelids. If she couldn't see anything, that meant the fall would be long. The drop could be deadly.

"Are you . . . sure?"

Oro sighed. "Fear of heights. Fear of falling. Fear of bridges. Should we make a list of your fears, Wildling?"

Isla glared at him. Instead of pointing out that those all likely classified as one single fear, not *three*, she nodded toward the hole. "Go ahead, King."

He held her gaze as he stepped forward and fell completely away.

Isla tensed. It was her turn now.

She didn't move an inch.

Oro could *fly*—no drop would be deadly. He had a million ways to survive a fall. Isla had none.

All she had were his words, promising she would be fine. Her life relied on his honesty. Something he seemed to pride himself on, if his demonstration was any indication.

Still. If she died this way, technically he wouldn't be breaking the rules . . .

Was this an easy way to get rid of her?

Were all the other rulers, except for Celeste and Grim, in on it?

Seconds ticked by. The whispers from the storm became louder. More insistent.

She was afraid. Though Terra had trained her not to fear death, she did.

But it wasn't what she feared most.

Her greatest fear was the one she faced in Celeste's trial—not living. Being trapped for eternity in a room without having done everything she dreamed of.

They were so close to finding the bondbreaker. Whether she liked it or not, Oro had become an integral part of their plan. He was the key to getting into the Sun Isle library.

Before losing her nerve, she took a deep breath.

And jumped.

It was like tumbling between worlds, worse, so much worse than falling from the cliff or portaling. The hole was just big enough for a body, and there was barely any air, nothing but the musky walls, and the smell of mold, and her screams, her voice scratching painfully against the back of her throat, her eyes shut so tightly that her head pounded, ached—

Isla was swallowed up.

Before she could process the cold, the freezing water biting into her like a thousand mouths, two strong arms pulled her out, onto cool stone. She pushed him away with as much force as she could manage and gripped the ground, hair a wet fan around her head as she alternated between panting and coughing up water.

When her breathing slowed, she looked up through her curtain of hair and saw Oro standing there, completely dry. He was frowning. "Took you long enough."

She was on her feet at once, in front of him in less than a second. Her hands fisted and pulled back and struck—

But she was soaking wet, and her head was spinning, and he was too fast.

Oro gripped both of her wrists tightly. "This was all a test, wasn't it?" she yelled. Her back teeth clattered together. "You wanted to see if I could trust you."

The untrusting king, the paranoid ruler who always thought everyone was after his power. It was hypocrisy. He wanted her to trust him—when he trusted no one.

Oro stilled. And that was answer enough.

"I knew it." She fought against his grip, but his giant hands might as well have been chains, wrapped more than fully around her wrists. If only she had brought a sword, a dagger, *something* other than her knife-tipped earrings, which wouldn't do nearly as much damage as she wanted—

Isla spat at his feet and hoped that told him what she thought of him.

Oro's frown deepened. "Listen closely, Wildling. I don't care if you like me. But if we're going to work together, you need to trust me."

She bared her teeth at him. "How am I supposed to trust you if you haven't even told me what you're looking for?"

He considered her for a moment. Dropped her hands.

Then he said something that sent her rearing back in surprise.

"Are you going to divulge what I tell you to Grim?"

What? Why would he ask her that? Did he think she and the Nightshade were working together?

The Nightshade *was* constantly seeking her out. It was an easy conclusion to make, she supposed.

Isla wondered if perhaps that was the reason Grim made such a show of wanting to be near her. Was it for others to think they had allied?

"No."

He seemed to believe her, because the next thing he said was "I'm looking for Lightlark's heart."

Isla raised an eyebrow. "Its what?"

"Its source of power. Its life-force."

She tilted her head at him. "Isn't that . . . *you?*"

Oro gave her a strange look. "No. I'm the island's conduit, if anything. My connection to Lightlark, through blood, binds me to it. Through that bond, I can funnel power."

"But if you die, Lightlark dies."

"If its power cannot be funneled or is unbalanced, the island will crumble. Not because I am its heart, but because everything we have built, everything we are, relies on the power I channel."

"Oh. So . . . it has an actual heart?"

"Yes," he said. "But it doesn't look like the type you eat." *Interesting.*

"Then what does it look like?"

The king shook his head. Already annoyed. It seemed to Isla that he only had an allotted amount of patience and number of words for her, and she had already run out of both. "I don't know. Every time it blooms, it looks different."

*Blooms?* She had so many more questions. Why he was looking for the heart. How it even fit into the prophecy. How he thought she could help him find it.

But before she could say another word, Oro was speaking again. "Yes, Wildling. This was a test of trust. But we did come here for a reason."

For the first time, Isla looked around at where she had landed.

An oasis at the center of the mountain. Impossible. Beyond the stream she had fallen into stood hundreds of plants, growing right out of the cave floor, as if the rock was fertile.

The cave was freezing. She still shook from the cold of the water dripping down her face, her clothes soaked tightly against her skin. It was a wonder *anything* grew down here without sunlight or soil, let alone hundreds of different species. It didn't make any sense. This cave had to be infused with Wildling enchantment.

"What is this place?"

He frowned down at her dripping clothing. It pleased her knowing she likely looked terrible, the long, oversize fabric swallowing her up, her hair in wild strands stuck to her cheeks. He made a move as if to dry her using his powers, then didn't. Good. She didn't need his warmth. "Wildlings built a garden in the center of a mountain, to protect all of the island's flora. This cave harbors plants from every isle on Lightlark."

Something in her chest tightened. So many Wildling plants had died since she was born, thanks to her powerlessness. She had believed them to be lost forever. But perhaps they still lived on, here.

"The heart of Lightlark blooms every hundred years, attached to a living thing. A plant. If you could identify which types of plants something like the heart might be drawn to, they could guide our search. We could go to where they originate on the island." So that was why he needed her.

This, she could do. She had never seen most of these Lightlark species, but growing up raised by Wildlings meant she knew how they worked. What to look for.

She bent down, studying the plants closest to her. "For the heart to blossom regularly, it needs to feed off life on the island. It needs a willing, nurturing host."

Isla made her way through the garden, and, after a while, the king followed her, deeper into the center of the mountain. The floras were fascinating. She saw a tree with leaves every shade of a fire. A small cactus that grew a single, stunning, no doubt poisonous flower. A bush with vines that curled and uncurled like beckoning fingers.

One wall was covered completely in a mess of dark red roses. Isla could have sworn they were humming.

"Are they—"

"They only grow over dead bodies," he said impatiently. "Or where blood is spilled. It is said they capture the last words of the dead who give them life."

*Oh*. "Like the willow strands," she said quietly. In Wildling, there was a crop of ancient, sacred trees where the memories and voices of the dead were kept. Twirling some of the limp branches around one's wrist could make them speak.

Did that mean there were bodies buried in the mountain? Or had the Wildlings simply replanted them here?

Only when she reached the back wall of the garden, an hour later, did she speak again.

"Those," she said, pointing at the uncurling and curling plants. "Something can be hidden in their middle. I've seen even birds live in plants like them. We call them purses. They . . . carry things. Without killing them." She looked pointedly at a plant on the other side, a carnivorous one that looked almost exactly like the purses except for the row of teeth she knew lined its core. She turned again. "And those," she said, pointing at two trees with thick trunks. "We have something similar called coffiners. They have been known to grow around living things . . . almost like a shield. Or, in some cases, as a prison." Poppy had told her about a girl she knew who had gotten lost in a forest for weeks. A tree had grown around her in seconds, trapping her in its trunk. It had fed her and given her water but had tried to keep her. It had taken three Wildlings to free her. She shrugged. "It would be a perfect place for the heart to hide while also leeching off a living thing."

Finally, she pointed at the pond she had landed in.

"Those water lilies have roots," she said. "It could be stuck to a root like that, at the bottom of the water."

Oro nodded. Made to turn around.

"So, what now?" she asked.

He worked his jaw, irritated, like every piece of knowledge he shared sliced against his very core. "I will decide on a place to start. One that has the plants you've indicated."

That sounded fine. She smothered a yawn, exhausted. Her eyes searched for a way out of the cave. But there was no other exit. Only the hole, a hundred feet up, visible even from this side of the cave. She frowned. "How—"

He turned to look at her. And there was something wicked in his eyes, something that took great pleasure in the horror that overtook her face.

"Absolutely *not.* You must have spent too much time under the moon, you lunatic, if you think that I—"

"It's the only way we get back to the castle before sunrise," he said.

She opened her mouth, ready to refute that claim, but he interrupted her.

"Trust me, if there was another way, if there was a way to do this without *you,* we wouldn't be here."

Isla waited to feel the sting of his words, but none came. He disliked her just as much as she disliked him. And she was fine with that.

Quickly, before she could warn him what she would do if he dropped her, one arm knocked her legs from under her and the other caught her back. He looked down at her, sighed when he saw her blinking back at him, eyes wide in fear and threats—

Then shot up into the air. He must have angled in such a way as to go through the hole that hadn't been directly above them, but he certainly did not stop or slow down—he flew fast as a shooting star, a strike of lightning in the opposite direction.

Isla screamed so loudly in his ear, it was a wonder he didn't simply let her go, especially when her nails dug so deeply into the back of his neck, she was sure they drew blood. Feigning bravery felt impossible. They propelled faster than the wind for just a few moments before everything went weightless.

He was simply . . . walking. Had they reached ground already? She moved to jump out of his grip, but he hissed and his arms gripped tighter, almost painfully so. Only when she opened her eyes did she see that they were still very much in the air, hundreds of feet up. Oro was walking on nothing, an invisible bridge instead of the flimsy one, right toward the cliff. The exposed beach sat far below, rocks poking out of it like shards of glass. She gasped and promptly stuck her face tightly in the space between his neck and shoulder.

Oro laughed meanly, amused by her fear. She whispered words into his ear that made him frown. "It's almost like you *want* me to drop you."

Before she could say something she might regret—and that wouldn't have much bite, anyway, given how tightly she was clinging to him in terror—Oro took a step that felt much more solid.

Finally, they were back on the Mainland.

The second it was safe to do so, she stumbled out of his arms, relieved to be away from the king. She glared at him. "That was horrible," she said, lest he have any doubt about her feelings about flying—about being so close to him.

He returned her cold look. "I'll see you tomorrow," he said, baring his teeth, making it sound like a threat.

Then he shot back into the air, toward the castle, leaving her to walk home alone.

## CHAPTER TWENTY-FOUR

# SEEKING

Isla might have promised she wouldn't tell Grim about the heart. But she had said nothing about telling Celeste.

The first place she went once she reached the castle was her friend's room.

She knocked, and the door swung open immediately, even though it was nearly dawn. The Starling must have been waiting all night to speak to her.

The pairings had complicated their plan.

She told her friend everything. To which Celeste demanded, "Are you sure he said *heart*?"

Isla nodded. "He must believe it fulfills the prophecy. An original offense committed again, somehow. Maybe finding it was the original offense?"

Celeste shook her head. "I don't know. But I don't like this. Not at all."

"Me neither. The king is clearly desperate to break the curses this time," she said. "But I think this can be good."

Her friend looked at her as if she had sprouted a flower from her forehead.

"*This* is how we get into the Sun Isle library."

Celeste considered that. "You think you can convince him to show it to you?"

Isla winced. The king hated her. Still, she would find a way. She nodded.

"All right," the Starling said. "Get him to show you the library as soon as possible, then. There are just a few weeks until the ball."

*A few weeks until rulers are allowed to kill* were the words she didn't have to say.

On Isla's way to the door, her friend called to her once more.

"Oh, and, Isla? Be careful." Celeste bit her lip in worry. "The rulers . . . I'm afraid of what they'll do to win, now that we know Lightlark is in trouble. I don't trust any of them." She looked her right in the eyes. "Especially not the king."

Oro arrived at her room the next night, as promised. He barely spared her a look before leading her to their next destination.

This time, Isla didn't ask where they were going. She had been to some of the isles now, knew where nearly all of them were. She could figure it out herself.

Twenty minutes into their walk, she was positive they were going to Sky Isle.

Crossing the bridge confirmed it.

Oro thought this was the first time she was seeing the isle. Isla didn't go so far as to pretend she was in awe of the floating city, but she did keep quiet.

They left the base of the lower village and walked into a set of woods. Isla couldn't help but swallow. She wondered if the forests on Lightlark were like the ones on Wildling. Dangerous. Deadly. Even fools feared the forest. No one went inside without protection. It was why Oro's rash had been so surprising. Plants could be as wild as animals. They could strike, maim, kill. Terra said that was why powerful Wildlings were so important. Only they could tame nature. Protect others from it.

But Isla wasn't a true Wildling ruler. Plants did not obey her. She had many scars that had taken years of elixirs to fade to prove it.

What would the king think if they struck her?

Would he blame the fact that she was supposedly cloaking her powers, at his request?

Would he become suspicious?

Luckily, when she entered the woods, nothing happened. The trees stood tall, like everything else on Sky Isle, like the people themselves. They bore sky-colored berries the size of buttons and wore dandelions up their branches, like they had gotten caught on bits of cloud. The temperature dropped quickly, and Isla wished for a cape, one of the ones big enough to wrap around herself. She thought of the king's secret. It did get noticeably colder away from the endless hearths and fires on the Mainland.

Oro didn't consult a map, but he walked assuredly, the island seeming to have a gravitational pull just for him. "I've identified two places on Lightlark that have an unusual number of the plants you indicated in the garden," he finally said. "One here. One on the Mainland."

The forest ground turned into a steep incline, and they climbed it in silence. The king could have flown, she knew. It would have saved a lot of time. There must be a reason he wasn't. He had alluded to searching for the heart for over half a century. Perhaps he had flown over every inch of the island and had still been unsuccessful.

This time, it seemed he wanted to be thorough.

Finally, the hill crested, and Isla stared down into a valley full of purse plants. Relief was cool down her back. This variety of nature wasn't dangerous. She would be relatively safe here.

But there was a new concern. There were thousands, taking up every inch below, from mountain to mountain. Miles and miles. Searching the entire area as carefully as they needed to, on foot, would take days. "How will we know we've found it?"

"You'll know. The power it radiates is unmistakable. But only detectable from a very close distance." So *that* was why he hadn't abandoned her to fly the length of the valley in minutes.

Isla didn't trust her ability to sense the heart solely from its power. Not when she didn't have any of her own.

"Will it . . . look special?" she asked.

The corners of his lips turned down, their favorite placements. "Yes, Wildling," he said. "It will look *special*." He turned to the left without giving her a second glance. "I'll start over there."

Good. At least they wouldn't be searching side by side.

She looked back into the valley and swallowed. There really was a lot of land to cover. It all looked the same too. It would be easy to mix up where she had and hadn't looked, especially over days. She needed a strategy.

Isla found a pattern in the plants, rows that weren't clear cut but were easy to spot once she knew their shape. Now, she just needed markers to indicate the areas she had already searched. Her eyes took in the land, looking for a color that stood out. A different sort of flower, maybe. A special type of vine.

But there was nothing. The plants all looked the same. Even the ones in the forest behind her were too similar in shade.

*She* was the only thing that stood out in the entire valley.

Isla sighed and reminded herself this was the best way to gain access to the Sun Isle library before ripping the bottom of her favorite shirt.

There. That would have to do.

She was efficient. After four hours, Isla had covered a good chunk of her area. She had developed a system. Purse plants opened when their tops were stroked. It took a few long moments for their leaves and vines to uncurl, and a couple of more seconds to get a good look inside before they closed again. At her fastest, she was able to get to five a minute. Once she was finished with a row, she marked it by tying a strip of fabric to its last plant.

By the time Oro came to collect her, Isla had looked inside over a thousand purse plants. And her shirt had been reduced to ribbons. Before, it had nearly reached her knees. Now, it ended far above her navel.

The king looked horrified. She grinned, reveling in the fact that she looked as wild as he believed her to be, covered in dirt, her hair curled around her face, clothes cut to pieces.

"What did you do?" he demanded.

She crossed her arms across her chest. "What I *did* was cover this entire area," she said, motioning toward a large grove sectioned off by her fabric.

The king's eyes briefly darted to the spot she had indicated. He didn't look impressed.

He didn't look anything.

Isla narrowed her gaze. "I'm assuming this means you didn't find it?"

He didn't humor her with a response before turning around toward the way they had come.

The next morning, Ella arrived with clothing. More long-sleeved shirts that looked just like the one she had torn to ribbons. Pants that were like her other pair—now coated in a layer of dirt—but thicker, with reinforced fabric on the knees, better for the elements. Boots that were far better suited to the task of searching forests and valleys than her now soiled-beyond-repair slippers.

"The king sent this," the Starling said.

Isla rolled her eyes.

She almost wanted to rebel and wear her same clothes from before, just to spite him. But she thought about her mission. Get him to show her the library. He wouldn't honor her request yet. But perhaps if he saw her trying to help him, to find the heart . . .

Still. She decided she *would* wear her crown that night, as at least the faintest reminder that she was *also* a ruler of realm, not to be trifled with. Even if she had hidden most of it in the folds of her hair, so it wouldn't give her away to the mysterious ancient creatures the king had warned her about.

Before they parted ways to search each half of the grove, Isla asked something she had been wondering since he had shared his plan with her: “How did you find out about the heart in the first place?”

He said nothing.

She casually walked the few feet between them, smiling sweetly. She reached up and flicked his crown, just because she knew he had hated it the first time. “You should tell me. Because if you don’t . . . I’m not opening another purse plant.”

Oro’s eyes flashed with irritation like crackling firewood. Still, he said nothing.

Isla clicked her tongue. “An untrusting king who always keeps all of his cards close to his chest . . .” Her hands circled her waist, fingers pooling in the oversize fabric of her new long-sleeved shirt. She stared pointedly at his arm, where the bluish gray had started spreading. The sign of the king’s impending death. “Tell me, how has that worked out for you?”

Oro glared down at her. He took a breath that seemed to shake his shoulders. Power emanated from him in thick waves—a sharp wind she couldn’t see, a riptide she couldn’t pull free from. Suddenly, the cool air went hot as Wildling.

The force of him made her knees wobble. But she couldn’t allow him the satisfaction of seeing that. Instead, she smiled again, blinked her long lashes, and lifted on her toes so she was just inches from his face as she said, “Well?”

Immediately, his power was ripped from between them, swallowed up. He did not flinch away from her proximity. “I’ll take my chances, Wildling,” he said coolly before flicking her own crown. The movement sent her back on her heels, stumbling a few steps. Her head immediately throbbed. *How hard had he flicked it?* She reached up to trace her finger along the metal and came upon a deep indentation.

Something in Oro’s eyes glinted with wicked pleasure as anger twisted her features.

"You dented it!"

He simply turned away and began walking toward his side of the valley.

"Fix it!" she demanded.

All she saw was his back as he got farther and farther away, golden cape billowing softly in the wind.

"Wretch," she whispered angrily under her breath. "If we weren't paired, I really would gut you."

That made him stop. He turned like he had heard every word.

She made a gesture at him that she hoped proved just how much she had meant them.

Oro frowned and turned back around.

And only because he was her best chance at getting into the Sun Isle library and finding the bondbreaker did she fix her hands in angry fists and walk toward her rows of flora.

They spent three more nights searching the purse plants. They worked from after the sun went down to an hour before it went up, enough time for the king to reach the castle before day reached him. Just as her room filled with light, Isla would collapse into bed, sometimes without even a bath, exhausted.

Her fingers were stiff, the muscles in her palms sore. Her arms even hurt after lifting them one after the other, thousands of times. Her neck ached from straining to peer into the centers of the plants. Her lower back was a lost cause.

Every day, Oro and Isla got closer in proximity, starting from the edges of the valley and making their way to the center.

By the thirty-first day of the Centennial, they met in the middle. Both covered in dirt. Both tired. Both frustrated, if the look they gave each other was any indication.

"It's not here," Isla finally said. Her voice was raw. Sleeping for a couple of hours during the day and working at night had begun to take its toll. Especially since she hadn't started their search in good health in the first place. Her arm had fully healed, but the cold hadn't completely left her chest.

The king wasn't standing as straight as he normally did. He ran a hand through his hair, not seeming to care he was coating it in dirt. "No," he said. "It isn't."

She must have groaned, because he looked down at her, eyes ablaze, almost daring her to make a snarky comment.

She might have. If she didn't need him.

It took everything in her to take a deep breath and say, "Where is the second place?"

# CHAPTER TWENTY-FIVE
# SECOND PLACE

It was night, and the castle's lights were off. The darkness was so deep it seemed to seep everywhere, like spilled ink all around her.

Isla looked around for lights, for curtains she could open. She found a candle and lit it.

Her shadow loomed before her, trapped against the wall.

Another one joined it. Far bigger than her own.

She whipped around, and there he was. Grim. He was dressed in armor. Shining sheets of black metal.

He was the thing of nightmares, the monster in the dark.

For a moment, she was nervous. But not afraid.

Still, she took a step back, until she and her shadow were one and the same.

He stepped closer. Reached up to pull the helmet from his head. Dropped it to the floor with a loud clatter. Lifted her from the ground by the backs of her thighs, just as her hands fisted in his hair, and she said—

Isla gasped. Blinked at the ivy that snaked across her bedroom's ceiling, a thin shard of sunlight peeking through her curtains. She was in the Mainland castle . . . not the dark room.

Not with Grim.

*Fool.*

She blamed her exhaustion for the dreams. Her sleeping patterns had changed, and her body still hadn't gotten used to it. Yet—

Isla hadn't seen Grim in a week. Not since the matching ceremony.

*A week*. Before, he had sought her out whenever he could. Had he gotten whatever he had needed from her and moved on to the next step of his plan?

Her chest felt too tight thinking about it, but she sat up and tried her best to ignore the feeling. She would be a fool to spend another moment on him.

Isla should be focused on her *own* plan. That night, she and Oro would travel to the second location. It would be best to try to get more sleep . . . but the idea of dreaming of Grim again—and worse, *liking* it—sent her out of bed, toward her balcony. By the position of the sun, she guessed it was still early morning.

She got dressed, deciding to seek Ella out on one of the bottom floors of the castle. She remembered the recipe of a Wildling sleeping elixir. All it required were a few ingredients.

*Yes,* she told herself as she swept through the palace, *that* was what she needed. One cup of the tea, and she would sleep soundly through the day, no Nightshade haunting her dreams. No waking up every few hours clutching her blanket, covered in sweat.

She was just about to round the corner when she heard low voices.

Taking the abandoned old halls was second nature by now. It ensured she rarely saw any attendants and never ran into another ruler. It was how she had visited Celeste a handful of times undetected.

It seemed she wasn't the only one who used these empty halls for privacy.

Without making a sound, she pressed herself against the wall, straining to listen.

"Your plan is madness."

Isla froze. The voice echoed even in a whisper, deep and angry.

*Oro's* voice.

Another voice responded, too quiet for her to make out the words. But she knew who had spoken them.

Azul.

What were they doing, meeting in such a strange, hidden place?

Isla crept closer to the voices, walking silently, just like Terra had taught her. Tips of her toes, then the sides of her feet, her heels never reaching the floor.

"You will be sentencing thousands to death," Oro snarled.

She didn't dare take a breath. There was a pause.

"A realm has to die, Oro," Azul finally responded.

Isla took a step back, shocked—the heel of her shoe made the slightest noise.

The voices quieted.

A moment later, a door slammed shut, blocking out the rest of the conversation.

That night, they remained on the Mainland. Isla and Oro entered the vast woods to one side of the castle, which stretched all the way to the coast. She felt the familiar prick of fear down her neck. This forest was wilder than the one on Sky Isle. Energy coursed through the air. Branches seemed to curl toward her, as if straining for a closer look. Vines across the floor tightened as she passed, as if making to trip her.

The nature here seemed intrigued by her. Sweat pooled down her chest as she watched it. At least it hadn't hurt her. Yet.

Panic began to poison her thoughts, so she turned her attention to the king instead, hoping the less she looked at the forest, the less it would stare back. His eyes were squinted and slightly more creased at the edges. He walked more stiffly than usual.

"You haven't been sleeping at all, have you?"

He said nothing to indicate he had heard her speak.

"You could at least try to sleep during the day if we're going to work at night."

Oro continued through the forest, ducking to avoid branches that Isla could barely touch if she reached her arm up.

"Unless you have another ally you're working with during that time?"

"I don't have other allies," he said curtly.

"Really?" she said. "Not even Azul?"

Oro looked bored. "Eavesdropping is lowly, even for a Wildling."

So, he knew it had been her listening. Good. "What's his plan?" she demanded. Before she could stop herself, she added, "You promised to protect me from the other rulers. Should I be worried?"

Oro sighed, irritated. He turned to her. "Azul is harmless. You, of all people, have the *least* to worry about when it comes to him."

That didn't make sense. Azul had talked about ending an entire realm. If he hadn't been talking about Wildling, which realm *was* he talking about? "But—"

His sharp look silenced her. "I will not be revealing any more of our private conversation, so you can save your breath and be grateful you heard anything at all."

The way he spoke to her . . .

Oro wouldn't tell her any more details about their conversation. But perhaps learning Azul's story would help her understand his motivations. "Did something . . . happen to him?" she said a few moments later. The Skyling was always jovial, but she had caught a haunted look on his face a few times. She was willing to bet there was sadness, or perhaps anger, behind his good-natured mask.

Seconds ticked silently by, and Isla thought he was going to ignore her again. But he finally said, "Azul lost someone. Someone he loved."

*Oh*. Isla wasn't expecting that. She supposed all rulers had lost someone close to them the night the curses were spun. This seemed different. "A partner?" she guessed.

He nodded. "His husband."

Isla felt a knot in her chest. She didn't know Azul very well, but the thought that he had lost someone so close to him made her hurt in an inexplicable way.

"Was he also Skyling?" she asked.

He shook his head.

It made her think of Oro's brother, and the wedding the curses had destroyed. Two rulers were set to marry for the first time in centuries, a chance to bring the island together. She didn't want to ask directly about King Egan, but she did say, "Is marrying between realms common on Lightlark?"

"It has become more common" was all he said.

She frowned. "How does that affect power, then? Children . . . are they born with just one realm's ability?" She looked at him. "They don't get both, do they?"

He shook his head.

She waited expectantly, wanting a better explanation.

The king sighed. "They are born with one power, Wildling."

*Interesting.* Isla opened her mouth, another question ready, when Oro gave her a look that silenced her again.

Fine.

Though he was the one who had ended their conversation, not ten minutes later did he say, "The entrance to Wild Isle is near." He murmured the words, as if not really meaning to speak them.

Isla stood still. She knew Wildlings had their own isle on Lightlark, of course. She had even searched for it during her snooping. But she hadn't found the bridge anywhere.

"How do we know the heart isn't on Wild Isle?" she asked, suddenly desperate to see it. Oro had kept walking, and she raced to catch up. "Surely most of the plants are there."

The king looked over at her. "You said so yourself. The heart needs a willing, nurturing host to survive." He shrugged. "All the nature on Wild Isle is dead."

*Dead.* The word was a rock to the chest.

She shouldn't have expected anything different. But it still hurt to hear it spoken.

A moment passed. "What did you think of them?" she asked, even though she practically knew the answer, given the way he had sneered at her during their first dinner together. "Wildlings."

He frowned, and Isla readied herself for a string of insults that she might just slap him for. "They were my favorite realm, besides Sunling," he finally said.

She scoffed. "You can't possibly mean that."

He peered at her over a shoulder. "I said *were,* Wildling."

"Why?"

They kept walking. The trees began changing. Thinning. Until they entered a clearing.

"Wildlings were advisers in our court," he told her. "When I was a child, they taught me to wield a sword, how to pick the right berries. They were loyal. They were good."

Isla just stared at him. "And now?"

"And now . . ." They walked into another set of woods then, made up entirely of coffiners. Hundreds of them. "Wildlings are all the things they say."

They spent the entire night peeling back bark, peering into each coffiner tree. Oro did so without having to use a knife, thanks to his Starling abilities. Isla used her hands and a tiny dagger she had sneaked onto the island, disguised as a bracelet. With each cut of her blade, she winced, waiting for the tree to retaliate. But none of them made to hurt her. Isla moved quickly enough that she hoped Oro wouldn't suggest she unmask her powers for the task. Every hour that ticked by, she worried even more, waiting for him to say the words.

At the end, he finally did. "This would be easier with your abilities," he said, frowning.

Isla stilled, wondering if she should prepare to run. And what good it would do her.

"But the creatures it would draw out . . . I'm not sure it's worth the risk." Isla wondered about these creatures, the ones he had mentioned before. Who were they, and why did they hate Wildlings so much?

Why was even Oro afraid of them?

Isla had always assumed that the rulers were the worst things at the Centennial. The most powerful. Most lethal.

The way the king spoke about these ancient creatures made her think that wasn't true. Made her wonder how deadly they could be.

And also made her hope she never found out.

## CHAPTER TWENTY-SIX

# THORNS

It had been ten days since Grim had sought her out. She should have been relieved. But part of her wilted at the fact that Celeste had likely been right.

What other explanation could he have to suddenly avoid her after seeking her out so consistently? She really had just been a part of his plan—whatever it was.

*Fool,* she called herself, for believing anything else.

It was their third night in the coffiner forest. They had looked inside hundreds of trees, all heartless. Isla was starting to wonder if she hadn't paid close enough attention in the garden.

Was there something she had missed? She had identified the plants most likely to harbor the type of power Oro had described . . . but she could have been wrong.

On their way across the Mainland, she had asked the king more questions. Every day with him was a test, seeing how much he would tell her.

"Why didn't Cleo attend the last Centennial?" Azul had mentioned it before.

The woods hadn't hurt her yet, but she still felt their energy unspooling around her, as if the nature was simply waiting for the right moment to pounce. Even the king was careful where he walked, not underestimating the power of the forest for a moment.

"You should ask her. The two of you get along so well."

Isla might have thought that was an attempt at a good-natured joke, and might have keeled over at the possibility of the king making one, if his tone hadn't been so hostile.

She gave him a look. "It isn't my fault she's had a target set on me since I made that comment at dinner."

The king shook his head. He seemed in disbelief at her foolishness. "Cleo wouldn't kill you because she dislikes you."

Isla scoffed. He clearly hadn't seen the way the Moonling had studied her, as if she was counting down the hours until the fiftieth day of the Centennial. "You seem to think highly of her."

The king, to her surprise, nodded. "I do. Cleo thinks of the good of her realm above all else."

Isla remembered the Moonling's trial. It had tested one's desires.

Terra and Poppy had preached the same unrelenting commitment to one's people. Only on the island had Isla understood how big of a sacrifice it was to give up all the world had to offer. "Really?" Isla said incredulously. "She has no hobbies? No lovers?"

Oro didn't meet her gaze. "She did have different relationships, with both men and women, before she came into power," he said. "But since she has been ruler, she has focused completely on her realm's future. Her focus is admirable." He worked his jaw. "That does not mean she is not a problem, however."

*Problem.* Isla wondered if he knew about her legion. Her guards. He must.

"Wouldn't that commitment to her realm mean she would kill any ruler she could to fulfill the prophecy? To make sure she and her people don't die?"

The king came to a stop. "Any ruler?" he repeated.

She shrugged. "The first she had the chance to assassinate."

He had never looked as repulsed by her as he did then. "Don't you understand, Wildling? Killing a ruler isn't the hard part. We all have had several opportunities to fulfill that portion of the prophecy. Do you know why killing isn't allowed until the fiftieth day?"

He looked so upset, she didn't dare form a response.

"It's because choosing the *right* ruler and realm to die is the difficult part. Not just because we would be sentencing thousands to death. But because *all* of our futures depend on making the right decision." His voice became louder. She had never seen him more impassioned. Or angry. "All of our realms are connected. You can't begin to understand the consequences of losing one of them. Even if we did know for certain the offense that needed to be committed again, the decision of who needs to die would be nearly impossible. *That,* more than anything else, is why the curses haven't been broken until now."

Isla didn't know why she spoke her next few words. But she needed clarity. Answers. "Why not just kill Grim, then?" she wondered, even as the thought made her insides twist with a surprising amount of pain. Even if he seemed to have forgotten about her. "He's not part of Lightlark. Isn't he the obvious choice?"

His smile was mocking. Cruel. "I can't," he said. Perhaps it was because he was so angry, so eager to throw in her face how little she understood, he told her more than she expected he would. "Grim is the only thing standing between us and a greater danger you can't even begin to fathom."

*Greater danger?* What could be more dangerous than the Nightshade? Or the curses? Or the Centennial?

He looked down at her like she was a fool, a naive ruler. And it did seem now like she knew nothing. Terra and Poppy had always framed the Centennial as a survival-of-the-fittest game. One where the weakest link would be murdered, if the others were given the chance. If Oro was to be believed, the hundred days were more about making the *right* choice over the most convenient. Before she could ask anything else, he had stormed off.

The king was on the other side of the woods now. She could hear him every few minutes, slicing into the bark with his powers, just enough to look inside the trunk. He didn't get distracted, no matter how many hours they did the same task.

Isla couldn't say the same. Not when she now had so many questions on her mind.

She had finished her section for the night. No hearts. Just the occasional animal burrowed inside the trunk that would peek up at her with curious eyes.

Celeste had visited her that morning, looking for an update.

*I'm trying,* Isla had said. It just never seemed like the right moment to ask the king about the library. Too soon or out of the blue, and he would become suspicious of her request.

Now, she wondered if she had burned all her chances at getting him to take her to the Sun Isle library with their earlier conversation. The king had looked furious.

It was dangerous, stupid, but she walked deeper into the woods, hand trailing along the coffiners until they ended. The nature changed, becoming wilder. Flowers bloomed, red like the dresses she most often wore.

Rosebushes. Bulbous petals guarded by halos of thorns.

The last Wildling Eldress, the one she had found in the forest, had called her that once.

*You are a rose with thorns,* she said. A pretty thing capable of protecting itself.

If only.

Her blades should have been enough. She was a great warrior. But against power—metal might as well be paper.

The rosebushes became thicker, turning into another plant. One that had spines long and thick as fingers, jutting everywhere. It looked like a weapon. She didn't know why, but she followed it through the forest, watching the bush become larger, taller.

Until she reached an entire wall of spines and thorns.

Her pulse raced.

Thorns formed on plants to guard them. They were defense mechanisms, just like her own throwing stars and blades.

This entire wall of spikes had to be protecting something.

Maybe the heart of Lightlark.

Isla turned to yell for Oro, triumphant.

That was when it struck.

The thicket of spines came to life—wrapped her in its embrace.

And pulled her right into its nest of spikes.

Her scream was guttural. Dozens of barbs stabbed through her back at once, sharp as blades. Thorns needled themselves through her arms.

She was well practiced in pain, but this was not rehearsed. Not expected.

Isla tried to tear herself away from the wall, but she was stuck to it, the spines curved into her skin like hooks. Keeping her. Every push away sent them farther within. Blood ran hot down her back; tears shot down her face. A choking sound escaped her lips.

Then there were warm hands steadying her.

"Stop moving. You're making it worse," a voice yelled.

She wanted to spit at his feet for chastising her at a time like this. She wanted to warn him to get away from the evil plant. But she could barely even see. The pain had eaten all her senses.

The king cursed, and she imagined he was inspecting her back. "I'm going to have to break them to free you," he said.

Isla nodded and, a moment later, screamed at the top of her lungs as Oro tore the first barb in two with his Starling energy. No matter how steady or gentle his power was, she felt the spine in her back, twisting closer to her bones. The plant didn't like Oro's handling of it. It dug its other barbs deeper inside. It did not strike the king, however. As if it only had an appetite for her.

"There are . . . several."

She couldn't take another one. The first—

She cried out again. Saw flashes of hues behind her eyes, the pain so deep she swore it had its own color.

Again.

Again.

Again.

Isla couldn't control herself. The next time he broke one of the spines, and the plant retaliated by digging farther inside, she retched all down the front of her clothes.

If it got on him, he didn't say a word. He just held her steady as he broke the spikes in two.

Again. Again. Again.

Isla insisted on being the one to pull them out.

She was on the ground now, away from the wall, Oro kneeling in front of her. The rest of the forest had gone still. Watching her.

"How did this happen?" he asked.

Right. Of course he was confused. Plants wouldn't dare attack their ruler. Even if she was supposed to be keeping her abilities cloaked.

"I . . . tripped," she said, wincing. He kept studying her, and she narrowed her eyes at him. "Go, look for whatever the wall is guarding," she spat. "I'm fine. I can take them out myself."

Even when she was injured, even soaked in blood, the king had the nerve to glare at her. "You're covered in your own vomit," he said flatly. He reached toward her back to help her, but she reared back, then groaned.

"I said I'll do it myself," she growled.

Oro bared his teeth at her. "Are you truly this stubborn?"

"Are you truly this *overbearing?*" she demanded. "I said no. Now leave."

The king stayed put for a moment.

Then he got up and walked back toward the thicket, cursing beneath his breath.

*Good.*

When he was far enough away, Isla folded over and gripped the ground with all her strength, arms shaking in a sob. The pain—

It was like nothing else she had experienced. *Evil, wretched plants.*

And it wasn't over.

Wincing, Isla reached back and felt around for the first spike. Gripped it with shaking fingers.

And pulled with all her might.

Her scream echoed through the forest; she could have sworn it rumbled the trees. Their shaking leaves sounded almost like laughter.

She had never hated herself more for being born powerless than she did now. If she was a true Wildling ruler, she could control every inch of the woods. They would never have hurt her. They would have *helped* her.

Her hand shook as it released the bloodied spine. It fell unceremoniously to the ground.

Only ten more to go, if her count had been correct when Oro had broken her free from the bramble.

The king was back now, crouching next to her.

Her entire arm shook as it bent backward, feeling for the next one. "I told you to go look for—"

"I did," he said. "No heart."

Tears rolled down her temples from the angle her head tilted. All this. For nothing.

"You can—you can go," she said, closing her eyes tightly.

A few seconds passed. She didn't hear him move and wondered if he had simply flown away in that soundless way of his.

But when she opened her eyes, there he was, frowning down at her no doubt gruesome-looking back.

Oro reached toward her, and she flinched. He held his hands palm up. A peace offering. "The spines are all yours," he said, eyes clear. Reasonable. He motioned toward the dozens of thorns embedded in her arms, thin crimson streaks raining down from them like tears of blood. "I'll get these." She started to shake her head. "It's faster," he added. "The sooner this is finished, the sooner we can resume our search."

He had a point. She supposed she could let him help her if it meant completing their mission. And getting out of this wicked forest.

"Fine," she whispered.

His hands were hot against her skin but surprisingly gentle as they worked, pulling the thorns out, one by one. Each was followed by a prick of pain.

But nothing compared to the spikes in her back.

She wrapped her hand around another. Pulled. Screamed into her knees.

Another one. This one was curved, just an inch from her spine. She pulled, and a jolt tremored through her entire body, needles through her bones, poison in her veins. In the shock, her teeth bit down hard on her tongue, and an animalistic sound left her throat. Blood pooled immediately, dripping from her mouth.

"Here." Suddenly, Oro was offering her something to bite into instead. "You're going to bite your tongue off," he said. "I've seen it happen before; you have to have something in your mouth for something like—"

Isla pulled another barb out, knowing it was impossible to feel more pain than she was feeling now.

But she was wrong. It doubled, tripled, and she bit down hard on what he offered.

Again.

Again.

Her eyes were closed so tight, her head hurt. She slipped in and out of consciousness. But she pulled every spike out herself.

It wasn't until she was done and slumped against a tree that she realized she had been biting into Oro's hand. It was covered in bite marks. She had pierced the skin in various places.

She was too tired to feel shame. All she could do was count her breaths as Oro used a canteen of water and his Moonling abilities to close her wounds.

By the time she stopped bleeding, it was time to leave. Dawn was approaching.

"What now?" she said, her voice barely making a sound.

Before the wall of spikes had attacked, she had already finished searching her assigned trees. She assumed Oro had too. The heart clearly wasn't in this forest.

His jaw clenched. "There are too many places with the plants you indicated. I thought—because of the quantity, we would . . ." *Get lucky* were the words she filled in.

Isla almost wanted to laugh. Or cry.

If there was any luck in the world, she and the king had never encountered it.

He shook his head. "I have another plan. One I hoped to avoid." He looked her in the eyes. "You know those ancient creatures I told you about?"

She nodded.

"Well," he said, "I think it's time we meet one of them."

## CHAPTER TWENTY-SEVEN

# THE HARBOR

Oro hadn't knocked on her door in five days. He was supposed to be attempting to seek out the ancient creature, to make a deal that would guarantee their safety.

"Would one of these ancient creatures really try to hurt the king of Lightlark?" she had asked.

"I can't be sure," he said. "Though they would certainly not hesitate to hurt you."

Isla had been grateful for the break. Oro had healed her back with his Moonling powers, but her body had shut down for two days after they had returned to the castle. She was wrecked. Exhausted. Broken.

But her mind had never been clearer.

Her encounter with the barbs and thorns had only made her want to break her curses more. Not just for the freedom . . . but for the power.

Never again would plants harm her. Never again would she be powerless against them.

After the third day, when she was ready for their next mission and still hadn't heard from the king, she began to worry.

Had he decided a Wildling who had been attacked by plants wouldn't be much help to him? Had he decided to continue the rest of his plan on his own?

She refused to sit in her room and wait for him to fetch her. If his plan had changed, so had theirs. She needed to speak to Celeste.

Isla had slipped a note under the Starling's door, asking her to meet her in the agora. Since they weren't paired, she thought they needed to start forming a superficial friendship seen by the islanders, so if they were somehow caught together, it wouldn't be so suspicious. They were supposed to serendipitously run into each other in the Starling weapons store. Isla *did* need a dagger—one that didn't double as an accessory.

But, more than that, she needed to speak to her friend.

She had been so focused on her work with Oro that she had nearly forgotten the Starling had been forced to spend time with Cleo. What had that been like? Celeste was the type to avoid telling Isla things, so she wouldn't worry. But she wanted to be there for her. Just as much as the Starling had always been there for her.

The agora was busier than even before, vendors filling their storefronts with their best accessories—silk hats, crystal-covered gloves, gowns that were as puffed up as the pastries sunbathing in the nearby bakery windows. All in preparation for the ball.

It was just ten days away.

Ten days until killing was permitted.

Ten days to find a way into the Sun Isle library.

Ten days to find and use the bondbreaker.

Ten days to break their curses and get off the island.

Isla stopped in front of the Starling store. Just as she was about to enter, someone bumped into her.

Strange. Usually the islanders gave her a wide berth, as if her skin was poisonous.

Then she felt the note that had been slipped into her hand.

It was a small piece of paper. The words made her go still.

*You are in danger,* the paper read.

What? Isla whipped around, looking for who had given her the warning. She spotted a white cape weaving through the market, head down. That had to be them.

A Moonling?

She wasn't going to sit around and solve the riddle of who might want to harm her. There were too many people on that list.

Instead, she followed whoever had slipped her the message.

Music was playing in the streets, a quartet no doubt hired to build excitement for the ball. Stores kept their doors open, and young boys and girls shouted advertisements—*special offer! Two pairs of gloves for the price of one! One-of-a-kind hats for one-of-a-kind islanders!*

Isla rushed through the crowd, pushing past shoppers holding stacks of boxes tied with ribbon. Children holding cones of cream. She whispered apologies that were met with frightened gasps as she nearly collided with a wagon holding ripe fruits and freshly roasted nuts. But there, far ahead, she saw it. A flash of white fabric, disappearing around a corner.

Celeste was suddenly in her path then, on her way to the Starling shop. Her friend's eyes narrowed with confusion as Isla ran past, whispering, "I'll be right back," leaving without waiting for a response.

Her arms tight by her sides to slip through the busy road, she moved like a ribbon in wind, her feet finding free places on the pavement, her body filling gaps in the sea of people. Moments later, she was turning that same corner, onto a street that was almost empty. So empty she could see the Moonling racing away, the trail of their cape billowing in the breeze.

This tendril of the marketplace went down instead of up into the mountains. The air was heavy with salt and fish and brine. The rough cobblestone became wet beneath her shoes, and she nearly slipped in her rush to catch the Moonling.

She turned another corner. And they were gone.

*Too slow.* She had lost them. The sea was near. She was in the remnants of what must have been a harbor, hundreds of years before, when the island wasn't entrapped in its curse.

Isla forced herself still, refusing to give up. She looked around, squinting, searching for a sound or a ripple of fabric.

She turned in the other direction—and found it. The curl of the white cape, disappearing behind a ship that had somehow made it onto land. It looked like a washed-up whale, flipped on its side.

Isla took a step and gasped.

Chains from nowhere locked around her wrists and ankles.

And the cool edge of a sword pressed firmly against her throat.

"That was a little too easy," a low voice said in her ear. Isla yanked against the chains and found that they weren't chains at all. They were braided water, firm as a rogue wave, strong as the tide.

Five more men peeled away from where they had been hidden, behind ancient boathouses and landlocked ships. They wore crisp white suits, with diamonds in place of the top button of their shirts.

Moonling nobles. She recognized them from the demonstrations.

A growl escaped her throat. She became a little more of the beast they believed her to be.

The person in the white cape appeared then, and Isla bared her teeth at them, her gaze promising violence. The figure didn't even glance her way before it was handed a handful of coin and slipped away.

A trap. She had been tricked.

*Fool.*

No. *They* were the fools.

She lifted her chin high and said with as much venom as she could manage, "Release me, and I will show mercy. Keep me bound, and you will all see what happens when you try to trap a Wildling."

The men only smiled.

"Wild, even captured," one said. His white hair was slicked back, and he gingerly held a cane with a crystal top, though he clearly didn't need it. He pointed the cane in Isla's direction, and the water chains tightened, forcing her onto her knees. Isla seethed as her bones screamed and her skin broke against the damp stone floor. "But even wild things can be tamed. And caged. Tell me, will you beg for your life, Wildling?"

Now, it was her time to laugh. "So, your ruler sent you to do her dirty work?"

It wasn't the fiftieth day yet. Either Cleo had skated past the rules by not exactly *ordering* Isla's assassination . . . or the Moonling ruler didn't care about breaking the rules. Perhaps she wasn't after the prize of the power promised after all.

So much for Oro's theory that Cleo wouldn't kill her just because she disliked her.

Though, admittedly, Isla sneaking into the Moon Isle library likely had more to do with it.

The Moonling with the cane stiffened, insulted. Others turned to look at each other, and that told Isla enough. Cleo might not have sent them to assassinate her, which would have directly violated the rules. But their efforts were sanctioned.

"I'm sorry," one of the men said, surprising her—and the rest of his group, it seemed. "But the Centennial isn't just a game for rulers. One of the realms must fall. And we have families . . ." He shook his head. "We don't want it to be us."

She *did* understand. The Centennial was a deadly game with many players. And grave consequences.

She spat at the man's feet anyway.

"Enough." Isla was hauled up by the man behind her, sword still against her throat. "Say farewell, Wildling," he rasped into her ear, pulling the blade back for a clean, clear sever.

Isla yanked at the watery chains with all her strength, made to escape—

But her efforts did nothing against their Moonling power.

Back in the Mainland forest, Isla thought she had never wanted her Wildling powers more. She had been wrong. Now she not only wanted them—she *needed* them.

Words pummeled through her mind, the last she would ever hear: *Too late. Failure. Powerless. If only—*

Before she was ended, she heard another word.

"Farewell," a voice said, stopping the blade just an inch from her throat.

And the man was hurtled back through the air.

Celeste made a fist, and the water chains went limp, disappearing in a mess of silver sparks. She must have followed her. One of the nobles sent a wave of sea hurtling toward her, and the Starling spun on her heel to meet it with a stream of energy.

Unshackled, Isla was unleashed. She reached both hands toward their opposite wrists and unchained her bracelets, which snapped into throwing knives. She sent them flying with ease, each finding their marks.

Two Moonling hearts.

The men slumped to the ground, and Isla turned—only to be thrown by a wave of power.

Her hand managed to grip a shard of glass from the floor, then the world went sideways as she was slammed against an old ship.

Isla tasted blood on her tongue; her head pulsed between her eyebrows. The man's hand was around her neck, lifting her up. She heard a roaring that was not the sea and made a terrible sound when she tried to breathe.

Still, she smiled.

She might not have been a match chained up.

But the restraints were gone now.

Isla wrapped her fingers around the long shard of glass in her hand—and stuck it through the man's throat.

He released her immediately, reaching for his own neck, trying to speak. No words left his mouth.

The other Moonling nobles hadn't fared any better. She raced back to Celeste, only to find her standing in the middle of a mess of dead, laid out across the wet harbor stone.

"She tried to have you killed," Celeste said, voice surprisingly steady. "You need to leave a message. One that shows you're strong. One that makes her think twice before another attempt on your life." They worked together to scrawl a response in blood.

When they were done, Isla looked down and smiled. Once, she might have had the urge to vomit. But she had been on the island forty days. In that time, she had dueled against famed rulers. Survived countless trials. Swallowed down unspeakable pain. Pulled barbs from her back with her bare hands. She stood straight and steady, remembering how the men had threatened her. Remembering how weak she had felt, chained in place. Powerless against power. Never again, she promised herself.

*Try harder,* the message read.

## CHAPTER TWENTY-EIGHT

# PLACE OF MIRRORS

Isla had never wanted power more in her life. First, the barbs. Then, the assassination attempt at the harbor that was proof her blades meant little on Lightlark.

They *did* serve well as an outlet for the anger that roiled through her like a storm, though.

She had marched straight into the Starling shop after the assassination attempt and purchased her dagger. One with a curling snake around its hilt, fit for a Wildling. She held it now, cutting the air to pieces. The metal was weightless in her grip. She twirled it around her fingers, threw it up in the air, and caught it without having to look. Mimed stabbing someone right in the gut.

The Moonling nobles flashed in her mind, and she carved her blade through the air, through *them*.

Her lip curled. She stabbed them all, one by one, the men and the memories.

"Did the wind do something to offend you?"

Isla whirled in an instant, and her dagger flew—piercing the stone of the palace, right above Grim's dark hair.

He grinned. With a fluid motion, he dug out her dagger and threw it back at her.

She caught it without her gaze ever leaving his.

*Grim.* Her stomach stumbled for a moment at the sight of him. Then, anger swelled. She glared at him. "I never thought the ruler of Nightshade would be so indecisive."

"Indecisive?"

Isla took a long step toward him. "*Indecisive.* You can't seem to make up your mind. One day, you act like we're friends, and the next, strangers. You disappear for weeks."

Grim did not shy away from her gaze. "Which would you prefer?" he asked, as though he truly wanted an answer. "Friends, or strangers?"

She swallowed, begging her emotions to stay in check. "Neither," she lied. "I just want you to stay away from me. Consistently."

He stepped toward her. Grinned, just a little. "Is that *truly* what you want, Hearteater?"

Her breath hitched. He felt her everything.

She turned away before he could feel any more.

Grim's grin vanished. He suddenly became deathly serious. "We really should stay away from each other," he said. "That is why you didn't see me."

So, he *had* been avoiding her.

"Why?" she asked, though she could fill in a thousand answers.

He shrugged a shoulder. "I'm the famed Nightshade warrior—thousands of kills on my blade. Everyone hates me. No one trusts me. For good reason. They shouldn't." He peered down at her. "*You* shouldn't."

She wanted to ask what he meant. But before she could, he took a step closer. Her hair was wild around her face, and her shirt seemed too tight against her skin—she had changed into pants and a shirt to train. Even though her gowns were all designed for a fatal temptress, at this moment, these training clothes seemed far more revealing.

"You know what it's like to be hated, don't you, Hearteater? To be seen as a monster? A savage?"

It was true. Still, it hurt to hear the truth spoken.

"You're feeling irritated, Hearteater. Do you deny what you are?"

She was breathing heavily. She didn't even really know why. "No. Do you?"

Grim shook his head. He took a step toward her. "Never. I am the monster."

Isla knew she should probably run away, or leave, or do something other than take a step even closer. He tilted his head. Something about the way he looked at her, the way he stood so close. Closer than anyone had ever dared.

"I'm not your enemy," he said, voice softer than she had ever heard it.

Then why couldn't she trust him? Why was he pushing her away? Why did she even care?

"Prove it," she dared. "Tell me something."

"Anything."

She remembered the king's words in the forest. The reason he had given for why the rest of the rulers hadn't simply decided to kill Grim to fulfill the prophecy. "Oro said you are the only thing standing between us and a greater danger. What was he talking about?"

Grim didn't look particularly surprised by her question. Though he took his time answering it. "There are worse things in this world than the curses. Or even me."

"Like what?"

He shook his head. "I could tell you. But it would only distract you. Believe me, right now, the curses are the more pressing danger."

Isla scowled. Who was he to decide what would and wouldn't distract her? What was too much to know? Still, she could tell by his tone that he wouldn't budge.

"Fine. Show me something, then."

"Anything," he repeated, though the word meant less now that she knew it had limits.

"Show me where the Wildlings lived when they were on Lightlark."

The request surprised even her. She still hadn't found the entrance to Wild Isle. Oro's comments about it in the woods had only fed her curiosity. There was so much about her realm she didn't know.

And now, she was more curious than ever. She wanted the endless power her Wildling ancestors had once possessed. Perhaps they had left something behind. Something that could help her now.

Grim stared at her, and Isla held her breath, wondering if he knew how much she had thought about him in the last few weeks. Wondering if he knew that however hard her heart was beating, however many times his words had already echoed through her mind, he was right—she couldn't trust him.

And he couldn't trust her.

"Of course, Hearteater."

Isla did not speak a word as he led her into the Mainland forest, in the shade of the castle. Not far from the crop of coffiner trees, but in the opposite direction. The way was wild. The stone path had long been overtaken by weeds, untamed plants that smothered it completely. Isla flinched as she watched the woods, bracing herself for another attack. Her back prickled, as if remembering. But the forest did not dare strike her in Grim's presence. They stepped over vines thick as limbs and under spiderwebs large as umbrellas. Soon, the trees lost their leaves and became sharp, bare branches that resembled clusters of swords. Stones that might have lined a riverbank replaced the grass. She couldn't see the end of it until she was out of it.

Sunlight blinded her momentarily, and she stilled.

There was a bridge. It was broken in many places. The sides were made of braided vines.

The isle on the other side gave no indication of life. But something about it called to her. Isla stepped onto the bridge first, without hesitation, and was on the other side before she knew it.

The king had been right. There was no life left here.

Wild Isle had been reduced to a forest of hulls. The trees were bare and twisted, skeletons swaying in the wind. The vines and roots along the floor were dry and crunchy beneath their feet. The ground was a mess of broken branches, in the shapes of striking snakes. No animals. No green. No . . . anything.

In the center of death stood a structure.

Grim was by her side. "They call it the Place of Mirrors."

Every inch of the palace was covered in reflective glass that cast back the bare forest, mirroring its surroundings. Its edges winked in the sunlight.

The Place of Mirrors looked fragile, like a strong wind could shatter it. But it had survived when everything else on Wild Isle hadn't. It was shaped like the carnival tents she had seen on the outskirts of the Skyling newland with her starstick—bulbous, as if blown up by air, and pointed in three places.

Somehow, though the outside was mirrored, the interior was clear. She stepped inside and saw the razed woods through endless windows, cut in a million shapes. The ceiling was curved.

It was almost empty. Just a few statues remained, along with leaves that had swept inside. Isla walked deeper into the Place of Mirrors to find that the rest of the large palace was not made of glass at all. The walls became stone and opened into what must have once been interior gardens, where the ceiling ended altogether. Dead vines grew up columns. A small fountain now held dark water. She kept walking, into rooms and corridors that had been left abandoned and overtaken by the dead forest, until she reached its very back wall, which was sturdier than the rest, carved into the base of a mountain.

It was covered in markings, the most prominent a large swirl. The rest depicted battle—men and women dressed in armor, holding swords and shields. Some rode giant beasts she didn't recognize. She traced the drawings with her fingers.

"Is it everything you hoped it would be?" Grim asked.

She turned. "It's much more."

"Even if it's almost empty?"

Isla hadn't gotten to explore the entirety of the palace, but she guessed she would find it cleared out, the same way the other rooms were.

"The fact that it's still here . . ." She pressed her palm against the wall. "Gives me hope. That Wildlings can survive all of this."

Grim was somewhere else—she could see it in his eyes. She wondered what he was thinking about. Every move he made was confusing.

"What are the Nightshade lands like?" she asked, not really knowing why.

Even with her starstick, she hadn't dared travel to their territory. Terra's warnings about them had kept her away.

Grim looked at her for a long time. "One day," he said, "I'll show you."

Isla waited for the cloak of darkness before leaving the castle. Oro still hadn't returned to her door. The night was hers. And she made careful use of it.

She wished for Grim's power to see easily in the dark as she took the path through the Mainland, the moon her only guide. On their way back, she had made sure to study the route to Wild Isle intently, but everything looked different touched by night.

The path continued too long when it should have disappeared under overgrowth. She must have taken a wrong turn or missed it completely. Soon, she was back at the Mainland castle.

Isla cursed and tried again. She strained to remember the curve of the trees, or the number of steps she had counted hours before while trying her best to mask her emotions around Grim. He couldn't know that the entire time he was answering her questions, she was thinking about what she had spotted in the Place of Mirrors—and how soon she could go back. Alone.

She squinted through the darkness, then bent so that her fingers could trail the path, waiting for the wildflowers to begin smothering the stone, marking the place she needed to follow.

If she had Wildling powers, she could simply call to the forest and listen for its reply. Follow its song to the palace.

But she didn't. So, she continued stumbling blindly through the night.

Finally, grass brushed against her fingers, a second path veering from the first. She followed it to the forest and hesitated. The moon was locked out of the woods, blocked almost completely by hunched-over trees. She would have to feel her way through. And hope the forest was satisfied with the amount of blood she had already shed for it.

Isla ducked her head lower, wondering if she should come back in the morning. She wondered even as she continued through the woods, thorns catching on her ankles. Even as she tripped over a vine and landed on her hands and knees.

No—no one could know about her midnight journey to the Wildling palace.

Not even Grim.

By the time she stumbled into Wild Isle, her hair had been tangled out of its braid, and she felt the sharp sting of cuts across her palms. But even the pain stilled as she regarded the building in front of her.

At night, the Place of Mirrors reflected only darkness. Her light-brown clothes cut through it like a blade. She watched herself peel from the shadows of the bare woods like a specter.

Inside, moonlight showered down once more. The floors above groaned, as if awakened from a slumber. Wooden walls somewhere cracked. *Normal ancient palace noises,* Isla told herself. Something thudded against the glass above. *Just a fallen branch.* Still, she quickly made her way through the halls and rooms, only stopping at the back wall.

She had seen it, earlier in the day, with Grim. And knew she had to go back.

Isla recognized the spiral on the wall as a door. It was the same shape as the one hidden within her chambers, beneath a broken panel in her closet. The same place she had found her starstick, tucked within her mother's things.

If the Wildlings had a secret door, whatever was inside must have been important enough to hide. And it must still be intact, unlike the rest of the palace.

She had a feeling whatever was inside could help her now. That it held something she needed.

Isla had to get into the vault.

She pushed against the spiral door with all her might, expecting it to creak open with enough effort, just like the one in her room had.

But this one didn't budge.

Isla studied the wall and spotted a gap. A place for a key. No . . . it was too long for a key to fit. Unless it was massive.

She looked around for something that matched its intricate design, a strange pattern like a miniature mountain range. A short candlestick holder seemed close to the right size. She tried to shove it into the hole, but it didn't fit. Not even close. She tried getting some vines and fashioning something similar. But when she turned it like she would a key, the vines snapped.

Her back teeth slammed together. If there was a way to open the door, it had to be inside somewhere.

Isla walked up a winding staircase, covered in dead leaves that were a symphony of crunches beneath her feet. She roamed through hall after hall, into room after room, shards of moonlight her only guide. Minutes later, she had an armful of objects that might fit into the hole. An old, abandoned comb. A thin champagne flute. A vase just big enough to hold a single flower. A miniature harp.

She shoved object after object inside, trying them like keys, until dawn peeked through the palace, bathing the glass entrance in violet. But none of them worked.

The door remained closed.

## CHAPTER TWENTY-NINE

# THE ABBEY

Isla was more convinced than ever that the Wildling vault held something she could use to find the bondbreaker. Or help her in some other critical way.

And if anyone on the island would know the secret to opening it, it was Juniper.

She walked into his bar the very next day. It was empty, save for a man sitting at the back corner, hat over his face, as if he was napping in the pub, waiting for the livelier evening crowd.

"My favorite Wildling," Juniper said from behind the bar. He wrung his hands together. "To what do I owe the pleasure?"

Isla needed to make this quick. Hopefully no one had spotted her entering the pub, and she wanted to keep it that way. "Moonling nobles attempted to assassinate me." There. That was her secret.

Juniper's head reared back, as if this news surprised even him. "What information do you seek?"

She leaned in closer. "The ancient Wildling palace on Wild Isle. What do you know about it?"

He pursed his lips. "Admittedly, not much. Is there something specific you're wondering about?"

"Is there something hidden inside? If so, would you know how to find it?"

Juniper frowned. His brow creased. It seemed he wasn't used to not knowing about a subject. Isla had to admit it was a long shot.

Wildlings hadn't lived on Lightlark for hundreds of years. She doubted most islanders knew the palace even still stood, if its abandoned state was any indication. "I apologize, Ruler. I have never heard of something hidden inside the Wildling palace. From my understanding, anything of value was looted long ago."

Isla nodded sharply. She had known the chances were low that anyone knew about the vault. Her secret would have to be used another time, for another sort of information. She made to leave, but Juniper spoke once more.

"I do know *something* about the Place of Mirrors, however."

She sat down again. Juniper had used the castle's name, the same one Grim had told her. "What is it?"

"The Place of Mirrors is the only place on the island where all powers other than Wildling's are repressed. Only Wildling ability works inside."

*What?*

Only powerful enchantment could do such a thing. She didn't even know ability like that existed. Something in the vault must be responsible.

It wasn't the information she was looking for, but it was enough to make Isla desperate to know what was behind the door.

And more positive that whatever it was could help her now.

Isla walked back out into the agora with more questions than answers. A storm was on the horizon. The sky above was filled with dark clouds like a pack of wolves circling, gray fur and all. They seemed to mimic her troubled mind.

"How do you think that dress would fare in the rain?"

Grim. He was leaning against the outside of the bar, waiting for her.

She blinked. "Are you following me?"

Going from completely avoiding her to trailing her . . . it made no sense. What had changed?

What was he after?

Grim raised an eyebrow. "No. I was here for my own reasons, and I sensed you."

"Sensed me?" *Own reasons?*

He nodded. "Your emotions, they have a tinge . . . a color, almost. I knew you were nearby."

She didn't know how she felt about that. Wanted to know what color she was but didn't ask. Instead, she raised her chin and said, "Creep."

Isla turned to walk out of the marketplace, and Grim easily matched her pace. "You know, if you're asking Juniper for information, I might recommend taking precautions. I can make him forget your conversation, if you would like. Or simply threaten him for his silence . . ." She glared at him while simultaneously considering taking him up on his offer. Juniper had helped her, but it was impossible to trust a barkeep who traded secrets.

She really had hoped Juniper knew how to open the vault in the Place of Mirrors. It clearly required a key—one she had no time to look for.

Finding the bondbreaker had to be her focus.

She couldn't describe it . . . but the door pulled to her, spoke to her. Told her in its own silent language that she needed to get it open.

If only she had the time and resources to make that happen.

"You're disappointed, Isla." She blinked, and there Grim was, stopped in her path, watching her. The castle loomed far ahead, high on its cliff like a crouching giant.

Her back teeth clashed together. She stopped too. "I told you not to read me."

"And I told you I couldn't help it."

She crossed her arms, mouth already open in reply—

When the sky cracked open like an egg.

Rain soaked her clean through in an instant. It stormed so hard that she could barely see through her lashes. Grim was just a dark figure before her. She heard him, though, his deep laughter like a rumble of thunder.

Wind blew her hair and dress back, hissed in her ears. The trees at their sides arched, their leaves dancing wildly.

Grim reached out a hand. And she took it.

The castle was too far, and Isla wasn't sure any of the Nightshade's powers could shield them from rain. He led them to the closest building, the abbey she had seen many times before, with the stained-glass eye at its front.

Grim opened the front door with a blast of dark power and pulled them through.

She was panting, freezing. Drenched. Her hair stuck to her face in wild strands, and her dress—her dress clung to her, outlining her every inch. She reached up to take her crown off and found it knotted in her hair.

Grim stood a few feet away, watching her.

He was soaked too. Dark hair splayed against his forehead, dripping tiny droplets down the sides of his face. The black fabrics he always wore now seemed too fine, barely even there, the muscles beneath them now perfectly defined. His cape dripped softly against the wooden floor of the convent as he slowly walked over. And when she looked into his eyes, she found no humor there, no amusement.

Grim stopped just inches away, and Isla stopped breathing. He reached toward her, and she went still—but his hands simply went to her crown. His fingers gently, carefully, pulled at the strands of her hair wrapped around the metal, unknotting it from her head.

He pulled a little too hard on one piece, and she made a sound that made Grim immediately meet her gaze. Something wicked danced within his eyes, something that made the bottom of Isla's spine curl.

There were no lights in the abbey, no flame. Only the single, rounded stained-glass window offered muted daylight as the storm raged on, rain pattering violently against the glass. And Isla could have sworn the dusky corners of the room darkened further, ink spilling over, shadows lengthening toward the rows of pews.

She took a tight, shaky breath and convinced herself it was because of the cold. Grim watched her mouth and said, "You're feeling . . . distressed, Hearteater."

He was so close she could feel his breath on her cheek, cold as the rain outside, cold as the fingers that were still partially knotted in her hair.

"And you?" she said, her voice just a rasp. "What are you feeling?"

Grim grinned. "Oh," he said, eyes trained to hers, as if he wanted to make sure she heard every word, "what I'm feeling can't be said in a place like this."

Her breath shouldn't have been catching; her pulse shouldn't have quickened at his proximity or words. She still didn't know why he had come to the Centennial, what he was after. Isla had judged her people for their recklessness with love. Now, she understood them a little better.

And herself a little worse.

What was she doing? She had always thought herself above such desires. Stronger than her mother. More focused. Grim had told her she couldn't trust him. He had proven it time and time again.

Why did that make her want to get even closer to him?

With a final tug, he freed her crown. He frowned down at it, and Isla watched as his thumb ran across the dent Oro had made days before. It smoothed over instantly. He handed it to her, in the limited space between them.

She took it with treacherous, trembling fingers.

Then he turned, leaving her standing there, words caught in her throat. She gripped her crown so hard, its rough edges pierced painfully into her hand. *Get a grip.*

Celeste's warning flashed in her mind then. He was a distraction. He was playing her.

She could play him too.

"Where were *you* that night?" she asked, voice still a little breathless. "The night of the curses."

He looked over his shoulder at her. Shadows danced at his feet, their sharp edges ebbing and flowing. Like night itself was seeping from him. "Do you really want to know?"

"Yes."

"I was in bed."

Isla's eyebrows came together. "You were *sleeping?*"

He stared at her. "No."

*Oh.*

Suddenly the stained-glass window seemed very interesting. Isla studied its four illustrations intently, hoping the heat she felt on her face wasn't visible in the darkness.

Grim sat at one of the benches in the abbey, elbows on his knees. He watched her—she could feel his gaze on her but couldn't bring herself to look back.

In an instant, he was behind her. She felt his breath on her bare shoulder and tensed.

"When I left my chambers, everything was burning. And all of the rulers were dead." She turned and found his face drawn, more serious than she had ever seen it. "I was a ruler of realm. When all I had ever trained to be was a warrior."

Darkness billowed out of him in waves, snuffing out even the limited light creeping in from the window. A flash of lightning struck outside, but its light did not reach them.

Isla swallowed. Turned to face him fully. "I know what it's like to have responsibility you never wanted . . . and never thought you deserved."

Grim's hands were tightly wound by his sides. She tentatively reached out and opened one of them. Ran a finger across his palm and felt him tense in front of her.

"Will you show me?" she asked, knowing she shouldn't.

He seemed to know she meant his powers. The extent of them, beyond the simple demonstration he had given weeks before. And she seemed to know that he needed a release.

Grim looked intently into her eyes. "Are you sure you want to see?" he asked.

She almost said yes immediately, then remembered the bite of disappointment she'd felt at his answer the last time he had prefaced his response. He was warning her, she realized.

Warning her that she might see something she wouldn't like.

Still, Isla nodded. She wanted to see it. Raw power. The thing she wanted more than ever.

He was so close his nose almost touched hers. "Not here." He glanced at the window. Isla heard the rain, still raging, but not as violently as before. "Do you mind going outside again?"

She shook her head and followed him back out of the abbey.

Isla felt it all once more, the water in sheets, but she was already wet, already cold. Her eyes stayed glued on Grim as he walked to the cliff, to its very edge. His back was tense, his cape glued to his shoulders, and the muscles there rolled back.

Fast as lightning, he turned, hand shooting in front of him—and darkness erupted in a violent line, a wall of ink that rippled like water, peaked like flames. It whipped right past her, inches from her face. She stumbled back, the force of it almost making her fall over.

As quickly as it had struck, the darkness dissolved. Isla took an unsteady breath. In the places night had touched, life had been ripped away. The grass sat charred and matted; trees were reduced to hulls that decayed into ash right before her eyes.

If that power had been unleashed on a human, she could imagine their skin would melt right from their bones. And those bones would splinter and crack until they were fragments in the wind.

This was worse than fire.

Grim's darkness left nothing behind.

He had turned back to the cliff, hand fisted at his side. A hand that wielded terrible, terrible power.

Grim went still when she trailed two fingers over the back of that hand, against her better judgment. When she said, "Show me more," he grinned.

And gripped her by the waist.

They shot off the cliff, to the sand below—and this time, Isla didn't scream. Because somehow, they had skipped the entire middle of the jump.

The sea foamed and raged like a crazed animal in the storm, clouds bubbling and frothing above, melding together to form a gray gradient. She couldn't see where the ocean ended and the sky began. They both churned and eddied, desperate to touch.

Isla stood close enough to Grim that she heard him over the rain, over the wind that blew in from the sea, whipping against every inch of exposed skin and leaving it numb. She still had her crown in her hand and, for a moment, considered simply throwing it into the angry ocean, wondering if that would solve her problems.

"Hearteater," he said.

She looked up at him, only to see something peculiar in his expression. He looked *worried*. Devastated.

Worried that she would cower from his terrible display of ability? Hate him for what he was?

She remembered his words.

*I am the monster.*

Part of her was afraid of it.

But she wasn't afraid of *him*. Even though part of her screamed that she should be.

"Tell me how I'm feeling," she whispered. She could try her best to control her thoughts, her actions—but if the Nightshade had taught her anything, it was that her emotions were far more difficult to bridle.

Rain fell from his hair and onto her cheeks.

He swallowed, reading her. "You're feeling . . . intrigued."

She motioned toward their surroundings and shrugged. She had asked him to show her more. "Well?"

Instead of grinning again, Grim's expression darkened. The ocean curled with a giant wave that crested before them and collapsed into cliffs just feet away. His mouth was suddenly at her ear. "I could open a black hole that would swallow the beach. I could turn the sea dark as ink and kill everything inside of it. I could demolish the castle, brick by brick, from where we stand. I could take you back to Nightshade lands with me right now." His voice was deep as dreams, dark as nightmares. "I could do all of those things." His lips pressed against the top of her ear, for just a moment. "And I might—if I didn't think you would hate me for it."

Isla's shoulders and fingers shook—from the cold, or the rain, or his proximity, or his proclamations, she wasn't sure. She looked down at their bodies, pressed close. Just flimsy, drenched fabric between them. Red dress against black, a rose dipped in midnight. Like tea in boiling water, darkness still seeped from him, around him, ribbons of it that reached toward her before recoiling. "Why do you care what I think? You barely know me."

Grim's shadows flared, though his expression did not change. "I know enough," he said.

"What about staying away from me?"

His lips were right above hers now, his words practically pressed against the corner of her mouth. "I gave it an honest effort," he said. "But it turns out . . . I'm not that honest."

Isla stumbled away from him, afraid of what she might do if she stayed so close, close enough to feel the power that leaked from him, close enough for it to brush against her as harshly as the wind—it was magnificent.

But she was a fool. He had been hot and cold for a reason. He had his own plan.

*If anything, he'll use* you. *Us.*

Grim took a step back. Another. The shadows at his sides flinched, hissing over the rain. "You're afraid," he said.

She didn't know what else to do, so she nodded. Because she was terrified. Terrified of the way her heart was beating wildly, of how her head was as fogged and clouded as the sky above.

Her people deserved better than her, an unproven leader who was at that very moment gambling away their salvation.

What was she doing?

What was *he* doing?

He must have felt all her emotions, fear weaving with confusion and desire and shame. Because he said, "Let's get back to the castle." And all the darkness and shadows fell to his feet before being washed away by the rain.

# CHAPTER THIRTY
# SPECTER

On the forty-third night of the Centennial, the king finally knocked on her door again.

She opened it. Looked him up and down. "It's been eight days," she said.

He was expressionless. "It took five to find her. Two to coax her out of hiding. One to make a deal."

Isla stared at him, wondering if she could trust him. Wondering if she even had a choice. She had spent the last few days trying to find another way to get into the Sun Isle library. Unsuccessfully.

Part of her considered simply walking straight inside herself, without an invitation, without a disguise, and allowing the king to make his own conclusions. She had proposed the plan to Celeste, who had gotten back to her a day later, with bad news.

*Sun Isle library is heavily guarded and monitored,* she had said after asking around. *It is also always full. It would be impossible to search for the bondbreaker unnoticed.*

She needed the king to allow her an unmonitored invitation. Which meant earning his trust.

So she accepted his explanation. And followed him to their next location.

Star Isle was silver. The ground glimmered with cosmic dust. Trees stood thin and crooked, turning into themselves in spirals, tiny glittering leaves growing from even the trunks. The castle was a monstrosity with endless arches, bright jewels tucked into the stone itself, like stars had been stolen and used to fortify the palace, trapped in stone before they could fly home. Celeste once told her that to Starlings, the stars looked brighter than they did to everyone else, like millions of moons, or shining fruits ripe for the picking. Only they could see how brightly they truly glowed.

Starlings manipulated energy from the stars, concentrated power so bright and shining that it could once make buildings topple over, throw bodies soaring without a touch, and shatter all a palace's windows. Now, with their curse, Starling masters no longer existed.

The isle was glittering, beautiful. But in ruins. Unlike Sky Isle, run by its people and their representatives, or Moon Isle, run by the strict Cleo and her harsh nobles, these lands were unkempt. Overgrown. It was a wonder the castle still stood. All other structures looked either unstable or were already partially fallen apart.

That was what happened when an entire realm died before twenty-five, she supposed. Their government was almost nonexistent, run by nobles who were practically still children when they died.

A pity, Isla thought, as she walked through Star Isle. Something about the realm dazzled her, every living thing coated in a shining gloss, like someone had dipped their hand inside a star and smeared its silvery glow across the land.

A bird that looked crafted out of shining metal sat in a tree nearby, beneath a cluster of silver acorns. A metallic snake crept along a branch, its scales like chain mail. They walked through the strangely hued forest for just minutes before coming upon a stream, water silvery in the moonlight.

Isla's skin prickled, not just because of the cold, but because of nerves. They were about to meet one of the ancient creatures. The ones Oro had warned her about.

"Do as I say," he had said. "They are tricksters. Some more violent than others. Some will eat you for dinner and pick their teeth with your bones. Others are more scheming than murderous. They are as old as the island itself."

The king had promised the one tonight would not try to kill her. He had made sure of it during his final meeting with her the night before. But Isla was still on edge. There had to be a reason this hadn't been Oro's first plan.

The trees stopped suddenly, revealing an ancient building, all arches and columns. The windows had long been blown out; the stairs had partially fallen away. Silver roots and vines swept inside, curling around the pillars, in and out of the entrance, around its base, then back into the woods, like the forest was desperately trying to keep the structure from floating away.

Oro took the stairs two at a time, careful to avoid steps that had long since crumbled into powder. Isla followed and once inside saw just how much the forest had taken over. The ceiling was high and vaulted, split into shards—and covered in leaves. Trees had grown up the sides of the interior columns, and brambles swept across the walls. Smaller plants had budded between the stones of the floor, some sporting flowers, others sprouting silver berries that resembled bells, thick thorns between them. They were much smaller than the ones that had pierced her, but even looking at them made her stomach turn.

Oro took one of those thorns and pricked his palm with it. The drop of blood that formed dripped onto the floor.

And a woman stepped out of the wall. She wore a simple dress that floated around her, just like her hair, both suspended as if she was underwater. Her body was silver and slightly transparent.

A specter.

*This* was the ancient creature? A ghost?

"My king . . . you have returned for me," she purred, her voice like wind chimes.

The temperature had suddenly dropped. When Isla breathed out through her mouth in shock, a cloud puffed from her lips.

The specter turned sharply to face her. Her smile deepened. "And you brought me a gift."

"Not a gift," Oro said. "But yes, what you asked for."

Isla took a step back. "Asked for?" she said, tripping on a vine. She barely caught herself before falling.

Was this his new plan? Was he going to trade her for the heart?

The specter approached quickly, hair moving like a whip behind her head. "Ah, yes . . . exactly as I requested. How were you able to find her on such short notice? I've never seen a face quite like that." She frowned. "The clothes do not flatter her, but I see the hint of a nice figure there . . ."

Isla pulled her new dagger from her waist and brandished it. "Don't take another . . . float," she said, looking down and not seeing any feet.

The specter's head fell back at a gruesome angle as she laughed. "That metal would just go through me, girl." She squinted milky eyes at Isla and said, "Now knot that shirt. I want to examine the body I will be wearing."

"Wearing?" Isla whipped around to face Oro, who seemed content to watch.

He sighed. "It's just for a few seconds."

The specter pouted. "I had hoped you had changed your mind about that."

Isla was a moment away from plunging the blade into Oro's side. "You have one second to explain before I run from this place screaming and never speak to you again," she said through her teeth. He conveniently hadn't mentioned *this* on the walk over.

His expression was bored. "The specter's price for helping us is being allowed to walk in a body for a few moments."

Her hand tightened on the knife's hilt. "Why not yours?"

"I offered. But she requested . . . something specific."

The specter was suddenly at her side. "The most beautiful girl on the island, that's what I requested." She reached out a silvery finger, making to touch Isla's cheek. "And you're *perfect*."

"Absolutely not," Isla said, stepping back. "How do I know she won't stay in there? That you're not in love with her and just want a body for her to inhabit for eternity?"

Oro gave her a look, just as the specter turned to regard him in a way that told Isla that was exactly what she was hoping for.

"Well?" Isla demanded.

"Do you trust me?"

"No! You didn't even tell me about this until you summoned her!" But that wasn't completely true. She did trust him, at least a little, after all they had already been through.

Anger burned down through her chest. *This* was the deal he had made with the ancient creature?

Oro sighed. "What will it take?"

*Nothing!* she wanted to scream into his face. But then her heart began beating faster, doing a little dance in her chest. This was her chance.

This was the moment she had been waiting for.

She was so excited, so nervous, she didn't bother glazing the request. "Take me to the Sun Isle library" was all she said. "Let me look inside. Alone."

Oro frowned. "Why?"

Isla straightened. "I like books. I want to see what your isle has to offer," she said casually. Then, to draw attention away from her admittedly random request, she added, "Sunlings do *read,* don't they? Or do they prefer to spend their time frowning, sulking, and burning things like their ruler?"

That did the trick. He stared down at her like he wanted to throw her off the nearest cliff but finally said, "Fine."

Something cold plunged into her chest.

He had stabbed her—that was her first thought as her mind went dark and she drifted far, far away.

She was suspended, weightless, a whisper in the night. Free and bound, loose and tethered. Dancing. Falling.

"*That's enough.*" Oro. She gasped.

Isla blinked. Oro blinked back—an inch away. Her body was pressed firmly against his, her fingers were laced through his golden hair, and her lips were almost against his lips. He wasn't holding her at all, but she was clinging to him.

She startled and likely would have fallen back and cracked her head open on the stone if he hadn't reached for her.

A true Wildling wouldn't have been so fazed by the king's proximity, but Isla didn't have a long list of conquests like the proud temptresses of her realm.

Isla turned to glare at the specter, who floated nearby, beaming. "You're lucky you're already dead," she spat.

Her cheeks burned and she refused to look at Oro again, who said with just as much venom, "You got what you wanted. Now tell us what you know."

The specter sighed. She sat in an invisible chair. "What you seek is not on Star Isle. Not this time." *This time?* Before Oro could leave, she said, "A warning, King. The underbelly of the island is rising up. Darkness is at work . . . We feel it."

"Feel what?" Isla asked.

"Dread." With a final smile at Oro, the specter disappeared through the wall. Isla wanted to turn to Oro, to scream something at him, but she knew it would make him even more suspicious of her.

Besides, she had finally gotten what she wanted.

Though—it seemed too good to be true. She needed to make Oro fulfill his word tonight, lest he go back on his deal. It was still early. They could go right now. "Great. That was traumatizing," she said. Her shoulders hiked with a chill as she thought of that ancient being wearing her skin. Even if it was just for a moment. Of being close enough to the wretched king that she could feel his breath against her mouth. "Now you know the heart isn't on Star Isle. Thanks to *me*. I'll admit, it's valuable information. Must narrow locations down significantly." She looked him right in the eyes. "Now, take me to the library."

Oro turned and walked back through the Starling forest in silence.

He was really taking her. She couldn't believe it.

Sun Isle's was the only library they hadn't searched. The bondbreaker had to be inside. She could find it and break their curses that very night.

Celeste would be thrilled. She couldn't wait to tell her—

At the bridge, the king took the wrong turn.

She stopped. "Isn't your isle that way?"

He just kept going as if he hadn't heard her.

"You made a promise, King," she yelled at his back.

"I will take you to the Sun Isle library," he said over his shoulder. "But I don't recall specifying *when.*" His gaze narrowed. "Perhaps when you have helped me find the heart, as promised in our original deal."

Her fingers spasmed, itching, pleading to choke him. She shook her head, so angry she felt the prickle of tears at the corners of her eyes. She was so close. He had *promised*. Had she not done enough?

"Come back," she said. He did no such thing. He ignored her, a specialty of his.

Her body was broken and tired—this was all she asked for in return.

This time, Isla's voice shook with rage. "You . . . you are a self-centered, heartless wretch."

That made Oro turn around. He took a few steps back toward her and grinned meanly. "Is this your plan, Wildling? To try to win my heart by tormenting me?" His wide eyes searched hers, waiting. He was serious.

Isla had felt the sting of tears, but now she laughed. Breathless, infuriated, she laughed and laughed. She took a step forward and said slowly, so he could hear every syllable, "I have absolutely no interest in you whatsoever, *King.*"

She waited for him to call her a liar. To say she was just like the countless Wildlings before her who had undoubtedly also been instructed to seduce the king as part of their strategy.

Instead, Oro looked taken aback. Shocked. Was it really that surprising that a Wildling wasn't trying to make him fall in love so she could steal his abilities and bring that power back to her realm?

Could he tell by her anger that she was telling the truth?

"Then what *are* you interested in, Wildling?" he demanded. "Why do you want access to my library? What are you looking for?"

She stood very still. And said nothing.

He took a step closer. "I have watched you. You are a chameleon, becoming everything everyone wants you to be, all of the time. Except around *me*—you don't seem to give a damn what I think of you." His gaze was fire. "The lands I have been entrusted with are dying. *I* am dying. I will do anything it takes to break these curses. You, or whatever you are planning, will not keep me from that end." He looked down at her so closely, it was as if he was trying to see right through her. "So, I will ask you again. What do you want, Wildling?"

The king was suspicious. And perceptive. He knew she was looking for something.

She had ruined it.

Hurt and a million other emotions pooled in her stomach. Her voice had never been so cold. "You are taking me to the library. Now."

Oro's expression did not change. "I will take you once we find the heart," he repeated.

His tone was final. Isla knew he would not change his mind, and they were nowhere near finding the heart. She couldn't wait until then. Not with the ball a week away. Not when Moonling nobles had nearly succeeded at assassinating her even before then. The handwritten note in the agora might have been a trick, but it was true. She *was* in danger.

"No," she said, laughing without humor. She felt her sanity unspooling around her. "You know what? I'm *done*. With you, with this plan." Her voice became louder and wilder the more she spoke, but she didn't care. "I have bled. I haven't slept. I have been possessed. I have had the thorough displeasure of being in your presence for far too long. I am *done*. Our deal is off. And guess what? I don't need you to get onto your isle, King," she sneered. "Unless you want to stop me?"

She kept her eyes locked on his. Daring him to deny her access.

He did not.

"Good. Perhaps I'll go during the day, then," she said, hands in fists at her side. She spoke her last words right in his face before passing him by. "That way, I'll have your land all to myself."

## CHAPTER THIRTY-ONE

# FIRE

Terra had been right. She had always scolded Isla and her emotions. *Your feelings will be your ruin,* she had said countless times. They made her weak. Vulnerable.

And now, they had ruined her plan at gaining access to the Sun Isle library.

She shouldn't have gotten so angry at the king. She shouldn't have expected him to be anything but insufferable.

Of course he would use her own words against her. Of course he would have a specter use her body for his own purposes yet deny her a simple request.

Isla had gone about it all the wrong way. She knew that now. But she refused to tell Celeste she had failed them. Again. Not when her friend had gone to such great lengths to secure the gloves.

She wouldn't give up. Not yet.

Sun Isle was empty during the day, as expected. There was no one to gape at her bright-red dress. She hadn't bothered wearing a more neutral shade. Any hue other than gold would stand out immediately, anyway.

The isle was gilded, just like its king. Gold everywhere. She didn't waste time looking at its wonders, or lingering. She marched right up to the castle with resolve.

She didn't care if all the guards in the palace tried to stop her, she was getting into that library.

As soon as she entered the castle, the sunshine from outside died. The only light came from fiery orbs and chandeliers. They filled every inch of the ceiling, doing what the king couldn't.

"Isla, ruler of Wildling?"

She turned around to the guard who had spoken, ready to tell him he couldn't keep her from the isle. That she was *allowed* to be here. But before she could, he spoke again.

"We've been expecting you. Please, follow me." The guard's gold-plated armor clinked as he turned on his heel and made his way down the hallway.

*Expecting you?* She took off after him.

"You . . . have?" she said, looking around carefully, expecting to see more guards soon. To possibly be brought to some sort of dungeon.

He nodded. "I've been given orders to take you to the library." Isla was silent. That couldn't be right . . . it had taken her three days to find her nerve to venture into the Sunling land. The guard had been waiting right at the doors. There was no way he, or others, had been waiting for her to arrive.

Before long, he stopped in front of an entrance. "The king has ordered the library to be closed this week. You will be alone and are to have full access to any of the floors."

She blinked. Oro had refused to take her here himself, yet he had given her exclusive privileges?

It had to be a trick.

Though, as long as she was able to search the library . . . she didn't care. Isla bowed her head in thanks, pasting a smile on her face as if this was all normal. Expected. "Thank you," she said.

"I will be out here, should you need anything."

The library doors closed behind her with a thud.

The guard was right. She had the entire space to herself. Ten floors of books. Galleries so long, she couldn't see their end.

If she didn't have a specific task, she would have loved to spend days in here, exploring.

But that wasn't why she had fought so hard to get inside this room.

Isla took off, not knowing if more guards were coming to trap her, or if the king himself would appear any moment, to demand she tell him what she was looking for.

She fetched the Starling gloves from a hidden pocket in her cape and pulled them on with only minimal disgust. With so little time, she needed to touch everything and hope she got lucky.

The books were beautiful. Their covers were gold, gems up their spines. Knowledge seemed to be prized on Sun Isle.

Dozens of tables filled the space, unlike any other library she had visited on the island. Did this mean Sunlings were granted full access inside?

No time to wonder. She looked for anything out of place, anything that looked special at all.

At the very end of the hall sat a hearth, big enough to swallow her whole. The flames inside crackled, almost like a beckoning.

She stopped in front of it.

The Skyling hidden section had been at the very top of the tower, high in the sky. The Moonling one had been engulfed in water.

Perhaps Sunling's secret section was hidden in flames.

Before she could think better of it, Isla reached one glove toward the fire, knowing it could very well wilt to pieces. She braced herself for the pain and smell of double layers of flesh burning.

It did not. The fire vanished immediately, and she stepped into the mouth of the hearth. Pressed another hand against the stone wall behind it. And watched the brick fall away.

Her chest felt too tight. Her throat too dry.

This was it. The last library. The last place to search.

She stepped inside.

Sunlings had more relics than any of the other realms combined. There were shelves of them, sitting in the near darkness.

Isla didn't waste a moment.

She was thorough. She picked up every single enchantment in the room. Held it for a few seconds. Pulled some apart, making sure nothing was hidden inside. There were dozens.

None of them resembled a giant needle.

None, besides a few swords, even had a point.

No. This couldn't be right. They had searched *every* library on Lightlark. The text had said—

It had said the bondbreaker was in a library centuries ago.

More than enough time for it to have gone missing.

Or to have been destroyed.

Or maybe . . . it never even existed in the first place.

Her chest filled with fury, then worry, then sadness. Celeste and Isla had planned for years. *This* was their way to break their curses. *This* was the key to her freedom.

*This* was the plan that guaranteed she would be off the island before the fiftieth day.

Now, the ball was just three days away.

And there was no bondbreaker.

## CHAPTER THIRTY-TWO

# NEXT

Celeste took the news surprisingly well.

The Starling paced for a few minutes before saying, "There must be another library, then."

Isla loved her friend. But in that moment, she felt like shaking her by the shoulders.

There was no other library. No bondbreaker.

"We need to consider another plan," Isla said. "This one failed. We searched every library. Every isle. The fiftieth day is almost here."

The Starling shook her head. "Exactly. The Centennial is just halfway over. We have time to find the library. We—"

"I don't have time," Isla yelled, cutting her friend off. She tensed. She had never raised her voice at her. But the words had come flooding out. Isla swallowed, and her tone became gentler. "*I* don't have time," she repeated. "Cleo means to kill me. She will, after the ball."

Celeste frowned. Grabbed her hands. "I know, I know," she said. "But didn't I protect you last time? With the nobles?"

Isla sighed. "Of course. But you said so yourself. You can't protect me from all of them. And I'm not sure Cleo is the only one who wants me dead."

Her friend insisted on continuing their search for the bondbreaker. But Isla had made up her mind.

They needed another plan.

And she knew just where to find it.

***

Isla found him in front of a crescent window in the Mainland castle. He stood watching the moon, as if staring at it hard enough might make it a sun.

The king stiffened as she entered. But he did not move an inch. Not when she crossed the room. Not when she walked to his side. His eyes remained firmly on the window.

Clearly, she would need to be the first one to speak.

"Thank you," she began. "For allowing me access."

He stared straight ahead. "You said so yourself. You did not need my permission."

They both knew that technically wasn't true. If the king hadn't wanted her on his isle or in his library, he could have kept her out.

Silence stretched on, seconds tripping over themselves.

"Did you find what you were looking for?" he finally asked. Only then did he glance over at her.

"No," she said sharply, and he faced the window again.

More moments ticked by, cartwheeling between them.

"Did you?" she whispered.

It had been five days since she had seen him. More than enough time to have sought out another ancient creature for help. If he had somehow found the heart without her, she would have no other plan. Her only hope was that Oro would take her back. Would honor the terms of their deal again. She would get his protection after the ball, and a chance at still saving her and Celeste.

"No," he said. Relief tasted sweet on her tongue.

"Good." She turned to face him. Oro turned too. "What's next?"

# CHAPTER THIRTY-THREE

# THE BALL

At the midpoint of the Centennial, on the fiftieth day, the Betwixt Ball took place. It was the Lightlark event of the century, a beautiful excuse for a party that was intended to muddle the anxiety and anguish of the Centennial with bubbling drinks, gowns made of gossamer, and a feast that celebrated each of the isles.

It also marked a turning point in the games. At midnight, killing could begin.

Her guardians had designed a specific outfit for the ball. Precariously placed leaves trailed across her chest and along her stomach, leaving strips of skin exposed across her ribs. The green leaves continued down her middle, just past the tops of her thighs—below there was just sheer material, the occasional leaf sewn into the tumbling fabric. Her cape was deep green and offered at least some sort of modesty.

It also hid her weapons. Throwing stars disguised as brooches. Blades tucked into the folds. Chain mail was stitched into the fabric, making the cape into a shield.

She knew how useless it would all be against a ruler set on assassinating her that night. But she refused to die without a fight. As much as it annoyed her, she would have to trust that Oro would hold up his end of their newly re-inked deal. They were set to seek out the next ancient creature—one the king had promised would *definitely* try to kill her—the very next night.

A knock sounded at her door. Ella. "They're ready for you," she said.

Isla knew exactly what to expect. Nevertheless, her fingers shook at her sides as she walked down the halls, trailed by staff who carried baskets of crimson rose petals, crushed leaves, and freshly picked wildflowers.

Too soon, she stood before double doors, and Ella left her side. Her spine straightened. Her chin rose.

The doors opened, and Isla stopped breathing.

The ballroom had six grand staircases—one for each ruler. She locked eyes with Celeste across the room. Her friend looked determined, seeing through this glittering ball's mask into its bloody underbelly. By the next morning, one of them could very well be dead.

It had been twenty-five days since the rulers had been paired together, with the task of figuring out all aspects of the prophecy. Who knew if someone *had* identified the offense that needed to be committed again and now just needed a ruler to die?

She thought of the king's words in the forest. He claimed the reason the curses hadn't been broken wasn't because it was hard to kill another ruler but because *choosing the right ruler and realm to die* was the difficult part.

Cleo's assassination attempt negated all that he had said about her and the games. Isla spotted the Moonling then, at the top of her own staircase. Anger curled in her stomach. It was the first time she had seen Cleo since she had tried to have her killed.

It was quickly replaced by a dark satisfaction. *That didn't go the way you planned, did it?* her smile said as she stared at the Moonling from across the room. The ruler met her gaze, but there was no triumph in it. Or *anything,* really. Her face was a mystery, revealing nothing.

Snow fell in sheets from clouds that crowded the glass ceiling, shadows danced along the walls, trees grew from the marble floor, silver stardust was smeared like paint down the stairs, and dozens of rings of fire hung above their heads.

Isla knew exactly what to expect.

But it was still magnificent.

The rulers began their coordinated descent.

Lightlark nobles and, in Skyling's case, representatives, awaited below. Many stared at her dress. Some whispered and grinned at each other behind ornate fans, as if gossiping about her impending assassination. Coins clattered as they were exchanged between hands. Were there bets on rulers' deaths?

Some Moonlings regarded her with clear malice. Perhaps the nobles she and Celeste had killed were their friends. Or family.

Isla stared them down and hoped they feared her.

As soon as her heel reached the marble floor, a single brave man peeled away from the crowd. A Starling in a silver suit. Other nobles gasped at his foolishness. He bowed his head and offered his hand. "Would you honor me?" he asked.

Normally, Isla might have refused. She already felt on edge and off-kilter, the snow and smeared starlight and flames bright in every corner of her vision.

But it was important she appeared unaffected by the prospect of the first rule expiring at midnight. Fear would only make her an easier target.

Isla took the Starling's hand, and he immediately whisked her into the center of the ballroom. Poppy had taught her all the traditional dances. She moved effortlessly through the steps, as easily as twirling her blades in her hands, and the Starling kept up, spinning her perfectly, keeping a firm hand on her lower back and his feet away from hers.

The song changed, and she had another dance partner. Then another. Another. Celeste was nearby, dancing with just as many people, doing a better job at looking like she was having a good time.

Cleo was sitting in one of the corners of the room, surrounded by Moonling nobles.

Watching her.

Waiting?

Azul stood by a long spread of food, goblet in hand. He wore a cape entirely made up of Skyling jewels, his every knuckle glimmering with gems. From across the room, he gave a nod of appreciation to the large diamond teardrop earrings she wore that skimmed the sides of her neck.

She smiled back politely.

Some nobles tracked the exchange, perhaps suspecting an alliance.

*Good. Let them suspect anything but the truth.*

She thought back to the conversation she had heard between him and Oro. Had he really not been speaking of her realm?

If so, which realm had he been speaking about ending?

No one was busier than Oro, who lingered by his throne. He wore gold, as always, with sleeves covering every inch of the bluish gray she now knew was growing down his arm. Dozens of nobles surrounded him, asking questions he answered lazily between sips of drink. But his eyes were alert. A handful of women seemed determined to get a bit closer to him, not afraid to discreetly push each other out of the circle to do so. Isla rolled her eyes. Just when she was about to look away, he met her gaze. And nodded before taking another swig of wine.

She looked around for the last ruler . . . but didn't see him anywhere.

After yet another dance, she excused herself, her head spinning and throat dry from small talk. She stumbled out into the hallway, into the closest room, and closed the doors firmly behind her.

It wasn't a room at all. At least, not one with four walls. Her steps echoed against the stone floor until she reached an interior balcony. There were more of the same levels, above and below it, like layers of a cake crafted out of marble. Her eyes closed and her fingers gripped the railing as tightly as if it was a starstick that could transport her anywhere else.

Isla hated the fake smile she had worn all night. She hated the nobles who had watched her every move. She hated how closely *she* had watched the clock, every bell marking the hours making her stomach sink with dread. She—

"Looking for me, Hearteater?"

Isla whipped around, and Grim was there, towering over her. He wore a much nicer version of his typical clothing, a black suit with a shining cape.

He took in her every inch and grinned. "Now you look satisfyingly terrifying, don't you?"

Sparks twirled around her bones, and his grin widened, sensing it . . . sensing how he made her feel.

She didn't even bother hiding it. Not tonight. Not with everything else going on in her mind. Grim was the least of her worries.

"I didn't see you," she said.

He shrugged. "Sometimes the only way to keep people from bothering you is to not let them see you at all."

Isla wished she'd had that power an hour ago. "Then why bother going visible again?" she asked, her voice barely above a whisper.

Grim took a step toward her. Took her hand into his with such brazen possession that she nearly took it back. "To dance with you, of course."

Before she could say a word, she was whirling around, the sheer bottom of her dress draping across the marble floor, leaves crinkling. His hand, cold as night, was at the base of her spine—the other wrapped completely around hers.

His grin was devilish, and she swallowed, knowing exactly what he was sensing as her hand gripped one of his wide shoulders, as she looked up at eyes that might as well have been two pools of ink, the space between stars.

Did it frighten him? Everyone in the six realms lived in fear of having a Wildling love them. It was a death sentence.

And she didn't love him . . . she barely knew him.

But shouldn't he be afraid of what she was feeling now?

She pressed herself closer, completely against him, reading his reaction, surprising herself with her boldness. And Grim only laughed darkly. His hand ran a slow trail down her spine—then up once more. "Hearteater," he said into her ear. "You're killing me."

Isla didn't breathe. His breath was against her cheek. He smelled like stone and storms and something spiced, like cinnamon.

She bit her lip, and he watched the movement, swallowing.

Then he was gone.

No, not gone. Invisible.

And so was she.

A crowd of nobles entered a moment later. Their voices were high-pitched with the pleasure of passing along gossip, though Isla didn't pay attention to their words. Grim was shadowed next to her, visible . . . but not truly there. Her own body looked similar.

The sight of the nobles made her sick. Betting on lives. Looking at her as if she deserved to die, simply for being born.

Suddenly, she craved a distraction. The ball would soon turn bloody. She would either stand and fight—or flee to a safer location. She still wasn't sure. What she *was* sure about was that these could be the last few minutes that she didn't have to watch her back, the last hour she might enjoy just for herself.

"Let's go," she whispered. They were both leaned against the balcony, facing the crowd.

Grim raised an eyebrow at her. "Leave the ball?"

"Just for a bit. Right now, I want to be anywhere else."

Grim grinned wickedly. He wrapped his arm fully around her waist. "Then allow me to whisk you away, Hearteater."

He fell back and took her with him. They plummeted right off the interior balcony, backward, to the floor below.

Grim's hand was over her mouth before she could scream—half a moment later, she was in his arms. It was all a blur, the marble and ceiling lights and the sheets of her gown mixing to make their own galaxy, and then she was on the ground.

Isla looked at him like she wanted to gut him, and he just laughed. The nobles were huddled like wolves above, oblivious to them. She ceased being shadow, and Grim went solid before her. He took her hand once more and said, "Night is a wicked time, Hearteater . . . you can get into all sorts of trouble."

*Trouble.* That was exactly what he was, leading her through room after room before turning into a hall. He knew the way well, and Isla had almost forgotten that it had been his home once. Centuries before.

Grim went down a set of stairs, and Isla matched his pace. Around and around they went. Down, down, down. She was smiling—*why was she smiling?*—even as she could barely see the steps before her. No light shined there, the brightness of the ball far behind them.

"Where are we going?" she asked, and only got a grin in the dark in response. She almost tripped on the folds of her dress, but he held her firmly, all the way until the bottom of the stairs.

They must have been at the base of the castle—underground, maybe. Orbs holding white light crowded the corners of the room, floating like balloons. The walls were arched, held up by columns, and beyond them sat a slice of dark water like a piece of the nighttime sky trapped below.

It shimmered, startling her, and she took a step back.

Right into his chest. She stilled.

Grim placed a hand on her waist. Her shoulders hiked up, his body ice-cold but leaving heat blooming beneath her skin. His fingers trailed down to her hip bone. His thumb circled the delicate skin just beyond it. Closer and closer to even more sensitive places. Isla pinched her lips together.

In her heels, she was tall enough so that when she leaned back, her head rested against his shoulder. From that angle, she imagined he could see down her dress, only a few leaves keeping her from being completely exposed. Still, under his piercing gaze, she felt bare. Breathing became difficult. One hand gripped her hip harder, pinning her to him, while the other traveled across her stomach. His knuckles trailed up her ribs, only stopping once they reached the heavy underside of her chest. They grazed her there, and she was suddenly aching, her skin prickling, heat pooling. She met his eyes and found them dark with—

She didn't know what that was.

Was it desire?

Was it . . . sadness?

"What are you thinking?" she asked, turning to face him.

Grim looked at her like he knew her, like he saw her for what she truly was and not what she pretended to be. She felt naked before him, not just because he had touched her where no one else ever had but also knowing he sensed her every change in emotion. The pulsing desire for him to touch her *more,* for him to pull her dress down and touch her everywhere without any fabric between them.

"I'm thinking . . ." he said darkly. *Thinking what?* He reached for her.

And blinked. His entire expression changed.

The hand he had reached toward her now reached inside his pocket.

". . . that I have something for you." He pulled out a necklace. It had a dark chain, holding a black diamond as large as a plum.

Isla's eyebrows came together. He was giving her jewelry? She didn't know what to say. Her face was still hot. The diamond was beautiful, but she didn't want a gem—she wanted him, pressed against her. Immediately.

Grim grinned, sensing everything. He looked ready to take her into his arms once more but seemed to think better of it, because he turned his attention to his gift. "May I?"

She nodded, hoping he didn't mistake her disappointment for not liking his present. She lifted her hair, and he clasped the necklace into place, tight around her neck, his fingers lingering for just a moment.

"I know you are more than capable of protecting yourself," he said, head bent low, breath against her nearly bare shoulder. "But should you ever need me, touch this. And I will come for you."

She glanced down at it again with greater appreciation.

*I will come for you.* He had said it like a promise.

She needed any protection she could get. Something like this would be useful, especially after seeing his display of power. Especially now that they were minutes away from killing being permitted.

Yet—

"Grim. I can't . . . I can't wear this." It would be a statement. Oro had already suspected they might be working together. This would all but confirm it. She couldn't do anything that would compromise her and Oro's alliance, not when it seemed like the only chance to break her and Celeste's curses.

"I know." Two of his fingers pressed against the chain, against her neck, and it went invisible.

She looked up at him. Didn't know what to say, wanted to thank him . . . but the words formed and died in her throat.

Grim reached toward her again, all restraint gone, and trailed his knuckles down her cheek, the necklace, her collarbones. Down the center of her chest. "Hearteater," he said gently. "You don't want to know what I'm thinking," he finally answered. Her body tensed in anticipation, taut like an arrow a moment away from careening through the air. She wanted his hand lower, higher, everywhere . . .

But he dropped it instead.

He did not touch her again on their quiet walk back to the ballroom. She wanted to say something, do something, tell him . . .

When she opened her mouth, he was already speaking.

"I need to go," he said, looking over her shoulder. Was he looking for someone? He almost looked nervous. Wary.

Of who?

"You're leaving?" she asked, eyebrows coming together.

"Don't worry, Hearteater," he said. "I'll be back before midnight." His gaze shifted to the corner of the room where Sunlings had gathered, Oro at their center like a sun they all revolved around. "In the meantime . . . perhaps you should dance with the king," he said.

*Oro?* Isla frowned. Grim had just run his hands down her body. He had gifted her a necklace. Why would he suggest she dance with someone else? Especially his enemy.

It didn't make any sense. Before she could ask anything, he was gone.

Isla turned around, back to the party, slightly dazed. She trailed a finger across the chain of her necklace, invisible to everyone else. It felt like another secret.

One she actually enjoyed keeping.

"There you are." Celeste casually slipped to her side, pretending to study the table of desserts nearby. "Half an hour until midnight. What will it be? Fight or hide?"

The rules required they attend each Lightlark event. But nowhere was it specified they had to stay the entire time. She and Celeste could leave, barricade themselves somewhere safe. Her friend had suggested portaling to Star Isle and staying there awhile.

But their alliance would be compromised. And though their plan had gone to shambles, secrets were still sacred during the Centennial. Letting their friendship be known could endanger them both.

"Fight," Isla said, surprising herself by the conviction in her voice. At the beginning of the Centennial, she would have said *hide* without any hesitation. But though she didn't have power, Isla refused to be a coward. She would face Cleo's rage head-on. *That* was how she would survive. Not by hiding.

"Are you—"

Before Celeste could say another word, the floor lurched. And Isla was suddenly careening through the air.

She landed on her side, temple banging against the marble.

Air shattered with high-pitched snaps of metal chains as the fiery chandeliers fell, taking most of the ceiling with them. The floor split into fractures, strikes of lightning across the marble. Cracks of collapsing stone and hissing fire filled the world—everything solid turned out to be delicate, crumbling like cake, breaking as easily as glass.

As the castle collapsed, nothing and no one was safe.

Isla only had time to reach an arm up in front of her eyes as a ring of fire fell, right at her face—but before it broke her skull, Celeste was suddenly there. The Starling raised her own arms, and it stopped midair.

Screams echoed against the stone walls, the metallic scent of both power and blood filling the room. There was a roaring, a ringing, as the world stumbled, then straightened, only to fall again.

The woman to her left, a Skyling in a cornflower-blue dress, was swallowed up by the floor. A Moonling man stood still in shock—he took a step, but it was too late. A chunk of the ceiling crushed him, no water around for him to wield in defense.

She turned to where Celeste had been. But her friend was gone. Isla's heart pinched. She raced to her feet. Dust clouds bloomed, and she squinted through them, searching desperately for the glimmer of her silver dress, fearing the worst—

But Celeste was nearby, lifting debris off a group of Starlings.

Isla backed toward the wall, her mouth opening and closing, her lungs frozen in her chest, her hands outstretched, but doing nothing.

It wasn't even midnight yet. What was this?

Azul was at the other side of the room, his arms working in wild strokes, creating a shield of air under which dozens of guests hid. Cleo was healing a group of Moonling nobles who had been badly burned by the fallen flames.

*Oro.*

She found him on his knees, at the back of the room. His face was twisted with pain, and his fingers had gone through the marble floor.

That was when she realized what was happening.

Lightlark was falling. It was just as the king had described. People dying, structures collapsing. For hundreds of years, the rulers had failed to break the curses. It was finally taking its toll on the island.

But why now? Why at the ball?

She reached toward a group clinging to what was left of the floor, a bloody bridge snaking across the room. One she was able to pull up. Another fell through the cracks.

Her blades could do nothing. Her cape might shield some debris, but it was useless against the thick slabs of marble raining down around them.

If she had power, she could save them. She could wield the vines decorating the room, use them to pull people to safety.

She might not have abilities. But Oro did. He needed to get up—he could stop this.

She shouted his name. But he remained hunched over, forehead now nearly against the floor. The roar muted her voice. Furniture fell through the ceiling. He was across the ballroom. The space between them was half-gone, the rest falling without warning.

Isla cursed as she kicked her shoes off and ran toward the king. She jumped over the largest hole, sharp pieces of rubble embedding themselves in her heels upon landing. The pain was a whisper compared to the spines she had pulled from her back—if she could live through that, she could live through anything. She dodged a chair that nearly crushed her, pushing a young Moonling away from its path too and earning a look of disgust that she had dared touch him.

*Next time I'll let it crush you,* she thought as she ducked beneath a piece of the ceiling that had concaved and finally made it to the king.

"Oro." She knelt before him, the same way he had when she was on the forest floor, full of barbs and thorns.

He didn't acknowledge her presence.

Nothing new—but this wasn't just about her.

She grabbed him by the shoulders and said, "Get up! People are dying. They need you!"

Oro raised his head enough to meet her gaze. His eyes were hollow. As if every ounce of energy had been drained. Another tremor shook the floor, and he growled, his fingers going deeper into the marble. The pain must have been unbearable to have brought the king to his knees.

"*Please,*" she begged. A few feet away, rock rained down into a pile that crushed half the group Azul had been trying to block. He rushed to fling the rubble away with his wind, but blood coated the stone. It was too late.

Oro did not move an inch. But she heard him say "*Leave*" through his teeth.

No. When Isla was hurt and had demanded he go, he had stayed. She wasn't leaving. Not until he stopped this.

Isla took his shirt in two fistfuls and shoved him against the wall with all her strength, tearing his fingers from the floor. She screamed right into his face. "You might be dying, but you're not dead yet, you miserable wretch, now get up and do something before you allow your brother's sacrifice and everything we all have lost to be for nothing."

Oro did not meet her gaze or get up.

But, with a groan that shook his shoulders, he leaned forward, pushing past her—and his hands fully pierced the marble. Power erupted from his touch, filling the room.

Forcing it still.

Then he collapsed against the floor.

Screams and calls for help and final breaths became a symphony that overtook the violins and harps that lay in splinters in the corner of the room, along with most of the orchestra.

When Celeste found her, and they rushed out of the room, Isla thought about the king's words—that this Centennial was not simply *another* chance at breaking the curses . . .

But perhaps the last chance.

Dozens were dead. The wing of the castle had been reduced to little more than rubble. And it would get worse, Isla knew, if they didn't break the curses soon.

She had somehow found herself in an alliance with the king. They had a plan to find the heart. Grim, Celeste, and Oro had all promised to protect her.

Even without the bondbreaker, it had all seemed almost possible to survive the Centennial and break their curses before it ended.

But as the broken ballroom doors managed to slam closed and the screams were swallowed up, Isla wondered if the island would even last the rest of the hundred days.

## CHAPTER THIRTY-FOUR

# ORO

The aftermath of the ball left the island fractured in more ways than one. Part of the castle was in ruins. The streets of the agora were so empty, wind whistled down them. Store windows shuttered, and their walls did not fold open at night. Islanders were afraid to leave their homes, let alone their isles. There were whispers that the tragedy at the ball was Grim's doing, after his demonstration weeks before had shown the same thing happening. Except this hadn't been an illusion.

The Mainland became a place only for specters and rulers.

They did not pretend any longer. Cleo abandoned all pretenses of working with Celeste and moved to her isle, breaking tradition. Oro uncharacteristically pushed their excursion back a few days, needing to deal with the wreckage and keep the nobles from rebelling. Tensions had never been so high.

They had always known that the Centennial had a timeline. A clock of a hundred days.

But it seemed as though that clock had changed.

"Tell me more about the heart," Isla said on the fifty-third day.

A screech echoed through the night, so loudly the wood beneath her hands quivered. Isla took a steadying breath, keeping her grip, refusing the siren call in her head that dared her to look down at the hundred feet below her toes.

Oro paused for a moment, waiting for something. His gaze flicked to the sky. Then his arm reached up for the next branch. They were climbing up a lattice of wood, thick trunks that had been woven into webbing. Oro couldn't fly wherever they were going, Isla assumed. She hadn't asked why.

Isla had many questions. Which meant she had to be selective.

Another second passed without a response, and she was very close to pulling him off the grid by his foot. But he said, "It was made during the creation of the island and contains pure, concentrated energy from its creator."

"Who created it?"

"Horus Rey."

"And Cronan Malvere?"

Oro paused before his fingers could reach the next branch. She watched the muscles in his back tense. Slowly, very slowly, he looked down at her.

She stared back, eyebrows slightly raised. It seemed he didn't have the energy to glare at her any longer. More than two dozen nobles had died at the ball, and each life lost weighed on him. She saw it in the firm set of his mouth, the tense shape of his shoulders. "Did Grim tell you that?" he finally said.

"He did. He's much more forthcoming than other rulers of realm," she said pointedly. Part of her wanted him to glare at her. Wanted him to do anything but look so hollow.

Oro still hadn't reached for the next ring. She climbed up to his level so they were matched. "Is that all he told you?" he asked.

She nodded.

He frowned. "Not as forthcoming as you think, then," he said. Then he climbed up to the next level.

"What is that supposed to mean?" she asked.

Oro said nothing.

"Hello?"

He turned to look down at her and said, "Ask Grim. He's the most *forthcoming* ruler."

Isla's mouth was already open in response—when a hand reached through the lattice and pulled her through.

She was dragged forward, into an endless maze of wood. She couldn't see her attacker; the moonlight was far behind her back. Isla reached for her dagger, which she had tucked into her waist, but another hand bound hers together. There was the unmistakable burn of rope against her wrists.

A moment later, she was on her knees in total darkness.

She was trapped again—but this time, it was on purpose. Isla had proposed using herself as bait. Oro had agreed, seeming willing to take more risks after the disaster of the ball.

And it had worked.

Light erupted, illuminating everything. The walls were honeycombed. She and Oro must have been climbing the outside of it.

*Oro.*

She saw the unmistakable curl of his cape as he stepped next to her. He wasn't bound, he was simply standing there, looking down at her.

"Release her," he said sternly.

Isla looked around to see who he was talking to. That was when she saw them, standing in the gaps of the hive. Dozens of them.

They had long, transparent wings that hung limp at their sides. Their skin was light blue, like someone had stuck a paintbrush in the air to get the color. Their eyes were too large, limbs too long.

Not one of them moved.

Oro bared his teeth. "Did you not hear me?"

Steps sounded before her, at the center of the hive. From the shadows stepped a man as tall as Oro. He had the same light-blue skin as the others, but his wings were larger and perched high, the tops peaking above his muscled shoulders. His hair was dark as Grim's. "Oh, no, they heard you, *King,*" he said. "They are hesitant to listen to a ruler who has abandoned them, however." He angled his head at Oro. "You can understand, I am sure."

Oro made to step forward, but a sword appeared from thin air—and pressed firmly against his throat. The winged man had a hand raised, keeping the blade hovering in place.

Oro's finger twitched and the blade drew closer, sending a droplet of blood spilling down his neck.

The winged man clicked his tongue. "A move, *King*, and we'll see just how easily you can die like the rest of us."

She had to think, do something. Stall, until she could come up with a better plan. "You would destroy the island just to kill him?"

Slowly, the man turned to her, as if noticing her for the first time. She expected a sword against her throat next. Oro had said he would try to kill her. That he, like other ancient creatures, hated her kind.

But he only grinned, pleased. "The island is well on its way to destruction," he purred. "And it would be a gift . . . We all have suffered enough, *Wildling*."

He turned to Oro, amused. "Did you think you could disguise her from me?" He smiled, and Isla saw too many teeth in his mouth, all crowded together. "That might work on others . . . but me?" He laughed. "Or did you think she would be enough to convince me to work with you? Are you truly that cornered, King, to ask me for aid? You fool."

The winged man turned to face the others. Their hair was blue, not dark like his. And they looked too pale. Sickly. The way their wings hung made Isla think they didn't work anymore. Was it because of the Skyling curse? Did it affect them as well?

"What do you say?" he said loudly, a leader rallying his people. "Are we ready to be free of this island? To see how we fare on the other side?" His hand turned to a fist.

And the sword sliced across Oro's throat.

Isla gasped. The blade had not cut deeply. But blood streamed down his neck, staining his shirt. They had to get him to water so he could close the wound before he lost too much.

Even with the gash across his throat, the king's face did not change. He did not wince.

They needed to abandon her plan. He had been right—

It had only taken a few seconds of the winged man speaking to his people for Isla to retrieve her dagger. A few more to cut through the rope. She felt cool metal in her fingers.

And then her arm flung through the air.

The blade flew true, aimed perfectly, right at the winged man's heart. It whizzed fast as an arrow, blade glimmering in the light.

An inch before hitting its mark, the dagger froze.

Isla stilled, preparing for the winged man to send it back through her chest.

But he had not frozen the blade. His eyes were wide; he looked as shocked as anyone to see the tip pointed at his heart.

It wasn't alone. The sword that had been at Oro's throat was now at the man's neck.

*Oro* had stopped Isla's blade.

Everyone stilled. Not by their will, but by Oro's. His nostrils flared. "Perhaps *you* are the fool for believing you could immobilize a Wildling with a bit of rope." He stepped forward. Blood still flowed steadily from his wound. He did not reach up to wipe it away. Oro grinned meanly. "Yes, she knew she would pique your curiosity enough to get us into your hive. And I knew you would be prideful enough to believe you could capture us so easily." He reached the platform the winged man stood upon. His voice became almost a growl. "Now, tell us where we can find the island's heart."

The winged man was silent for a moment. Then he smiled. "How I love a surprise . . . and *she*"—he looked curiously at Isla—"*she* certainly is a surprise. More than you know . . ." Isla froze. She could hear it in the edge to his voice—he knew. Somehow, he knew she was a Wildling ruler born without powers. She braced herself, waiting for him to say it.

Waiting for what Oro would do with that information. But the winged man simply laughed. "Curious, so *curious, Wildling*. Born so strangely."

He turned to Oro, still smiling joyfully. As if he had not just sliced the throat of the king of Lightlark.

"What will you offer me, *King?*"

Her blade drew closer to his heart. "I'll offer you the chance to keep your hive, and people, intact."

The man's expression didn't falter. "I want the Wildling."

Before Isla could make a move, Oro's hand was at the man's neck. And it was coated in flames.

They danced in the man's eyes as he calmly said, "I want the Wildling *to visit me*. Once this is all over." He glanced at her. "She will come willingly, I assure you."

Isla stepped forward before Oro could make another move. "Done," she said. His skin was too pale. He needed to be healed immediately. She sighed, feigning boredom. "Now tell us where to find the heart. I'd like to get at least a *wink* of sleep tonight."

The winged man's smile widened. "Very well. The heart blooms somewhere new every time. I have seen it. I know not where it is now . . . but it seems to always choose a place where darkness meets light."

Isla had no idea what that meant. But Oro plucked her dagger from the air and held it firmly as he turned his back on the man and the rest of the winged people. He grunted as he walked past her, a sign for her to follow.

They walked through the maze of the hive until they reached its outside layer. He handed her back her weapon. Isla began to climb down, but Oro stumbled through one of the openings and grabbed her before falling. He soared for a while, breathing a little too fast. His blood stained her cheek, her hair.

"A plan," he said, voice hoarse. "We have a plan."

"Oro," she said as they half flew, half fell, the trees just inches below. She tried to keep the panic out of her voice. "*Oro*."

He glanced at her—and his eyes were bloodshot. Had he been sleeping at all? They closed for a moment.

And they began to fall.

They hit the trees, and Isla screamed. His hands tightened around her, and the air flurried, shattered as something like a shield appeared around them. Branches snapped, wind roared in her ears as they tumbled, dropped—

She hit the ground with a thud. Even with the shield breaking their fall, the breath was knocked from her lungs. She gasped, gripping the dirt, leaves crunching between her fingers. Stars dotted her vision, mixing with the real stars, and darkness threatened to swallow the rest.

Isla forced herself up, her bones screaming in defiance. Oro was a few feet away, sprawled across the ground. Blood pooled at the side of his neck. The cut didn't look deep, but he must have lost too much for him to have been weakened so thoroughly.

Water—he needed water. Then he could heal himself with his Moonling abilities. She forced herself to go still. To listen.

Her breath was too loud, so she held it. Her lungs pulsed in pain, her head spun, but finally, she heard it. The trickling of a stream.

Not nearby, no. She grabbed Oro's hand. "Get up."

He didn't stir. But blood was still flowing. That was a good thing.

"*Get up.*"

Nothing.

She slapped him across the face as hard as she could.

His eyes opened at that. And began to close. "I can't carry you," she said. "You need to help me."

Slowly, with her help, he rose.

"Can you call the water to you?" she asked. But it was like he couldn't hear her. So, she half dragged him toward the sound, his weight on her like a boulder.

He was too heavy. She wanted to stop. Wanted to crumple to the ground.

But if Oro died . . .

All Lightlark would.

She needed the heart now, just as much as he did.

He needed to live.

She walked until her legs burned, until her breath was hot against her lips. Until Oro's skin began to cool, the unmistakable Sunling heat dying down.

Just as her knees threatened to buckle, the dirt softened beneath her boots. And the roaring of the stream was in front of her.

Her legs nearly collapsed with relief. She pushed him into the water with all her remaining strength. He seized for a moment before falling still.

She worried it was too late. But the water seemed to know him. It glowed faintly and got to work. He began to sink, but she kept his head out of the water. She held him firmly by the shoulders, the back of his head in her lap, the rest of him deep below.

His sleeves were rolled back. The grayish blue he had shown them before had spread. A lot. It now covered his entire left arm, down to his hand. Was this why the cut had weakened him so quickly? Why the ballroom had broken in half during the ball?

Isla stayed like that, gripping him, her legs in the cold stream, for a long while. Waiting. Waiting for the island to begin to crumble around her, like it had at the ball. For trees to fall. For Oro to stop breathing.

The water worked intently, all through the night. Slowly, slowly, the slice across his neck knitted together, new skin replacing the broken shreds. The blood on her dried. She could feel it on her cheek, smell it in her hair, but didn't dare wash it off. She just kept holding Oro.

And waiting.

She must have drifted off, because her head knocked against her shoulder. Her spine straightened, and fear gripped her chest. *Had she let him go?*

No. There he was. She hadn't let him slip. His wound was nearly healed.

Still, his eyes remained closed.

A stream of light had begun peeking through the trees. The first dewy, honeyed tinge of day. Isla's first thought was that this was good. Maybe the heat would be good for him, maybe he could draw upon its strength . . .

Dread stabbed her through the stomach.

*The curse.*

She had to get him inside. If the sword hadn't killed him, the sun would. And the water wouldn't be able to heal him from that.

"Oro," she said, shaking him.

He didn't move.

"Oro," she yelled into his ear. "The sun's coming up. We have to go."

His eyes did not open.

Light had almost found them. It made lazy lines across the forest, peeking through the trees. Day had almost broken open.

He was going to die. She was going to watch him burst into flames, the same way, using her starstick, she had watched a child burn to ash in the Sunling realm, years before, helpless—

*No.*

Not helpless.

She spotted an opening in a mountain twenty feet away. A cave.

Isla didn't know if they would make it inside before the king became fire. She had no idea how she was going to get him there.

But she gripped beneath both of his shoulders and pulled.

## CHAPTER THIRTY-FIVE

# THE CAVE

It was midday by the time the king finally opened his eyes. Isla was curled against a corner of the cave, watching him. Still covered in his blood.

"You saved me," he said, frowning.

Hearing him say the words made her realize how absurd it was. Oro was the most powerful person in all the realms . . . and *she,* a powerless ruler, had saved him.

Perhaps she really wasn't as powerless as she thought.

She gave him a look. "I'm not as weak as you think I am."

He didn't return the glare. "I've never thought you were weak."

She blinked. He couldn't mean that. "Well, now we're even, I suppose." That day on the balcony seemed realms away.

"I suppose we are." Oro took in the cave. They were at its mouth, sunlight spilling inside, just a few feet away. Those streaks of gold had nearly seared him through. She had pulled him to safety with a second to spare.

Oro turned his attention to the other side of the cave, the tunnels that led through the underground. Pretty blue lights illuminated the ceiling like a constellation of stars.

"We're beneath a Skyling graveyard," he said gruffly. He nodded toward the bright blue. "Glowworms. They eat the bones."

Isla scowled, the mysticism of the place ripped away. But she remembered the winged man's words. "Is it a place where darkness meets light?"

He nodded and winced. "One of the few on Sky Isle. Once the sun goes down, I'll search it." He seemed to sense her confusion about the winged man's information, because he said, "Nightshades did build the island, along with Sunlings. When they were banished from Lightlark, their lands were built over. But some parts, and some creatures, still dwell in the in-between."

"So, this is our plan," she said, needing confirmation. "We're going to check all the places on the island where Nightshade and Lightlark meet? That's where the heart is?"

He bowed his golden head. His crown was covered in mud. Both of them were caked in dirt and blood. "There aren't many. Especially with Star Isle off the list, thanks to the specter's information." He stretched. "Besides the graveyard, there is only one other place on Sky Isle that qualifies."

"How about Sun Isle?"

"I will search those locations myself."

Isla gave him a look. "Yourself?"

Oro sighed. "Do you truly not trust me yet?"

She frowned. "Do you trust me?"

Oro did not answer her question. Instead, he said, "I never break promises. I do not break deals on a whim." He looked at her pointedly.

Isla rolled her eyes. "And what about Moon Isle?"

"There are a few. But that's the last place we check."

"Why?"

"Because Cleo has her isle heavily monitored, and if she thinks we're looking for something there, she'll try to find it herself."

Oro was being unusually forthcoming. She needed to get every detail out of him that she could. "How many total places are left, then, where darkness meets light?"

"Eight."

*Eight*. That wasn't a large number at all. Hope bloomed in Isla's chest.

"Don't get too excited," he said, frowning. "There are risks."

Isla didn't care. They had a firm strategy and a manageable number of places left to search. Still, something made her uneasy. "The plan is entirely based on what others have told you. The specter. The winged man." She swallowed. "Did it ever occur to you that they could be lying?"

"They can't lie to me," Oro said simply.

Isla didn't know what that meant. Was it because he was king of Lightlark? Could all his subjects not lie to him? She certainly could. And she had.

She asked another question, since it seemed like he might answer it. "In the oracle's prophecy, it says the original offense must be committed again to break the curses. You believe the original offense was wielding the heart of Lightlark, don't you? Using its power?"

Oro glanced at her. Nodded.

So that was why he needed the heart of Lightlark. To fulfill part of the prophecy.

"You said that when Sunling and Nightshade created Lightlark, they trapped a fraction of their power in the heart." Her eyes widened, realization dawning. "That's why you invited Grim here for the first time," she said, the words toppling from her mouth. "You don't think he or any Nightshade spun the curses. You think someone used the Nightshade power trapped in the heart to cast them."

Oro nodded again. Something in his eyes, a gleam, looked almost impressed.

She lifted her chin. "That means you didn't know about the heart until after the last Centennial. Or else you would have invited him to the previous ones . . ."

Oro's silence confirmed it. But his expression had turned wary. "You should go," he finally said, not meeting her eyes. He was stuck there until dusk . . . but she could leave at any time.

Her dry lips pressed together. Part of her wanted to run out and up to the surface. Take a bath and wash the hair that was stuck to the blood on her face. The mud that covered her clothes. The film of dirt across her skin.

Another part wanted more information. The king had never been this forthcoming before. And she had one more question she needed answered.

"I'll wait with you," she told him.

Oro blinked, surprised. Then frowned, annoyed. She ground her teeth together—*wretch*. The king tensed as he trailed a finger across his neck, making a line through the dried blood.

She shot a look at the light at the mouth of the cave, a carpet of gold across the floor. "Seems like we'll be here awhile longer," she said. "Let's play a game."

"A game," he said flatly.

Isla nodded, undeterred. "Questions, back and forth. I'll answer one. And then you will. Honestly."

She expected he might say her proposed game was foolish or might even decide to brave the fiery sunlight rather than spend another moment stuck with her. But he leaned the back of his head against the wall and looked at her, chin lifted. "Fine, Wildling. You start."

She sat up. Her important question barreled through her mind, but she couldn't ask it. Not yet. She had to start small. "Be honest—do you ever tire of wearing gold?"

Oro gave her a look that said, *That's what you want to ask me?* He sighed. "Yes, Wildling. Though I can wear blue, white, or silver if I choose."

Right. He was an Origin—he could wear colors from all the realms he had powers from. She wondered if he did wear other shades, outside the Centennial.

"Your turn."

He studied her for a few moments. "What is your life like, back in the Wildling newland?"

It wasn't the question she might have expected, but it was an easy one, so she was grateful. "It's . . ." She opened her mouth. She had an answer queued up, ready to go, about how wonderful and exciting it was.

But she had promised to be honest.

Isla wanted him to trust her, so they could find the heart and break her and Celeste's curses.

Which might mean trusting him in turn.

"It's awful." She studied the ground, running her fingers along its rough patches. "I love my guardians—they're my only family." She took a long breath. "But—" She squinted, not knowing how to say it. She met his gaze and found him watching her intently. "Have you ever felt like a bird in a cage?"

She expected him to sneer at her.

But he nodded, just a slight dip of his raised chin. "Every day for the last five hundred years."

*Of course.* Her limited existence locked away in her Wildling castle was nothing compared to the centuries Oro had endured.

"Who trapped you?" he asked, though it wasn't his turn.

Isla winced, then cursed herself for even suggesting this game. Why would someone with so many secrets do such a thing? He had no idea how close his question was to the truth . . . to unraveling all the lies she had built up like a fortress around her and her realm.

"Not *trapped* . . . just . . . protected."

Oro didn't push the subject, and she was glad. She hurried to ask a question of her own. "Have you ever been in love?"

His answer was immediate. "No."

"Why not?"

"Kings of Lightlark do not fall in love. It makes us vulnerable. Our power becomes unprotected." He glanced at her. "I suppose we are similar in that regard . . . in our inability to have that."

*Because of the Wildling curse.* "I suppose so." She thought of Grim. His hands across her dress. Clutching her to his chest. It wasn't her turn, but she had to know. "Do you think it's possible for a ruler to love another ruler? Truly, without any agenda?"

"No." He shook his head. "Not truly."

A part of her wilted inside. But he had to be wrong. Just because he had never experienced love didn't mean it wasn't possible. "So, your brother really wasn't in love with his bride-to-be?"

Oro shrugged a shoulder. "Egan loved Aurora. But not in that way."

"How would you know?"

Oro met her gaze. "They didn't share abilities." Falling in love meant sharing access to one's power with their beloved. It was what made rulers falling in love so dangerous.

"Your turn," she said quietly. She had asked several questions in a row and was surprised he had answered them.

"Did you know Grim previous to the Centennial?"

Isla stilled at the mention of him, as if Oro had plucked him from her thoughts. She answered honestly. "No."

He looked at her strangely.

She rolled her eyes. "I'm not working with him against you, don't worry." It was true.

Oro's expression settled into something she hadn't expected . . . relief mixed with surprise. Isla immediately shifted the subject away from the Nightshade ruler. "What's your favorite part of Lightlark?"

He scratched the side of his head, just below his crown. "There's this secluded stretch of beach on Sun Isle, along a cliff . . . with giant coals in the water that sizzle when the sea hits them." He lifted his gaze, eyes on the ceiling. "The sea is a strange shade there . . . dark green. The color of your eyes."

Isla glared at the word *strange* to describe her eyes but mumbled, "Sounds beautiful."

His arms stretched over his head. "Your singing," he said simply.

She blinked. Part of her had forgotten that he had heard her, so many weeks before. "What about it?"

He shrugged. "Tell me about it."

Isla looked toward the mouth of the cave. The sunlight still glittered brightly. "It's calming to me. Something I was born being good at, without really trying."

"Like swordplay?"

"No. That was hard. I wasn't naturally good at it, not like the singing. It used to frustrate me to no end . . . Terra, my fighting instructor, would scold my impatience constantly." She sighed. "So, I practiced. A lot. Every day, all day, all the time. Until the sword was weightless in my hand. Until it was a part of me, just as much as my voice was. I *forced* it to be."

Oro studied her but said nothing. It was her turn.

Finally. It was time to ask her question, for the sake of her own sanity. Just to make sure she had made the right decision in calling off her search. It was a risky thing to say aloud. But now, on the fifty-fourth day of the Centennial, every action seemed like a risk. "Is there a relic on the island that can break any bond? That can break the curses of the ones that wield it?"

She studied his face desperately, looking for any sign of recognition, any hint of surprise. The king's eyebrows *did* come together. But, more than anything, Oro looked confused. "No," he said firmly. "If there was, I would have found a way to use it."

She believed him. It was a foolish thing to do, but she did.

Which meant the bondbreaker either never existed . . . or was destroyed before the king had learned about it.

"Is that what you were searching for?" he asked. He knew she had been looking for something in the Sun Isle library. And that she hadn't found it.

No use in hiding it now. She nodded.

It was her turn again. "How long have you been able to gild?"

Oro looked surprised by the question. He blinked. Isla wondered if this was the one he would refuse to answer. A few moments passed in silence before he said, "Since I was a child." His eyes were trained on the ground. Deep in thought. "I was told to hide it," he said, frowning, as if he hadn't expected to be telling her this. "Egan was the eldest. The heir. He was supposed to be the strongest."

"But he couldn't gild," Isla guessed.

He met her eyes. Nodded.

"So why now? Why show everyone?"

Oro sighed. Shrugged a shoulder. "I figure I'm dying. Might as well share all my secrets." He said it casually, but his eyes were hard. Serious. She thought of the bluish gray she had seen hours before. How much it had spread since he had first shown it to them in the throne room. Moments mounted, and silence stretched between them. She wondered if he wouldn't take his chance to ask a question, right up until he finally met her gaze and said, "What was your secret, Isla?"

*Isla*. He so rarely called her by her name, instead referring to her as *Wildling* most of the time, as if to remind both of them of what she was. Or, she supposed, what she was supposed to be.

She felt her throat get tight. "What?"

His stare was unrelenting. "Your secret from my demonstration. What was it?"

She swallowed. Shook her head no.

The king laughed without humor. "I didn't think so." He scratched the side of his neck. "How about this—why did you let me win our duel?"

So, he *had* known. The duel seemed so far away. So much had changed. "I didn't want to make myself a target."

"Ah."

Her turn to be bold. To prove that, even though he had proclaimed that he wanted to share all his secrets, there were still some he wasn't willing to divulge.

"What is your flair?" she asked. She had wondered for a while if the king had one of the rare powers that didn't relate to their realms, the ones rulers so often possessed.

The way Oro paused made her positive he did. The Sunling inclined his head at her. Considering. "Share your secret, and I'll tell you."

*Wretch*. She said nothing.

And the king smiled. It unnerved her. She had never seen him smile, not really. Not genuinely. "How about this?" He sat up straighter. His eyes were not hollow at all—they were full of something she couldn't read. "Tell me your secret, and *you* can be the one who wins."

Silence. Her heart was beating so loudly, it was a wonder it wasn't echoing through the cave. "What?"

Oro did not so much as blink. "When we find the heart, you can brandish it, fulfilling the prophecy. *You* can win the great power promised." He shrugged. "But only if you tell me your secret."

*Win?*

Isla had never even thought of winning. She had been too focused on surviving. On breaking her and Celeste's curses. Lately, on finally getting her Wildling abilities.

He couldn't be serious.

"Why would you do that?" she demanded. "Don't you want the power for yourself?"

Oro shook his head. "I do not wish to become a god," he said. "Too much power is dangerous. I have never wanted to win. I simply want to save Lightlark."

Isla scoffed. "You would give it to *me?*"

"Who else? Do you suppose Cleo should have it?" Isla bared her teeth, and Oro looked ready to grin at her reaction. "Precisely."

"How about Azul?"

Oro shook his head but did not offer an explanation.

*Power.* Isla had wanted it more and more. The power promised was prophesied to be endless. The things she could do—

*No.*

Isla hadn't ever handled even a drop of power. What would she do with a sea of it?

Especially since the price was revealing her secret.

Isla shook her head.

The king looked surprised. Then he frowned. "Either you are the only other ruler not interested in the Centennial's prize," he said, "or your secret is worse than I suspected."

"That's not a question" was her only response.

For the rest of the time, they barely spoke, their game over.

Isla watched the sunlight streaming from the cave entrance until it withered and disappeared.

## CHAPTER THIRTY-SIX

# ORACLE

Each day after the ball held ruin. An ancient building fell into the sea. Another elder died. Another crack formed overnight, dividing the Mainland. The cursed storm grew along the coast. Still trapped in place, it began to rage. Thick bolts of lightning would strike at the same time every night, loud enough that Isla heard them wherever she was. Counting down the days.

The heart was not in either location on Sky Isle. Or Sun Isle, which Oro searched himself.

It was the last place Oro had said he wanted to look. But on the fifty-ninth day of the Centennial, the time came to search where darkness met light on Moon Isle.

Isla wondered about the guards. Oro had hinted at not wanting Cleo to know they were looking for something on her isle.

But the king had a solution. One that Isla didn't appreciate.

"I'll go slow," he said, surprising her.

Isla gave him a look.

"Slower," he amended.

She didn't want to ever experience flying again, but she also couldn't think of another way past the guards that didn't require telling him about her starstick. "If you drop me—"

"You will gut me, I am aware."

Then she was in the air. She buried her face in his chest, scrunching her eyes against the wind. His hand was splayed across her back, his grip a bit too loose for her comfort, so she clung to his neck tightly.

"You know," he said into her ear, "I used to wonder how Wildlings carved hearts out with only their nails." One of the hands that was supposed to be holding her securely reached back and smoothed down her own fingers, one by one, until they didn't dig into his skin any longer. "Now, I know they're sharp as daggers."

Isla poked her head up to give him a withering look. "I wouldn't have to cling so much if you held me properly."

"Properly?"

She nodded. "More tightly. More securely."

Oro shifted his hands. Suddenly, instead of being loosely held in front of him, she was cradled against his chest. Her entire body warmed from his heat. It was almost comfortable. "Better?" he asked. She expected his tone to be mocking. But it wasn't.

"Better."

Before she knew it, Oro landed, his arms tightening around her as they made contact.

The second she was away from him, frost filled her chest. Moon Isle had gotten significantly colder since the last time she was here. Her eyes darted to Oro. *He* was the reason. Since Lightlark and his control of it was weakening, he could no longer keep it warm. Or bright. The days were dimmer. The sun set sooner. All parts of the island were noticeably cooler. Dozens more hearths and torches had been added across the Mainland and inside the castle. But they were only a temporary solution.

They had landed on the edge of a forest of trees that looked more like knotted, twisted roots, delicately braided at the top. Streams navigated between them, transporting water lilies and fat white flowers as big as her palms. It was so silent, she could hear the snow falling. She shivered, cold air puffing from her lips. Her fingers already felt frozen; her toes were tiny blocks in her boots. Wind bit against her cheeks and nose, and her eyes watered and stung.

Suddenly, Isla screamed.

In the middle of the silence, a dark-blue bird like ocean made into wings landed on her shoulder and screeched right into her ear.

Oro turned and struck immediately, without waiting to see what the threat was. His fire curled through the night, right to where the bird had been—but it was too fast and went flying away, back through the woods.

His arm dropped as he watched it. When he turned to Isla, his eyebrows were slightly raised. "Aren't you supposed to be good with animals?"

"Not when they blow out my hearing," she said, gingerly cupping her ear. "Aren't *you* supposed to have more care with your fire?"

Oro's jaw tensed—she had struck a chord, it seemed. "Yes," he said tersely.

They walked in silence until the ground turned to ice. She could see the roots of the trees below the crystal-like veins, dark as night. They reached a cliff where snow began to cake the ground like frosting. Her boots quickly got stuck in it, so she trailed behind Oro, whose steps melted a path. Snowflakes got lost in her hair and piled on her nose, and she felt as cold as one of the ice statues that sat in front of the Moon Isle palace.

After an hour, her breathing became panting, and she must have slowed, because Oro finally turned. One look at her, and he offered his hand. "I can warm you."

She wanted to say no. But she was done being proud. She gripped his hand with her own, and he frowned.

"You're freezing." He said it like an accusation.

Isla wanted to glare at him, but her eyes stung too much to make the movement.

In a quick sweep, he removed his golden cape and draped it around her. It was so large, it wrapped Isla like a blanket. She wanted to reject it, but the moment it touched her skin, her body was flooded with heat that seemed to melt through her bones. Her face buried in the fabric, shoulders shivering as she tied it closer around herself. It smelled like honey and mint leaves, deliciously soft against her skin.

When she finally peeked her head out of the cape and buttoned it around her neck, Oro was watching her warily. "Are you . . . all right?" he asked, as if the idea of hypothermia and dying of cold had never once crossed his mind.

"I'm fine," she said quickly, raising her chin as if doing so did anything to make her look less ridiculous. She walked past him, into snow that drenched her ankles in cold. "Thank you."

Oro followed behind, and she must have been walking in the right direction, because he didn't say a word. She did not stop until she reached a slab of ice so large, it was like a glacier that had gotten trapped on land.

Isla squinted at it. There was something inside. She inched closer and wiped at it with Oro's cape. Some of the frost cleared, and she startled, tripping backward, right into Oro, who steadied her before she could fall into the snow.

Three women were trapped within the ice.

"The oracles," he said, hands falling from her shoulders.

She blinked too many times. "I thought there was *one.*"

"Only one has thawed in the last thousand years."

"Why are they here?"

Oro stepped to her side. "A king far before me trapped them in ice, so they would never leave, or die. Three women born with the gift of prophecy. Enraged at being imprisoned, two of them joined forces with Nightshade, calling to the dark part of the island. When Night Isle was destroyed, they froze forever."

"So, this is a place where darkness meets light."

Oro nodded as he placed a hand against the ice. It immediately began to thaw.

The middle woman's eyes flew open. She floated in the water, her white hair a halo around her head. Her gaze went to Isla, then Oro, then back again.

Her voice echoed, sounding like a million voices trapped in one throat.

"It's been a long time since I saw a Sunling and a Wildling side by side." She angled her body toward them, her face just inches from their own. "I've been warned not to help you . . . but this is just too curious . . ."

*This* was the woman who had spoken the prophecy of the curses. The key to breaking them. Her words were the ones they followed like law. The ones she had learned from the time she could talk.

"Warned by who?" Oro demanded.

The oracle shook her head. "*That* I cannot say. But I will say more than I've promised not to."

Cleo. It had to be Cleo.

"So many secrets, trapped between you," she continued. The oracle scratched along the ice with a long nail, and the sound made Isla wince. "But, just like this wall, they too will one day give way and unravel and fall . . . leaving quite a mess and madness."

Isla avoided meeting Oro's gaze. The oracle met her eyes with a knowing look. Knowing everything. She grinned.

"Enough of your riddles," Oro said. "We seek the heart of Lightlark. Is it here?"

The oracle smiled wider. "It is near. Nearer than you know."

"So, it's on Moon Isle?" Isla said.

The oracle nodded. Relief nearly brought her to her knees. "Where?"

The woman shook her head. "That I cannot divulge. You both must find it on your own. That is the only way to successfully wield the heart."

Isla glared at her.

The oracle stared back. "You . . . have many questions. There are so many things I could tell you . . . though I should not." She looked at her knowingly. "All will be revealed soon enough."

Isla's stomach puddled. Could she truly mean that her secret would be revealed? *No*.

"Know this," the oracle said. "There are lies and liars all around you, Isla Crown."

*Lies and liars.*

Who?

"And one of the six rulers will indeed be dead before the hundred days are over." Which ruler? Did that mean the curses would be broken?

Isla took a step forward, willing the right words to form in her head, the right question. But before the words could leave her lips, the oracle smiled.

And the water hardened into ice.

Isla banged on it with knuckles that immediately spotted with blood. Still, she kept pounding, over and over, her hand raw and throbbing.

Finally, Oro placed his hand over hers, stopping it. "She's gone," he said. "And she will not awaken again anytime soon."

Her hand stayed splayed across the ice for another long moment before she tore it off. She turned to Oro. He had secrets too. The oracle had confirmed as much.

So much for sharing them all.

*Lies and liars* . . . Had the oracle meant him?

Or someone else?

And which one of the six rulers would perish?

Though she was disappointed, terrified . . . the oracle's information had been invaluable.

"How many other places on Moon Isle qualify?" she asked, voice barely above a whisper. The oracle had warned her that her secret would be revealed. They needed to find the heart soon, before that happened. Before the island was no more than rocks and ruins.

"Three."

*Three.* Isla breathed out and leaned against the ice, relief making her limbs go weak. The cape kept her warm, and she cradled her bloody knuckles against the fabric. "Three," she repeated. "Can we go tonight?"

Oro shot a look at the sky. "No," he said quietly. "We . . . *I* don't have time. One place is easier to access than the others. And, for both of our sakes, let's hope that is where the heart is."

Isla nodded, though her teeth locked in disappointment. She wanted to find the heart that night, as soon as possible, so she could break the curses, free her people, and get the power before the oracle's words could come true. Before her secret came to light and made her a target for fulfilling the rest of the prophecy.

"Tomorrow?" she said, cape wrapped tightly around her.

"Tomorrow," Oro agreed.

## CHAPTER THIRTY-SEVEN

# PUDDLE

Later that night, Isla stood in her room, holding her starstick.

Before the Centennial had even started, she'd promised herself she wouldn't use the relic to look at her home. Part of her feared she would miss the Wildling newland so much, she would make a rash decision and leave the game, portaling away.

Now, so much had changed. She wasn't the same person who had arrived on the island two months prior.

Before, she had never even spoken to a man unsupervised for more than a few minutes. Now, one had touched her up and down her body.

Before, she thought she would cower before the rulers. Now, she had beaten them in trials. Threatened them. She had even saved the king.

Before, she believed it was wrong to want anything other than to break her and her realm's curses.

Now, she wanted everything.

She drew her puddle of stars, almost hoping that her old self would click back into place at the sight of her realm and people.

The edges quivered, alive—spilled ink and diamonds. The stars faded into different colors, the hues sputtering and forming quickly before her eyes. They scattered until she was looking at Wildling.

Blood drained from her face. Her heart became all she could hear, beating unsteadily in her chest.

It was gone.

The forests had been razed. The Wildling palace was nearly destroyed. Villages were empty.

This had to be a trick—an illusion.

Her hand trembled as she touched the starstick, leading it somewhere else. The colors scattered until she was looking at a woman, sprawled across what was left of the forest floor. Her tan skin had hardened, turned to sheets of bark. Strands of her hair had become vines. One hand was already roots in the ground.

It was Terra.

Isla stopped breathing.

Her guardian had started to be taken by nature, just like the Eldress. The first steps of a Wildling death. Isla's stomach went watery, her mouth went dry, her vision blurred—

She was about to jump into the puddle, to go to Terra, but forced herself still.

There was nothing she could do. She was powerless. Reversing a Wildling death that had already begun required endless ability and enchantment.

And her realm had none of that to spare.

*Terra.* Her fighting instructor, the closest person to her in the world. The one who had taught her nearly everything she knew.

Poppy was kneeling next to her, applying an elixir that would delay the transition. But it wouldn't save her. It wouldn't save their realm.

"I reach my hand into the dirt, to speak to the trees," Terra told Poppy, voice frailer than Isla thought possible. "But the dirt is dead in my hand."

Poppy held Terra's few soft fingers. "We still have time," she said. "Our little bird is still fighting for us."

Terra only closed her eyes. "How many more are like this?" she asked.

"Almost all of them," Poppy answered.

Isla had thought her people would be just the way she had left them. Wildling had weakened during her reign, but it had been gradual.

How was this possible?

The land had been without power for too long. The ground was demanding its due. Taking powerful Wildlings, one by one.

Breaking her curse and theirs wouldn't save them. The Wildling realm was too far gone. Even the powers she was supposed to have been born with wouldn't be enough. Not when they had weakened with every ruler's generation.

To save them all, she needed more—more than even a single ruler could give.

Tears streaming down her cheeks, Isla remembered the prize. The single person who broke the curses was fated to be gifted immeasurable ability—more power than the realms had ever seen. The type that could save the Wildlings. The type that could save Terra. The entire Centennial, Isla had been focused on making sure she didn't lose.

Now, she knew she had to win.

Isla felt like she was going to be sick. She had cried for so long, it didn't seem possible her body had any liquid left.

"What happened?" Oro's voice was surprisingly gentle when she found him, pacing around a room in the Mainland castle. "I just saw you a couple of hours ago," he said in confusion, in anger, muttering almost to himself.

Her eyes must have still been swollen. She didn't answer his question. "Does your offer still stand?"

Oro seemed to know she meant the one he had extended in the cave. To her relief, he nodded.

A tear ran down her cheek. "Can I trust you?" she asked.

Oro stared at her. "Yes. I've never lied to you, Isla. Not once."

She hoped that was true. Her stomach felt like it was flipping inside out. If Celeste knew she had willingly shared her greatest secret with the king, she would be furious. But the Starling would understand.

Isla had no choice now.

Oro was directly in front of her. His hand went to her forehead. He was frowning. Did he think she was sick? He studied her body quickly, clinically, looking for damage. Did he think she was injured?

She wished she was. Physical pain would hurt less than this.

Isla couldn't believe she was going to tell him her secret. She closed her eyes, unable to look at him as she did. Every bone in her body and vein and muscle and swath of skin screamed against it.

*Your secret is your greatest weakness. You can never reveal it.* The rule was like a favorite blanket. She had learned it before she had learned anything else. All other lessons were birthed from it. She needed to know how to fight because she was powerless. She needed to hide in her room because she was powerless. She couldn't meet anyone alone because she was powerless.

She was a disappointment because she was powerless.

She had to follow the rules because she was powerless.

Terra and Poppy had to rule in her stead because she was powerless.

She had to survive the Centennial and lie, cheat, steal, and kill because she was powerless.

*No.* She forced her eyes open. Forced herself to look right at the king as she said the words she had built her entire life around—the foundation of everything.

"I was born powerless."

There. The words were out. Birds let free. Their cage propped open. Nothing and no one could take them back.

Oro went still. She could see it in his eyes—he had expected anything but that.

His brow creased, confused. He squinted at her.

A million thoughts were going through his head, and Isla imagined none of them were good.

It was too much to ask for her to stand there in the aftermath. She was strong enough to say the words—but not enough to stay.

Isla turned on her heel, but Oro stopped her with a gentle hand.

He looked strange. Slightly horrified. "Are you saying you have never used power?" he demanded.

She blinked. Was she going to have to repeat it? "Yes," she said, her voice trembling. She swallowed. "You can't use something you don't have."

For once, Oro was speechless. She might have enjoyed seeing him so flustered if she wasn't having the worst day of her life.

And she supposed the oracle had been right. Her secret was revealed.

Just not in the way she would have ever imagined.

She turned to leave again.

And this time the king did not stop her.

## CHAPTER THIRTY-EIGHT

# TOMORROW

The next morning, Isla entered the throne room with her head held high. She had told Oro her secret and survived.

The king claimed he was a man of his word. Which meant now, the power promised would be hers. All they had to do was find the heart. And now they knew it was on Moon Isle. There were only three locations left. They would search one of them that very night.

They were so very close.

Hope was the only thing keeping her from falling to pieces.

*I'm coming for you,* she whispered to Terra. *I'm coming to save you, just as you trained me to.*

Killing was permitted. Isla should have been scared, walking into a meeting with the other rulers of realm. But she wasn't. She had Oro. Celeste. Grim.

The king had called the rulers together for an update. Isla was safely by his side. Grim appeared next. She hadn't seen him since the ball, but every night she ran her fingers across her necklace, wondering when she would get the courage to pull the diamond and summon him to her room.

Cleo strolled inside wearing a cape that buttoned down its front, with a slit for her pants-clad legs. She looked at Isla with little interest, but Isla didn't make the mistake of believing it meant the Moonling didn't want to kill her. Cleo likely knew she couldn't get near Isla with Oro as her partner.

Good.

Celeste joined them. Then Azul.

They all stood far away. Their eyes alert. Ready for attack. Ready to wield their powers, should they need to.

Oro finally spoke, his voice filling the room. "It has been sixty days since the start of the Centennial. Would anyone like to share their progress?"

No one said a word. Isla wondered what, or how much, she should say. They hadn't discussed the meeting beforehand.

To her surprise, Oro said, "Isla and I have scoured the island for a relic we believe might have been used five hundred years ago. We think wielding it was the original offense, and that its power created the curses."

The truth. Nearly all of it. She blinked, shocked.

Azul frowned. "What sort of relic could possibly have cast curses?"

"One infused with Nightshade power," Oro said simply.

Again, the truth. Isla stared at him, lips parted. Hadn't he said he didn't trust the others? Why hadn't they discussed this beforehand?

The Skyling ruler whirled to face Grim. "Could such a relic exist?"

Grim had gone still. "It could if it was created long enough ago that a Nightshade ruler could afford to sacrifice a part of their power."

Azul looked incredulous. "Then shouldn't we all search for this relic? Shouldn't the Nightshade look for it? Perhaps it would call to him."

Isla glared daggers at Oro. Why would he give so much away?

"No," the king said, his voice absolute. "We cannot take the risk of focusing our efforts on one avenue, should we be incorrect. Not with the urgency of our situation." He lifted his sleeve, showing them how far the bluish gray had spread. His body was like a map, demonstrating the crumbling of the island. She straightened. At least he had the good sense to keep the others away from their plan. "*However,*" he said, "I believe it's time for a change in matches."

The blood drained from Isla's face.

Oro turned to the Moonling ruler. "Cleo, would it suit you to be matched so we might search Moon Isle for this relic together?"

Isla wasn't breathing. A roaring had overtaken her hearing. She had to have heard him wrong . . . had to have misunderstood. Could he even change the matches?

She knew she should have shielded the outrage in her eyes, burning angry holes in Oro's face. Or the shocked set of her mouth.

But the king did not even turn to look at her.

Cleo's smile was feline. "Are you sure, King?" she said. "It seemed you and the Wildling were getting along so swimmingly."

Oro matched Azul and Celeste next. Then Isla and Grim. But she barely heard his voice over the roaring. Her body hardly resisted barreling over the table and slicing the king's throat with his own crown.

The realization hit her like a boulder to the chest.

Oro had been using her—up until she had become useless. Just as Celeste had warned.

Now that they knew the heart was on Moon Isle, he had changed alliances to suit his plan. He had chosen Cleo.

For the entire time she had known him, every choice Oro had made was for the good of his people. *I will do anything it takes to break these curses,* he had said.

Even if it meant betraying her.

"Are you really sure, King?" Cleo said, staring at Isla with pursed lips. "I have to admit, I'm suspicious . . . This isn't just a strategy between you and the Wildling, is it?"

A sprig of hope grew in Isla's chest. They had worked together for weeks. She had saved his life. He had saved hers. Maybe he wasn't betraying her. Maybe this *was* a strategy . . .

Oro's smile was pure mirth. "I'll let you in on a secret that might explain my decision," he said loudly, for all to hear. He turned to look straight at her. "Isla Crown doesn't have powers."

The world froze.

Then shattered.

She was a fool. A fool for believing the king would let her have the power promised in the prophecy. A fool for believing his promises held any weight. A fool for believing he would keep her secret.

The oracle's words rang through her head, to the tune of dread.

*There are lies and liars all around you, Isla Crown.* She had been talking about Oro. Trying to warn her.

Betrayal seared through her stomach, iron being formed into a blade. She wanted to stab Oro through the heart with it.

Cleo turned to face her, seeming to put together that Isla was unprotected. Alone. Powerless.

She took a step forward—

But before any of the rulers could make a move on her, Grim took her hand and they were gone.

## CHAPTER THIRTY-NINE

# PROMISE

They knew. All of them knew.

The secret she had kept for her entire life, the reason she had been trapped inside her room, the one thing that would make her the number one target at the Centennial.

Because Oro had *told* them.

The pain was a hand unraveling her insides.

No. This couldn't be real.

He had said he had never lied to her. He had said she could trust him. He had gotten kinder, more caring—

*Fool.* Even now, she was defending him. Even after he had ruined her chances at breaking her curse and saving her realm.

Oro had sentenced her to death. He had used her. This *was* real.

One moment she was in the throne room, watching the look of horror on Celeste's face. Watching Cleo take a step toward her. The next, she was on the other side of the Mainland, down the cliff, on a beach.

Grim still clutched her hand.

*Grim.* He was the reason she wasn't dead. But how did he—

Isla must have looked confused, because he said, "My flair."

His flair. *This* was what it was.

It was a dangerous power. Isla thought Grim could simply turn invisible—she had never imagined he was able to travel across the island within a single breath.

She remembered his proclamation on the beach, then.

*I could take you back to Nightshade lands with me right now.*

Did the other rulers know? Or did they simply suspect he had made her invisible?

What *was* clear was that he had risked his flair being found out, for her.

"Thank you," she said, tears prickling the corners of her eyes. "I—"

He watched her carefully. His eyes were crowded with worry.

Of course. Grim knew her secret now.

Did he think less of her?

She took a step back.

Did he regret potentially revealing his flair to save her?

She felt ashamed. Weak. Foolish.

"I knew," he said gently.

A second. Another. "Knew what?"

He stepped closer. Until he was right in front of her. He pressed two fingers to her chest. Pushed. She shivered. "I knew that you aren't bound by the curses. And that you've never wielded power."

Isla's entire world blurred, tilted.

He *knew.*

"What?" She imagined her emotions were a tidal wave of feeling, fear and shame and surprise and anguish dueling each other.

"Nightshades . . . our powers include curses. I can sense all the others. I knew from the first time I saw you that you weren't bound to them."

She remembered how he had saved her from eating the rest of the heart, demanding it be taken to her room during the first dinner. He had known then.

He had known the entire time.

"I'm not a danger to you, Isla," he said, voice firm. Eyes clear. "I would never hurt you. Or divulge your secret."

"Why?" she said, breathless. Why wouldn't he tell the others? Why hadn't he given her up the moment he had sensed that she wasn't bound to the curses?

Grim grinned then. It was unnerving the way, even in this moment, it made her insides puddle. "Because we're monsters, Hearteater," he said. "Or, at least, that's what they think." His grin widened. "And monsters stick together."

*I am the monster.*

The puzzle began to form. Grim's immediate fascination with her. His pursuit of her, without fear of her curse.

The parts of her that had recoiled in fear now settled. Half of her felt bare and broken in front of him. Flawed. Powerless.

But the other half slackened in relief. He knew her secret. And hadn't told anyone.

She had suspected him of using her during the Centennial. But he hadn't. Every interaction with him had been genuine.

Her lips quivered. She willed them to stop, but they didn't.

Grim took a step forward, feeling her everything. Her sadness. Her lingering self-hatred. He squinted at her, confused, then trailed his knuckles down her cheek. A tear had fallen, and she hadn't even noticed.

"Grim . . ." she said, voice unsteady. "What's wrong with me?" A ruler born without power was an oyster without its pearl.

Grim's eyes flashed with anger. "Nothing, absolutely nothing, is wrong with you, heart," he said.

Then he took her into his arms. She stayed there, trembling.

"I think they're going to kill me," she said quietly, then looked up at him.

He surprised her by smiling. He placed his hand carefully against her cheek. "If anyone makes a move to harm you, I will ruin them and their entire realm." His fingers trailed down her face, past her throat, then tugged gently on the pendant at the end of her necklace. "Pull this," he said. "And I'll be there."

Isla believed him.

She believed *only* him.

## CHAPTER FORTY

# TOGETHER

Oro's betrayal was a glacier in her chest, throbbing and raw. She had *trusted* him. They had been through a flurry of challenges and obstacles. Together.

Didn't that mean something?

The weeks she had spent helping Oro had been wasted.

The only thing that thawed her pain was Grim. He filled her dreams, then her days.

Isla knew they were numbered, not just because the island was crumbling around her. Cleo and Oro would be close to finding the heart . . . had possibly already found it. And when they did, and they wielded it, only one last part of fulfilling the prophecy would be left—killing a ruler, and their entire realm.

Soon, Isla would be dead. She would never have her Wildling power. Terra would be gone.

And there was nothing she could do about it.

For a week, Isla thought only of survival.

With Grim's help, she had moved into the Place of Mirrors on Wild Isle. If Juniper was to be believed, only Wildling power could be wielded there. It was the only place where she and Cleo, or even Oro, would be matched in power, should they attack. Her blades were not meaningless there.

She had taken over one of the abandoned rooms upstairs.

Every morning, she wondered if it was her last. She locked her door and put furniture in front of it, knowing all it would do was give her notice before someone struck. She tried to stay awake at night, every creak of the castle making her jump—but eventually her body shut down, forcing her asleep.

Her hand was never far away from her dagger.

Ella risked grave danger in the deadly forest, venturing to Wild Isle to bring her whatever she needed. Food. Water. One of the last times she had stopped in, Isla had handed her most of the gems she had brought to Lightlark, a sack full of diamonds and precious stones. "Hire a healer," she had said.

She had wondered if the Starling wouldn't return after that, having gotten what she wanted. But she did. Every day, she returned.

So did Celeste.

Right after the betrayal, she had called Isla a fool for trusting the king. Then she had pulled her into her arms, and they had cried.

Isla had wondered if that would be the moment Celeste would leave her behind. Her friend had her own life and realm to worry about. It was foolish continuing to ally herself with Isla.

But Celeste was still convinced the bondbreaker was an option.

"I'm searching for it," she said. "I'm making progress."

Isla spent most of her days drawing her puddles of stars and looking inside until seeing Terra made her stomach twist with guilt. The entire right side of her body was part of the ground now. She could barely speak.

Once, she wondered if she was being selfish by hiding. If Cleo and Oro did indeed find and use the heart of Lightlark and fulfilled most of the prophecy, didn't it make sense for Wildling to be the ones to die?

Her newland and people were nearly gone. She was powerless. Isla and her realm offered nothing to the future of the island.

Perhaps they made the most sense . . .

Isla mentioned it to Celeste, who had looked ready to slap her.

"We need Wildlings," her friend had said. "To rebuild. To grow. You and your realm are more important than you know."

That night, she had wandered the Place of Mirrors, stopping in front of the carvings of her people and the vault she had tried and failed to open.

Celeste was right. Wildlings were once great. Integral to the island.

What a shame they had such a weak leader, she thought, staring at the wild animals that once roamed free here, the glorious floras thousands of Wildlings once grew, the weapons they had wielded before their focus became hearts and blood.

What a tragedy this was how their chapter ended.

## CHAPTER FORTY-ONE

# LETTER

The next morning, Isla found Celeste at her door in the Place of Mirrors. "You have sulked enough," she said.

Isla blinked. *Sulked?* She had been trying to survive.

"You really are a massive fool. Do you know that?" Celeste said.

Isla nodded weakly.

"Good. But you know what you are not, Isla Crown? A failure. And neither am I. So, you got betrayed? We expected this. We *knew* we could trust no one. Or did you forget?"

Isla's back teeth bit together painfully.

"We didn't plan for years to be stopped by this," she said. "And all hope is not lost, not yet." She surprised Isla by grinning. "I've been speaking to the Starlings who work in the castle, your Ella included. About the hidden library."

Isla resisted the urge to scream. The bondbreaker was a lost cause. She knew that. Her friend's insistence on finding it was getting infuriating. Isla needed a *real* solution—not a legend.

Still. Celeste could have abandoned her the moment the rest of the rulers had learned her secret. But she hadn't. So, Isla said, as gently as she could manage, "Do any of them know where it is?"

"Not yet—but they're looking. I have them each searching a specific section of the castle and asking around to anyone they—"

Isla gave her friend a look.

Celeste lifted her arms over her head. "So, what's your plan? Sit and hide here until the island falls apart around us? Wait until Cleo and the king find the heart—if it even exists—and kill you? Wait until the Wildling realm is officially extinct?" Isla bristled. Even though that was exactly what she had been doing.

She had told her friend about what she had seen in her puddle of stars. She had shown her.

*I will help you,* her friend promised. But Isla knew nothing short of the power promised in the prophecy would save the Wildlings in their state of deterioration.

Her problems seemed insurmountable.

How was she supposed to find the heart of Lightlark when everyone now not only wished to kill her but knew they easily could? The moment she stepped out of the Place of Mirrors, she would be a target.

How was Isla supposed to win now?

She looked down at her hands. Her shaky words surprised her. There was a lump in her throat, and the corners of her eyes prickled. "I don't want to give up," she said honestly. Every time she closed her eyes, she saw her guardian. Suffering. Slowly becoming part of the forest. Poppy and Terra were counting on her . . . and Isla had purposefully gone against all their plans and preparation. She had truly thought that she could fulfill her duty and get what she wanted most on her own terms. How foolish she had been. "But how can I not? We have no plan. No allies."

Celeste took her hands in her own. There was something bright in her eyes, an intensity like two glimmering stars. "We have exactly what we started the Centennial with. Each other."

If only that were enough.

If she had power, she could face off directly against Cleo and Oro, maybe even get the heart from them, instead of waiting to be slaughtered.

The Starling ruler paced the room quickly, as if invigorated by her own words. "This game is not over. We've been on the island over two months. We must have made some sort of progress, some connection. Someone here must be able to help us."

*Connection.*

Celeste's word gave her an idea. Her breath caught. Her thoughts scattered. One person had proven useful, time and time again. Someone who dealt in secrets.

And if Isla had learned anything during the Centennial, it was that secrets were everything.

"Parchment," Isla demanded.

The Starling ruler smiled. "I'll be right back."

An hour later, Celeste returned with parchment, ink, and Ella. The Starling now knew of their friendship, but Isla didn't worry. Not when Ella had been loyal and was one of Celeste's people. It was in her and her realm's interest to keep their secrets.

Isla wrote the letter quickly, showing it to Celeste before folding it in half and handing it over to Ella to be delivered.

Finished. Isla had done something . . . She wasn't giving up. Not yet.

As Ella left with the letter, Isla felt a spark of hope. She might be young and powerless and foolish. But if Oro and Cleo *had* found the heart, they would have already used it. One of them would be dead, and the curses would be gone.

Something had gone wrong.

Celeste was right. The game was not over. Not yet.

The letter was for Juniper, whose bar had been closed since the ball. If anyone knew the location of a rumored hidden library, or anything at all that could help her win, it was him.

It read, *Details of my greatest secret in exchange for yours?*

Isla couldn't sleep. And, it seemed, neither could Grim. He stood with his back to her in the long room, staring out a window—a threshold he could not pass. He took a deep breath, and his head fell back as he exhaled, as if just seeing the dark beyond invigorated him.

She took a step, and he whirled around.

He looked surprised. Relieved.

"Heart," he said quickly, forgetting the last part of his name for her again. Was she no longer "Hearteater," now that he didn't have to pretend not to know her secret? Grim took long strides toward her, never once breaking her gaze, and, before she could say a word, he swept her into his arms.

She made a sound she had never made before, and he touched her possessively, like he knew her every inch and wanted more, wanted everything. Soon, his armor was on the floor, next to her puddle of a dress, and—

Isla gasped as she sat up, blinking away the bits of dream like the scraps of dress that Grim had . . .

She swallowed.

*Just a dream.*

*Just another—*

Dream.

The next day, Isla could hardly meet Grim's eyes when he visited her in the Place of Mirrors. He came whenever he could, walking into the castle like anyone else, unable to use his flair to get inside. Juniper hadn't replied yet, but she hadn't lost hope that he would. The barkeep wouldn't be able to resist her secrets. Not if he had heard about her powerlessness.

Grim had brought her chocolate from the market. She thought all the shops in the agora had closed after the ball, when the island had started crumbling in earnest. But she supposed Grim could be very convincing when there was something he wanted.

Isla had almost been able to feel his hands on her during her dream. It had been so vivid, the way he had—

"Hearteater?"

She blinked.

He grinned. So wickedly that Isla scoffed. Her eyes narrowed into a glare.

"Did you—did you *send* me that dream?" she asked, voice very tight. Nightshades had that ability. With her own eyes, she had seen him create illusions during the demonstrations. "Have you been sending me all of them?"

Isla thought about Grim more than she should. But the number of times she had dreamed of him was absurd. He filled her head nearly every night.

She should have known. All those dreams she'd been having lately . . .

"What dream?" was all the Nightshade said. But his eyes looked devious.

She got up from her makeshift bed and stormed over to him. Something about him planting the dream in her mind felt invasive—no matter how much she had liked it—and her hands made angry fists at her sides. "You know very well *what dream.*"

Grim had the nerve to still feign confusion, though the corners of his lips twitched, fighting not to grin. "I'm not sure what you mean," he said. "But . . . from what I'm hearing . . . and *sensing* . . . it might be one I would enjoy hearing more about . . ."

She fought the urge to stomp on his foot before sending him away for the day.

Isla tentatively stepped out of the Place of Mirrors the next morning.

She expected to find Cleo's legion waiting, or Cleo and Oro themselves, jumping at the chance to kill her.

But no one was there.

No one was waiting.

Isla didn't want to leave. It was too soon and seemed reckless. But Juniper had sent a reply—and it had hinted at something worthwhile.

*I know who cast the curses,* he had written.

It wasn't the type of information she had been anticipating, but it seemed crucial. All this time, she had been focused on how to break the curses instead of who had created them.

She didn't know how this would help her win the Centennial. But it was a start. It was the only lead they had.

When she and Celeste entered the agora, Isla's pulse quickened. Again, she anticipated an attack. Just like at the harbor. People jumping out of the shadows.

But it was abandoned. No islanders lingered. The only sound was the creaking of shop signs, coated in dust, moving in the wind.

Celeste scrunched her nose as they walked into the pub. Isla squinted. Though it hadn't seen patrons in weeks, the smell of alcohol had intensified, so strong it burned her eyes.

And there was something else—another scent.

Isla raced to the bar and peered over it, only to gasp. A scream scraped the back of her throat.

There was a message.

Scrawled in blood.

No, not just a message. A response. She remembered the words she and Celeste had painted after the attempt on her life at the harbor: *Try harder.*

Written across the wooden cabinets that housed shelves of bubbling drink were the words *Hard enough?*

And below the words, Juniper was dead.

## CHAPTER FORTY-TWO

# CLEO

The island was built from hearts and bones and blood. Death was at its very core, from the duel that had killed Cronan Malvere to the lives lost since. For the three days after Juniper was found dead, Isla remained in the Place of Mirrors, knowing she was next.

Cleo hadn't killed her yet—but her influence was everywhere. She had intercepted Isla's note or found out about it somehow. No communication was safe. And her bloody message was clear.

The Moonling hadn't come for her yet . . . but she would.

Sometimes, late at night or early in the morning, Isla slipped out of the Wildling palace and ran. It was the only activity lately that cleared her head of the never-ending images of her realm dying. Every day she went farther, risking venturing deep into the wicked forest. To the cliff. To the outskirts of the castle, even.

At least it made her feel something.

She felt useless, doing nothing to win.

But where would she start? Oro hadn't—purposefully—shared the remaining locations on Moon Isle where darkness met light. She couldn't go search them herself. Even if she did know where they were, Oro and Cleo had likely already looked. Which meant they must have the heart . . . or must be close to getting it.

Guilt piled onto her shoulders and stacked high, weighing down her every step. She had failed her people. She had failed her guardians.

And she had failed Juniper. Cleo had killed the barkeep because of her—because of the knowledge he had been about to share.

Which meant his clue had been important.

Isla wouldn't let Juniper's death be for nothing. And, as she ran through the woods, she felt a tinge of hope.

If Cleo and Oro had already found the heart, the Moonling ruler wouldn't have bothered sabotaging Isla.

The island was a pastry, crumbling into the sea, day by day. But at dusk, it was pretty. The sun was a running yolk, smearing gold and orange and red across the sky, as if desperate to leave its mark. The clouds were cotton dipped in pink dye.

Isla watched the sunset from a cliff, hands on her knees, panting. She had just run for over an hour. The roots of her hair were wet with sweat, the day's heat reminding her of Wildling. A salty breeze blew her braid back and receded, sticking her hair to the side of her face.

She was wearing the clothes the tailor had made her during her first week on the island. Clothes meant for running and fighting. The fabric was thin but offered protection against the elements. Isla had planned to wear this same outfit to find the heart—

Together.

She sat down as the last of the sun reluctantly dipped below the horizon. Her hands gripped the grass, and she felt it—power, coursing through the soil, though weaker than before. Power she could not access.

"Mom," she said to the incoming darkness. "I don't blame you." She spoke to her sometimes.

Isla had never known her mother. She was killed the day Isla was born, by Isla's father, before he had turned the knife on himself. Both were victims of the Wildling curse. Her mother had refused to kill her love, so the curse had demanded its blood.

And their daughter was born without abilities.

"I couldn't do it either," she said quietly.

Isla thought about it, sometimes. The impossible choice. Killing a beloved . . . or dying. Before, it had seemed obvious. Now she knew she could never kill the person she loved.

Perhaps that made her mortal. Perhaps that made her weak.

No. Not weak. A weak ruler wouldn't have made it this far into the Centennial without powers.

"I understand you. And I don't blame you. And . . ." Her voice shook for just a moment before smoothing again. "And I wish I'd known you."

By the time she walked back into the woods, the moon was a wide eye in the sky, watching her. She sneaked through the shadows, keeping at its perimeter, watching the Mainland castle through the darkness.

She missed her room there. She missed her secret and the safety it had allowed.

Isla was about to turn back into the Mainland forest when she saw her.

Cleo.

Her first reaction was to freeze, draw her dagger. But the Moonling hadn't spotted her. She was too far away.

As Isla watched Cleo slip through the night, her white cape pale as bone, her fear dimmed.

Celeste was right. She had sulked for too long.

Soon, she would be forced out of hiding anyway for Carmel, the twenty-four-hour-long celebration that took place on the seventy-fifth day. Attendance was mandatory, lest she wish to officially take herself out of the game.

She couldn't. Not with the state of her realm being what it was.

Isla would be forced to face Cleo there. Part of her wondered if that was when Oro and the Moonling planned on killing her—if they wanted to make it dramatic, in front of the attending islanders. Her heart hammered at the thought.

She wouldn't live any more days afraid. If her destiny was to die, she would face it head-on.

Sweat sticky on her forehead, Isla began to trail the Moonling ruler through the night.

Perhaps she would lead her right to the heart.

Cleo swept across the Mainland, white clothes shining through the night, illuminated by the spotlight that was the moon. The Moonling ruler basked in it, stopping for a moment to roll her shoulders back and lift her face to it. It was said that Moonling had become the strongest realm since the curses had been spun. Unlike Sunling or Nightshade, they could still access their power source. And, unlike Starling, many of their members were still ancient. Their curse, if anything, affected them the least. Thousands of Moonlings had died at the hands of the sea over the years, that was true, but the survivors hadn't been physically weakened.

Isla's stomach twisted. She didn't know how she hadn't thought of it before.

Cleo must have spun the curses. *That* was what Juniper had tried to tell her. *That* was why the Moonling killed him.

Had she created the curses and given her realm one to erase suspicion? A curse that wouldn't weaken her in the slightest?

She hadn't suffered at all. She was still as strong as ever.

If that was true . . .

Cleo wouldn't want the curses to be broken.

Did Oro know? Was that why they hadn't yet wielded the heart? Was Cleo making sure Oro never did?

Isla was breathing too quickly. Cleo was dangerous. Deadly. But she did not turn around and go back to the castle, to Grim or Celeste.

She followed Cleo to the Moon Isle bridge.

For the first time, there were no guards there. The Moonling ruler must have removed them after she and Oro had been paired. *Why?*

She didn't have time to wonder and took their absence as a positive sign.

Isla waited a few minutes for Cleo to disappear down the bridge.

Then she crossed it.

***

Cleo walked past her palace. Isla trailed her through the same forest she and Oro had visited two weeks before. Where was she going?

The Moonling's white dress floated gently above the foliage, not staining in the dirt or getting wet in the weaving streams. The water shifted its current in her direction as she passed—called to her, it seemed.

Isla's outfit kept away much of the cold. Her cheeks and nose stung, but her chest was warm. Her boots kept out the frost. Cleo walked easily, unbothered by the snow. Perhaps it invigorated her, the same way the moon did.

Without warning, Cleo stopped, and Isla stilled before diving back into the cover of the forest. The Moonling ruler had paused before a mountain, coated in ice like armor. Her arms raised overhead, fingers splaying—and she dropped them with the grace of a snowflake falling from the sky.

Instantly, the ice began to thaw, slipping down in sheets that hit the ground, then hardened again. Isla squinted through the darkness. What was Cleo doing?

She needed a closer view. Isla stepped forward, one foot out of the forest. She squinted as the ice continued to fall, revealing a hole, almost like a portal. Or a hidden passageway. Her eyes narrowed. Was this where she and Oro met? Was it where she was keeping the heart? Or something else entirely?

Isla took another step—and a loud screech pierced the air.

The dark-blue bird from before swooped through the trees, aimed right at her head. She ducked just in time, but it looped back around, snapping its beak wildly. It squawked loudly—an alarm, Isla realized too late. The bird was a spy for Cleo, alerting its master that she was being followed.

Isla dared a look up. The Moonling ruler had turned. They locked eyes.

In a flash of crystal blue, she was hurtled through the air by a thick sheet of water. Her breath was ripped from her chest. Cleo flung her against the side of the frost-coated mountain, and Isla cried out as her spine seemed to shatter. The pain was shocking, blinding, and she screamed again just as the water that had flung her back crackled into ice.

Cleo stepped forward, looking surprised.

"I have to admit," she said, "I'm impressed by your stupidity. A powerless ruler, following me onto my own isle?"

She was going to kill her. Just like she killed Juniper.

Isla tore against the ice—

But it might as well have been iron.

"Oh, as the night grows colder, the ice will only get stronger," Cleo purred. "Now tell me, Wildling, why have you followed me here?"

She had to be smart, keep Cleo talking as long as she could. And pray it would give her enough time to come up with a plan.

"I know," Isla said, her voice coming out deep and fractured. She took a shaking breath, the pain in her back like daggers through the gaps in her spine. "I know why you killed Juniper."

Cleo looked curious. She took a step closer to Isla. Her white hair glimmered in the moonlight as she shook her head. "You are a fool."

*Fool.* The word was an old friend, or maybe an enemy, waving hello. Though she had done foolish things, Isla was not a fool. "But a courageous one, showing up to the Centennial without abilities . . ." She raised an eyebrow. "And using the skin gloves to get into protected sections of our castles? Ingenious." She pursed her lips. "Let's see if you are clever enough to get yourself out of this mess."

The Moonling snapped her fingers, and the ice keeping her in place expanded. Thickened.

Anger warmed her core, though not enough to keep the frost from turning her numb. Her lips were two chips of ice when she whispered. "You're afraid," she said. "Because I know . . . I know you spun the curses." Isla raged against the ice, pounding over and over. But it was no use. "I know, and if a *fool* could figure it out, so can anyone else."

Cleo raised a hand, and the ice traveled from Isla's collarbones all the way up her neck, like a crystal choker. Isla gasped, every breath now frozen. "You don't know what you think you do, Wildling," she said. "But even if you did . . ." She smiled. "Corpses can't talk. And corpses can't break curses, can they?"

With that, Cleo smirked before disappearing into the icy hole.

Time ticked differently when you were dying, Isla realized. The seconds were miles long, and the minutes were endless howls of wind. It might have been hours, or only half a chime, but soon, Isla stopped feeling the pain in her back like a hundred knives. The ice had frozen it over, just like it had muted the limited heat that her outfit had provided.

She remembered the first time she had portaled to the Moonling realm. How she had hated it. The snow and ice and frozen everything had looked beautiful—but had felt like a bite. Mosquitoes, all over her body. She had only stayed minutes, which was long enough to watch the full moon swallow a ship whole.

Never did she think that something as simple and natural as the cold would be the thing that ended her. A curse or a blade to the heart, maybe. But never the cold.

First Isla was sad. Then she was afraid.

And then she was angry again.

Cleo was right . . . she was a fool. She had followed the Moonling ruler without a plan, so desperate to get answers. And the heart.

And revenge.

She took all the words to her mother back, calling them from the sky, roping her prayers down. If she had powers, she could maybe lift a finger and access the rock deep below the ice. Or a tree. Or call to an animal that would help her free.

*I do blame you,* she said in her head. *If I die, I blame you. What kind of Wildling falls in love, knowing the costs?* She wondered what her mother would look like now. An older version of herself, she supposed. Once a ruler had children, they began to age more properly, looking older and older the more their family line grew. Each family only had access to so much power. After the curses, the island and realms grew weaker. But in a way, some people, by losing their families, became stronger.

Isla had no family. And she was still weak.

Alone.

No . . . not alone.

Her necklace. Grim had told her to touch it any time she needed him. He could save her. Her hands were too far—she had no chance of breaking them free. But her chin—maybe she could touch it to the chain . . .

A sound from deep in her throat echoed against the surrounding mountains as she strained, the nerves at the base of her neck crying out in pain. She angled her head the farthest she could, head pounding.

But with the ice Cleo had trailed up her throat, it was not enough.

She collapsed, her head hitting the back of the mountain. She barely processed the ache. Even if somehow she could touch the necklace, Grim couldn't be out at night, she realized. He couldn't get to her until morning.

And by morning she would be dead.

## CHAPTER FORTY-THREE

# LIES

Hot breath puffed against her cheek. She heard splitting ice—someone was heaving a blade against it. Cutting through the frost to get her out like carving a statue.

Isla couldn't open her eyes. They had frozen over, like the rest of her. Her eyelashes had glued together. Though she could not see, she knew it was still night, for it had gotten colder.

Her lips tried to part, to thank whoever was setting her free. But they were sealed closed, knitted together by frost. Whoever they were, they banged their weapon hard against the ice, over and over, the vibrations going through her bones. They were going to strike her if they weren't careful.

"It's her, isn't it?" a voice said. It was wickedly deep—and amused.

Another voice. "Look at that face. Of course it is." She felt something sharp against her cheek. A blade? No, a nail. A long one. "We'll make a broth from her bones that will fill us with power. We'll burn her hair and inhale the smoke to make us beautiful again."

Isla stopped breathing.

The first voice said, "She's awake, isn't she? Do you think she can hear us?"

"I don't care. Where is Thrayer? This ice isn't breaking easily."

Something rustled nearby. Then, "I'm here. You found her like this?"

The first one squealed. "Trapped like a rat in honey."

"Good. Very good . . ."

The ice went warm, shifting into water. She slipped down the side of the mountain, landing at its base. Even though her body was freed, she couldn't move a muscle, even to reach her neck.

Someone gripped beneath her shoulders and hauled her up.

Who were they? Cannibals who would roast her on a spit and eat her charred flesh?

It was so cold, the promise of heat was almost welcomed.

Whoever they were, a Moonling was helping them. Someone had unfrozen the ice.

They carried her through the forest. And she could hear that ridiculous bird, the one that had announced her presence. *Cleo's* bird. Was she watching her, somehow? She imagined the Moonling ruler would take great pleasure in seeing her roasted alive.

"Shoot the bird. It's making my ears bleed."

She heard the familiar sound of an arrow hissing through the night. For a moment, there was silence.

Then more screeching.

"If you can't shoot a bloody bird, why should you get her heart?"

"I found her!"

"Perhaps I'll shoot *you* and keep her for myself."

The bird screeched and screeched, almost happily.

The forest went still.

She felt a current through the air, metal in her mouth.

One of her captors screamed, and the heat of flames roared past her face. The smell of stars shattering something nearby, blood splattering against her skin. The one holding her dropped her.

But before she landed on the ground, someone else's arms were around her.

And she was in the air.

She was metal being fashioned into a blade, filled with so much heat she screamed and wondered how she even had strength to make the sound.

"Just a little longer," someone said.

At the sound of that voice, she stilled—and kicked with all her might, moved any limbs that had been thawed.

A hand came over her eyes, warming them, and finally, she could open them.

Oro was standing above her, frowning.

"*You,*" she said through her teeth, her voice venomous. Her hands pleaded to choke him. To gut him, slice a blade right up his center, tear his heart out with her bare hands.

Was he here to kill her? Had he finally found the heart of Lightlark?

"Before you do whatever horrific thing I am sure you are imagining," he said, "let me speak."

She would have lunged at him without hearing another word if her body wasn't still so numb.

Oro sighed. "I did not betray you, Wildling." Isla opened her mouth, but he kept talking. "Though you believing so helped tremendously . . ."

"Helped what?" she growled. He was lying. She didn't trust a word that came out of his wicked mouth.

"One of the places where darkness meets light on Moon Isle was impossible to access without Cleo. It had been encased in a maze centuries before to keep others out. I needed her . . . so I changed the matches."

Isla's nails dug into the flesh of her palm. She could move her fingers now. Maybe, if she was quick enough, she could choke him. She attempted to get her hand up. But it barely got an inch off the bed.

*Bed.*

She looked around, wildly.

She wasn't in her room. She was in *his*.

The walls were plain, but the ceiling was solid gold. The floors were stone. All the windows were covered in heavy fabrics.

Oro took a step back from the bed, noting her gaze—and possibly her panic. "I brought you here after I found you. I figured you wouldn't want others to know what had happened."

None of it made sense.

Why had Oro saved her?

He claimed he hadn't betrayed her . . . that their plan was still on. That all his actions were in *service* of their quest to find the heart.

Lies. Too many to count.

*There are lies and liars all around . . .*

Oro continued. "She finally took me there tonight. That's how I found you. I was on Moon Isle, in the maze. The heart wasn't there, which is good, because I suspect Cleo would have tried to take it . . . But now we have just two places left to search."

*We*. There was no *we* anymore.

She shook her head. Tears fell down her cheeks, his betrayal still raw. "This isn't just about changing matches." Her voice broke. She hated it. "I trusted you. I— *You*. You told them. You—"

Oro closed his eyes for just a moment. "I know. I'm sorry. Truly. Cleo had become suspicious. She knew we had visited Moon Isle the day before, somehow." Isla thought of the bird. Her spy. It had spotted them. "The only way to convince her to help me was to discard you. Publicly. Your reaction and actions in the last few weeks had to be genuine."

That wasn't a good enough reason. She opened her mouth to tell him so, but he continued.

"And," he said, "my sources told me Cleo has become increasingly convinced that Starling must be the one to die."

*What?* Isla barely resisted the urge to shoot up in alarm.

"That makes no sense. She wants *me* dead."

Oro frowned. "Cleo would have killed you tonight if she wanted you gone."

"She nearly did," she said, exasperated. If Oro hadn't saved her, she would have been someone's meal. "Why would she choose Starling?"

"She believes Starling is the weakest of us. It is the smallest realm. The least developed in the last five hundred years due to their curse."

Isla's voice shook as she said, "You . . . you don't agree, do you?"

He shook his head. "No. Starling is essential. I told your secret not just to get Cleo to trust me but also to cast doubt on her decision. Before, when Cleo and Celeste were paired, she couldn't kill her. When I changed them—"

"She could have gone directly for Celeste," Isla finished.

Oro nodded. "Exactly."

Isla didn't think Cleo even cared about following the rules or winning the power promised. Not if she was the one who had spun the curses.

Though, if Oro was right, and sharing her secret had saved Celeste . . . she was grateful.

Everything he said sounded logical. If he was telling the truth, then everything he had done in the last two weeks was to keep her and their plan safe.

She shook her head. "I don't believe you."

"I have never lied to you, Isla." He took a step closer. "Even though you have lied to me repeatedly." Another step. "You told me your secret. Now let me tell you my flair. No one can lie to me." She remembered his words from the cave. "Because I know when people are lying."

*His flair.* Isla blinked.

She had lied to him too many times to count, throughout the Centennial. Throughout their time working together. And he had known, every time.

He narrowed his eyes at her. "All you did was lie to me, and I still told you about the heart. I told you everything, except for this. Because Cleo *loved* how betrayed you looked. It was why she was willing to finally take me anywhere on Moon Isle I wanted. She was *thrilled* that I exposed you and chose her as a partner instead. That I revealed such a critical secret." He stopped just a foot away. Her hands were still in fists, and she briefly considered how good it would feel to slap him across the face.

"You put me in danger," she said. "Cleo could have killed me!"

“I was never far from you,” he said. “I knew when you moved into the Place of Mirrors. I guarded its entrance. Had guards stationed nearby. How did you think Ella was able to get through unharmed? Wherever you went, I followed. And when I could not, I had guards monitoring Cleo so I could ensure she wasn’t anywhere near you.”

Isla laughed without humor. “And tonight?”

“Tonight, I went to meet her. You slipped through the cracks by trailing her. But I found you, didn’t I?” He shook his head. “Cleo is planning something. She has been forming a secret legion.” So, he *did* know about it. “The heart is on her isle. If she gets her hands on it before us, I’m afraid of what she will do.”

He was right. Isla was convinced Cleo had spun the curses. If Oro was correct about his theory, that meant she had used the heart before. What was keeping her from doing it again?

Oro’s gaze was relentless. “I trust you, Isla, though you have given me countless reasons not to. Are you going to trust me? For the sake of both of our people?”

*Our people.*

Isla never wanted to speak to the king again. But she didn’t have a plan. Celeste was still helplessly pursuing the bondbreaker.

And her people were dying.

“Your offer holds, then,” she said, every nerve ending in her body screaming at her not to trust him. To stab her blade through his back and let him see how it felt.

Oro nodded. “When we find the heart, you will wield it. You will receive the power promised.”

Isla would be a fool to trust him again after what he had done. But part of her hoped he wasn’t lying—that there was truly a chance to save her people, and herself.

She also couldn’t ignore the fact that Oro had saved her life. Again. It didn’t make any sense. If he was working against her, why wouldn’t he want her dead? It would fulfill part of the prophecy.

She released her hands from their fists, and the dagger she had swiped from a hidden pocket in her pants while he had been talking clattered to the ground. Oro eyed it on the floor, unsurprised.

"Fine." She pinned him with the coldest look she could manage. "You know now that I don't eat hearts," she said slowly. "But betray me again—earnestly or otherwise . . ." Isla bared her teeth at him. "And for you, I'll make an exception."

## CHAPTER FORTY-FOUR

# CARMEL

"Cleo spun the curses," Isla told Celeste the next morning. She told her friend everything: The attack. Her and the Moonling's conversation.

At that, Celeste had frowned. "To what end, though? If she did create them, she hasn't acted on it. It's not like she used the other realms' weaknesses to invade them. She's done nothing."

Isla had been thinking the same thing. "I don't know. Maybe she *has* done something and we just don't know it yet."

She also told her that the Moonling wanted Celeste dead. And her friend only shrugged. "I figure everyone here except for you does. I'll be more careful, of course. But I've never trusted her for a moment."

Finally, Isla told Celeste that Oro had saved her. And what he had claimed.

She had readied herself for Celeste's judgment, for her disappointment. But the Starling almost looked pleased. "This is good," she said.

"Good?"

Celeste nodded. "I told you, I've been looking for the hidden library. I'm positive it's in the Mainland castle. And he must know where it is. You can ask him. He told everyone your greatest secret—he would need to tell you. To earn your trust again."

Celeste's insistence on continuing to search for the bondbreaker made her want to scream, but Isla promised she would ask when the time was right, just to mollify her friend.

Since the ball, islanders had sequestered themselves on their isles. The lack of power being used on the Mainland had quickened its crumbling.

It was no time to celebrate. Isla and Oro needed to search Moon Isle's last few locations as soon as possible, before time ran out. Before Terra was nothing more than wood and vines.

But Oro was bound to the rules of the Centennial with his life. And Isla had to follow them if she wished to win.

On the seventy-fifth day, Carmel went on as planned.

A twenty-four-hour carnival meant to celebrate the last quarter of the Centennial, Carmel was a celebration of the realms for all islanders, not just nobles. Isla didn't think anyone would show up for the event, not with what had happened at the ball, but, sure enough, the day before the carnival, shops opened their doors once more. People started filling the streets.

Isla didn't need to attend the entire event—just some of it. She skipped the picnic in the morning. The festivities on the east side of the Mainland in the afternoon.

She wondered if Cleo would make an appearance, given her suspicion that the Moonling didn't care about the rules. If she *had* spun the curses, she would want to keep them intact . . . not break them.

The Moonling would also want to keep anyone else from breaking them too.

Isla waited in the castle all day, listening at her window for echoes of the festivities. Music played far away. Glasses clinked as the celebrations moved toward the castle, into its gardens.

If tonight hadn't been Carmel, she would be on Moon Isle, searching the final locations. Both of Terra's legs were underground now. Flowers bloomed from the crown of her head.

It wouldn't be long before the forest took her completely. It wouldn't be long before there was no forest left.

*One day of rest,* she told herself. Then she would find the heart and get everything she wanted.

"You look ridiculous," Celeste said.

It was just after dusk. The Starling had just returned from the festivities to call upon Isla. Isla had moved back into her room at the castle, at Oro's insistence, since they were working together again. He promised he would take precautions to keep her safe.

Guards heavily monitored their hall. The king himself checked on her throughout the day.

Celeste and Isla were both dressed in elaborate, gleaming representations of their realms. The Starling ruler was covered in crystals, from the top of her neck to her long gloves and down to the fabric that puddled at her feet. Her hair was spotted with tiny diamonds that looked like stars that had been coaxed down from the galaxy just for the day.

That night, Isla was a rose in bloom. A crown of flowers had been placed atop her own, bright red against her dark hair. Pink petals had been pressed against her neck and trailed onto a bodice split into three parts. They became more and more elaborate until her waist—cinched tightly by ribbons crisscrossed down her spine—before blossoming from her hips in giant sheets. Rows of petals, all knitted together, trailed all the way to the floor. Her cape was a train of roses that ran five feet behind her.

They couldn't walk into Carmel together. Oro likely knew of their friendship if he and his guards had been tracking her movements. But that wasn't particularly alarming. Of course the youngest rulers would become friends. Still, they didn't want anyone suspecting their alliance had predated the Centennial.

Celeste promised to be close by. And Isla only planned to stay a few minutes. Vendors lined the streets outside the castle, selling pickled porridge, elderberry scones, spun sugar that really did spin, and goblets and goblets of drink. Revelers from all daytime-dwelling realms roamed through the festivities, dressed in elaborate versions of their colors, their wariness fading with every second that passed without a disaster. Starlings wore glitter, Skylings wore hats that floated precariously above their heads in the breeze, and Moonlings wore white formal suits and dresses.

Everyone was staring at her. She imagined news of her powerlessness had spread. Though most of them had seen her at the duel. They had witnessed what she could do with a blade. She twirled one through her fingers, watching them back. Daring them to make a move.

Isla immediately noticed she was being followed. But not by Cleo.

Oro had arranged a guard of about half a dozen to trail her through the gardens. They were discreet, but Isla could feel their eyes on her.

Their protection made her bold. When a Starling carrying a tray of drink passed her by, she took one of the goblets.

She knew the odds of finding the heart and getting its power. This could very well be her last celebration. Her last chance to try wine.

Isla swallowed the drink.

It tasted like malted honey and burned its entire way down her throat.

The guards continued to trail her throughout the gardens. It only took a few moments before she began to feel weightless.

Wine couldn't be that strong, could it? Had it been some sort of celebratory drink that was more potent than usual?

Celeste would know. Nobles stared at her as she walked past, searching the crowd for her friend. She didn't see her anywhere. Perhaps she had left. Maybe she hadn't been able to find Isla and went searching for her in her room.

*Time to go,* she thought. She had been at Carmel long enough to satisfy the rules. And the drink's effects were firmly taking hold.

By the time she stepped up the stairs of the castle and into the halls, the world seemed to be stumbling. Or maybe that was her. She was *hot,* too hot, the ridiculous outfit sticking to her like molasses. She took off her flower crown and let it drop on the ground. She peeled off the petals that trailed down her neck, choked by them. The entire outfit was entirely too much. She undid her cape and let it fall behind her. Already, she felt so much better. *Freer.* Wilder.

Isla imagined the guards trailing her finding the bits of her dress and laughed.

All her worries had fizzled away like bubbles in champagne. She couldn't even think of one of her fears for more than a few seconds if she tried—they were slippery in her mind.

Isla smiled as she began picking the petals off her dress. "I bet a flower has never picked itself . . ." she said to absolutely no one. Then she laughed as she ripped the bottom layer off, stepping out of it with relief.

She turned around and found herself in a hallway she didn't recognize. Had she already passed her room? Had she been too busy ruining her ridiculous dress to notice? She shrugged and kept going, unraveling herself until the flower dress ended high above her knees, leaving behind a trail of petals. She walked until she reached a dead end. Isla frowned at the wall, then whipped around at the sound of a voice.

"Isla?"

She smiled far too wide, excitement flooding through her veins as quickly as the wine had. "Oro," she said, his supposed nonbetrayal feeling worlds away. All she remembered was she was supposed to be nice to him and hope he kept his promise. She walked over to the king, bare feet stepping over petals. She must have taken her shoes off at some point. Isla laughed at herself for what she was about to do, barely keeping it together enough to stand high on her toes and flick his crown.

He blinked at her. Then he frowned. "Are you all right?"

Isla rolled her eyes. "You're always so angry . . . *why?* Do you ever smile?" *Yes.* He had smiled at her, just once.

She was still on her toes, and the ground seemed to slip under her like a rug. Before she could fall back, Oro grabbed her elbow to steady her. He immediately dropped her arm.

Isla scowled at him. "I'm not *poisonous,*" she said, rolling her eyes again for good measure.

She turned and swayed down the hall to music that seemed to be playing through her bones.

"I'll take you to your room . . . if you would like?" he asked.

She shrugged. "Fine. I was going there . . . but the hallways changed." She looked at him for explanation, and he glanced at her like she had said something ridiculous. Isla blinked, not knowing what it could possibly be.

He suddenly looked alarmed. "Did you drink the haze?"

Isla nodded enthusiastically. Was that what the wine was called? She was humming something. No, she was singing. She opened her mouth, and her voice flooded the halls. She liked the way it echoed, and she sang louder.

She had never felt so alive . . . like her throat and arms and face were on fire and glowing, buzzing.

Why hadn't Poppy and Terra ever allowed her such pleasures?

She didn't realize she was partially speaking her thoughts aloud until Oro said, "Your guardians?"

Luckily, Oro was leading the way, because she hadn't processed any of the last hallways or turns. She nodded. "Did you have guardians?"

He was silent for a few moments before he said, "No, I didn't. I was never supposed to be ruler, or king. My brother was the one with guardians."

"So, what did you think you would be?" Words slipped off her tongue so easily, she wondered why it had ever felt hard to ask him anything.

"I led our armies."

Isla stopped in the hallway. She placed her hands on her hips. "*You* commanded the Lightlark armies?"

She expected him to glare at her, but he didn't. He just nodded. It made sense, though. That was why he had been so good at dueling. She started walking again, slower this time. He matched her pace. "That's why you hate him, isn't it?"

He seemed to know she meant Grim. While she had heard of the Nightshade's previous title, Terra hadn't ever told her about Oro. She wondered why. Did she even know herself? She supposed the Sunling king's reputation and history prior to the curses had been smothered by everything that had come after them. "We both lost many warriors," he said. "And I didn't agree with the way he fought." He didn't explain further, and then they were at her door. "Are you going to be all right?" he asked. Oro looked over his shoulder, verifying the guards had followed. They had and stood in their places against the wall, guarding the entrance to the hall.

Isla nodded. "I'll be fine." When he turned to go, however, she caught his wrist. "Wait. I still have so many questions. Will you come in?" Oro looked like that was the last thing he wanted to do, but Isla wasn't deterred. "I'll make tea," she added.

She entered. At her insistence, he followed. Oro warmed some water, and she found the pouch of Wildling spices and flowers that made her favorite drink, a tea she called yellow bee.

"Why yellow bee?" Oro asked before taking a sip. He seemed to like it.

Isla plopped down next to him on her couch and shrugged. "The plant that grows these flowers was always swarming with bees," she said. "I used to get at least three stings every time I tried to collect them for tea. But it was worth it."

Oro gave her a strange look.

"You haven't been sleeping well, have you?" she asked, leaning toward him, squinting at the purple beneath his eyes.

She expected him to ignore her question, like he had before, but he said, "No. I haven't for a long while."

"Why?" Her voice, surprisingly, was gentle. Not judgmental, the way it always had been with him.

Oro looked at her tree, its fruits ripe and swollen with juice and so heavy the branches dipped. "I have a lot of guilt," he said quietly. "That keeps me awake." *Guilt.* She knew the word intimately.

"How did you find me?" she asked suddenly. She remembered that night in shatters, like a broken, scattered mirror.

"In the hallway? I followed the trail of petals."

She shook her head. "No . . . before." *In the Moon Isle woods.*

The air cooled and stilled, and Isla hummed softly to its current. "I heard the bird," he said. "That's how I found you. I followed the bird."

*Stupid bird,* she thought. The same one that had almost gotten her killed. At least it had done some good.

She was suddenly tired, her energy unraveling as easily as her dress had. Her eyelids were heavy, and she smiled. She lay down on the couch, her head against his leg. The drink made her mind spin behind her eyes, and she groaned. "I have honey in my head," she said, because that was exactly what it felt like.

Oro laughed, and it was such a surprise that she wished her eyes would open to see if he really had.

Isla woke up warm. Wine still fogged her mind, but it was more of a mist than its previous storm. She remembered the celebration in pieces—Celeste coming for her. Noticing the guards. Drinking wine. Going to the castle. Ripping her costume off. Her eyes flew open.

Her head was in Oro's lap, her cheek against his leg. He was leaned back against the couch, exactly as she remembered him.

Except he was asleep.

She wondered what in the realms went into wine. And knew why Terra and Poppy had kept it from her. Isla remembered her conversation and shuddered—her questions had been so brazen. But Oro had answered them, hadn't he?

How long had they been asleep? She turned to the balcony. The curtains were closed, but no sunlight peeked through their slight gap. Night, then. Which meant a party was going on at that very moment, in the gardens below.

Oro looked more peaceful than she had ever seen him. It almost pained her to poke him in his chest. But he had to attend at least the last few hours of Carmel. He startled, a hand going up quickly in defense, almost reaching her throat. His eyes were wide for half a second when he saw her across from him in the darkness. Then he straightened and lowered his hand.

"You fell asleep," she said. "Thank—thank you for staying with me. I'm sorry, I think you missed part of the . . . party."

Oro's eyebrows came together a bit, and Isla wondered if he had forgotten about it. He did look better. The purple crescents beneath his eyes were fainter, the set of his jaw stronger.

Isla remembered the sound she had fallen asleep to—Oro, laughing. And not meanly, the way he always had. She had never heard him truly laugh before. As she looked at him, she wondered if she really had imagined it. He was frowning as he studied the room. As if he regretted having agreed to step inside it.

Isla rose. She didn't dare look down at her dress, which she knew was in shambles, ripped high up her thigh. Oro didn't look either as he stood.

"I should go to the celebration," he said gruffly.

Isla nodded. "You should." Without thinking, she reached up and fixed his crown, which had gone wayward while he was sleeping.

Her eyes met his when she was finished. And there was something like anger there. She fell back on her heels, surprised.

"Two more places on Moon Isle," he said flatly, unmoved by her expression. "Tomorrow, we'll go to one. The next day, the other. Then we're done."

"Good," she said curtly before turning to her balcony and slipping through the doors.

The night air was like a caress, rustling the remaining petals on her dress. Far below, she could hear the celebration—the clink of glasses and hiss of conversation and pluck of joyful music.

She was still on the balcony an hour later when pounding sounded against her door. Her eyes rolled, expecting Oro might have returned to check on her, on his way to bed. She opened it with a sigh.

And found Ella standing there, red in the face. That was when she noticed that the party she could hear from her balcony had gone quiet. The music had died.

"What's happened?" Isla asked, retrieving her dagger in a flash.

Ella didn't even wince at the weapon as she said, panting, "A ruler has been attacked."

"Which one?" she asked, roaring filling her ears, filling the world.

Ella's silver-gloved fingers shook at her sides. "Starling."

## CHAPTER FORTY-FIVE

# VANISHED

Isla moved through the castle like a storm. If she'd had power, it would be everywhere. She ran like she was running from something, wielded her dagger like she might throw it; her teeth chattered like the marble beneath her feet was ice.

Ella, a Starling, was alive. Which meant her ruler had to be too.

*Had* to be.

As she approached the screams and rushing islanders desperate to get out of the gardens, she remembered her mask.

She wasn't supposed to know Celeste, beyond the last few months.

She wasn't supposed to care so much.

Isla pinched her palm to keep from crying. Smoothing the worried lines across her face was like trying to move metal, but she did.

Still, when she entered the gardens, she was running.

She gasped. Stilled.

Celeste floated in the middle of a miniature maze, looking a lot like she was sleeping. Silver fog and string thin as spiderweb wrapped a thin veil around her.

The only other ruler there was Oro. He turned to her, face drawn. "This is old enchantment. I haven't seen it in a while. It's a poison."

*Cleo*. She had gone after Celeste. Just as Oro had suspected.

"How do we fix it?" Her voice was breathless.

Oro shook his head. "We can't. Only her body can mend itself. Moonling healing ability strengthens this poison." Isla's lips trembled. She watched Celeste like watching a corpse in a coffin.

During the last seventy-five days, she had begun to feel strong. So unlike the unsure, inexperienced Wildling girl who had stepped foot on the island.

Now she felt completely powerless again.

*No.* There had to be a way to heal her. She couldn't just not do anything.

"Whoever did this was interrupted," Oro said, studying the webbing around the Starling ruler. "It should have killed her immediately. That's the only good news."

Her hands were in fists. "When will she wake up?" Isla demanded. Her voice was too loud, too raw.

Oro eyed her. "If she does . . . it could be days. Weeks." The island might not last that long.

"It was her," Isla growled. "Cleo."

Oro didn't meet her gaze. "Perhaps."

"Perhaps?" Isla wanted to scream. She wanted to cry. But she did neither of those things and patiently waited for Oro to leave.

When Isla had almost been assassinated, Celeste had saved her. When she had almost been crushed by the ceiling at the ball, Celeste had been there. When Isla was reeling from Oro's supposed betrayal, Celeste had pulled her out of her gloom.

She had always been a good friend. The best friend.

And Isla had failed her. She had been full of drink and moody on her balcony when her friend had needed her most. She had left Celeste *alone* at the celebration, knowing the risks.

She felt the air change as Grim appeared, in the safety of the closest room to the gardens. Finally.

"I need you to do something for me," she said, her voice finally steady.

"Anything."

Isla took a breath that felt like there were leaks in her lungs.

"Whoever attacked her will come back to finish the job. I need you to make her disappear until she wakes up."

She was grateful when he didn't question her request. Grim simply nodded.

And a moment later, Celeste's body vanished.

## CHAPTER FORTY-SIX

# POISON

Everything changed in an instant. Now, Isla wasn't just fighting for herself, or Terra, or her people.

She was fighting for Celeste.

Tears streamed down her cheeks as she left the castle just past dawn. Isla had failed her friend in so many ways—and she had been blind to it until now. Seeing Terra slowly die should have reminded her that her friend would suffer the same fate if they weren't successful. Instead, she had quickly abandoned the plan they had spent years formulating, partly because it wouldn't benefit *her* realm. She hadn't thought enough about Celeste's.

She couldn't fix the past, but she could try to help Celeste now.

Oro claimed that she couldn't be healed by Moonling ability . . . but perhaps she could be by Wildling remedy.

Soon she was cutting through a path covered by wild grass. Through a forest that seemed determined to mark her skin a thousand times. Crossing a perilous bridge.

Until she saw herself reflected in the barren woods. Against the Place of Mirrors.

She had to open that vault. By any means necessary. There could be ancient Wildling remedies inside, plants that could draw Celeste's poison out. She hadn't seen any in the oasis Oro had taken her to so many weeks before, but perhaps they had been locked away here instead.

Isla knew the door wanted her to open it for a reason. Maybe this was it.

She walked steadily to the wall, not willing to leave without figuring out the lock. It was a strange, long shape. First she tried her fingers. Stuck them in painfully, shoving part of her palm inside to fill the gaps. But when she tried to twist her hand, all she did was scream out as her skin got caught in the metal. It took her nearly an hour to free herself, and by that time, she had cuts across her hand, dripping blood.

She did not give up. She searched every room of the enormous palace that had been her home for weeks. There were strange, curved weapons. Instruments she didn't know how to play. One, a thin wooden box with holes, she shoved into the lock so forcefully it broke. So, she spent a while trying to get the splinters out, cutting her fingers again in the process.

By noon, she was furious.

Vowing to return, she went back to the castle empty-handed.

Isla had wanted to kill Cleo for a long time. Especially after the assassination attempt at the harbor.

But now . . . seeing Celeste lifeless, floating like a specter, wrapped in webbing . . .

Now she wanted to kill Cleo and take a long time doing it.

Isla was thinking about all the ways she would make the Moonling ruler suffer as she stepped foot onto Moon Isle with Oro by her side.

*Two more places,* she told herself. Celeste couldn't play the game anymore. Isla would have to play for both of them—make sure she won and saved her friend's realm. It was all that mattered now.

Only two more places left to look.

Snow fell with the hurry of rain, soaking into the crown of her head and dripping in streaks down her cheeks. This time she had worn a thick cape over her long-sleeved shirt and pants to shield her from the cold. Still, it didn't do much, and she didn't veer far from Oro, who radiated heat like a sun that had slid down from the sky.

Soon they came upon a tower sticking out of a mountain of snow. Oro climbed through its only entrance, a window, and she followed him inside, down, then through a hall, until she realized they weren't in a tower at all.

They were in a palace.

It was abandoned but still ornate, built completely out of white marble. They had entered from its highest peak—the rest was buried in ice, trapped in the forever winter that was Moon Isle. She followed Oro down floor by floor until they reached the top of a grand staircase.

The wide steps led down to what must have been the main floor once upon a time.

Now it was completely underwater.

Somehow, the furniture remained tethered; everything in the room below looked perfectly in place. Just . . . submerged.

Oro began taking off his clothing.

Isla whirled to face him. "What are you doing?"

He glanced at her. "There are creatures in that water that won't be easy to face. I don't need to be weighed down or give them something to choke me with." His cape was now discarded on the ground. His shirt soon joined it.

Isla stared, though everything in her mind told her not to. Oro looked remarkably like the marble statues on Moon Isle, his chest and arms muscled like a warrior, toned as sharply as a blade.

More than half of him had now been overcome by the bluish gray. He was part gold, part ice sculpture. She studied him, wondering if it hurt to lose one's powers, to die slowly, inch by inch.

She looked for other reasons too.

Oro stared back at her, surprised. "I'm sure you've seen plenty of bodies before," he said flatly.

Isla bristled. He hadn't said it meanly, more matter-of-factly, and she supposed she couldn't blame his assumption. A *true* Wildling, even a powerless one, would have seen countless naked bodies. They were famed for their romantic conquests.

A fact—nothing more.

Isla swallowed. "Of course I have," she said a bit too quickly.

Oro raised an eyebrow, sensing her lack of curse wasn't the only thing that distinguished her from her people.

He took a step forward, still shirtless. Tilted his golden head at her. "Tell me, Wildling . . . how *many* people have you been with?"

Isla's face flushed. She barely resisted the urge to slap him. "What kind of question is that?" she demanded. In her realm, love was forbidden. But intimacy was not shied away from. It was *celebrated*.

He seemed to know it, and his expression became even more surprised. "A curious one." He shrugged. "I've been with many women. It's not something I deny."

Isla sneered at him. "Well, that must have been a long time ago, judging by how uptight and insufferable you are."

The sides of Oro's mouth twitched. Amused. "That might be so. But you didn't answer my question."

"And I won't," she said, glaring at him. He grinned. Was he laughing at her?

For some reason, she was compelled to prove him wrong. To wipe the smirk off his wretched face. Without breaking Oro's gaze, she unbuttoned her cape and let it fall to the floor. She slipped off her oversize shirt and pants until she was only in the clothes she wore beneath, over her underclothes. A tiny tank top that reached just above her navel and a pair of high-waisted, tight shorts that ended high on her thigh.

She wasn't in her underwear, but only wearing scraps of fabric, she felt bare in front of him.

Oro stood very still.

She shrugged, trying her best to look carefree. "It's just skin," she said, her voice slightly breathless.

"Just skin," he repeated, his mouth barely moving.

She walked past him, down the steps of the stairs. Until her feet splashed. Until the water reached her knees. She heard him slip off his shoes, then socks, then pants. She shivered, the cold biting every inch of exposed skin.

A moment later he was by her side, just in undershorts. This time, she looked away. A bit reluctantly.

"Water lilies grow here," he said, not looking at her either. "The ones you pointed out in the mountain." Isla remembered that day, which seemed realms away. "You said something like the heart might attach to their roots, correct?"

He glanced at her, and she simply nodded.

"These waters house ancient, vicious creatures," he said. "Be on guard."

The water rippled as he dived into it. Isla took a deep breath and followed him. He swam quickly, out of the main hall and into the corridor. She stayed near the stairs. The ceiling was fifty feet tall, and she was at the top of it, diving down toward a room that looked nearly perfect except for a painting that had slices through it, ribbons of what had been a landscape curling in the water.

Her gaze traced the edges of the floor, beneath the furniture. No sign of any plant. She turned, to try a different room, and almost swallowed a mouthful of water in shock.

A face, lovely and vicious as a nightmare, floated before her.

Half of the girl's face was scaled; half of her hair had the transparent silkiness of a koi fish's tail. Her arms and legs were scaled too, creating the effect of submerged silk around her limbs.

Mesmerizing.

Isla squinted. Her mind had suddenly become just as murky as the water. She was there for something . . . but she couldn't quite remember what that was.

The girl smiled and reached out a scale-covered hand with nails sharp as knives. *To help,* Isla realized.

She didn't know why . . . but she took it.

And the girl led her deep below. Through a bedroom, into a hall. Isla saw the water lilies then, sunken, their roots like braids that went down for yards. Something about them seemed important, but she didn't know what.

Luckily, she had the girl to lead her. Lead her *where,* though? she wondered.

Something drummed in her ears, an echoing or roaring, as her chest contracted. The pain was muted, as far away as the surface. But the beating continued. Beating like . . .

*The heart.* That was what they were there for, Isla remembered now.

She stopped following, and the girl whipped around. Pulled at her arm.

Isla shook her head, the movement making her dizzy. Her eyes had started to close. She needed something . . . air, maybe.

The girl was insistent. She yanked her arm, dragging Isla along.

Something wasn't right. Isla slipped out of the girl's grip.

The creature didn't like that. She whirled around and sliced across Isla's middle with her razor-sharp nails.

Clouds of crimson stained the water like blotches of ink.

Isla began swimming out of the room again, not knowing anything, but knowing she needed to get away. She made it through the door, back through the bedroom, until she could see the stairs. But the steps were too far, and her legs had gone stiff.

She wasn't here alone though, she realized, the fog in her mind thinning. She could call to him—

Something pulled her foot so sharply she gasped, swallowing water, and sank again.

It was fire in her throat, burning her lungs, the salt water straight from the sea. She jerked, her organs pleading for air, for relief, just as she turned to look at her feet, at the girl who had claimed her once more.

She grabbed the dagger she had hidden in the middle of her chest, tucked into her underclothes—dropped it. Her free foot caught the blade with her toes.

And she stabbed the dark figure right in the eye.

It hissed, disappearing far below in a flash.

She was at the top of the stone stairs in an instant, coughing up the water from her lungs.

In the air, her head cleared completely.

What happened? she wondered. Why had she followed the girl like a fool?

"That was a night creature," Oro said somewhere close by. His voice was tight. "They can invade your mind. Shut it down completely."

He knelt beside her, and she wondered why until she screamed out, her pain rushing at her in full force. There was a long gash along her side where the girl had cut her.

Oro made a gentle, calming sound that seemed totally at odds with his hulking presence. He towered over her even on his knees.

She shivered on the cold stone floor, and he placed a hand against her bare stomach. At once, heat flooded her core, followed by a sting—he was healing her. Oro made the calming sound once more when she flinched, and Isla looked at him, really looked at him, grimacing as her skin knitted itself back together. He stared back.

Something about his proximity, maybe, or his hands on her—or the blood she had lost, more likely—made her feel a little dizzy.

Isla groaned again, the healing like electricity against her skin. He flinched as her hand came over his own, both pressed against her wound. It was hot as a coal beneath her fingers, and enormous, spanning almost fully across her stomach. Before long, it moved.

She watched his knuckles trail down her ribs, healing the very edges of the wound.

"Finished," he said, just as Isla braced herself for another sting.

Isla blinked at him. She had been panting, the salt in her wound like flames against her skin. Now, her breathing settled.

Oro slowly removed his hands from her bare skin. As soon as he did, she shivered, the cold rushing back.

At that, he touched her again, this time against her knee.

She straightened, willing her strange thoughts away, remembering why they were in the wretched palace in the first place. "Did you find it?" she asked.

Oro's gaze darkened. "No," he said. "It wasn't there."

She closed her eyes, disappointment hurting almost as much as her wound had. She was Celeste's and her people's only hope. She couldn't fail, not again. When she opened them, she forced herself to look more confident than she felt. "It can only be in one place, then, right?"

"Yes. But that place is one I had hoped to avoid."

"Why?"

"It's right at the center of Vinderland territory," he said.

Her face scrunched in confusion.

"The group that tried to kill you."

*Oh.*

"Who were they?" she asked. She hadn't seen them, but their voices . . . what they had wanted to do to her . . .

Oro blinked. "I thought you knew."

*Knew what?*

"They were Wildlings."

*What?* Her face twisted. "There aren't any left on the island, and they were *men*—"

"There aren't any left. They *were* Wildlings. Their group left your realm long before even the curses. They had already renounced their power, so their kind wasn't affected."

So, they ate hearts and flesh out of desire . . . not because of a curse. She shuddered. There was so much about the Wildlings she didn't know.

Why had the group left their realm in the first place?

"I can go alone," Oro said. Unlike every time he had said similar words before, there was no mean edge to his voice. "If you would prefer not to take the risk."

But she had made it this far. If she was going to win, if she was going to save the people she loved most, she needed to be there when they found the heart. "I'm coming," she said.

That same night, Oro took her to a place she never would have expected to be invited to—the castle's ancient store of weaponry. She grabbed too many things—arrows, bows, knives, throwing stars, swords. Celeste and Terra were on her mind—the strongest people she knew.

She left the vault ready for the next day.

Ready to take on the former Wildlings who had almost picked her apart.

## CHAPTER FORTY-SEVEN

# BLOOM

As soon as they stepped foot on Moon Isle the next night, the dark-blue bird found them. It harped loudly, and Isla pointed her arrow at it. "Make another sound and you're stew," she said, wondering if she was speaking directly to the ruler of Moonling herself. She should shoot Cleo's bird right in the chest for what she had done to Celeste.

It squawked once more, then flew away, far from the sharp tip of her arrow.

"On edge?" Oro asked. He didn't have any weapons on him. And Isla supposed that was strategic. The ex-Wildlings couldn't know the king of Lightlark considered them a threat.

Most of all, it was a message to Cleo. Wherever she was on Moon Isle, whether or not she was using the dark-blue bird as her spy, she would know they were on her land again. Oro entering her isle so many times unarmed sent the greatest message of all.

The Centennial was a game. And Oro was still its most powerful player.

Isla tried not to think of the white-haired ruler as they made their way across the snow to the final location. Instead, she thought of the heart.

Would it bloom as beautiful as a primrose?

Would it be as cold as the heart of the king of Lightlark?

So close.

They were so very close.

She turned to Oro and found him watching her. His expression was resolute, hard as the slabs of ice at their sides. He nodded once, as if able to read her thoughts.

*One more place. Then it's all over.*

Vinderland territory sat far beyond the reaches of Cleo's snow kingdom. At its northeast corner sat a stretch of land so treacherously cold it was almost uninhabitable. Isla relied on the warmth blooming from Oro like a shield. He extended it so that it engulfed her fully, and she barely felt the frost on her nose.

Ice, sharp like teeth, stuck out from the ground at an angle, a cluster of swords. Isla held the hilt of hers tightly, eyes alert. Studying everything. They entered a forest of dead trees, skeletons covered in snow.

They came in a wave.

One moment there was silence. The next, the night split apart in screams as bodies leaped from trees, right into their path. Others had been hidden behind trunks, and they showed themselves now, arrows pointed at their necks.

But Isla was ready.

She smiled, just a little. And unleashed.

Three of her arrows flew at once, each finding their targets. Bodies fell from the high branches. She ducked, barely missing a flying blade, then turned, her sword now in her fist. She gutted the man in front of her who had a dagger to her heart, turned and did the same to a towering woman who had a rusty hatchet aimed at her temple.

Throwing stars from her pocket flew from her other hand, into the neck of a man half a moment away from burying his blade in Oro's back. They landed in a perfect line across his throat like a macabre necklace.

Oro's fire hissed and roared as he took out five people at once, their metal weapons dropping into the snow with barely a sound. He froze one against a tree. Another, he sent hurtling back with a burst of Starling energy.

Isla whipped around, fast as a twirling top, her blade finding flesh and slicing through it as easily as Wildling teeth sinking into a heart's soft tissue. Her metal clinked against other metal before she hit the weapon away and cut down the one who wielded it. She did the same to another. And another.

With a grunt, she was knocked onto her back. The ground was coated in ice, and she gasped but felt no relief, her lungs turned to stone.

A man towered over her. His teeth were sharp as blades—cut into weapons. Tools to eat with, she realized.

He reached a hand toward her neck. To break it. To make a clean kill so that the flesh would be unmarred by injury, suitable to feast upon.

Isla watched, frozen. She lifted a shaking hand from the ground, gasping, willing her body to get over the shock of the impact—

And a blade went right through the man's chest. He made a gurgling sound, then choked on his own blood before falling over onto the snow.

Oro stood there, holding a sword.

But he hadn't been armed . . . or so she had thought. She watched in wonder as the silver sword disappeared in a burst of sparks. He had *created* it from Starling energy. She hadn't known a thing like that could be done.

When her breath returned, she stood, looking around at bodies that never would again.

Dead. They were all dead.

"There are more," Oro said quickly. "Who will come to investigate. Let's go."

Isla took his hand, still gasping at air. He heated her through their touch, and they ran, Oro pulling her so quickly he was nearly flying, only stopping the moment it came into view.

A tree of white feathers, blooming from the ice.

Of course. The perfect host for the heart. A secluded tree, frozen in time. It could be hidden in its feathers or even among its roots.

She stepped forward. Once. Twice. Then she ran.

Finally. After everything . . .

There it was. Their salvation. Her chance at being the ruler and friend the people she loved deserved.

She heard Oro right behind her. His heat grew, relieved that it was all over. The months of searching.

The centuries of suffering.

Isla reached the tree and began searching its branches. The feathers were soft as snow. They danced quietly in the wind, rustling together, tiny bits of feather falling.

When she didn't find anything in its brush, she looked down at the roots. The ice allowed her to see their every inch, thick and twisted into braids.

"Isla."

She studied the tree again. And again.

"It has to be here," she said, hands going through the feathers furiously now. Desperately.

She fell roughly to her knees to get a closer look below, biting down the pangs of pain that nearly blinded her vision. She pressed her hands against the ice and searched closer, studied every knot.

But there was nothing intertwined in its roots.

"It's not here," Oro said. His voice was as hollow as his eyes had looked that first night at dinner.

They had been wrong.

Or they had been right, and Cleo had gotten there first. Perhaps Cleo had sent her bird to mock them when they had first stepped on the isle.

Isla stilled. If Cleo had the heart . . .

She heard Celeste's warnings and doubts—the ones she had ignored—echo through her mind as she pressed her head to the ice and cried.

## CHAPTER FORTY-EIGHT

# HIDDEN

Twenty days of the Centennial remained. And Isla didn't think the island would make it ten.

Terra wouldn't make it five.

After all Oro and Isla's searching across the island for the heart, they had failed.

Isla had made countless mistakes in the last eighty days. She had trusted the wrong people. She had made the wrong plans. She had followed the wrong leads. She had blindly chased power when she should have done everything to protect the people who loved her.

But she refused to give up. Not this time. Not when Celeste would have demanded she didn't.

Isla banged on Oro's door three days after their last journey to Moon Isle, her knuckles still raw from the cold of the Vinderland expanse, even after she had repeatedly smeared Wildling elixir over the broken skin.

At the feathered tree, Isla had seen the light go out of his eyes—she had watched him fold back into himself, ready to become the same king she had met that first night. More closed off and guarded than his own cursed island. When the heart hadn't been where it was supposed to be, part of him had vanished, the same way Lightlark would if they failed. This time, perhaps forever.

Oro opened the door just as her fist was coming down in its wide swoop. He caught her arm before it could crash into his chest. He held her wrist and looked down at her, confused.

Isla pushed past him into his room, and he let her.

"This isn't over," she said, nostrils flaring and voice cracking in half as if she was still trying to convince herself of the fact.

Oro stared at her. He said nothing.

She took a step toward him. "I refuse," she said, shaking her head. "I refuse to believe this is how it ends." She jabbed a finger in his chest. "You are the king of Lightlark, the most powerful person in all of the realms." He raised an eyebrow, seeming surprised that she was speaking about him in any manner that didn't include the words *wretched* and *insufferable.* "There has to be another way. Another ending."

Her finger was still against his chest, and he looked down at it before looking at her. "What do you suggest?" he asked.

Such a simple question . . . but one he had never asked.

Even in her search for the bondbreaker, she had been following Celeste's plan.

For the first time, Isla made her very own.

"We start from the beginning," she said firmly, turning, taking in his room. "From the most basic truth, the root of all of this." She bit her lip, thinking. Thinking about the first thing he had told her, the basis for their entire search. A question she had asked before, that he hadn't answered. She turned to him. "How *did* you find out about the heart?"

He frowned. "I read about it."

"Where?"

"In a book."

"What book?"

"An old one. One I found in a hidden library."

The world went quiet. All of Isla's senses began to fade.

*Hidden library.* Just like Celeste had said.

Why hadn't she listened to her friend?

She tried her best to mask her surprise, her knee-wobbling relief, and her crushing guilt as she said, very quietly, "What library?"

Oro did not hesitate as he walked across the room and opened the door of his balcony. He pulled the door all the way back until it pressed against his room's largest wall and turned the handle again—this time, pushing forward, against the solid stone.

It opened.

Isla followed him into a room tall as a tower, wide as the king's chambers. Filled to the brim with books and enchanted objects.

A library.

Isla barely breathed, barely moved, hoping her treacherous heart, beating far too loudly in her chest, wouldn't give her away. All she saw were books. The bondbreaker must have been well hidden. Not that it mattered now.

Celeste was on the brink of death. Isla couldn't use it with her in that state. And, even if she could, the bondbreaker wouldn't save Terra. Only an excess of power would. Only the power promised to the person who broke all the curses would.

Oro walked to one of the shelves assuredly, as if he had done so countless times before. He plucked a book from the rest and opened it.

Markings had been etched across the page in swirling ink, an ancient language she didn't understand.

"You can read this?" Isla asked.

Oro nodded.

"Read everything," she said. "Everything about the heart. Please."

He agreed. But instead of looking down at the page, he looked at her. "Before I do, there's something you should know, Wildling." He was serious, no amusement or meanness in his expression.

Her stomach sank on instinct. Ready to be disappointed.

"I would have informed you at the beginning. But after what Grim told you . . . I was waiting for him to reveal the information himself." She swallowed. Tell her what? What could be so important? "I'm guessing he never did."

Isla just stared at him. Waiting.

"My ancestor, Horus Rey, and Grim's, Cronan Malvere, created the island."

She nodded. She knew that.

"And so did yours."

She blinked. No. That wasn't true. Isla placed a hand against the table just to feel something steady. Wildlings weren't even really accepted on the island anymore . . . they didn't help *create* it. "That doesn't make any sense."

"Lark Crown. She made the land we stand upon. The island was named after her."

*Lark Crown.* She didn't know that name.

"You're lying. If that was true, everyone would know it. It wouldn't be a secret."

Oro's eyes darkened. "I've never lied to you," he said. "And it wasn't a secret, not for a long while. Until, like much of our knowledge, it was lost to time. Thousands of years went by. Sunlings ruled for so long, *who* created the island was forgotten. But not by everyone."

He was serious. And Isla knew he had nothing to gain from a lie like this.

If it was true, why hadn't Grim told her when they had discussed the creation of the island? She remembered what Oro had said after she had called Grim the most forthcoming ruler.

*Not as forthcoming as you think.*

Her lips pressed together. No, it was not a lie. Now she understood why Oro had wanted to make a deal with her. Why he hadn't yet truly betrayed her.

"That's why you needed me," she said, her voice very tight. "To find the heart."

Oro's expression did not change as he nodded. "It can only be found and unlocked by one of us. Sunling, Wildling, or Nightshade. I assumed . . . with both of us . . ."

*Only joined can the curses be undone.*

He was simply following the prophecy. An inexplicable part of her shriveled inside.

All Oro's words had edges, and they cut into her mind. Oro had confirmed, weeks before, that he believed the *original offense* was someone using the heart of Lightlark to cast the curses. He now claimed only a Sunling, Wildling, or Nightshade could access the heart's powers.

Which meant one of *their* realms had spun them.

Not Cleo. That didn't make any sense . . .

Had Isla's ancestor used the heart to cast the curses? Or Oro's brother, King Egan?

Or Grim's late father?

No. It had to be Cleo.

Isla looked carefully at the book, though she could feel his eyes on her. Studying her reaction to this new information.

"What does the book say?" she asked through her teeth, willing her mind still. Willing herself not to give away a single thing.

Finally, Oro's eyes left her face. And he began to read.

Two chimes later, Isla and Oro sat hunched over in the library, countless books and frustrated silence spread between them.

The book's details had been scarce. It spoke of a heart containing pure, unfiltered Sunling, Wildling, and Nightshade ability. Energy greater than their own, the type of power that had only existed thousands of years before.

*The heart is hidden until it blooms and becomes a part of Lightlark when it is needed most.* That was the translation Oro had offered her.

By the time Isla stood again, her legs had cramped, and she was surprised to see light shining through the very bottom of Oro's curtains. They had spent hours reading and weren't any closer to the heart than before.

But Isla hadn't lost hope.

In fact, she was more hopeful than she had been in a while.

"This is the key to finding it," she told him, motioning to the books. "I know it is." Oro offered a nod, but his eyes were more tired than ever.

Purple rings and creased edges. When Isla had suggested they rest for a bit before meeting again, he had only refused once. Then, thankfully, he had relented.

Isla walked the halls, quiet as a specter, the castle opening up and dawn's reddish fingers peeking through long, uncovered windows. She was far from Oro's quarters. Far from her own.

Celeste appeared as soon as Isla walked into the room where Grim had hidden her. She looked exactly like she had every night that Isla had visited. Still as a statue. Floating peacefully.

Tears stung the corners of her eyes. From the beginning, Celeste had been intent on finding the bondbreaker—a plan to break their curses without killing another ruler. Without needing anyone else except for each other.

For so many weeks, Isla had hunted for it.

Though Celeste couldn't hear her, Isla's voice shook as she finally said, "You were right, Cel. About the hidden library."

She grabbed her friend's hands, knowing how excited she would be if she was awake. And that was when Isla noticed one of them was curled into a fist. As if she had been fighting, right before the poison had made her go still.

*Not fighting,* Isla thought, as she carefully pulled her friend's fingers back.

Sending a message. To Isla.

There was something in Celeste's fist, something she had managed to grab, to tell Isla who had done this to her. A clue. She finally fully pulled her friend's pale hand open.

And the diamond ring she had given Azul fell to the floor.

## CHAPTER FORTY-NINE

# DIAMOND

Azul had poisoned Celeste. He wasn't the jovial, haunted ruler who had charmed Isla with his music. He was a calculating ruler with a plan.

She remembered the conversation she had overheard, so many weeks before. Oro had been fighting with Azul over a strategy to end one of the realms. The king had assured Isla she was safe. She had assumed Azul had meant to destroy the Moonling realm.

Now she realized he must have been talking about Starling. Celeste. Worse—Isla hadn't even told her friend about the overheard conversation. After her best friend had been paired with the Skyling, she should have at least warned her *then,* but she had been too focused on Oro's betrayal. On herself—always herself.

How had she not considered the possibility that Azul might be targeting Starling?

But why?

What was his plan?

So many questions, pieces that didn't make sense. Every time she thought she knew something for certain, the truth shifted and scattered. But not for long.

Isla remembered what the oracle had said.

*You . . . have many questions. There are so many things I could tell you . . . though I should not.*

*All will be revealed soon enough.*

Isla stood in the Place of Mirrors, spine straight. Dead leaves blew lazily at her feet, wind peeking in from a fracture in the glass. She faced the grand staircase that led to rooms that once were full and now sat empty, cobwebs and cracked mirrors instead of laughter and music.

She could almost hear them, their voices just as honeyed as her own, as she reached up to her neck to the giant black diamond that sat against her throat and pulled.

A minute ticked by. His power didn't work in the Place of Mirrors. He would have to appear at the edge of its forest on Wild Isle and get to her on foot.

The door slammed open so hard it seemed close to shattering, and she whirled around to see Grim, running, frantic.

His eyes were wide—filled with fear. His breath was wild. There was a sword by his side.

He was in front of her in an instant.

"Heart—are you hurt?" His giant hands cupped both sides of her face, thumbs at the corners of her lips, studying her for any damage. He looked down at her as if she was made not of blood and bone but of ice and mist, a moment from vanishing . . . panting from the run . . .

"I'm fine."

Noting her tone, he dropped his hands.

No need to skirt around the reason she had called him here. "Why didn't you tell me that Wildling created the island with Sunling and Nightshade?"

His expression did not change. Not the way she had thought it might. For a moment, all he did was study her.

Finally, Grim said, "Some things are better uncovered ourselves." His gaze was steady. "There are many things others told me that I would have preferred to have learned on my own. In time. When I could understand it all better . . ." *What things?* she wanted to ask. But she stayed focused.

"Were you ever going to tell me?"

“In time, of course. I brought you here . . . answered your questions . . . but I didn’t want to force everything onto you at once.” He shook his head. “You had just arrived somewhere new. Not knowing much. Forced to carry the burden of the curses, to represent your entire realm. Powerless. You were terrified. I couldn’t make it worse. I didn’t want to.”

Isla shouldn’t have been shocked he had been able to sense her terror throughout the Centennial. Her confusion. Still. That was no excuse.

“Is there anything else you’re hiding from me?” she demanded. She couldn’t trust anyone. Azul had poisoned Celeste. Cleo had tried to kill her on multiple occasions. Isla remembered the oracle’s warning.

*There are lies and liars all around you, Isla Crown.*

Was Grim one of them?

His eyes flashed with something. She knew him well enough now to recognize it.

She took a step back. “There is, isn’t there?”

Grim tensed. Nodded.

“What is it?” Part of her was angry. The other half was scared. And he felt all of it.

Grim took a step closer. She stepped back and almost lost her footing. “There are a *few* things I haven’t told you,” he said. “Not explicitly.” Another step.

*Just say it,* Isla thought. She couldn’t take another moment of wondering.

He frowned. It was an unfamiliar expression on his face. He frowned at other people, a *lot,* but never at her. With her, he always grinned. “I haven’t told you what you do to me.”

She blinked. “What?”

“I haven’t told you that you’ve ruined me.”

“Ruined?”

He nodded. “*Ruined.* Tortured. You haven’t stopped tormenting me since the first moment I saw you.”

Isla opened her mouth. Closed it. Considered apologizing, even.

Grim continued. "A few conversations with you, and I was ready to make the most disadvantageous trade—all of me in exchange for any part of you you'd be willing to spare." He shook his head. "You have invaded my mind. I have questioned my sanity. I think about you all the time."

The way he said *all the time* had her cheeks burning with its insinuations. "All the time?" she repeated, voice breathless.

"Late at night, I ache for you. I ache for you *all the time,*" he said, face truly looking tortured. As if he had waited a long while to say those words. As if she had been a curse worse than all others.

Then he kissed her.

She gasped, just a little, and he pulled away. *No.* Before he could get far, she pressed herself against him, arms around his neck. She tilted her head back to meet his gaze. All anger was gone, replaced with emotions that made Grim's eyes darken.

Before he could grin, she pressed her lips to his. He was cold as stone, and she became even colder as he pinned her against the glass. Their kiss deepened, mouths opening, heat burning its way down her center. Her head fell back, and he kissed the length of her neck, teeth just slightly grazing her throat, below where her necklace sat.

He moved her cape aside and ran his lips along her bare shoulder. She made a sound, the cold making her skin prickle, and his hands gripped her waist, pressed her harder against the wall. She reached up to unbutton his cape, and it fell soundlessly to the floor.

His eyes snapped to hers. But she was already pulling at his shirt. He let her take it off in one quick movement. Then she paused. And stared at him.

Built for war. Toned completely. A ruthless warrior towering over her. A large scar marred the center of his chest. It sat inches from his heart. She pressed her hand against it, and he watched her movement, his breathing a bit unsteady, as if he was trying very hard to stand still.

"What is this from?" Her pulse was already racing. So was his.

Grim shivered as she traced the scar's jagged mark. "Just someone trying to kill me." He placed his hand over hers. "Hearteater," he said, the ghost of a smile on his lips. *The name was back*. "Right now, *you're* killing me." His voice was deep as the dreams she'd had the last few weeks. The ones he had sent her. The ones she now wanted to make real.

She took his crown between her fingers. Let it drop to the ground with a loud clatter. She did the same to her own.

The ruler of darkness and the ruler of the wild, both breathing a little too quickly. She stepped over her crown, to him, and he took her into his arms. This time, his kiss was desperate, like the sun was setting and they only had a few more minutes left, like the glass room was just a moment from being blown to pieces. He held her tightly, as if afraid she might just float away, a bird uncaged.

Her legs locked around his center, and she could *feel* him—every inch of him against her, even through the fabric of their clothes. *I haven't told you what you do to me*. His words echoed through her mind as she found their meaning. *I ache for you* all the time. He was aching for her now. She moved herself against him slowly, and a low growl escaped his lips. With a burst of unchecked desire, he gripped her by the backs of her thighs, fingers digging sharply into her skin, and ground himself even closer. Her eyes fluttered closed at the friction, her head falling back. He leaned her against the glass as his hands went to the front of her dress, making quick work of the ties and straps. Before she knew it, the fabric was gone, and Grim's mouth was on her chest.

The world could fall to pieces, and she wouldn't notice. Her sole focus was on the path of his tongue and teeth. She was burning for him, for his taste, his touch, the way he made her skin feel like a path lightning had struck.

"More," she said, or moaned, she didn't know, all she knew was that she wanted every single thing he had to offer her. "*Please.*"

He held her close to him, and she gripped his arms, bit down against his shoulder to keep from making more sounds as he lifted her higher and his hand finally reached right where she wanted it. Over fabric. Then, under it. Isla groaned at the first press of his calloused fingers against her, and they quickly began to wander slowly, steadily.

*More.* He gave it to her, and she gasped against his mouth as he used them to explore her deeper. Deeper. Need overpowered everything else, and Grim cursed as she started to move against his hand. "That's it." His voice was barely above a growl, coaxing and strained, as if he was enjoying this just as much as she was.

Before she could wonder what she might do next, he angled her head back up at him and said, "Look at me, heart. I want to watch you come undone."

She dug her nails into the back of his neck. Their foreheads pressed together, and she had never felt more alive, more bare, than she did in that moment, having him watch as endless sensations overcame her. Grim looked her right in the eyes as every feeling intensified, saturated, more than she had ever thought possible.

And something about it all was so familiar, like falling asleep, or humming to the rain, or breathing. Like she had already done it all a thousand times in her dreams.

## CHAPTER FIFTY

# SLEEPLESS

Isla did not sleep. She spent her days and nights in the library, and they slipped away as easily as the rain racing down the hundred windows of the Place of Mirrors, during the storm that had locked her and Grim in the glass box for hours.

As she flipped the pages, she felt the memory of his hands against her skin, his lips against her shoulder. They hadn't done everything she had wanted to in the moment, and part of her was relieved that instead of making any move to remove his clothes, he had pulled her into his lap on the floor. That they had watched the rain instead, her head against his chest. His chin resting where her crown should have been. Before they left, she had made him promise to find Azul, wherever he was hiding. And bring him to her.

Oro watched her like he could sense the places Grim had touched. She knew he must have noted her daydream eyes. But he hadn't said a word. Part of her didn't want him to know. To suspect.

Isla dug her nails into her palm, forcing herself to focus. Breaking the curses and winning was now more important than ever. She was her, Terra's, and Celeste's only hope.

Also—the heart was the key to unlocking the life she had always wanted. Not only power, but also, perhaps, a future to look forward to . . . with Grim.

"Anything?"

Oro's voice was a bucket of water over the simmering thoughts in her head. She blinked and noted his expression, knowing she wasn't focused on the text at all.

She closed the book and cleared her throat. She had read the same paragraph ten times, and none of the sentences had anything to do with the heart, or curses.

"No," she said, leaning back in her chair. "You?"

He shook his head and stared at the stack of ancient books in front of him as if he was just seconds away from incinerating the entire pile with a flick of his finger.

Isla rubbed her hands across her face, over her eyes, down her temples. She sighed. "This isn't working."

Oro just watched her.

She was exhausted. Her neck and back ached from being hunched over, reading. Her mind was tired from all the work it had been doing, thinking, scheming—and also daydreaming.

"Talk to me," she said, laying her head in her arms. The wooden table was cool against her skin and smelled of pine. "Tell me everything we know."

Oro didn't balk at the order the way he unquestionably would have months before. Instead, he leaned back in his chair and thrummed his fingers against the table, close to her head. "We know the heart is on Moon Isle. We know it contains immeasurable power from Wildling, Sunling, and Nightshade. We know it was used to spin the curses. We know it blooms regularly when it is needed, in different places. Where darkness meets light."

*Where darkness meets light.*

Behind her eyelids, there was only darkness. She imagined it, darkness meeting light. What it would look like. What colors it would make. She frowned against her arm. She didn't *have* to imagine it. She had seen it countless times, thousands of instances throughout her life.

Isla's head shot up so quickly, pain pulsed through her forehead.

Oro's eyes widened slightly. "What is it?"

She stood, pacing, her mind working too hurriedly, her words coming out too slowly. "What if it's not a place, but a time?"

"What?"

She stared at him. "Dawn. Dusk . . . when darkness meets light."

Oro considered this, eyes narrowing. "Remlar said it would be *where* darkness meets light." That must be the winged man's name, Isla thought.

"What if it's both? What if it's in a place where darkness meets light, but only appears during dawn or dusk?"

Oro blinked away fatigue like clearing cobwebs. Thinking. He was so focused Isla could almost see his mind working behind his eyes, spinning possibilities. He gazed at the table, hand splayed on its top. He shook his head. "I searched the island for decades and never found it . . . Perhaps this is why."

The cursed Sunling king couldn't be out at dusk or dawn, both times too close to sunlight. They had always searched for the heart at night, long after the sun had disappeared. It would explain why the heart hadn't been in any of the places they had checked. Maybe it *had* but had been hidden. He looked up at her. "Isla, I think you might be right."

She stood. Oro did too. They faced each other, and he smiled. *Smiled.*

She had never seen him this happy.

Something about his smile made her remember another happy memory. The moment she had felt the flames against her arms, prickling painfully along her frozen skin, relief sweeter than a mouthful of molasses. The moment she knew, surrounded by the Vinderland, that she had been saved. By Oro.

He had found her, against all odds. *I followed the bird,* he'd said.

She smirked. The same creature that had almost marked her death had saved her life.

Oro raised an eyebrow at her, wondering at her thoughts.

Isla froze. She felt the blood drain from her face, and Oro shot out a hand to steady her just as she braced herself against the table.

The bird had followed her relentlessly every time they had stepped foot on Moon Isle. She had assumed it had been Cleo's eyes and ears, but what if she had been wrong?

What if it had been trying to tell her something?

"I know where the heart is," she said.

## CHAPTER FIFTY-ONE

# HEART

Isla's steps were silent against the snow. Her breath was steady. Her entire world had narrowed into a tunnel. Her normally endless thoughts were replaced by a predatory calm, the sensation right before making a kill, the moment before releasing a bow, the string taut.

She was right this time. She knew it with every one of her bones.

Oro had been waiting for her in the castle foyer that night. The room had buzzed with invisible energy, emanating from him in ripples. He was excited. Hopeful.

She had smiled, in spite of herself. Because she was excited and hopeful too.

Isla had walked over to him, stood on her toes, and flicked his crown. She had grinned at him, testing him, seeing how their months of working together might have tamed his disdain for her.

Oro had frowned. Then he had surprised her by taking off his crown.

And placing it on her head, around her own.

"If you're right about this, Wildling," he had said, "you might become more powerful than even me."

His words had nearly made her knees buckle. He was truly giving her the win. No—acknowledging that it *was* her win.

Isla had figured it out when even the king couldn't.

She had taken off her own crown and placed it in his golden hair. It was laughably small on his head, and her lips twitched. "Wildling suits you, *King*," she had said before walking out the doors.

His crown was still warm and heavy on her head. It was so large, it sank down to the middle of her forehead. But she found she didn't mind it.

It was just under an hour from dawn. Just enough time to search for shelter for Oro. Once they found it, all they would have to do was wait.

Isla's skin itched; her entire body was covered in sparks. Still, she stayed in her tunnel, focusing all her energy on the other side.

The heart. The ones she loved. Her future.

Power was the last thing on her mind. If she could save Celeste and Terra, she would be content. They meant so much more than abilities ever would. She knew that now.

She just hoped she hadn't realized it too late.

"What will you do?" she asked him as they took their first steps across Moon Isle. "When we break the curses?"

Oro walked steadily, eyes trained on the sky. "I'll rebuild," he said. "These past centuries, the focus has been on the curses. How to break them. How to live with them. How to survive them. With all of that erased, I could be free to bring Lightlark to its previous glory."

Isla raised an eyebrow at him. "With Sunling as the reigning realm?"

Oro shook his head. "No. Before that. When the realms were united."

She let out a long sigh. *United.* That would mean Wildlings returning to Lightlark. The ones that were left, she thought, dread dancing in her stomach. "I'm not sure the people of Lightlark would be thrilled if Wildlings returned."

"They will have to learn to be," Oro said. And his voice was so firm, she glanced at him. He met her gaze. "And perhaps you would want to stay."

Isla blinked. She had never considered staying on Lightlark. During the limited times she had allowed herself to dream about *after,* about what her life might look like if she managed to break the curses, she had imagined bits and pieces. Her and Celeste, back in the Starling newland. Celebrating all her friend's birthdays without sadness or fear.

Leading the Wildling newland with confidence, Terra and Poppy strong beside her. And, more recently . . . visiting Nightshade. Spending time with Grim.

None of her futures included the island.

"Perhaps," she said. But it was a lie. And because of his flair, Oro knew it.

They walked the next half hour through Moon Isle in silence.

The wind whipped her cheeks so violently, she wondered if Azul was responsible. *Azul.* She hadn't told Oro about the proof that he had poisoned Celeste. She told him then.

Oro frowned. "There must be a mistake," he said. "Azul has never wanted to hurt another ruler. He has never even tried to form an alliance."

She had just told him how the Skyling had poisoned Celeste. Wasn't that proof enough that he wasn't innocent?

Why was Oro defending him? She wanted to demand an explanation but reared back as something screeched in her ear.

The dark-blue bird.

Its wings flapped slowly, as if its feathers were too heavy for its small frame. It squawked again. This time, Isla did not threaten it.

She followed it.

Isla and Oro ran quickly through the snow, and she squinted, trying not to lose the bird in the dark. She didn't feel the cold, or the hill dipping below her legs, or anything at all as she trailed after the bird, through the forest with branches like skeletons that caught on her clothes as if pleading with her to slow down.

She kept going. Panting.

The bird wasn't the heart. She knew that.

But it would lead her to it.

Ice mountains came into view. The oracles were not far. *Where darkness meets light.* She remembered what the oracle had said . . . that the heart wasn't in her ice but was *near, nearer than you know.* The trees grew farther apart here, with more room for snow to pile. A river snaked through them, the sound of the water splitting then refreezing again like the tiny cracks of firewood splintering.

Another screech through the night. She found the bird as it dipped down and flew up, into a tree.

Into a nest.

"Here," Isla said. She knew the heart was there, somewhere.

All they had to do was wait until dawn.

They found a cave carved into one of the ice mountains, within view of the tree. Oro made a fire, though she knew he could heat them both without one. It seemed as though he needed something to do with his hands, to distract him from the time that moved too slowly and the bird just yards away.

Or maybe he couldn't warm them. She had seen how much of his skin the bluish gray now covered. She had felt the island getting colder and darker with every day that passed.

Its flames popped and peaked in beautiful curls. Oro's fire was still orange and red, but also tinged in something different . . . a strange shade of dark blue. A signature of his, it seemed.

Isla traced a finger around his crown, perched precariously on her head. She frowned up at it, squinting so she could see its edge, right above her eyebrows. "It's unreasonably sharp," she said, sucking on her fingertip where the skin had been broken by one of the points.

Oro laughed. It was a glorious sound, making her smile immediately. Genuinely. Perhaps because, as far as she had seen, she was the only one capable of making him laugh.

But then he doubled over.

Moon Isle shook. Icicles fell from the mouth of the cave like daggers, some shattering, some digging into the ground. Isla narrowly avoided one that would have gone clean through her arm.

Oro's hands were in fists, and he arched, grunting, face twisted in pain.

Snow slid off the mountains, threatening to bury the entrance of the cave. The bird screeched angrily, its pitch so high it made her wince. A crack like thunder sounded as a glacier split open.

As quickly as the shocks had started, they ended.

*The island is crumbling, and me along with it.*

Oro panted, fingers dug into the stone. His back trembled like he still felt the tremors, still ached everywhere.

She took a careful step toward him. Knelt until she was right in front of him.

He leaned back against the wall, eyes shut tightly.

"Are you all right?"

Oro nodded just as his entire body seized again, as if he'd been struck by lightning. He slammed a hand against the ground, and long cracks erupted from the place he had hit, Starling energy making the cave smell of sparks.

She couldn't imagine the pain. His connection to the island meant he felt its power . . . but also its destruction.

Isla placed a careful hand on his shoulder, and he stiffened. She quickly withdrew it.

Oro yelled out again, his fingers digging deeper into the stone, fire forming then dying in his palms, ice freezing then melting, sparks coating them, then vanishing. "What—what can I do?" she asked, panicked. There had to be something she could offer.

His eyes were still shut. He swallowed, and she watched the movement, watched him wince once more. Found herself wondering if she would take his pain for herself if she could.

"Sing for me, Wildling," he finally said.

Isla thought she must have misheard him. But he took a shaky breath in, and out. Quiet. Waiting.

She remembered that night on her balcony. Singing when she hadn't known anyone had been listening.

He had clapped. And she had assumed he had done it to be mean.

Perhaps he had liked it.

She began to sing a Wildling song. Her favorite song. The one she sang when she wanted to hear her own voice echoed back to her. When she was alone in her chambers and hoped someone far away might hear her. When she wondered if there was someone realms away, listening.

She sang that song.

Her voice was thick as honey, high as bells, deep as rumbles of thunder. She could do wild things with it, and she did, sitting back on her heels, her knees grazing his legs. Her voice echoed through the cave, harmonies weaving together.

Oro's eyes opened at some point. He watched her, taking steady breaths. Slowly, his fists began to uncurl. He rested his palms against the cool stone and listened.

She smiled at him when his shoulders settled. His expression did not change. She continued to sing, because he hadn't told her to stop, and the sun hadn't come up. She sang until her voice went hoarse and the sound changed. She liked when it got like this, smoky, different.

Part of her wondered if he had let her go on to be polite. But when she closed her mouth, Oro frowned.

"Why did you stop?" he asked.

Isla motioned toward the mouth of the cave, breathless. "Because of that," she said.

The dark sky was brightening. The moon was fading.

Oro was on his feet in an instant. They both rushed to the entrance, watching. Waiting.

In the rising light, Isla noticed something. She squinted. Right below the nest, something was floating in the air, untethered to gravity.

"Is that an egg?" she asked.

Just as the words left her mouth, the egg fell. Slowly, too slowly, it plunged to the ground—

And cracked open.

From its shell emerged a shining, gold yolk. It rose from the ground in tandem with the sun rising from the horizon, just across the cliff.

"The full egg represented the moon," she said, her voice hoarse from singing. "The yolk . . . is the sun." How many times had she thought the full moon looked like an egg? That the sun looked yolky?

She turned to Oro, eyes wide. "That's it," she said. "That's the heart."

*The heart is hidden until it blooms and becomes a part of Lightlark.* Oro had presumed it was a plant. But this time, the heart had returned as the very basis of life. An egg.

Oro watched the floating yolk and its discarded shell with such awe, she wondered if he might sink to his knees. He met her gaze and smiled so brightly, it was as if the sun itself was shining right through his skin.

He swept her into his arms and spun her around. She laughed, so close to crying in relief her eyes prickled, her lungs burned. She was immediately flooded with his heat, down through her bones. A moment later, she was back on her feet.

Oro shook his head in disbelief. He reached toward his crown on her head, and she wondered if he was about to take it. Instead, he straightened it, smiling. "Go ahead, Wildling. Get our heart," he said.

She grinned back at him.

*Finally.*

She was not weak. She had solved the riddle of the prophecy, found the heart, *her way.* She had been right. She was going to save those she loved. She was going to do what even her guardians had thought her incapable of.

She was going to win the Centennial.

Isla set off toward the tree. The bird screeched happily. The yolk was bright as the sun, small enough to fit in the center of her hand. It glimmered like pure gold. The source of all Lightlark power. Its heart.

She reached for it. Gripped it. Felt the force of it shoot through her skin, along her bones, the power like a bolt of cold water, a tidal wave through the crown of her head, flames licking her every inch—

And felt it all rip away as an arrow plunged through her chest.

She choked, falling to her knees. Her chin dipped, and her eyes settled on the long tip of an arrow, sticking right through her heart.

A perfect hit.

A roar erupted somewhere behind her. She thought it might be Oro, right before fire swallowed the forest, burning people . . . there were *people*.

Vinderland. Here to get revenge. Arrows still drawn. They pulled back their strings to strike her again and died. Oro had killed them all in an instant.

A second felt like a lifetime. Her head lolled over her shoulder, the king's oversize crown falling from her head. Oro was there, reaching for her, just yards away . . . but he could not take a step out of the cave to heal her. Not during the day. His face was strange, etched and lined in a million ways. With a desperate jolt, he reached farther, only to roar again in pain, the sun splitting his skin in two. Blood pooled below her in a crimson puddle. Its warmth was almost a comfort in the cold.

She had survived too long already—stolen seconds the heart's power had no doubt given her.

Isla clutched the heart of Lightlark with one hand, her own sputtering its last beats. With the other, she reached up and pulled on her necklace.

Grim appeared from thin air before her fingers could uncurl from the diamond. His eyes widened at the sight of her covered in blood. She was in his arms in an instant.

"Please," Oro said from the cave, and Isla hardly recognized his voice. Why was he begging? Did he want her to leave the heart? Her hand went limp, and the yolk fell to the ground.

The last thing she saw was Oro's face, fragmented into a handful of emotions, each more surprising than the last.

And then she was gone.

***

The heart *had* been keeping her alive. She knew that for certain when she dropped it, and the world had gone dark.

And then she was falling through an endless puddle of stars.

The realms were just spokes on a wheel, turning, turning, turning. She was somewhere in between them, drowning, gasping, fading.

*Mom*. Would she finally get to meet her? *Dad*. And the man who had been worth death, worth bearing a cursed child?

Death was not quiet, and it was not quick.

## CHAPTER FIFTY-TWO

# PROPHECY

"Hearteater."

The word was a bell, somewhere far away. A rumble of thunder. The quick shut of a door.

"Come back to me."

*Come back*. Had she ever really left?

A shaking sigh. Words drenched in pain. Agony. Whittled down into a whisper. "What did you do to me?" he said, voice pleading. She felt a finger run down the side of her face. "What did you do to leave me completely at your mercy?" Isla opened her eyes.

She was in her room. Grim was clutching her remaining bottles of Wildling healing elixir in one arm.

Isla was in Grim's arms before she could take another breath. He pulled her to his chest, cradling her head, hand behind her knees. His eyes searched hers desperately.

She pressed her forehead against his mouth. He was cold as stone, and it dulled the ache. She was too warm . . . coated in flames, in energy, in sparks.

*The arrow.*

A hand went to her chest. Nothing. The sharp tip of it was gone. She looked down and saw her shirt, shredded. Ripped open to address the wound. She pulled her underclothes aside and saw it. An angry mark, right over her heart. Where the arrow had pierced.

She should be dead.

"How . . . how . . ."

"I don't know." He held her again, careful as cradling glass.

But she did. The heart had saved her . . . its energy had been enough to keep her alive for the moments it had taken to heal her.

She remembered Oro's words. Only those in Wildling, Nightshade, or Sunling could claim the heart. Use it.

Isla didn't have powers . . . had it still recognized her?

Had she truly been able to wield it?

She swallowed. If she *had* used the heart, then part of Oro's interpretation of the prophecy had been completed.

*Only when the original offense has been committed again.*

Isla slipped out of Grim's grip and winced at the pain that pulsed through her chest. The sun still shined, but it was fading. She had been recovering all day . . . too much time had been wasted.

"Thank you," she told Grim, hand going to the invisible chain around her neck. To the diamond large as a small potato. She wrapped her arms around him, hands interlocked behind his neck.

"There's something else," Grim said. He was so serious that Isla's stomach sank. What had happened while she was healing? "There is a Moonling shop in the agora, a hidden one long abandoned. I went there, to try to find more remedy, while you were sleeping. And I found something, hundreds of years old. A rare Wildling elixir that does what Moonling healing cannot."

Isla drew in too much air. She blinked at him, a question in her eyes.

He nodded solemnly. Grim looked at the floor, not at her. "Celeste is awake."

"I need to go," she said quickly, both delighted and panicked. What if Azul came to finish the job now that Celeste wasn't hidden any longer? If Grim had found the Skyling ruler, he would have already told her.

Grim looked at the mark on her chest, then up at her. "You need to rest," he said.

She shook her head. No.

Isla turned to leave but stopped when she heard, "*Hearteater.*" His voice broke on the word. She faced him. "I thought you were dead."

*I did too,* she thought. But she didn't say that. Instead, she said, "I'm alive. Because of you." She closed the space between them. Moved her head so his nose grazed her neck. Her mouth was at his ear. "And I want to do a thousand things with you," she said, shuddering as her chest burned, the wound still tender. "But first . . . there's something I must do."

Grim nodded.

And she pushed past him, out of her room. She ran to her friend's chambers as fast as she could.

Before she could knock, the door flew open. Celeste stood there, eyes wide.

She threw her arms around her friend, even though it still hurt to move. Pain barreled through all her bones, her organs tightened, and she choked the words, "I thought you— Celeste, you—"

"I know," Celeste said quietly. "It was Azul."

Isla pulled back to meet her eyes. "*I* know. I got your message." She held her hand up, revealing the diamond on her finger once more. "Why?"

"I have no idea. He must be planning something."

Isla wanted to sit and speak with her friend, allow herself to feel relief for more than just a few seconds.

But she had to move again.

"I did it," Isla said, voice breaking. "It's a long, terrible story, but . . . I found the heart. And wielded it."

"What?" Celeste said, like she might not have heard her correctly.

Isla smiled. "I'll tell you everything later, but for now . . . stay hidden and wait to hear from me." She gave her friend another quick embrace. "All of this will be over soon."

She turned to leave, then stopped. There was something she needed to say.

"I'm sorry, Celeste. For everything. I've been a terrible friend. Terrible partner. But I'm going to make everything better. I promise."

With another final squeeze of her hand, Isla raced down the hall. Celeste frantically called after her, but she didn't stop. It was dusk. The sun was setting.

She raced back to her room. Grim was gone.

A moment later, her balcony doors burst open.

Oro flew through, landing in the center of her rug, his skin marred and healing right in front of her. He had flown through the waning light, she realized, when the sun still barely shined. Enough to burn him, but not kill him.

She froze, staring at him.

"You're alive," he said sharply, like an accusation, his chest still heaving. His eyes were wide.

She nodded. There was a pause.

"Good." He straightened. Swallowed. His fingers unfurled, and the heart sat in his palm, glowing like Oro had reached a hand into the sun and taken a fistful of its shine. It looked less like a yolk now and more like an orb. Golden. Fiery.

"We did it," she said, breathless, hand going to her aching heart. She smiled, even though her chest felt like it had been halved.

He handed the heart to her. It gleamed in her palm, winking.

"Bathe, Isla," he said. "Get dressed." Only at that moment did she register the dried blood in her hair, the dirt on her clothes. "Then meet me in the library."

Before she could say a word, he flew back through her balcony, into the night.

She gripped the heart in her hand, wondering how Oro could possibly trust her with it. The king of Lightlark, untrusting of everyone, had handed over the island's most prized possession. The key to ending the curses. The key to her future. The key to the island.

Even *she* thought he was foolish for doing so.

Isla didn't part with it, bringing it into the bath with her as she scrubbed herself down quickly, not lingering too long on the mark on her chest, which had further healed but still looked pink against her skin. A permanent bruise.

She put on a dress. Red, like the blood she had spilled.

*Ten days.*

They had found the heart with ten days to spare. But there was still a rush. The island could crumble away at any minute. Terra could die that very day. Isla had watched her through the puddle of stars before going to find the heart with Oro. The only part of Terra that hadn't succumbed to the forest floor was the right half of her face, her eye still opened wide. The other was closed.

Isla clutched the heart tightly on her walk to the library, and it pulsed in her hand. Glimmering. Speaking to her in its strange language, a siren call that promised power.

Power it had already started to give her, if her miraculous healing was any indication.

Oro was sitting in the library, lost in thought. Looking at a text, but not reading it.

As soon as she entered, he stood. Nodded. Sat again and motioned for her to do the same.

He was oddly serious. The king of Lightlark sat before her, not her companion on many adventures. Not the person she had come to trust with her life.

Isla sat down and placed the heart between them, carefully.

"I think I used it," she said firmly. "I think it saved me."

Oro only nodded.

She repeated the prophecy from memory.

> *"Only joined can the curses be undone*
> *Only after one of six has won,*

*When the original offense*
*Has been committed again*
*And a ruling line has come to an end*
*Only then can history amend."*

Isla swallowed. "*We* were joined . . ." she said. "Throughout the Centennial. And all of the rulers were joined on the island. That's the first part. Then, I committed the original offense, by using the heart."

Oro leaned back, his crown's sharp tips pointing toward the back corner of the library. He must have retrieved it, along with the heart, once the sun had gone down.

He hadn't returned her own crown. Her head felt empty without it . . . and also weightless. She found herself not rushing to wear it again.

"You will receive the power that was promised. You will officially be the one who *wins,*" he said, looking unbothered by the fact. "When you complete the final part of the prophecy."

Isla nodded, chin high.

"The last step, then, is the matter of which realm will perish." Oro leaned back in his chair. "As promised . . . the choice of which realm to save is yours."

"Starling," she said immediately. Her shoulders settled a bit. She was safe . . . and so was her best friend. Oro's brow furrowed, surprised. *Why?* she wondered.

Then her blood went cold.

"Who dies?" she asked quickly, not bothering to hide her fear. Not anymore.

Oro's eyes softened. But the rest of his expression remained firm. The face of a king. "Nightshade, Isla," he said gently.

Something had punctured her lungs—another arrow, maybe. Her breathing became panting. She was drowning from the inside out.

"But you said he couldn't die. You said he's the only thing standing between us and a greater danger." From that point on, she had assumed Grim was safe.

Oro nodded. "That was true . . ." he said. "Until we found the heart."

The realization was a boulder to the chest. The heart held unparalleled Nightshade power. With it, the king didn't need Grim anymore. He could kill him and still protect the island against the mysterious threat.

"What about Cleo?" she demanded, voice angry. Fingers curling. "I don't know how, but she spun the curses. She must have teamed up with someone else who could wield the heart. She's the reason for *all* of this." Her voice shook. Her eyes prickled with tears that did not fall. "She tried to kill me. Twice."

Oro's expression did not change. "That might be. And if she did spin the curses, she will be tried."

"*If* she did?" Isla yelled, standing.

Oro stood too, towering over her. "There are thousands of Moonlings on this island. I will not sentence them all to death because of the actions of their ruler."

Her arms shook. But he was perfectly fine allowing the entire Nightshade realm to die. Her hands clenched and unclenched. Her head throbbed. "What about Azul?" He had nearly killed Celeste. "He obviously has some sort of plan to overtake power on Lightlark. He can't be trusted."

Oro shook his head. "I told you. At the second Centennial, Azul's husband died. Each Centennial since, he does not work to break the curses, or form alliances, or overtake anything. He only tries to speak to his beloved one last time."

"What about his plan?" Isla demanded. "I heard you both."

*Your plan is madness,* Oro had said. *You will be sentencing thousands to death.*

*A realm has to die, Oro,* Azul had responded.

"His plan?" Oro said, taking a step toward her. "His plan was to *sacrifice* himself. Give himself up as the ruler to die to end the curses. He knew the island's days were numbered after my demonstration. He was willing to sacrifice himself, his people, if it meant saving everyone else. They have a democratic rule. His realm *agreed* with him. They voted for it."

"That's not true. He tried to kill Celeste," she growled.

"I don't know why he would do that. I'm sure there's a reason—"

A *reason.* The king seemed to have endless excuses and empathy, but only when it suited him.

Azul and Cleo both had their own agendas, she knew it. But Isla realized then that they must have had help. Cleo had killed Juniper after somehow finding out that Isla planned on meeting him. Celeste had been found away from the Carmel celebration in the gardens, as if she had been led there . . .

Only one other person knew about Juniper's letter to Isla and Celeste.

One person knew about Celeste's poisoning before anyone else.

One person had complete access to the castle and could move freely, practically unnoticed.

Ella.

Isla's eyes burned; her throat was dry. She didn't know anything anymore. Was she wrong? Or right?

She had worked tirelessly to find the heart.

Little did she know, the entire time, she had only been guaranteeing Grim's death. If Isla refused to kill him, Oro would. She knew that.

*You could choose him,* a voice in her head whispered . . . choose his realm to save. And see if Oro might choose Moonling or Skyling to die over Starling.

No. Isla knew Oro would choose Starling then. It was the weakest of Lightlark's realms, with the smallest population, because of their curse. Celeste was the youngest ruler, besides Isla.

The choice was clear. Either Celeste, or Grim.

Tears streamed down her face. Angry, hot tears.

"Not him," she demanded. "Please."

Why did she think he would choose Cleo? Just because the Moonling ruler had tried to assassinate her? Because Oro had saved her?

She was a fool to think he cared, to somehow allow herself to believe that Oro was anything but the king of Lightlark. A cruel ruler who would do wicked things to serve his people.

And Nightshade was their enemy.

Oro's face was expressionless. He was the king at the dinner table sneering at her wet hair, putting a heart on her plate and demanding she eat it.

"I saw his flair, Isla. He can travel between Lightlark and Nightshade in a moment. Do you know how dangerous that is? When the curses are broken and Nightshade decides to attack again while we are still vulnerable, still healing, he can transport his entire army here in the blink of an eye. Without warning."

"But you didn't even *know* about his flair until now! Which means he could have done that exact thing in the war. And he didn't, did he?"

Oro shook his head, furious. "You don't know *what* he did," he said, baring his teeth. "And that was a long time ago. *Before* he became ruler and inherited immense power."

Isla's hands trembled at her sides. She looked up at him, eyes gleaming. Pleading. "Please. Reconsider."

He shook his head.

She bared her teeth. "You can't make this decision on your own. You said so yourself. The choice is important. It's harder than the killing itself."

Oro's expression was sad—pitying, even. "I'm not making the decision alone, Isla," he said.

He must have Cleo's and Azul's support, then. A majority of the rulers.

He had gotten their approval of his choice behind her back.

Her blade was in her hand in a moment. She lunged at him before he could make a move, pressed her dagger against his throat.

He let her. He did not strike her down with his fire, the way she knew he could with half a thought, even weakened.

Oro stared at her with his honeycomb eyes. Hollow. Emotionless. "Do it," he dared. His connection to all the people on the island prevented her from killing him. But she could make him bleed, make him hurt.

Isla's hand shook, the dagger trembling against his throat. She stared at him for a long while.

Then she took her blade and left.

## CHAPTER FIFTY-THREE

# CHOICE

Isla had a plan. It wasn't perfect, and it made her a liar, thief, and hypocrite.

But it was nothing she hadn't already been in the last ninety days.

Celeste opened the door, and Isla started talking. "Tell me that you're my friend. And that you'll forgive me."

The Starling straightened her spine. Her expression became resolute, ready for anything. "I'm your friend. And I'll forgive you," Celeste said firmly. Still, Isla heard the hint of fear there that everything had gone wrong. And it had.

Isla had everything. The heart. The promise of power. The chance to save her realm.

But it all had a cost: Grim's life.

For as long as Isla could remember, the thing she wanted most was freedom. Then, as the Centennial went on, she wanted power.

When Oro had declared that Nightshade would die, when Terra and Celeste were in danger, Isla had realized that there was one thing she wanted a little more than both.

A future—happiness. A life with the people she cared about. Terra and Poppy were the closest things she had to a family. Celeste was her best friend. Grim made her feel things she thought had been denied to her as a Wildling ruler. She had always thought freedom, or even power, would change everything, fix her. But they wouldn't . . . She knew that now that she had begun to fix herself.

So, she made a plan. One that would still save her realm. Still save Celeste. It wouldn't give her the power promised. It wouldn't be a permanent solution for Terra and the Wildlings.

But it would give her Grim.

"I think I know where the bondbreaker is," Isla said. "And I have a plan for us to use it . . . but not only us." She took a steadying breath. "Let Grim in on our original plan. Let us split the blood cost of the bondbreaker three ways."

She would save him. And in exchange, he would have to agree to help save her people. She didn't know what love felt like, but this, this sacrifice . . . rulers in love could share power. If he loved her too, she could bring whatever power they shared back to her lands, to save her realm.

Or, if that was not possible, when her curse was broken, Isla would attempt to trade the Wildling abilities she would gain in exchange for Terra and the rest of the Wildlings that had been taken by the ground. The forest on the newland was known to make deals—and a Wildling ruler's powers were too valuable to refuse. It was a sacrifice she was willing to make to right everything.

She *wanted* to win the Centennial; she wanted that immense power that was promised, longed for it like a lover. She wanted the Wildling power she had been denied at birth.

But she wouldn't choose it over Grim. Or anyone else she cared about.

"I know you don't trust him. But please . . . for me," she said. "I'm begging you, Celeste. We don't have much time."

It took a minute for Celeste to say anything. Isla waited, expecting more reasons this was all wrong, more pushback. But her friend must have heard Isla's desperation, must have known how important it was to her. Because she finally said, "Where is the bondbreaker?"

They had a new plan. A last-ditch effort. Celeste was going to make part of the castle crumble to lure Oro out of his quarters long enough for her to sneak into his secret library and find the bondbreaker.

"We need a place to use it," Celeste said. "One where Oro won't be able to interfere if he finds out we have it."

"The Place of Mirrors," Isla said. Oro's powers would be nullified there, but enchantments like the bondbreaker would still work.

Celeste nodded. "I'll get the bondbreaker. You bring whatever remaining healing elixir you have to close our wounds after the blood is shed. And that's it. That's all we bring, so no one becomes suspicious." Her friend swallowed. "If anyone finds out . . ."

One of them would end up dead. Isla knew that.

Oro had looked so cold. So *himself*, she realized. She had begun to believe that the insufferable, untrusting king had been a mask Oro wore to protect himself and his island.

Now, she wondered if the person she had glimpsed—the caring, trusting partner she had worked with for months—had been the costume instead.

Isla rushed to her room. She had a feeling she wouldn't be returning to it. After they used the bondbreaker to break their curses and Oro found out . . . she would have to flee, with Grim. And Celeste. At least until the hundred days were over and Oro either chose someone else to kill to break the curses or the island disappeared again. Perhaps forever this time.

Isla stood at the foot of her bed, trying to take it all in. The wall of leaves. The bathroom of white marble.

The chair where Oro had sat and offered her a deal.

The couch where she had laid her head in Oro's lap and first heard him laugh.

The balcony where he had heard her sing and saved her life.

She shook the memories away with a scowl. All he cared about was his people and breaking the curses. He didn't care about her.

Something shattered nearby. Tremors rippled through the palace. *Celeste*. Yells filled the halls, echoing. She braced herself against her wardrobe and knew it wouldn't be long before her friend got the bond-breaker and made it to the Place of Mirrors.

Isla had to be quick. The heart was beautiful in her palm, a slice of sunshine. Part of her had considered stealing it and using its abilities to heal Terra and her realm. But taking it would officially doom Lightlark and the thousands who lived on the island. She wanted power—but she wasn't that selfish.

And, as much as she hated Oro in the moment . . . she wouldn't hurt him.

Her hand shook as she wrote the letter to Oro. Explaining whatever she could.

When she was finished, her chest ached, her wound still pulsing in pain. It brought her to her knees, and there she stayed for a while, until the hurt dulled enough for her to move without groaning.

Satisfied she had given Celeste enough of a head start, she pulled her necklace.

Grim appeared immediately. She nearly sagged over in relief, seeing him still living. The determination in Oro's eyes had been clear.

They didn't have much time. Even weakened, Oro's power was endless. And this was his territory. He wanted the Nightshade ruler dead and likely had a thousand ways to do it.

She strode over to him. Grabbed his hand. "Do you trust me?"

Grim looked at her. Blinked. "Of course, Hearteater."

"Oro's going to kill you to end the curses. Celeste and I know each other—we have an ancient relic that will help the three of us. We're going to break our bonds, tonight. And then . . . we're going to have to run."

She studied Grim's face carefully. Watched his features twist. But he did not look surprised. Had he anticipated Oro would try to assassinate him?

"You would do that for me?" Grim asked, gripping her hand tighter.

It was foolish, caring for other players in a game as cruel as the Centennial. But she couldn't help how she felt. "Yes. And you're going to have to help me too. I might need some of your power to save my realm. I—"

"I'll give you anything," he said immediately. "Anything you need. Anything of mine. It's yours."

She smiled.

"Isla—"

"We don't have time," she said, squeezing his fingers. "We need to go. Now. As close as you can get us to the Place of Mirrors."

Grim's eyes shot to the window, where darkness cloaked everything.

He hadn't been outside at night in centuries.

"Do you trust me?" she asked.

He did not answer. He only pressed his hand against her heart. She shuddered, his fingers cold, a rush going through her. "Your *heart,*" he said, frowning. He shook his head. "It does not only belong to you." Isla didn't know what that meant.

Before she could ask, she fell through the ground, to somewhere else.

They landed, and Grim braced himself. If Isla was wrong, his skin would begin to split open, just like Oro's had under the sun . . . he would die—

But nothing happened.

They were at the edge of the woods on Wild Isle, enchanted by ancient Wildling power, shielding it from all abilities other than Wildings' own. She had a theory that the Wildling forest might be a little like her—that its quelling of powers also meant other realms' curses would be nullified.

And she had been right.

Grim's jaw went slack. He stared up at the sky through the treetops in wonder. He couldn't access the dark power that thrummed through his veins, but it seemed the view of the dark sky above was enough.

She gripped his wrist. "Quickly," she said, hoping Celeste had already made it inside.

Isla ducked into the dead forest, and Grim did not move an inch. He watched her. Eyes filled with something like despair.

"Heart," he said.

She stilled. Something about that word . . . about how he said it . . .

"Will you ever forgive me?" he wondered, reaching out and tucking a piece of her hair behind her ear.

Her heart beat once. Twice. "For what?" she asked, taking a step back. Another.

Grim shook his head. Frowned. "You asked me, just minutes ago, if I trusted you. When you should have asked if *you* could trust *me*."

The forest did not make a sound. The dead leaves did not rustle. As if stunned, just like her.

She stumbled away. Said, "What?" so quietly, she doubted he had heard her.

"Heart," he said. He took a step closer. "Your dreams, the ones you asked me about . . . are not dreams."

"What?"

"They're memories."

*Memories.*

Him standing before her in full armor. Her legs wrapped around him. His lips on her neck, on her collarbones, on the sides of her knees.

The dreams she'd had for weeks, the ones that had made it hard to look Grim in the eye.

"What are you talking about?"

He shook his head. Reached for her, then recoiled when she flinched. "You appeared in my castle one year ago. And you returned . . . several times. Using your Nightshade relic."

Isla was drowning, she was sure of it. The ground shifted below her feet. She gripped a decayed branch for balance. "I've never been to Nightshade lands," she said, shaking her head. Backing away another step.

Grim swallowed. "You have. You just don't remember. I had to take away your memories. All of the ones with me in them."

She was panting. *Like he had offered to do with Juniper.*

A memory raced to the surface of her mind—the second thing that had come out of her mouth when she had first stepped foot on the island, ninety days prior.

*Have we met before?*

Grim had touched her shoulder afterward, and she had forgotten all about it. At the sight of him, something must have peeked through the veil he had put on her memories. And he had snuffed it out with that touch.

Isla blinked too quickly. Nothing made sense. Though it was the least important thing he had said, her head was full of cotton, and all she could focus on was, "My starstick is a *Starling* relic."

Grim's eyes were sad. He looked like he was falling apart and trying very hard not to show it. "No, it isn't," he said. "It's Nightshade." He frowned when she shook her head again. "Who do you think its power came from?"

She wasn't breathing. Grim's flair was the power to portal anywhere he wanted to go. The same power as her starstick.

"No," she said. "I've never been to Nightshade lands," she repeated, her mind spinning, voice breaking. She hadn't dared, not after Terra's warnings.

Grim's voice was gentle. "Heart," he said steadily. "Where do you think you were before you portaled back to your room for the Centennial?"

Isla remembered arriving at her room, through her puddle of stars, right before Terra and Poppy had entered it. Right before fixing her crown atop her head and addressing her people.

But she didn't remember where she had been. She searched her mind, digging, begging the memories to appear.

They did not.

If what Grim said was true . . . she had been with him that morning.

He had taken her memories. Then, just minutes later, he had pretended not to know her. She had looked upon him like a familiar stranger.

It couldn't be true. None of it made sense. None of it.

*There are lies and liars all around you . . .*

She didn't know what to do, what to think, who to trust. But she certainly didn't trust herself.

Or him.

So, she ran into the forest her ancestors had created. Grim waited a few moments before taking off after her. And outside these woods, he might have caught her.

But she was fast as the arrow that had pierced her heart. Quiet as a hummingbird. Before, she had cut her cheek and arms in this same forest. Today, she jumped over all the right vines. Ducked under all the trees.

Until she saw her own self, reflected back at her.

She ran inside the Place of Mirrors, hearing snaps and cracks outside. Through the glass, she watched as the dead trees wove together and formed a wall, encasing her inside.

The forest was enchanted. Did it sense her fear? Was it finally protecting the ruler of Wildling who couldn't protect herself?

Isla didn't have time to question it. Grim couldn't use his powers here, but he was a warrior—it would take just a few good swings of his blade to get through the brush.

She almost slumped over in relief when she saw Celeste inside, eyes wide.

"What's wrong?" she asked, and Isla realized she was still panting. Celeste was holding something in her hand.

It looked like a giant sewing needle, long as a dagger. Sharply pointed at both ends. It was gold and part glass and glowed brightly, just as the heart had.

*The bondbreaker.*

"Nothing," she said, then shook her head. "Everything."

Celeste nodded, seeming to understand that Grim wouldn't be joining them. "I don't know what you needed from him. But I'll help you with whatever it is. We'll figure it out . . . together."

*Together.* She had ruined everything. But she believed Celeste when she said that they would find a solution.

"We need to hurry, then," Isla said.

Celeste extended the needle toward her. "It's a quick thing. We just pierce our skin with this."

The bondbreaker's cost was said to be at least a gallon of blood from a ruler. Isla wasn't sure how the needle was supposed to hold that much. But perhaps it didn't have to *hold* it. The needle likely made a puncture that wouldn't close until they'd lost the required amount. Isla had brought her remaining healing elixir to close their wounds once they were done.

A crack sounded through the night. Isla whipped around to see that Grim had made a path through the tree hulls, quicker than expected.

They faced each other through the glass. His eyes widened in sight of the needle.

"Now," Isla whispered, and Celeste stuck the needle into her own hand, wincing.

"Heart, no," Grim yelled before she could do the same, loud enough to make her pause. He ran as fast as he could, hurdling through the door.

But Isla felt a sharp stab through her palm. It was done.

She cried out, something critical rushing through her, burning like smoke in her lungs, salt in her throat, sparks in her stomach. Only it wasn't blood. It wasn't anything she could see.

Isla turned to face Celeste. Her friend's eyes had changed. They were darker, a deep silver instead of gray.

She grinned wickedly.

Isla froze. She didn't recognize that smile. Celeste's silver hair began to float around her head. Her back arched just as Isla doubled over, suddenly light-headed—her skin felt too thin, yet Celeste's skin gleamed far too brightly. The bondbreaker was *taking* something from her and giving it to Celeste. Something important.

Grim grabbed Isla's other hand, tried to pull her away from the needle.

And was flung back against the glass. By *Celeste*. But her powers didn't work in here—

The Nightshade thrashed violently against chains that looked like vines. His arms strained. Just then, the door crashed open once more. Oro stepped through. How had he found her? His amber eyes went straight to the bondbreaker, and he paled.

"Isla," he said softly, looking more panicked than she had ever seen him.

Then he doubled over, falling to his knees. Was the island deteriorating again? But this was different. Grim slumped over at the same moment. Both weakened in seconds—like her. How?

Suddenly, she was shoved straight down to the stone, away from the needle. It fell to the floor just as her head cracked against the marble.

She blinked, vision blurred, and Celeste took a step toward her. Blood dripped from the puncture on the Starling ruler's palm.

Six droplets.

One sizzled. One floated. One burst. One became dark as ink. One froze. One hit the ground and bloomed into a crimson rose.

Celeste's blood contained abilities from all six realms.

*Impossible.*

It was as if she had just drained Oro and Grim of all their power. But she hadn't even touched them . . . and it didn't explain *all* six droplets . . .

Celeste's head fell back as she laughed. Her eyes met Isla's, and she sneered. "You're not very good at following rules, are you?"

Isla was frozen on the ground, mouth parted. She had a thousand questions and couldn't form a single one, except for, "What?"

"You were supposed to stay *away* from Grim, remember? I warned you . . . and the king of Lightlark! You weren't supposed to seduce him, that wasn't *your* plan, it was your guardians' . . ." She grinned. "Good thing I counted on you breaking the rules, little Wildling."

Oro had managed to get on his feet somehow, though the color had completely drained from his face. He took a step forward, hand raised—

And was flung against the glass, next to Grim. By a wild root.

Celeste couldn't use her Starling abilities in the Place of Mirrors.

She was using Wildling power.

"How?" Isla said. She must be dreaming. Or having a nightmare. It didn't make sense . . . her best friend.

Isla was at Celeste's feet, staring up at her. Not searching the room for exits. Not reaching for the dagger at her hip.

This couldn't be real.

Celeste's smile only grew more serpentine. The Centennial was a big game—she and Celeste had repeated those words countless times.

And Isla had been played.

"Why don't you ask them?" Celeste said, motioning to Oro and Grim, who both looked like they were a moment away from going into a hundred-year slumber, their muscles slackened, eyelids drooping. Still, they fought against their restraints in vain. Celeste sighed. "Love on Lightlark is a dangerous thing, isn't it?"

Isla knew that. Falling in love meant handing someone else complete access to your abilities.

"I really thought it would be harder . . . but you played your part well. These two ancient, famed rulers fell at your feet like cut-down stalks of wheat." Celeste walked over to them, sneering. "Grim was easy. He already loved you . . . you two have *quite* a history . . . though I suppose you don't remember any of it, do you?"

Celeste turned to Isla for confirmation, and she didn't move an inch. She didn't recognize her friend. It couldn't be her . . . Isla refused to accept it. Celeste shrugged at the lack of response and stopped in front of Oro. His nostrils flared. If he'd had his powers, his gaze alone could set fire to them all.

But in the Place of Mirrors, only Wildling power was permitted.

"The untrusting, cruel king . . . fell in love with a Wildling?" Celeste shook her head, grinning. "It was torture, wasn't it, King? Trying to fight it. Believing yourself under her spell . . . not knowing that she had no Wildling powers to begin with, until she told you her secret."

Oro's gaze shot to Isla. He looked panicked.

She looked at him, really looked at him. *Fell in love?* Celeste had to be wrong.

The Starling stepped closer to Oro. Ran a silver-painted nail down his cheek. "Of course, you were never under any spell." She shrugged. "That, at least, should make you feel better about losing every drop of power you ever had."

Oro tore against his chains. Grim was very still next to him, looking at Isla. She felt his gaze all over her.

But she didn't know where to look. Nothing made sense.

Oro couldn't love her. She didn't even think he *liked* her.

At least, that was how it had started out. But the more time they had spent together, after everything they had been through . . .

Celeste clicked her tongue. "To think, they handed over all of this power to you." She looked down at Isla, still on the floor, and sighed. "And now you've given it to me."

It still didn't make sense. Even if Oro and Grim *were* in love with her . . . she couldn't simply give that power to Celeste. The bondbreaker—

Celeste must have read the confusion across Isla's face, because she said, "There never *was* a bondbreaker, little bird. *This* is a bond*maker.* The only enchanted device that allows a transfer of ability. Created to help Sunling kings shift their power to their heirs without having to die. Isn't that right, King?"

Oro growled and tore against the vines, so hard he almost broke them with a single motion.

When Isla had been pricked by the bondmaker, it had allowed Celeste to take all the power she had access to, even if she didn't know it—Oro's and Grim's.

"*Celeste.* You're my friend. You wouldn't do this." She would fight for their friendship. Fight for the person she loved.

Celeste frowned. She bent down to where Isla was still on the ground and took her face in her hand, like she had countless times before. Isla let her. The Starling ruler sighed, a hint of pity swimming in her bright eyes. Then her mouth twitched. She smiled, wide mouth sweeping across her face. "Don't you understand, you beautiful, beautiful fool? You did everything I wanted . . . and I didn't even have to make you."

The Starling transformed. Her nose shortened. Her eyes changed color. Her cheeks hollowed. Her lips became redder.

A different face. A different person.

An impossible power—a flair.

Celeste wasn't Celeste at all.

Oro finally looked ready to collapse. His eyes flashed with pain. "*Aurora.*"

*Aurora.* Isla knew that name. The Starling ruler who had died the day the curses had been cast. The one who had been set to marry King Egan.

"I watched you die," Oro said, his voice rasped.

Aurora turned and faced Oro. "An illusion, I'm afraid," she said.

"Why?" Oro's voice was guttural. Then realization hardened his features. "It was revenge, wasn't it?"

Aurora only smiled.

"What do you mean?" Isla demanded. Her head was swimming. Nothing made sense.

Every word seemed to pain him, but Oro said, "My brother was supposed to marry Aurora." Blood dripped from the corner of his mouth. "But he fell in love with someone else. With her best friend."

*What?*

"With your ancestor."

Her ancestor. The one who had died the night of the curses. Her name was Violet. She knew almost nothing about her. Certainly not this.

Aurora laughed without humor. It had all happened centuries ago, but the pain was raw on her face. "They meant to marry, with a ring already on my finger. I was so angry . . . I used my shape-shifting flair to change into a beautiful Wildling and convinced *this* fool"—she looked pointedly at Grim—"that he would have me that night if he gave me the most beautiful flower on the island . . . one I knew had bloomed on the remnants of Night Isle, just weeks prior. The heart of Lightlark. Something Egan had told me about as children. I had tracked it, intending for it to be a wedding gift. Instead, Grim unknowingly unlocked the heart for me to use. The job was rushed. Since I had not found it myself, I could not wield it effectively. I cursed all the realms without really meaning to. Even my own. Only *I*, as the curses' creator, was left unmarred.

"Then I panicked. With all the rulers except for me dead, I would be the prime suspect. So, I faked my death with a Nightshade illusion, using the heart. You *saw* me die . . . but the person who truly perished was my heir, my foolish sister. I took on her identity, her face. Then, when I formed the Starling newland, I forbade attendants in the castle. Led from afar. Keeping secrets is easy in a realm where everyone dies at twenty-five. I became a new Starling ruler every Centennial. All the while, biding my time. Planning. Waiting."

"For what?" Isla demanded. Tears streaked down her face. This couldn't be real. She still refused to believe it.

"For the right moment to take everything I had been denied. Only this time, I wished to rule all six realms. Gaining access to all of Lightlark's powers proved difficult." She sneered at Oro. "Even with a new face, a new personality, every Centennial, you always rejected my advances. An untrusting king indeed. Egan had told me about the bondmaker. I began searching for it every Centennial. But, even if I was able to trick you, King, into using it with me, I would receive just *four* of the six abilities. A ruler can only use the bondmaker to gain ability once and lose ability once. I needed a way to get all six powers in one go."

She turned to Isla. She was still on the floor, watching as everything in her life, everything she thought she knew, shattered.

"And that's where you come in, little bird." Isla swallowed. "It was all luck, really."

Grim's voice bellowed across the room. "*Aurora,*" he said in warning. "Don't."

She only smiled. And continued. "Years ago, one of Grim's powerful, curious generals stole one of his relics and used it to visit the Wildling newland. There, he met a beautiful Wildling. And, though forbidden in every way, would you believe they fell in love? The Nightshade general was powerful . . . so powerful, he thought he could subdue the Wildling's curse . . . keep it at bay. And he did." She smiled at Isla. "Long enough for them to have you."

Isla shook with rage. "No."

"Yes, Isla. You are not only Wildling . . . but also Nightshade."

She shook her head. "I'm powerless."

Aurora laughed. "Quite the contrary, little bird. You're *very* powerful. Your Wildling abilities have simply been cloaked by your Nightshade powers. Made invisible. Unusable, unless a skilled Nightshade should untangle them . . . Manifestations of powers are so strange, aren't they?"

*Power.*

Isla had always had power.

And she had lost it. To her best friend. Who had never been her friend at all.

"I saw my chance to get all six powers and planned accordingly." Aurora pursed her lips.

"Then something I hadn't anticipated happened. I didn't know you had been visiting other rulers too. You apparently mentioned something suspicious about me to Grim, and the very next day, he appeared in my room."

Aurora turned to face Grim.

"And that was when he became my accomplice."

Isla stilled. Grim's face had gone ashen. He did not meet Isla's gaze.

"A person's emotions have colors, apparently. *Celeste's* had the same shade as mine. He figured out my identity right away and was about to slay me, knowing that my survival meant *I* had spun the curses. But before he could, I told him that the only reason I kept returning to the Centennial with a new face was because I could not rest until Egan's familial line was destroyed for good. I presented him with a plan that would kill the king without dooming everyone on the island, break the curses, and give him control of Lightlark. All he had to do was help me."

"Hearteater," Grim said, trying to get her attention. But she couldn't even look at him. He growled, tearing against his binds. But it was useless. "She told me the original offense was a Sunling ruler falling in love with a Wildling ruler—Egan loving Violet." His breathing was labored. "To break the curses and fulfill the prophecy, the original offense had to be repeated again. You had to make Oro fall in love with you. But we were already in love. You would have refused. So, I had to take the memories of us together away."

Isla could barely breathe. That was why Grim had avoided her for weeks when she and Oro were working together. She thought about his strange comment, encouraging her to dance with Oro at the ball.

His voice took a desperate edge as she still refused to look him in the eye. "It was the most difficult decision I've ever made, Hearteater. Knowing that succeeding meant you beguiling someone else. Making you forget our story. Our love."

She finally met his gaze then. "Difficult for *you*?"

His voice turned resolute. "I was going to give the memories back. Once Oro loved you . . . and you remembered you loved *me* . . . we could take all of Lightlark's powers and rule together."

Aurora pursed her lips. "And, once Oro was drained of his abilities and link to the island, I would be free to kill him."

Grim spoke again. "I did it for my realm. Your realm. For *us*, Heart."

It fit the prophecy perfectly. Rulers being joined. Winning immense power. A ruler and their familial line dying.

Aurora sighed. "You have to admit . . . it *was* a great plan." She grinned. "Too bad it was all a lie."

Grim thrashed against his restraints, bellowing in anger. Immediately, thorns from the vines tying him down dug into his skin, drawing blood. He winced, already weakened. And now Isla knew why. Both he and Oro had been drained of power.

And so had Isla. Though she hadn't been weakened . . . not like them. For she had never relied on power.

She couldn't miss something she never knew she had.

"I need to thank you," Aurora said, looking down at Isla. "You not only found the bondmaker for me . . . but you gave me all six powers at once."

Isla was shaking.

Everything had been orchestrated. A game much bigger than the one she thought she had been playing.

Isla finally rose. Grim had done everything for the same reason she had tried to win the Centennial—to save those he loved and bring power back to his realm. On every level, she understood.

The difference was Isla had been willing to give up everything for him. When, the entire time, he had used her as a pawn. She spat in Grim's direction.

Isla looked at Oro and hoped he read the apology in her eyes. Because of her, because he had been foolish enough to love a Wildling, his worst fear had been confirmed. He had lost his power.

He had been right not to trust her. Not to trust anyone.

She should have done the same.

Isla took out her blade, then faced Aurora. Everything made terrifying sense now.

Aurora had killed Juniper after he wrote them about knowing who had spun the curses. Not Cleo or Ella.

Azul must have somehow figured out Celeste was Aurora and tried to stop her during Carmel.

Isla swallowed, knowing she had to finish the job.

She was quick, faster than lightning striking—her blade was at Aurora's throat in a moment.

But before she could pierce flesh, the blade shattered.

Isla and Aurora met eyes. It didn't make sense. Aurora couldn't wield her abilities here. The Starling ruler laughed. "The dagger you chose at the Starling shop, the one *I* planted there. One I had enchanted so it could never kill me should you discover my plot. Of course you chose the one with a serpent on it . . . so predictable, little bird. So weak . . . so *foolish*."

Aurora lifted her arms, and vines crashed through the glass of the Place of Mirrors, sending shards everywhere. They filled the room, squirming like serpents, reaching toward them all.

Oro and Grim were instantly smothered. Trapped firmly against the remnants of the glass wall. Aurora would end them, even with their powers drained, just to squelch any other claim to authority. Isla knew that.

"Killed by your own abilities . . ." Aurora mused, hands lifted, ready to strike Isla down with all the forest offered. She paused, for just a moment. "I did like you, Wildling. But all the rulers must die today. Again."

Before Aurora could send the vines and roots to end her, Isla reached back down her spine, her favorite hiding place. Her fingers wrapped around something that was buzzing faintly. Glowing.

Aurora's eyes widened. "I told you not to bring anything, fool," she said.

Isla grinned meanly. "I'm not good at following rules, remember?"

Then she plunged through her puddle of stars.

## CHAPTER FIFTY-FOUR

# CURSED

Her room looked just like she had left it, though the outside was barren. No trees near her windows. No grass.

She had fallen roughly, collapsing onto the stone, her knees screaming in pain.

At the commotion, her door flung open. Just as it had three months prior.

Poppy was wearing sleep clothes. At the sight of her, the woman screamed out in joy. Her guardian rushed to embrace her, arms going around her neck. She smelled of cinnamon and blood. It must have been a feeding day.

"You did it, little bird!" Poppy said. She must have assumed Isla's early arrival meant she had succeeded in the guardians' plan. The first step of which was to seduce the king out of his powers.

And though her true plan had been different from the start . . . Isla supposed she had.

She did not embrace her back. Finally, Poppy let her go, and Isla said, "You knew. Both of you." Poppy had the nerve to look confused. Isla ground her back teeth together. "You both knew I had power . . . didn't you?"

Celeste—*Aurora*—had called her a name only her guardians had ever used. *Little bird*. And that was when Isla had realized that the Starling's plot required help. People from the inside.

"And you killed them, didn't you?" Isla said.

Only Poppy and Terra had access to these chambers. Isla had gotten all her information about Lightlark, her parents, and her curse from them.

*Lies.*

*And liars.*

Poppy's hand went to the single blade she carried.

Isla drew hers first, one she kept beneath her vanity.

"Why?" she ground out.

Poppy looked pale. "We did it for *you*. The Starling ruler gave us a choice—kill your mother and her lover so that their power would be transferred to you in time for the next Centennial and raise you to be able to seduce the king one day . . . or she would kill the entire Wildling line and end our realm. She demanded we convince you that you weren't born with ability . . . so that you wouldn't ever try to use it. She said it was dangerous, the mix of power, that it could kill you."

Isla stepped forward, pointing her dagger at Poppy. "You killed my parents," she said, the words barely making a sound. Not the curses. Not the fact that her mother broke the rules. *Them*. The people her mother had trusted most. Her head was full of mist. Her limbs were limp. Her chest still throbbed. "I should kill you," she said before uncurling her other hand, revealing her vial of Wildling healing elixir. "I should leave Terra to rot."

She downed the bottle, hoping it would work over the next few minutes, for wounds she hadn't yet gotten.

She dropped her blade. "But I have something more important to do."

Isla strode past Poppy to her wall of swords. She rushed to put on her full armor—shoulder plates, high metallic boots, chest plate, long metallic gloves, and, finally, her helmet. She grabbed two swords.

Then she drew her puddle of stars once more.

She had escaped Lightlark. She was safe, for now. She could flee. She could run.

Yet.

She couldn't leave them behind.

Grim had betrayed her on every level . . . He deserved Aurora's wrath, a slow death at her hands . . .

But Oro did not. She remembered his words, spoken true: *I've never lied to you, Isla. Not once.* He was the only person she could trust. The only person who hadn't truly betrayed her. She wouldn't abandon him.

Poppy gripped her wrist. "You're going back? You made it out. Don't be a fool."

Isla hissed. She shook out of her guardian's hold. "I might be a fool. But at least I have honor," she spat. "I will return with power for Wildling. I will save this realm, and Terra. But afterward . . . I never want to see either of you again."

She raised her arms to the ceiling, her two long swords pressed together above her head.

And portaled away.

The moment Isla landed in the Place of Mirrors, she was moving. The vines Aurora controlled reacted reflexively, lunging toward her from every direction, thorns and all.

Isla might not have had power.

But, unlike the other rulers, she was used to fighting without it.

Her blades made a slicing sound as she peeled them away from each other and turned them both in wide circles, at her sides, at her front, behind her back—and wherever she cut, plants fell.

Aurora had stolen Isla's power . . . and even dead, the enchanted forest sought to protect the Starling ruler. The decaying nature created guardians in response to Isla's threat, creatures crafted from bark. They hurtled toward her through holes in the glass, wielding weapons made of bone and horns from wild animals. Isla roared and lunged, fighting them just as fiercely as any foe, spinning on her heel, turning her blades, shielding from their thorns and bone daggers with the metal across her arms.

The world went silent. Every step was delicate as a dance, every move of her blade targeted, her arms pulsing not with pain, but power—she had trained every day before the Centennial since she was just a girl. She played not with dolls but with blades. She did not braid her hair but wove vines to make shields.

For a moment, she was back in the Wildling woods during a rare training excursion outside, Terra sitting in a tree above, watching Isla move, her sword cutting through the air. Her arrows shooting targets carved into trees. Her throwing blades hitting their marks every time, from any angle.

And she heard claps, somewhere. Terra used to clap only when Isla had conquered a fighting technique. One that would earn her a new blade to display on her wall.

But the clapping didn't come from Terra.

Aurora's hands rang together, and a thin vine punctured the glass, so small it made it through Isla's raised blades.

And wrapped around her neck.

Isla gasped. It gripped tightly as her breath was choked from her throat, thorn cutting against her neck, right against her larynx.

Aurora stood in front of her, laughing. Clapping once more. Amused. "You came *back?* You were free, little bird." She clicked her tongue, suddenly disappointed. "And you flew right back into your cage."

She closed her fist, and the vine tightened even more, bringing Isla to her knees. Isla sliced at its root, cutting it free. But the piece wrapped around her neck remained.

Oro and Grim watched her, both fighting against their chains, eyes wide in fear. Blood spilled down their temples, down their limbs. Aurora had cut them a thousand times with those thorns. It seemed Isla had interrupted her slow torture of the two rulers.

They hadn't even had a chance to stop it . . . hadn't had access to their pools of power before Aurora had stolen them, because of her, because *she* had suggested they meet at the Place of Mirrors.

Still . . . there was an advantage to being here. Grim and Oro might be trapped, but Aurora was limited to only Wildling power. Beyond this place, her new powers were limitless. She could wield all six realms' abilities. No one in history had been able to do that.

Worse—she wasn't bound to any of the curses, as their creator. Leaving the rest of the realms weak, easy to conquer.

No. Aurora could not leave the Place of Mirrors.

Even if it meant Isla wouldn't leave either.

Isla sliced her blade through the air in a flash, right to her neck. The vine choking her was only an inch thick. A centimeter off, and she would slit her own throat.

But Isla's swords were a part of her—without any powers to wield, she had focused solely on them her entire life.

The vine fell from around her neck.

She barreled toward Aurora, swords raised. The Starling ruler sent tree hulls through the glass, made spikes from bark, threw them in her path.

Isla cut them all down. She was fluid as water. Precise as lightning. Fast as a star hurtling to earth. Her swords moved independently, in tandem, in a rhythm like the blood pulsing through her veins, like the ringing through the glass dome, echoing the slicing and shattering as Aurora sent more of the woods inside.

As she neared, Isla felt the tears, hot on her cheeks. The greatest betrayal was not Grim's. Not Terra and Poppy's.

It was Celeste's. She had pretended to be her friend. Her *sister.*

Isla had been alone. And Celeste had preyed upon her loneliness.

Still, even after everything, a treacherous corner of her heart still loved her friend.

Aurora grinned at the pain etched into the pockets of Isla's face. "You could have done it," she said. "Broken the curses. I hadn't counted on Oro finding out about the heart. You two truly could have broken them, if *you* had just been strong enough to let one of the rulers die. And, of course, there is the matter of the original offense from the prophecy . . ."

Isla whirled around, bracing against the impact of a trunk. She fell to the ground, air leaving her lungs for just a moment before returning, the healing liquid she had just taken still running through her blood, aiding her. One of Aurora's thorn-covered vines sliced right down her side, sending blood streaming, and she screamed—but a moment later, the skin knitted itself together again.

Panting, Isla kept her pace toward Aurora, swords still drawn. "The original offense wasn't using the heart," Isla said through her teeth, grunting as she cut through a vine wrapped around her leg, thick as her limb. Another tried to take its place, to send her against the glass next to Oro and Grim—who were still fighting against their thorned constraints, bleeding in the process—but she cut that one down before it could get to her. "And it wasn't a Sunling falling in love with a Wildling. Was it?"

No, curses so cruel could only be spun through a truly sinister act. The original offense could not have been love or wielding great power . . . blood had to have been spilled to make something of a malice so great.

And not just any blood.

She had learned at a young age about the six rulers' sacrifice in exchange for the prophecy that would break the curses. Poppy and Terra had told her that her own ancestor had led the sacrifice, giving her life up first.

But Isla now wondered if perhaps her ancestor hadn't sacrificed herself at all.

Maybe she was dead before the other rulers had even learned about the curses.

The Starling's eyes glimmered. As if, for a moment, she felt pain . . . remembered the act that had changed her forever, that had been the basis for curses that had lasted five hundred years.

Her face shifted back to its wickedness a second later, and she raised her hands.

The ceiling shattered as a dozen trees crashed through it at once. Isla was showered in shards of glass. She screamed out, watching her skin break, then close, tear, then heal, the Wildling healing elixir fighting to keep up.

Trees pummeled into her, bringing her to her knees. Before they could crush her completely, Aurora twisted her fingers and wove their branches into a lattice around her.

Glass still rained down as Isla looked up at Aurora.

Through the gaps in her cage.

"Little bird," Aurora said, shaking her head from across the room. "You should have stayed in the wild."

But she wasn't caged. Not really. Even when she had been locked away in her castle, she'd always had a portal to the outside.

She gripped her starstick from where she had again tucked it down her spine, ready to portal out of her cage—

And it flew from her hand, whipped away by a vine. She watched it roll across the room, to Grim's feet. He looked up at her. Blood ran down his temples. He panted and winced, as if it hurt to breathe. But he managed to say, "Heart." He gasped, his words barely coming out. "Your *heart,* Hearteater."

Her heart? She remembered the arrow that had gone through it, a shocking pain like a lightning bolt skewering her. She should have been dead. Even Wildling elixir, even *Cleo,* couldn't fix an arrow to the heart.

Only a heart could.

Isla pressed a hand against her chest, and it burned—not from its injury, she now realized . . .

But because of what it now held.

Power in its purest form. When the heart had healed her . . . it had marked her.

*Your* heart. *It does not only belong to you.* She hadn't understood Grim's words then. But she did now.

Isla felt its pull from across the island. In her room, where she had left it, with the note for Oro. The heart sang to her, the same song she had heard the moment she had stepped foot on the island. A call like the bird screeching in her ear, a chill like the frost that had numbed her tongue on Moon Isle.

Isla felt it—and called for it.

Her arm outstretched. Her fingers flexed.

And something like an arc of sunlight came crashing through the glass. The heart hurtled into her palm, and she glowed.

Her hand closed, and her cage shattered. Wildling power rushed from the heart in an endless stream. Branches snapped, flying across the room. Something shined at her feet—the bondmaker—and she grabbed it with her other hand, sticking it in her pocket.

A moment later, she was running, jumping, a foot in front of Aurora.

Eyes wide, surprised, Aurora changed in an instant, features twisting, until she became Celeste.

*Celeste.*

Isla did not hesitate the way Aurora must have been hoping she would. She grabbed the bondmaker from her pocket. Stuck one of its sharp ends into her palm.

And plunged the other end into her best friend's heart.

Isla's scream was wild and guttural as it rang through the Place of Mirrors. Her face twisted in agony. Her best friend . . . her sister . . .

She felt power barrel through the needle, into her, as Celeste's eyes went wide, then dimmed.

Dimmed.

Until the original offense was committed again. A ruler of realm killing her best friend, in cold blood. A ruling line came to an end. And one of six won.

The world exploded.

Isla was thrown backward by a force wilder than the wind, stronger than a riptide. Tears burned and blurred her vision, hot on her face, dripping down her temples. She blinked once at the stars as she flew back, and they looked much brighter than they ever had before.

Before she landed on the ground, it collapsed.

The curses broke, and so did Lightlark. The floor had fissured, and Isla fell through the crack, after Celeste's body, which had already been taken by the island. The Starling ruler had fallen hundreds of feet, down into Lightlark's fiery core. The heart fell from Isla's hand and plummeted after Celeste.

Isla followed.

She fell, fell, fell, just like she had that night on the balcony. Behind her back, the ground churned, boiled, ready to receive her bones. She felt power streaming through her, everything she had taken back with the bondmaker. But as she reached to grab it, the energy slipped through her fingers. She didn't know how to wield it . . . had never used her own ability before.

Isla closed her eyes. Recognizing her fate.

She only had time to say goodbye to one person. She chose—

And something caught her around the waist. Her back arched painfully.

She stopped falling.

Someone had saved her. But that was impossible. Grim and Oro might have been released from their restraints after Aurora's death, but they couldn't use their abilities in the Place of Mirrors, even with the curses lifted. Even with Isla returning their powers.

Unless—

Isla opened her eyes to see that the thing wrapped around her was vine. It had caught her and now began to pull her back to the surface.

Wildling power.

But she hadn't been the one to wield it.

*Love on Lightlark is a dangerous thing.*

Someone she loved was using her abilities.

The thick plant lifted her to the surface, out of the pit that had opened right in the middle of the Place of Mirrors.

When she reached the top, Isla hauled herself over the edge, onto solid stone, panting. Her hair was a wild mess in front of her.

Through it, she saw Oro release his fist.

And the vine around her waist went limp.

Oro was wielding Isla's power. And she could see in Grim's face that he knew what that meant.

The look on his face, agony melting into surprise and finally anger, said that he had also tried to access her abilities. And found that he could not.

Isla opened her mouth. Hours before, her feelings had been different. Hours before, she had been ready to run away with Grim, to build a future together. To sacrifice all she wanted, for *him*.

But he had betrayed her in every way. He had taken away her memories instead of including her in his plan. Instead of trusting her to make her own decision. He had made the choice for her.

And Oro . . . he had been her true partner through the Centennial. He had handed her truths in exchange for her lies. She had cried in front of him. Laughed. Conquered her greatest fears. Faced many dangers. He knew her better than anyone else on the island—except for the friend she had lost.

Before Isla could say a word, Grim backed out of a gaping hole in the glass and disappeared into the night.

Celeste's blood was still hot on her hand. Down her sleeve. She fell to her knees and retched. Sobbed. Screamed.

The curses were broken.

But so was she.

## CHAPTER FIFTY-FIVE

# BROKEN

They had been joined. One of six had won. A ruler's familial line had come to an end. The original offense had been committed again.

And on the hundredth day of the Centennial, the island did not vanish with the storm.

Isla had not emerged from her room. She only returned to the Wildling realm once, to inject power into the ground, saving it and her people from total ruin. She didn't know how to use her power yet, but it had been simple. Digging her hands into the ground. Releasing part of herself into its soil. The change had been immediate. Shocking.

Then she had returned to the Mainland castle, using her starstick. She spent her days curled in her tub, the hot water substituting for tears, because she found she had none left. She was empty.

Hollow.

Celeste. Her best and only friend. Hadn't been a friend at all.

Grim. A year's worth of forgotten memories. And some she remembered. Huddled together in the rain. Her body pressed against the same glass that had then shattered and sliced her in a thousand places.

She knew now that Ella had never been working against her. The Starling kept her updated through the door of her chamber. Through her, she learned that Cleo had cut away the bridge to Moon Isle, separating her territory from the Mainland. Isla didn't know what that would mean, what she was planning . . . but it couldn't be good.

Azul had been seen on the beach, watching as the cursed storm finally cleared. Apparently, the storm had held the souls of those killed by the curses. Those were the whispers she had once heard. The bodies trapped inside had supposedly walked just a few steps as specters before disappearing to their peace before they reached shore.

Isla hoped the Skyling had finally gotten to see his husband one last time.

Azul had never been a danger to her—Oro had been right about that.

After two weeks spent in the darkness of her chambers, the curtains drawn, she had finally felt strong enough to brush her hair. Put on a dress. And walk outside. She stood on her balcony, staring down at the sun's reflection on the sea, a golden apple just like the heart of Lightlark. The enchantment they had spent so long looking for that had saved them all. Had saved *her* more than once.

It held unmatched power.

And so did she.

She still hadn't tried to touch her abilities beyond giving some to the Wildling realm. Didn't even know where she would start. She was worried that if she tried to pull just a thread of them, she would end up ripping a seam and they would all tumble out of her in a destructive flurry.

So, she had let them be. Even though she knew the time would come when they would need to be unleashed.

Grim had returned to Nightshade, scathed. Betrayed.

Isla couldn't deny the sinking feeling in her stomach at his name returning to her thoughts. She hadn't let herself look too closely at the shadows in her room. She kept towels over her mirrors, just in case, knowing Nightshades could use them to communicate. Sometimes she drank coffee late at night instead of falling into dreams that she now knew were memories.

Especially since, five days ago, she had heard a voice echo through her mind, just before she had opened her eyes.

*Remember us, Heart. Remember it all.*

*You will remember.*

*And when you do—*

*You will come back to me.*

Grim's voice had spoken so clearly, it was as if he was sitting in her room. At the edge of her bed.

But when she had finally blinked her eyes open, gathering the covers to her sweating skin, she had found it empty.

With their curse broken, Nightshades would be stronger than they had been in five hundred years. She remembered with a swallow Grim's demonstration of power in the rain. Remembered the words that had made chills snake down her spine . . . they did so now, again, though for a different reason.

*I could open a black hole that would swallow the beach. I could turn the sea dark as ink and kill everything inside of it. I could demolish the castle, brick by brick, from where we stand. I could take you back to Nightshade lands with me right now.*

Before, she had thought of his words as boasts. Declarations.

Now, they seemed like threats.

She braced herself against the railing, knocked out of her own mind as heat flooded her. It came from behind her.

Oro.

They hadn't spoken since he had helped her back to the castle. She had been a shivering mess in his arms, sobbing, screaming, Celeste's eyes as she died seared into her mind. He had left food, tea, water, comfortable clothing at her door. But she had only ever opened it after he was far down the hall.

Her shoulders stiffened. She stared down at the sea, thrashing beneath her, all white caps and sapphire swirls.

"You're not thinking of jumping again, are you?"

She whirled around and glared at him. "I did not *jump*. You made me fall."

His eyes were serious. But his tone was all mock concern. "Did I?"

"Yes. You and your snooping."

He raised an eyebrow at her. "I could hear you from my room. I went out to investigate. I'd hardly call that snooping."

She tried to keep her glare in place. But as she studied his face, she blinked. She hadn't ever seen him in the sun.

Oro's amber eyes shined just as brightly as the heart had. His hair was sun spun into silk. The sharp edges of his face were highlighted in the light. His skin shined.

The dark circles below his eyes had disappeared. His cheeks looked far less sallow. The grayish blue had all vanished.

He was radiant.

Isla swallowed. "You were insufferable that night," she said, her words coming out without any bite.

Oro took a step toward her. "So were you. Walking into dinner soaking wet, hair dripping. And all I could hear was your voice, ringing through my mind like a curse. I thought it was on purpose, that you were using your abilities to lure me. Then, you were so surly it seemed implausible that was your plan." He frowned. "When you told me your secret, I was . . . taken aback." He laughed without humor. "For centuries, I had shunned any meaningful connection. And when, for the first time, I began to feel something . . . it was for a Wildling that wasn't even trying to beguile me."

Oro was so close, she had to tilt her head up to meet his gaze.

For a moment, they looked at each other. He opened his mouth, then closed it. She did the same.

Didn't know what to say.

"*Isla,*" he said, her name so soft on his lips. She saw her own emotions reflected in his eyes.

Confusion. Not knowing how it happened.

Just that it did.

Love was strange She wanted him in so many ways. Had for a while, though she had tried her best to deny it. More than anything, she trusted him.

Was *that* the basis of love?

She still wasn't sure.

Of anything.

Isla reached a hand to his chest. Somewhere, she could feel his power, pulsing. An endless stream, gold and gleaming. Sunling, Skyling, Moonling, and Starling. When Isla had used the bondmaker, she had returned each ruler's power, through the same bridge that had allowed her to take their abilities in the first place. Though she still had access.

There was no armor between her and Oro's endless pool, since it went both ways. She could dip her hand in and take it all, if she wanted to. And he could do the same to her.

Oro closed his eyes briefly, as if he could feel her fingers running along the rivers of energy contained within him.

He mirrored her movement. And she wondered what he felt . . . for, when Isla had killed Aurora with the bondmaker, she had known exactly what she was doing. Not just getting her own power—and Oro's and Grim's—back, but also *taking* something from her. All her Starling ruler abilities. A loophole, to kill a ruler and their line, fulfill the prophecy and end the curses, while sparing the Starling realm.

Now, Isla had a Starling ruler's power. And she didn't want to begin to think of what that meant.

Oro pressed two fingers against her heart. Ran them lower, to the center of her chest.

A vine snaked its way across the balcony and bloomed a red rose.

Oro plucked it. Offered it to her.

She stared down at the flower. A rose with thorns, just like her. It was beautiful. Vicious.

Isla took it, then threw it over her shoulder, clean off the balcony. And stood on her toes so her forehead touched his.

Oro stilled. His eyes were amber and burning, nothing like the emptiness she had glimpsed the first day of the Centennial. He looked at her like she was the thing they had torn apart the island for, the heart he had been desperately trying to find all these years, the needle that had finally threaded him together.

Isla took a shaky breath.

Then she turned to face the sea.

*Grim.* He had wrecked her. And she had been reckless. Rushed in without thinking, without waiting.

She wouldn't make that mistake again. Even though she trusted Oro—no one else but him.

Isla climbed onto the railing, the same way she had that first day of the Centennial, when she had sung the song that had drawn Oro out onto his own balcony. He was behind her, an endless source of heat, so close that when she leaned her head back, it rested against his chest.

Her feet kicked air, high above the churning sea. She looked up at him. "Don't let me fall in."

His eyes met hers. "Never," he said.

Isla glared at him.

"Never again," he amended.

# CHAPTER FIFTY-SIX

# KEY

The Place of Mirrors had lost its glass. It was a skeleton of a structure, its floors covered in shards sharp as knives. They crunched beneath Isla's shoes as she walked inside.

Oro had worked to close the crack in the ground, using borrowed power, but a scar still ran down the length of the room. A reminder of what had happened here.

A reminder of the ruler who had been buried below.

He was at her side, watching her every move. Without him, she didn't know if she would have had the nerve to return.

No . . . she would. Because she was stronger now. And it had nothing to do with her newfound power.

She continued forward smoothly, head held high. Oro had returned her crown. He had told her about how he had clutched it in his hands after they had found the heart, during the agonizing hours in the cave while the sun still shined and he was unable to go to her . . . or even know if she had survived.

*That was the moment I knew I loved you,* he had said. *When that arrow went through your heart, and it might as well have gone through mine.*

Isla had felt her crown's absence in the days following the breaking of the curses. She had drawn its patterns on paper, had imagined it in her mind's eye, wondering how it had looked on her mother. And the generations of Wildling rulers before her. Including Violet.

That was when she had realized what it was. The only thing that connected her to her ancestors. The only important object that had survived the centuries.

She stood before the vault, at the back of the Place of Mirrors. Oro was next to her, eyes fixed on its peculiarly shaped lock.

Isla took a steadying breath before slipping her crown into the hole. Its every ridge clicked into place. She turned it, just the way she would a key.

And pulled the door open.

# ACKNOWLEDGMENTS

Once, I was a twelve-year-old, writing books in my room and reading acknowledgments just like these, in the hopes of figuring out how to get published. It was my only dream. One I pursued relentlessly. After hundreds of rejections, I finally wrote *Lightlark* for me. It was the place I wanted to visit, the story I wanted to read.

It would have stayed only mine, if it wasn't for those who saw its potential and changed my life.

Thank you to my team, who has made every win possible. To Katelyn Detweiler, for falling in love with this book first and finding a home for it. Your support is like a suit of armor. To my entertainment lawyer, Eric Greenspan, for taking me on and seeing the possibilities of everything to come. To my film/TV agents at CAA, Berni Barta and Michelle Weiner. To Sophia Seidner, Sam Farkas, and Jill Grinberg at Jill Grinberg Literary Management. To Aimee Lim, whose feedback helped shape this book into what it is.

To my unrivaled editor, Anne Heltzel, for believing in *Lightlark* before it went viral and for championing me to the Abrams team. You saw in me what others didn't and pushed me to make this book even stronger—for that, I am forever grateful. To Andrew Smith for believing in me and all that the future holds. To Kim Lauber, Hallie Patterson, Brooke Shearouse, Elisa Gonzalez, Melanie Chang, and Megan Carlson at Abrams, a supreme group I'm lucky to have in my corner. Thank you so much for everything you have done to get *Lightlark* into as many hands as possible.

To my family, who has had the pleasure of being in close proximity to a writer (wink). To my parents, Claudy and Keith, for making it possible for me to follow my dreams. Dad, you always told me the harder you work, the luckier you get, and I've found that to be true. Mom, you are the strongest person I know, and I now see so much of you in me. Thank you to my twin sister, Daniella, who is the reason I kept writing. Your requests for more chapters pushed me to create new worlds. You were my first reader and will always be my best friend. To Sean, who was one of the first fans of my work—I am so grateful for your enthusiasm and help. To Leo and Bear, for bringing so much joy into my life. To JonCarlos and Luna, for being my star and moon. I can't wait to watch you follow your dreams too. To Angely, for always being there for me. To Rose, Alfonso, Carlos, and Maureen, for your unlimited love and support. To my heart, Rron—this book is dedicated to you. You make the real world just as good as a fictional one.

To my friends, who have all helped me navigate this new world. Your support, advice, and friendship mean more than you will ever know. To Chloe Gong, my other twin in so many ways. Our brunches have become a thing, haven't they? To Adam Silvera, for always hyping me up and making me smile. To Marie Lu, Sabaa Tahir, Zibby Owens, and Brigid Kemmerer. How did I get so lucky to know you?

To anyone who follows me on social media. Your messages and excitement for this book got me through every deadline and made me determined to make it worth the wait.

Most of all, thank you to BookTok. *Lightlark* is here because of you. Every video, every comment, every share, every friend I've made there—*thank you.* You are more powerful than you know. I can't remember what I was thinking posting that video about the concept of an island that only appears once every hundred years, but I'll never forget the shock that millions of people wanted to go on this journey with me. We did it!

# Turn the page for an exclusive teaser excerpt from

# NIGHTBANE

the stunning second novel in

THE LIGHTLARK SAGA

# CORONATION

There were fewer Wildlings left than she thought.

Months before, she had addressed her people. Now, only a fraction remained. They looked weak. There were details she hadn't noticed before, when she had been so focused on her journey to the Centennial. Now, she saw the signs clearly. A woman with short hair, crudely cut, wore a torn top that revealed all-too-visible ribs. Another looked far too pale, lips chapped, face devoid of color. They had learned to make enough food; she had seen them. She supposed it would take some time for consistent nourishment to make them healthy again.

Some details were the same. A portion of her people had animal companions near them, just like the day she left. Wildlings were known for their affinity with creatures. Poppy had a hummingbird that flew around her hair. Terra had a great panther.

She had always wanted an animal companion. It would have made her life far less lonely.

Terra had always said no.

Isla opened her mouth to speak. Before she could, they did something she couldn't have expected. Didn't deserve.

One by one, they bowed.

"No, I—"

They had never done that before. Isla had never demanded it. It wasn't a custom she was used to.

She didn't like it. Anxiety thrummed across her skin, and she wanted to yell that they should be screaming at her, calling her names, telling her everything she had done wrong up until this point. They looked like they were still *dying*. She was a failure, not a hero.

Isla stepped back, words caught in her throat, when a woman with a capybara next to her said, "You broke the curses. You did what all other rulers for centuries could not."

She frowned. "How do you—how do you know that?"

"Terra told us."

*Terra?* The name was a dagger to the chest. How had her guardians even known she was the one to break the curses? Why had Terra told them, after being banished?

Had she defied Isla's order? Was she still here, on the newland?

"Where is Terra now?" the woman asked. "She was here . . . and then she vanished. And Poppy?" *No. Not still here.*

"I don't know," Isla said honestly. She thought about telling them about the banishment, but she needed to first get a sense of their allegiance. Would they be loyal to her . . . or to the guardians who had mostly ruled the Wildlings since her birth? "Please stand," she said. She told them everything else. That she'd believed she had been born without powers. That she had a device that allowed her to portal at will. That she now had Starling power. When she was finished, she said, "I have not been a good ruler. I don't know your struggles. Speak candidly, please. I know you must have questions. Ask them. Tell me what you need."

Something flickered in her vision. Isla turned, and for the slightest second, she saw Grim, standing among the crowd, watching her.

She froze. Panic dropped through her stomach.

A blink, and he was gone.

Someone asked a question, and she didn't hear it.

She shook her head. "Sorry, what did you say?" Her ears were ringing. First, the vision in the Place of Mirrors. Then, his voice in her head. Now, she was seeing him . . . What was next?

What was wrong with her?

"I asked what is happening on the island."

She wondered how much she should say. "There is uncertainty on Lightlark right now. The realms are divided. There are signs of rebellion. We also have reason to believe Nightshades might try to attack Lightlark, like they have in the past." She attempted a smile. "Once all of that is dealt with, I hope to have us all back on Lightlark one day," she said. "This has been our home for five centuries, but it is weakened. Lightlark is where we have always belonged."

There were some murmurs, but no one spoke out against her. She hoped that was a good sign.

She answered their questions as best she could, then sought out a woman who wore purple flowers through the ends of her hair, the color of leadership. She was tall, with light skin, dark hair, and sharp eyes. Her name was Wren, and Isla learned she led one of the larger villages on the newland.

"Why are some people standing apart from the rest?" Isla asked. Her people were not as united as they had seemed months prior. Some were huddled together, but others stood on the outskirts.

Wren looked at her for a moment. "I mean no disrespect," she said. "But you didn't have the curse. You don't know what it's like to have to kill others for food. To go hungry because there simply wasn't enough." She shook her head. "Most of us did things we're not proud of to survive."

Tears burned Isla's eyes. All her life, she had thought it a horror being locked in her room and training so rigorously. It was nothing compared to what her people had gone through; she knew that now. "What do you need?" she asked. "How can I help you?"

Wren pressed her lips together. "We have slowly learned to make food. It has been good for us, I think, figuring things out on our own. Any challenge now . . . it is a mere shadow of what we endured."

"You must need something," she said. "Some of you still look starved. I can bring more food. Bring people to help teach you to make other crops or help reconstruct houses." She had seen the state of the villages during her travels with her starstick. Some buildings had stood the test of time, and others had fallen to pieces. "I can—"

Wren cut her off. "How are the Starlings?"

"I don't know. I've asked, but I haven't yet visited the newland or isle."

"Help them," she said. "We are resourceful. Older. They are so young. They need you more than we do." She smiled sadly. "It would help," she said. "With the guilt. To know in some way, we are aiding another realm, instead of . . ."

*Killing them.*

Isla nodded. "I'll be back," she said. "With help and resources, after my coronation."

Wren nodded. "We will be waiting."

Bells rang at a distance. The air was sharp with salt from the sea and burned honey from the fair that had cropped up at the base of the castle, all carts filled with varieties of roasted seeds and bands holding their instruments, but not playing them, not yet.

Isla stood at the top of the stairs, just beyond the shadow of the doors, just out of view of the thousands of people waiting below.

It was the day of the Starling coronation, and it seemed everyone on Lightlark was in attendance.

Well, almost everyone.

"No sign of Moonling," Ella said quietly behind her, because Isla had asked her to look. The young Starling had been her assigned attendant during the Centennial. Now, Isla employed her to be her eyes and ears wherever she could not see or hear.

The bells came to an end. It was time.

Isla stepped forward.

Strings of silver beads made up a dress like spun starlight. Her cape glistened in a ripple behind her as she walked down the stairs.

It was still a shock to wear a color she had only dared to use on her prohibited excursions beyond her own realm. It felt wrong, it all felt so *wrong*, like she had taken her friend's life, robbed her of her silver, and put it on herself.

Was that what these people thought? That she had killed Celeste—Aurora—for the power?

She looked to the crowd for answers, stomach tensed, braced. Their faces were a mosaic of surprise, curiosity, hate, disgust, trepidation, vitriol—

*Breathe.*

Isla took another step, and her foot nearly missed the stair completely. She briefly considered gathering her gown in her hands and running back upstairs, locking herself in her room and going anywhere, *anywhere,* with her starstick.

She wasn't worthy of any of this. She didn't deserve to rule anyone. She didn't even know herself. Part of her past was missing, and that person—the one who had supposedly loved a Nightshade—felt like a stranger. She was sad all the time, and there were so many emotions pressed down, in the deepest depths of herself, that she knew one day would overpower everything else and claw their way out—

She felt it: a thread of heat, steadying her. It was honey in her stomach, a beam of sunshine just for her.

Him. She met Oro's eyes. The king was her destination. He stood tall and proud and golden, at the very bottom of the steps. There was a silver crown in his hands.

He looked at her like it was just them, no crowd, no crowns.

She took another step. Another. Until she was standing in front of him.

Oro didn't say anything. He didn't have to. She could read a thousand words in his amber eyes, like *you can do this. I'm here for you.*

The past few days, she had been avoiding him, knowing he would want her to begin her training. She felt ashamed. Her people needed her to be strong. He just wanted to keep her safe.

He raised the crown high above her, not wasting a moment, knowing she wanted this to be over as soon as possible.

"As king of Lightlark, I name you, Isla Crown, the ruler of Starling." He placed the crown on her head. It was done.

There was a rumbling.

Oro had turned to address his people, but he paused, his brows coming together slightly.

Nervous murmurs spread through the crowd. There was a second of stillness, the island righting itself, and the people silenced, their momentary curiosity instantly forgotten. But Isla watched Oro, and his expression remained the same. Her hand inched toward the blade at her side.

Before her fingers reached the hilt, the island broke open.

The ground beneath her feet parted like a screaming mouth. She would have been swallowed if she had not been on its edge, on a part that rose like a sharpened tooth. Her body soared back with the force; she closed her eyes. Pain across her side was the only sign she had landed.

Screaming sliced the air in half as a scar tore across the castle steps in a rippling sweep, stone crumbling and falling away.

Both were drowned out by the screeching.

Winged, monstrous creatures howled as they barreled through the open fissure.

Their necks were short, their limbs long. Their tails were nearly non-existent. Their anatomy almost resembled people, except for their faces—which were pure reptile—their black scales, and, of course, their wings.

In a few moments, they were everywhere.

Dozens of the creatures dropped down, aimed at the crowd. Isla put a hand above her, as if it would be any type of shield against the teeth that curved out of the beasts' mouths like slanted blades.

Before the beasts could reach them, a blanket of flames erupted into a barrier. *Oro*. The heat was scalding, steaming Isla in her clothes.

When the fire was pulled away, the creatures were gone, reduced to ash that rained upon them. Dozens were killed.

Before anyone could run for shelter, more creatures emerged.

The scar had to be closed. The beasts were rising in endless sweeps, squeezing through the gap. Groaning, Isla pushed herself up to her arms.

Oro was leaned over his knees, clutching his side. Any injury to the island hurt him as well. It must have felt like he was also being peeled open. Face twisted in pain, he lifted his hand and created another barrier, but the creatures closed their wings together in response, making themselves into sharpened arrows, talons at their fronts like blades. With cries that threatened to crack the sky into shards, they barreled through the protective sphere—

And feasted on them all.

Bones crunched, blood splattered, limbs were torn away. The beasts crashed down, undisturbed by Sunling flames, Starling sparks, or Skyling wind. Their talons tore through flesh as easily as swords through sand.

Azul shot up into the air, with a legion of Skylings surrounding him. They fought with bursts of wind, shooting the creatures down from the sky or slamming them against the island until they went still. Sunlings wielding swords covered in flames guarded people huddled behind the carts in the fair. All the islanders fought back, but many were no match for the creatures, whose hides resisted most uses of power. Before their strategy could be changed, most of them were torn in half by powerful jaws. Some islanders stopped using their abilities altogether, as it marked them as targets, and pressed themselves to the ground or ran.

Just like at the ball months before, Isla watched it all unfold, a helpless spectator. No. They might hate her, this might never feel like home, but she had to do something.

Isla stood on weakened legs, blood hot on the side of her face. She placed a hand over her heart. The heart that had been torn in two by an arrow. The one that was healed by the heart of Lightlark itself, the one that was linked to Oro's own ability.

A heart that had, more times than not, failed her.

"Please," she whispered, eyes on Oro, who was oscillating between killing swarms of beasts attacking his people and trying to close the scar the winged creatures were still flying through in droves.

She could help him. Wildling power included controlling rock and land. If she could manage to grasp some of that power, she could help all of them.

Isla closed her eyes. She focused on her breathing.

Nothing.

She stretched out her trembling hand. "Come on."

Nothing.

The powers she had been born with were twisted together, making them harder to access. Her Starling abilities were not, however. They were there, just below the surface. She summoned them.

Nothing happened.

Perhaps she could focus on the link between her and Oro instead. Use *his* power. She looked at the king, whose arms were both shaking with effort, one outstretched at each side.

She felt it. Tried to grasp it. *Nothing*.

She shook her hand toward the cut in the ground, picturing herself sealing it shut with ice or burned rock or energy, willing with every bit of her being for it to close. "Come on!" she bellowed.

Nothing.

Her yell had attracted the attention of the closest winged creature. It opened its mouth, and a severed arm fell to the ground.

Then, it lunged at her.

# Step into the enthralling world of THE LIGHTLARK SAGA

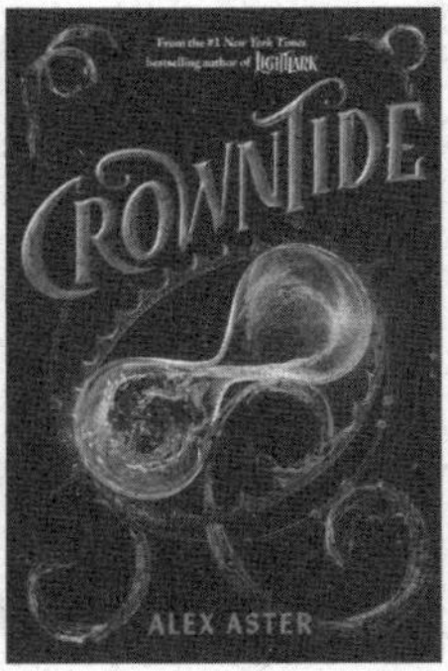

# Don't miss these deluxe editions!

**ALEX ASTER** is a #1 *New York Times*, *Wall Street Journal*, and *Publishers Weekly* bestselling author, as well as an internationally bestselling author and one of the most followed novelists on social media. She graduated summa cum laude from the University of Pennsylvania, where she studied creative writing, and is also the author of the Starside series and *Summer in the City*. Explore the world of *Lightlark* at asterverse.com.

FOLLOW ALEX ON INSTAGRAM AT @ALEXASTER
AND ON TIKTOK AT @ALEX.ASTER
SUBSCRIBE AT WWW.ASTERVERSE.COM TO
RECEIVE EXCLUSIVE CONTENT